A FAITH UNTAMED

A NOVEL OF BABYLON'S DESTRUCTION OF
BIBLICAL JERUSALEM

APRIL W GARDNER

BIG SPRING PRESS

Copyright ©2025 by April W Gardner

All rights reserved.

No part of this book may be reproduced or transmitted in any form or by any means, electronic or mechanical, including photocopying, recording, or by an information storage and retrieval system—except by a reviewer who may quote brief passages in a review to be printed in a magazine, newspaper, or on the Web—without permission in writing from the publisher.

This is a work of fiction. While the settings and some of the characters are drawn from scripture references and historical accounts, apart from the actual people, events, and locales that figure into the fiction narrative, all other names, characters, places, and events are the creation of the author's imagination or are used fictitiously.

Scripture quotations taken from the King James Version unless otherwise indicated.

Cover design: Indie Cover Design & Big Spring Press
Edited by L. Darby Gibbs of Inkabout Publishing

ISBN-13: 978-1-945831-47-8
LCCN: 2025909217

A Faith Untamed: A Novel of Babylon's Destruction of Biblical Jerusalem

Published by Big Spring Press

San Antonio, Texas, United States of America.

CAST OF CHARACTERS

Liora and Nebuzaradan (Arioch)
Chesed ben Ephraim, Liora's father/abba
Devorah, Liora's handmaid
Rimutu, Nebuzaradan's bodyguard
Idadu, captain of Liora's guard
Ishmael ben Nethaniah, prince of Judah, rebel leader
Zipporah, Liora's best friend, wife of Chesed
Gittel, widow
Sapir, orphaned girl
Omar the Kenez, captured Edomite
Nergal-sharezer, prince of Babylon
Jeremiah, prophet
Moreh Buzi, priest
Eitan, priest, son of Buzi
Hodaya, queen of King Zedekiah
Nebo-Sarsekim, chamberlain (rab-saris)
Keshet, rebel
Šulmanu, Liora's bodyguard
Haldi, Nebuzaradan's steward

CHAPTER 1

They hunt our steps, that we cannot go in our streets: our end is near, our days are fulfilled; for our end is come. (Lam. 4:18)

Days ago, Nebuzaradan made good on his boyhood name. Plundering and destroying, he roared his way through Liora's city. Arioch the lion was Nebuzaradan the Butcher, the victor over the fight for Jerusalem. He came next to conquer her.

Liora was filling her *abba's* cup at the morning repast—General Nebuzaradan's first in her home—when the man himself tramped, armor clanking, down the corridor. A giant among them, his every stride rattled her nerves.

He paused in the open doorway, peering down at them with the command of one who ruled her city, her home, her bedchamber. The first two were accurate. The third, Yahweh be thanked, hinged on whether Nebuzaradan could find a way around his vow to Yahweh, Judah's God.

The prophet Jeremiah would supply that *way*. Or so Nebuzaradan demanded.

Standing before them, he appraised her from head covering to sandals, taking his dear time at it, then slid a narrowed gaze at her abba seated at the place of honor.

Chesed ben Ephraim, her abba, scrambled to rise. He bowed and offered his place with a trembling gesture.

But Nebuzaradan was already taking it, nudging Abba aside and sinking his own muscled frame to the cushion. He plucked the filled vessel from Liora's hand and gave her a gracious nod. "A cheerful and blessed morning to you, wife."

Liora flinched at the new title.

Using a contract that her abba had no choice but to sign, as well as a slave's mark on her palm, he'd appointed himself her husband. He followed that with the shocking realization she was out of his reach—he would not touch her. Something to do with a rash vow he'd made to Yahweh as he and his soldiers stormed the temple gates.

She fidgeted where she stood, the hot clay pot stinging her skin but covering the single tongue of flame etched across the creases of her palm. Though expertly applied, the mark signified everything she no longer was—a free woman—and everything she had become: Liora bat Chesed, once privileged noblewoman of Jerusalem, now the property of Babylon's highest ranking general, the one gazing at her, expectant.

She lowered her head and replied in his formal Akkadian. "And to you, my lord. May the gracious God of Israel grant you peace this day."

Nebuzaradan grunted. "Impossible. Tomorrow, perhaps. If that god you've named allows me to live after what I must do." He swilled the steaming tea and ended on a satisfied hiss.

What he must do could take many forms, all of them likely to invite Yahweh's displeasure. Her mind leaped unbidden to his ongoing destruction of the Holy Temple, then to the covenant ark behind the veil in the holiest place.

What would become of it? What would become of Nebuzaradan? The Lord had slain men for presuming to touch His glory, and the general was no doubt under orders to gather the relic into Babylon's keep. Could she somehow protect them both? The ark from the power of Babylon and Nebuzaradan from the Power of the ark?

As he reached for a loaf of flat bread, she exchanged a questioning glance with her paling abba, who was descending to a cushion at the general's right. She received only a jerky shrug of confusion for guidance.

"If I may ask, my lord, what must you do today that might invite His wrath?" Sniffing, she dabbed her nose with the sleeve of her tunic. She stepped between the men, then knelt to fill an extra cup. "There is no violation of the law in calling on a prophet of Yahweh."

An hour ago, the general woke from a winter slumber and declared they would visit Jeremiah bar Hilkiah, the man she called *saba*. Not her true grandfather, he was a close enough, old enough family friend to qualify. It had been months since she'd seen him. He'd been in prison, locked away from any ears he might influence toward repentance.

Nebuzaradan angled an assessing gaze on her. "Are you ill?"

"No, my lord." She promptly sniffed again.

His eyes tightened.

"The ash is bothersome."

He stared on, scouring her features. For a lie? A pock?

She held steady. "It irritates the nose, the eyes. Others suffer the same."

Finally, he broke his scrutiny and reached for a dish. "Do not fall ill," he said, a commander's orders.

She cleared her throat to banish the humor from her voice. "At your will, General."

"Ben Ephraim, remove yourself from my right side." Nebuzaradan did not look up from the bread he ripped in half.

"A-as you wish, my lord." Her abba scurried around the mat to take the seat at Nebuzaradan's opposite elbow.

Nerves strung out, Liora ventured, "It pleases me to find my lord so rested. Was the bed to your liking?" She tipped the teapot to replenish the general's cup.

"You were not in it."

Her arms jolted, and liquid sloshed in the pot.

A wedded couple did not speak of such things outside the sanctuary of the bedchamber. And the general himself had said he'd promised Yahweh that, in exchange for his life, he would touch nothing that belonged to Him. Tattoo or not, as a daughter of Israel and a devout worshiper of Yahweh, Liora indisputably qualified. Praise a merciful God.

A FAITH UNTAMED

Nebuzaradan viewed things differently. The day before, when he realized his hasty, self-preserving vow included her, his composure disintegrated to a degree she'd never witnessed. Red-faced, he'd quaked with the force of anger and of impotence. The general did not appreciate being denied what he wanted. And what he wanted was Liora. That much was abundantly clear.

Eyes flaring, she darted another look at her abba, but he appeared to find the cheese plate particularly fascinating. "No, my lord," she said with a firm wag of the head and an uneven pour. "I would not dare enter your chamber without a summons."

A low laugh shook Nebuzaradan's shoulders and made the gold of his dangling earrings sparkle in the sunlight streaming through the open shutters. "Ah, my dearest dove. You are always welcome in my quarters, with or without my request. And let us not pretend you have not dared a great many things and quite without summons. Or concern for your life," he added with a wry twist of the lips.

At a loss, Liora clamped her jaw shut.

Abba filled the quiet with a nervous chuckle. "Yes, yes, quite. My Liora has always been rather—"

"*My* Liora." Nebuzaradan's eyes shot sideways. "What are you doing here, ben Ephraim?"

Mouth open, her abba gave the aromatic spread of food a pointed look. Wisely, he refrained from speaking the question on his face—*Is it not obvious?*—and slowly unfolded his legs, never straightening fully as he rose. "I am here to request that I attend my daughter on the morning's perilous journey through the city. This father"—he laid a hand across his heart—"would be better at ease if he were at her side."

Liora, too, would be better at ease. Her abba didn't know one end of a blade from the other, but she would like to give him the chance to redeem himself for not standing beside her when the streets swarmed with a stone-wielding mob. When they'd chanted her name, paired it with words like *adulteress* and *harlot*.

The memory was disturbing enough to tighten her airways, her most horrid memory flickering to life. And being caught in a compromising position with an Edomite was nothing to being named their conqueror's consort, to strolling at his side through their city. The people would see only a traitor, not the woman who wished to use her position for their good. How differently would they view her if they knew she looked for opportunities to preserve the ark from destruction?

"So it is your own ease that concerns you." Nebuzaradan selected a dried apricot from a dish. Then tossed it back on the pile. "Rather than your daughter's safety."

"Not at all! Well, it is both. Naturally."

Nodding, the general shoved bread into his mouth. Jaw muscle rippling, he chewed deliberately. The tension in the chamber grew so thick Devorah, arms laden with a dish, stopped upon entry, spun on her heel, and bumped into the door guard on her way out.

The home's quiet crowded in, and she almost missed her dozens of noisy guests. The prior evening, Nebuzaradan ordered that every person she'd saved from his sword-slashing soldiers the day of the

A FAITH UNTAMED

invasion must be gone from their home before sunset. Not even Liora complained. From the moment she'd ushered the first victim off the street, she hadn't found a minute that wasn't dedicated to filling hungry bellies and meeting demands, Nebuzaradan the most recent drain on her reserves.

Now, his throat worked a swallow before he ran a cupping hand down his mouth. In the silence, his chin whiskers rasped against his callouses. "I see," he said, tone dangerously soft. "You believe that I, commander of legions and of your doomed city, cannot protect my wife."

Liora's eyelids slid closed as, bless him, her abba stuttered and sputtered like a downed pheasant before an archer put it out of its misery. "Th-there is also my l-longtime standing with the prophet. Jeremiah is an old and dear acquaintance. My presence might smooth the way for your introduction."

"Babylon's victorious Butcher requires no introduction. Leave my presence."

Vibrant red replaced her abba's pallor as he lurched forward in a profound bow and sped out, robes rustling.

Liora stared after him, lips parted, betrayal a needle in her heart—not that he had a choice of abandoning her with her husband—until Nebuzaradan's intimate tones yanked her gaze to him.

"Do not be disturbed." The lines about his mouth softened. "Where it concerns you, he will learn to speak and to act with greater care."

Her fingers clenched about the vessel she still held. Did he want her to believe his handling was *benevolent* or intended to make her abba a wiser man? Of course, her abba should probably have sought Liora with his request, let *her* approach the general with it.

On reflection...maybe there was an element of truth to Nebuzaradan's claim. "Where it concerns a dear child," she replied, "a father is sometimes reckless and bold."

He snorted. "Chesed ben Ephraim is not bold. *You*, woman," he said, angling over his folded knee, "are reckless and bold. If the situation were reversed, you would not have left the room without another attempt to accompany him, and another after that."

"Chesed ben Ephraim, perhaps, understands better than others that some victories come from knowing when to stand down," she said her gaze steady on him.

"There!" He jabbed a long finger at her, then rocked back on his rear and laughed. "More of that. You do so please me, dove. Smart, bold, and beautiful. I am, indeed, a man blessed." He flashed his teeth in a cheeky grin.

"Blessed far beyond your deserving." She hiked a single eyebrow, a challenge to call her out on the reckless boldness he'd demanded of her.

He stilled, and his right eye twitched the scar that ran a puckered line through his eyebrow and down to his cheekbone. Did the wound still bother him on occasion? So it seemed as he rubbed his closed eyelid, grimacing. "I find no argument for that. Even the god of Israel would agree."

"Is your eye unwell, my lord?"

He made a noncommittal noise.

"The old wound? Or is it a bothersome speck? Something in the eye?" Ash would be her guess.

"There is," he said at a low register, the gravel of his voice going bitter. "But it is nothing either you or I can remove."

"Are you certain? Shall I look?" She set the pot aside and stood, intending to go around him for a better view. "Devorah, dear, bring a lamp!"

"No." He barked out the word, making her startle. "I said it is nothing."

In a moment, he was on his feet and towering over her, his brow turbulent. This was no mere speck.

And now that she looked more closely... What was that there, covering the eye? A forward lean to better see. Her breath stuck in her throat. The morning light slashed the side of his face, brightening the red of scabs and scrapes and revealing the thinnest white sheen over the bothersome eye, fading its midnight black to the darkest gray.

"Arioch," she breathed, his youthful name leaving her lips without thought.

The stern lines on his forehead wobbled and cut sharply down between his thick eyebrows. "It is visible?"

"The film over your eye? A little, yes. Only because the sunlight hits it just so." She drew closer and laid a light hand on his arm. Ignoring his jolt of surprise, she whispered, "Can you see through it?"

His jaw jutted to the side in an angry set. "Light and shadow. It is all he left me."

"Who? Did someone punch you here?" Two fingers to his bearded chin, she nudged his face to the side, but saw no evidence of a blow to the region.

That meant nothing. A thorough general, he'd not earned his brutal reputation by fighting at the back of his army. He'd arrived from the conflict nicked and cut, bruises bluing his limbs, and his head uncovered. Had someone struck him in the skull?

An acerbic laugh cut from his throat. "Struck? You could say that." He backed away until her touch broke. His fiery gaze fixed to her hand where it hovered between them, her marked palm on broad display.

She curled a hasty fist. But what reason did she have to be ashamed? And what reason did *he* have to look at his own doing with such contempt?

"My lady?" Devorah stepped hesitantly around the corner, a lamp held before her. Its flame trembled. "You called?"

Liora scooted back from Nebuzaradan's stiff bearing. "The general could use some tea for his contusions from b—" She caught the word *battle* as it hit the back of her teeth. Reminders of his violence did none of them any good. "Ginger and turmeric, I think."

"And a dash of black pepper." Nodding, Devorah backed out, spine bent to show the top of her veiled head. Her graying hair stuck out in a wiry array from the brown fabric. "At once."

A FAITH UNTAMED

Beside Liora, Nebuzaradan exhaled a mighty breath. Something indeed was wrong with his eye, but his position of unquestioned authority could not afford for it to become known. How weakened must a general be to lose trust among his men or, worse, his rank?

Liora would be happy to watch the entire Babylonian force march itself into the sea, but if she had her choice of commanders over the army destroying her city, it would be him, the man Yahweh had entrusted to her care. For all his butchery, Nebuzaradan inclined his ear toward her counsel. His heart also, remarkably, showed signs of softening toward the Holy One. Apart from being an unfortunate loss to any person, this eye trouble had all the markings of a threat to her fragile influence and to the general's tentative steps toward the God of Israel.

Whatever his personal motives for preserving his position—prestige, riches, favor—Nebuzaradan undoubtedly agreed. If his weakness was uncovered, it could unravel everything. He confirmed it with his next growled statement. "Prince Nergal-sharezer returns within days from Riblah." He ran a rough hand through his oiled, shoulder-length curls and angled abruptly toward the open window, as if he might spot the prince marching across Liora's courtyard.

A pigeon strutted along the retention pool's whitewashed rim, its head bobbing forward and back. Nebuzaradan scowled at the bird, and Liora had a fleeting thought to find the nearest projectile before she remembered the spread of food on the mat beside her. The hunger was over. The battle was lost, the bloodshed reduced to the last few rebel holdouts. The ideal time for an indolent prince to emerge from his luxury.

How like her own spoiled royals, waiting out the war in comfort, appearing only once the walls were down and the fires were burning. The king had not stepped foot inside Jerusalem, but his sons and officials, she'd learned, had set themselves up at the gate during the reprieve—the days she'd been in the Babylonian camp. Their presence, Yahweh's promised judgment in the flesh, had been the final terror that sent King Zedekiah fleeing into the night. Threat complete, the royals had evacuated to allow Nebuzaradan his violence, and their absence over the last days had given the general absolute authority. If Liora had a guess, that was soon to end, his eye notwithstanding.

Before it did, might she be able to shift the fate of the ark, prevent its desecration? A thought worth pursuing—right after those involving the Babylonian royal due to arrive. Time was short. Her head rocked in understanding. "How much of a threat is this prince?"

The general twisted back to Liora, his mouth tipped with the hint of a smile as he regarded her. One of the scars pitting his cheek drove deeper before he broke from her inquisitive gaze. "To my military rule"—he waved as though shooing a bad odor—"none. My king trusts him with Jerusalem's dismantling about as much as I trust a pig in the storeroom."

Though he snorted carelessly, Liora caught the unease clipping his words. His guarded worry fed her own. "Politically, however..."

"Politically, he is a different beast. Nergal will exploit any sign of weakness, even the hint of one."

If that *hint* included Nebuzaradan, it could mean loss of power, which could mean only bad for Jerusalem's survivors. The thin undercurrent of threat Nergal presented held all the promise of a cracked dam. "Then he will not know yours," she said with a downward jerk of the chin. "Guard!"

Metal clinked as the man stationed outside the chamber stepped in, his fist already positioned over his chest in a salute.

"Ah, it is you, Rimutu." She offered him a gracious smile, to which he blinked in surprise. Quiet and of average build, he'd latched himself to her memory with his overlarge ears. They jutted from either side of his head as if holding up his helmet. "From now until you are ordered otherwise, you will guard your general's right side when venturing beyond this house. You will do this as discreetly as possible, without err and without question."

The man shifted his blinking gaze to his commander.

In thanks for the soldier's deference, the general snarled. "Is that a question?"

Rimutu ducked his head, the tips of his bent ears turning crimson. "It is not, sir. I am honored to serve at the lady's command. Without err. Without question."

Nebuzaradan's chest bounced with a grunt. "Dismissed."

When Rimutu flicked her a glance, she refreshed her smile. "Thank you, Rimutu."

The man sank farther before he swiveled back to his post.

Nebuzaradan stayed fixed on the space the guard vacated. "This is not agreement to your precaution. If any learn of this weakness, I will become irrelevant to the crown. The guard will guess. He will know. Then I will kill him."

Liora frowned. "Choose another then. Which man can you trust?"

"I trust only fear and power. That of my sword and any granted me by the crown and my noble house."

"How very sad for you." She resisted reaching out with a consoling touch. "There can be more, you know."

"I do. For I see it in you, my dove."

Ignoring that, she pressed on, tone urgent. "You will not find it in fear and brutality, but in covenant mercy, the kind our God extends even to the undeserving."

"Who would I be if not the Butcher? As if such a thing were possible."

"With Yahweh, all things are possible."

"Yes, I see that belief in your eyes." He chuckled softly. "I see myself there too, more clearly than ever. The longer I know you, Liora daughter of a god, the better I know myself."

A FAITH UNTAMED

His statement clenched her heart. The first strides toward repentance included a right viewing of oneself, and Liora clung to the faith that Yahweh had a plan for her general-husband, one that went beyond the slaughter of her people. She *must* cling, or she would fall into an abyss of despair. But Yahweh was her portion; she would hope in Him. With that, the fingers of her faith gripped tighter to her Lord.

Turning to her, Nebuzaradan lifted a labor-roughed hand and traced the air beside her cheek, never touching. "I am a wretch and unworthy of such consideration as you show me. But *you*. You, my dove, are the purest light and deserving of every beautiful thing." His voice caressed her as his fingers could not. "Every foul soul should be struck from your presence."

She opened her mouth to protest, but lips twisting into a self-deprecating knot, he continued. "As I am an incurably selfish man, I will not remove my own foul soul. But I will banish those who have wounded you." His posture straightened; his voice firmed. "Starting with Chesed ben Ephraim."

Liora's chest bounced with a disbelieving laugh that dissolved under his rigid gaze. "My father? Did you say you will...*banish* him?"

He lowered his head a touch. "As he once banished you." His arm swung down and around to his back to join the other in a regal clasp. Shoulders pulled back, he showed her a closed-mouth smile, expecting...what? Praise?

He would wait a long time for *that*. "But those wrongs are ages gone! He has asked my forgiveness, and I have given it. Times are not as they were. We have since spent countless hours in pleasant company. In his chamber of scrolls, reading, analyzing prophecies, studying sacred texts together." Cherished hours. "We tread new ground now, my father and I."

Nebuzaradan's eyes flattened along with his tone. "Which is the only reason I have not whipped him to within three breaths of death."

She reeled back, hand flying to her throat as if to remove a choking hold. What insanity was this? "You would not do that to him. To me." No, she wouldn't believe it of him. The faith she had in her Lord and in the sliver of a soul this man possessed, foul though it was, would not allow it.

"*For* you," he said. "Not *to* you."

She stared at him, stunned.

He resented her abba; she'd suspected, had figured he would never respect him. But this, *this,* was unthinkable. Utterly irrational.

"Are you so hardened to violence, you cannot see they are the same?" Her clogged throat made her aware of the wet on her cheeks and of how foolish she'd been to submit to his insistence she give him the story of her pain.

When she'd told of how King Zedekiah underhandedly broke both their betrothal and her good name, nearly broken *her*, of how her abba then set her up in the Lower City with a pottery-painting shop for despised women, Nebuzaradan heard only that Chesed ben Ephraim sent her from his home for a sin she did not commit. That she'd later been sent to *him*, the Butcher, as a bargaining token had only fed his disdain.

"Be grateful I am *so hardened*," he replied, tone calcifying in kind, "and that I care enough to do the difficult things."

"Banishing the father I love is what you call *care*?"

He bent to eliminate their considerable height difference, putting his scarred face so near to hers there was no missing the intractable glint entering his eyes. "The man cast you to the filthy streets, Liora. *You*, the most honorable and loyal of women. Even now, you defend the coward. You fight for him."

"As I do for all those I call my own. As I fought for you only moments ago!" She thrust a stiff arm toward the door and the guard who'd tucked every scrap of himself out of sight.

Something flickered in Nebuzaradan's eyes, and she prayed it was doubt. On that hope, she pushed on, though she had the presence of mind to reduce her volume to a brusque hush. "Before I act in your favor next time, my lord, should I question myself? If this is how I am to be repaid, why fight for you? Why concern myself over a man who will only return it with threats on my father's life?" She wept in earnest now, tears sliding silently down her neck.

Nebuzaradan's gaze tracked the path with something resembling regret, but instead of conceding the point, he gave a soft huff. "I threaten no one's life. As I recall, I said I would *not* whip him." His breath, sweet from his tea, brushed her nose. "And whether your palm reflects it or not, you should recall my house symbol is an ax. Two, in fact." The statement cut toward her like a thorny whip. "And we do not use them to chop wood but to remind others of our authority."

He studied her, head tilted to view her through his good eye. One dangling gold earring tangled in his black, unbound hair. Did he detect the fury and defiance simmering beneath her skin. If he saw the hurt, if he cared at all that he'd driven her to the brink of impudence, his next words gave no sign of it. "Your enemies are my enemies. And my enemies, all of them, fall before me," he said, voice dangerously mild. "Do not forget who I am, dove."

The Butcher. The man reputed to have ravaged half a dozen cities before reaching Jerusalem. Forget? How could she when the streets of her own sacred city baked red with the blood he'd spilled?

But dwelling there, on his rampant brutality, would not draw him closer to the man beneath the sharpened blade. The one she wanted him to remember he could still be.

She took one long backward stride away from him and lifted her chin. "You are *Arioch*, and my father is no enemy." On that assertion, she ran both hands down her middle, smoothing wrinkles from her gown. "You will not banish him."

They exchanged implacable stares, his glinting with a trace of that amusement he'd claimed she provided.

Fury sparked in her breast. Was that what this was to him? Diversion from the toils of slaughter?

A FAITH UNTAMED

He must have seen the fire stoking in her, for he steeled his expression, swapping the amused glint with a proud slant of the chin. "Ben Ephraim will pay for his offense. Accept it."

Not a minute later, riled into a passion, she stormed up the steep wooden slats protruding from the west wall of her home's inner, open-air patio.

"Banish him?" she asked no one but the sooty sky above, as though General Nebuzaradan's glowering face hung there. *"Banish?"* How easily the man tossed the word around.

Was that what happened to Šulmanu? Had Nebuzaradan finally made good on his promise and banished the soldier, or worse?

Šulmanu, the soldier she'd saved from execution, had vanished three days before. She'd last seen him as he dashed up these very stairs in pursuit of her attacker. His absence gnawed at her, worry a brick in her stomach.

Would his general kill him for the slight lapse in guard duty? If so, she wasn't sure her budding trust in Nebuzaradan could survive it. The mere possibility of it twisted in her chest. How could she be wed to such a man? And how could she guide him toward Yahweh's light if he persisted in dragging others, herself included, into darkness? She knew the general's pride, his need to assert control. If he'd tracked Šulmanu down and laid the whip to him...

A little growl rumbled in her throat. She'd *just* nursed the soldier back to health. What good was she to anyone if the general insisted on undoing her efforts?

Head covering a-flutter on the ash-scented wind, Liora gripped her robes in one hand and with the other yanked herself along the wooden rail. Midway up, a stab to her palm hissed air through her teeth. She halted and flipped her hand over to frown at its soft, pale center.

"How appropriate," she muttered, less at the jagged flake of wood embedded at an angle than at the indigo image it pierced. His mark of ownership.

The only difference between herself and the plunder he collected during his systematic destruction of Jerusalem? She was not intended for his "exalted sovereign," King Nebuchadnezzar, but for himself.

Liora yanked the splinter from her flesh. Pressing her thumb against the bloody sting, she inspected the rail, worn smooth but for a fresh gouge, as if recently gouged by the edge of a careless soldier's shield. A thought she would keep to herself. She wouldn't put it past Nebuzaradan to punish whichever guard was responsible, not for the damage to the rail—the house would burn before the month was through—but for the drop of blood it drew.

Banish those who have wounded you...your enemies are my enemies...

Her nostrils flared. Where she was concerned, the man was not entirely in possession of his head.

Banish her father? Teach him to speak? Make him pay? What a child she'd been not to realize he would tamper so thoroughly with her life.

Then there were the twelve guards he'd assigned her. Every last one would escort them shortly into the city. Twelve! What a parade they would make. What an exhibition.

"Lady Liora?" Idadu, the captain of her guard, called down over the rooftop wall. "Is all well?"

Liora ground her molars. "No, Idadu. All is not well." But that was obvious. The soot-black sky said as much on its own.

The rungs vibrated once again beneath her stomping tread.

Idadu jogged to the top of the staircase, arriving before her. His dark eyes were round beneath his conical brass helmet, which gleamed beneath a dusting of ash. Not a wrinkle marred his bright red tunic. Hair combed smartly back and beard coiled and oiled, he was the picture of the polished Babylonian soldier. Fool was the man who did not look smart in the Butcher's guard.

Fool was the woman who mistook that Butcher's protective gestures for anything more than a display of control.

And what of me have you mistaken, child?

The godly thought, not prompted by her own angry mind, slowed her on the last step of the climb.

Admittedly, she was also the fool who put her own demands above whatever work Yahweh intended for a man lost to his own violent past.

"What is it? What has gone wrong?" A scabbard lay along Idadu's thigh, the hilt of a short sword protruding from its top. He held it in a ready grip.

She exhaled. "My heart, Idadu. My heart is wrong." Even as the confession left her mouth, she harbored the notion she could stop the city's unraveling. Must it *all* burn? Must *all* the temple's vessels be carried off? Little remained from the plundering of previous years, but the ark...

Trudging onto the landing, she swung her gaze around to the Holy Mount, the sight stopping her cold. The brass columns, once gleaming and proud, had been decapitated, their beautiful pomegranate capitals missing. Likely strapped to a cart bound for Babylon.

A wail throbbed in her throat, the urge to act, to fix, to *preserve*, welling up alongside it. She forced her breath to steady. There would be time later for grief. For now, there was work to be done. Starting with her soul.

CHAPTER 2

*I have set the Lord always before me:
because he is at my right hand, I shall
not be moved.* (Psalm 16:8)

In the street outside her home, Liora waited for Nebuzaradan to join her and the ring of twelve men parting to allow him through.

He gazed down at her through his good eye and held up her sheathed knife, the one he'd given her. The same she'd buried in Omar's leg yet kept forgetting to wear for dislike of the memory. Its leather thongs dangled about Nebuzaradan's large hand, accusing all on their own. Mouth pursed with silent rebuke, he tied it to her sash. Finished, he patted it against her thigh.

"Stay at my side, Liora," he said, voice stern with warning. "Not one foot outside the escort formation." Worded as if she'd *want* to stray.

In truth, she prayed the general's bulk and the guards' shield wall would block her from judging eyes. If they blocked her own downcast gaze from the char and destruction, all the better.

When he issued the command for a brisk march, Captain Idadu took up the position at her left. On her opposite side, Nebuzaradan walked so close she could turn her head, jut her chin, and snag the leather fringe of his shoulder guards between her teeth, if she weren't covered head to hips in a veil. Rimutu stayed at his general's right, his roving gaze on a constant scan of the narrow winding street leading through the Upper City.

The brown gauze rippling against the tip of Liora's nose was hardly suitable to keep out the fine ash, never mind the sights of tumbled walls, splintered doors, and skeletal structures, their beams warped and blackened.

Of her household, only her handmaid, Devorah, had seen the devastation. Two days earlier, she'd walked the distance from the Babylonian camp, through the Lower City, and up the mount to House Ephraim where Nebuzaradan sequestered Liora within the home's enclosing walls.

One glimpse of her surroundings, one collision with a set of eyes peering from a window—wide, sunken, condemning—was all Liora managed before her throat closed up. She would shut her eyes, too, if rubble didn't clog the path, threatening to trip her at every step.

Yahweh, holy and just, show me your grace this day.

Name her a coward, call her weak and prideful, but she wasn't sure her heart could stand up against much more. If she had a day, one quiet afternoon in which to sit and pray and *breathe*, she might scratch up some fresh energy.

Her rooftop prayers were a balm while they lasted, but the order to depart cut them short and set her heart to quivering. Her beloved city, once the crowning glory of the Most High lay in a heap of desecration. Of all the things she did *not* want to do that morning, walking through Zion's broken bones ranked highest. But for Saba Jeremiah, she would.

"My lord." Liora's soft inquiry drew the general's high, scanning gaze. "Have you received a report on the prophet this morning?"

"I have not." He resumed scouring the tiered rooftops. For what? Did he fear more than hateful eyes? What else remained of her city besides loathing strong enough to kindle a... Her confusion gave way to a name.

The Last Flame. Those who'd hidden in the hills during the siege.

If Devorah's whisperings were true, cloaked members of the so-called Last Flame had been spotted inside the city since the walls fell. She joined Nebuzaradan in scanning the street's shadowed corners.

Could he believe the resistance group would dare attack them? Attack *him*? Surely not.

"But I sent word," he continued, "that we will be arriving for an interview."

The statement returned her worry to Saba Jeremiah. She dearly prayed *interview* was not a veiled term for *interrogation*. If the prophet was as unwell as the captain of her guard claimed, he might not hold up to more than a few pointed questions. "Yesterday eve, I sent Idadu with bread and bones for broth."

"So I heard." Mouth a displeased slash, he passed a look over her head to Idadu.

Had he also heard the soldier's grim report? Per Idadu, the prophet was frail and ill to the point of alarm. So when Nebuzaradan announced the morning's visit, she'd thanked Yahweh and leapt to prepare, instructing Devorah to pack whatever herbs and other medicinals she could spare. Zipporah then dressed Liora in the sedate attire such a visit required. All was in readiness but her courage.

Liora didn't know which she feared most: finding her saba too broken to save from death, finding other survivors too bitter to receive help, or finding that her faith was too weak to save from destruction. Each presented its own challenge. If the Lord took His faithful prophet, she would weep for losing his guidance. If Jerusalem hated her for being favored, if they looked at her with even half of Gittel's bitterness, Nebuzaradan would not hear her pleas on their behalf.

I will banish those who have wounded you.

Even now, his declaration simmered her blood. What foolish things he'd said! And did he mean to take her into his bed or not? The way he veered sharply away every time their strides brought them within brushing distance, she might assume *not*—if he hadn't complained about her absence from his chamber the previous night.

And if her faith crumbled...

No. *Lord, I will not doubt your providence. I will set you ever before me.* She recited King David's song. *With you at my right hand, I shall not be shaken.*

"What do you know of the prophet's upbringing?" Nebuzaradan's question jolted her from prayer. He pointed ahead at a window, its blackened shutter on the ground in pieces. "Movement there."

A FAITH UNTAMED

A soldier broke off at a trot, sword drawn. Female cries and pleading tumbled into the street.

Quite on its own, Liora's hand darted to Nebuzaradan's forearm. She clutched his leather bracer, a demand hovering at her lips, until the soldier reemerged.

His sword hung relaxed, its polished bronze gleaming and clean. He sheathed it, nodded once at his general, and merged back into the advance guard.

"My arm, woman." Nebuzaradan's rumbled observation sprang Liora's fingers open.

She jerked her gaze back to the cobblestones, scrambling to remember his earlier question. The prophet. "Saba Jeremiah, he"—she swallowed thickly—"he is the son of Hilkiah and is of an ancient priestly line from Anathoth, a village in the hills of—"

"I know it."

Of course he did. His army would have passed it on the way to Jerusalem. "Does it…still stand?" Or had he ravaged it as he'd done so many others?

She tangled her fingers in the flowing fabric of her head covering as she waited for Nebuzaradan's narrowed gaze to release a darkened doorway farther down and come back to her.

"I stripped it of resources," he said, matter of fact, "as I do every house and hamlet. But, yes, it stands. The hill it sits on was of little strategic value."

And he'd had his eye fixed on a greater prize. Although, by the smoke coiling up from collapsed roofs and the scattered bones whitening in the sun,

Jerusalem could hardly be called that. Not by any standard man might set.

If not for Jerusalem's wealth, now gathered into Babylonian coffers, and the satisfaction of humiliating a rebellious vassal, it would have been a city to bypass, a place where death crept and disease festered in every shadow.

Even Saba Jeremiah had tried to leave during the reprieve when Babylon withdrew to confront the Egyptians. He'd intended to reassure his siblings he lived, then return to continue his ministry. But Yahweh had prevented it. Guards stopped him at the gate, directed there by city elders who'd accused him of defecting—a thin excuse to arrest him, since the Babylonians were nowhere about. His accusers demanded execution, but her saba was instead tossed into a pit that ruined his health.

Her heart still writhed over how Yahweh had permitted the beloved prophet to suffer. Why? To shape him? Was that why He allowed the mockery, the lies, the captivity? *Why* had he crushed His most faithful prophet?

Nebuzaradan's hand shifted to settle on the pommel of his sheathed sword. "If you were a rebel soldier, Captain, where would you attack?"

Liora's eyes widened. So he *did* consider them vulnerable to the so-called Last Flame.

"At the next block, General," Idadu replied. "It narrows considerably, and there is a sharp, blind turn with high views ideal for bowmen."

"Tell me it has been cleared."

"It has," Idadu said at once.

Nebuzaradan extended an arm to halt Liora. "How long ago?"

Idadu hesitated.

"Do it again."

Nebuzaradan's low, dangerous pitch sapped the color from Idadu's face. The captain knocked a fist against his chest and began issuing orders: four men to move ahead, the rest to close around the general.

Men peeled away, the others drawing in shoulder-to-shoulder, shields out. While the general issued orders with ruthless precision, Liora monitored the slight movements behind broken shutters. How long since their observers had eaten? Or did starvation continue to add to the tally of dead? The burden weighed on her heart, but she had no orders to issue, only prayers to utter.

Use me, Lord. How might I spare your chosen even a little suffering?

Nebuzaradan settled in with crossed arms and faced Liora. "Speak to me of the prophet," he said, though his gaze never stopped roaming the homes, the smelly single-story stable to her immediate left, or the pottery workshop across the street whose earthenware lay shattered in the doorway. "When did he become a mouthpiece of your god?"

Did he truly seek to understand the prophet, or did he use the questions as a distraction from whatever danger he perceived? Another report claimed Babylonian soldiers were mysteriously disappearing. Liora prayed Šulmanu hadn't fallen prey to their precision-strike tactics. She wondered which would be worse for a lone soldier—confronting a band of furious resistors or a general who controlled his troops through displays of punishment.

At least, for the moment, that general's focus was not on her loved ones or even on her. While he stared intently at a rooftop, she answered his query. "Elder Jeremiah has been at the Temple and at the royal court preaching repentance as long as I have been alive. He has always been there, in my memories, in my home." She tipped her head at Nebuzaradan. "Why do you ask, my lord?"

The question, though spoken at normal volume, echoed through the quiet street, and Liora suddenly felt small and vulnerable. Every muscle clenched except her heart. The thing began a rampage inside her chest.

Tension descended upon the guardsmen, Idadu among them. Not a foot shifted. Were they even breathing? Only their hair and the tassels on their tunics moved, rippling in the sultry breeze that cavorted in the street.

"General," she whispered, edging closer to the man.

"Yes, dove."

The *shhh-shhh* of swords slowly sliding from scabbards hissed like snakes disturbed in their den.

Nebuzaradan's was already out, held in a casual grip at his side, having made an exit without Liora's notice. Arms loose at his sides, he turned a deliberate circle, gaze angled high. "Captain," he said, low and tight. "The lady."

"With my life, my lor—"

Myriad twangs cut Idadu off. It wasn't until Liora heard the first thump against a wooden shield that she registered the sound as bowstrings being released—her last thought before Idadu wrenched her sideways to face him. He flung an arm about her, plucked her straight up, and pinned her to his chest. Her nose bent painfully against his leather armor, and her eyes sparked tears.

Then he was running, jostling her limbs like those of a doll. She scrabbled for a handhold, nails digging into his shoulder plates. Her legs flopped uselessly for the five pounding strides it took him to reach the nearest building. Mid-stride, he twisted and drove his shoulder into a solid object. Wood shattered, splinters pelting her shawl like hail. One stumbling step indoors winked out the sun, exchanging its brilliance for the murk and pungent aroma of a stable.

Shouts from the street, dim now through the stone walls, competed with the echoing slap of Idadu's sandals in the abandoned animal pen. His breath jagged in her ear, he dashed to a corner and released her. Before she could steady her wobble, he shoved her down hard by the shoulder. A pile of moldy hay cushioned her clumsy landing, and sour-smelling dust rose about her.

A cough gripped her by the throat, so she could only nod when Idadu commanded, "Stay down!"

He spun toward the entry. No one occupied its vacant center. The door hung lopsided on broken leather hinges, its fragments of decaying wood strewn about. There would be no closing that door again, much to the probable delight of their attackers.

Still coughing, she scraped the veil off her face and scooted back until her shoulders hit rickety wooden slats, a stall's short wall. The place was small, old, and half charred, a victim of Nebuzaradan's razing policy. That the flat roof remained intact was a miracle.

Idadu peered outside. "Their numbers are strong, my lady. I must join your guard, or they'll overwhelm us."

"Go, *go*."

He didn't bother responding. Sword going before him, Idadu darted into the daylight. His vicious snarl met the clang of metal-on-metal.

Whoever they were, they were well armed. But could this be any other than the hillside resistance? Who else would be foolish enough, desperate enough to attack the Butcher under the sun's full eye?

A projectile, its tip bright orange, zipped through the opening, another fast on its trail. The first drove into the wood above her head, its shaft vibrating at eye level. The second buried its head in the hay to her left. Flames erupted. With a bleat of shock, Liora kicked at it and scrambled back. The added hay only fueled its rage. It jumped, and the trailing edge of her shawl caught fire. She ripped it from her shoulders and surrendered it like an offering on a defiled altar.

A FAITH UNTAMED

Several ominous thuds sounded from the wood-slat roof. Already scorched and crumbling, the beams, the hay, the wall at her back, they could not resist the fire. There would be no sheltering in this stable. The clangor outside told her there would be no leaving through the front, either.

A glance back and up at the flames confirmed the decaying stable would not last long. Neither would her access to clean air. Black smoke was already thickening along the ceiling, scraping her airways with its claws.

"Yahweh, preserve me." She croaked the prayer, throat dry from the growing heat. She snatched up her robes and stumbled around the wall in search of another exit.

At the pen's rear, thin strips of light penetrated the smoky air. Was that a door? A sheep gate? Relief jerked her forward, but three strides from the goal, her sandal caught on debris and sent her flying. She sprawled in the ashy dirt, lungs stunned.

"Liora!" Nebuzaradan's bellow overrode that of the inferno.

Gulping for breath, she squinted through watering eyes.

His silhouette, a broad, blackened shadow, paced on the other side of the flaming barrier. "Liora, speak to me!"

Her chest kicked and air skidded down her throat, then racked her with a doubling cough. She curled in on herself, her cheek scraping along the dirt.

"I hear you, dove!"

She found a breath to shout, "Do not come, Arioch! There is—" Another cough gripped her, intent on tearing her ribs apart. "There is...a way out!"

A flaming beam crashed, sending up a shower of red sparks. Nebuzaradan's hazy form disappeared from view. Just as well. He could do nothing for her.

Give me strength, Lord. Liora lurched to her feet. At once, smoke engulfed her. At the gate, she tore her nails in search of a latch. Would she need her knife? No, *there*. Her fingers scraped across a latch. They'd only just released it when the door swung out. She fell forward with it, tumbling into strong arms.

Liora clutched at the man as he dragged her out. Coughing violently, she let him do the work, her legs bumping along and sandals scoring the dirt. Water streamed from her eyes, and no matter her heaving lungs, she could not catch her breath. Could not resist when he picked her up and ran into cooler air, then into the dark interior of another building.

She was unprepared when he pushed her against a wall and wrenched her chin up to look him in the face. One she did *not* expect.

This was no scarred Nebuzaradan or tattooed Idadu. This was no Babylonian at all, but a countryman. Red cording trimmed his black turban, and recognition struck like a knock to her skull.

That light-brown skin, those hazel eyes—all that was visible above the fabric shielding his nose and mouth—they could belong to only one person, a man she had not seen in years. Not since that terrible day he'd led her through the Lower City market on a supposed errand from the king.

Ishmael ben Nethaniah. Member of the royal house of Judah, captain of their offensive forces, and the man who'd looked away when cruel hands hauled Liora into darkness. Much as now. Just how cruel might these hands intend to be?

If her heart weren't in a frantic race to feed her lungs, it would have stopped cold at the thought. She'd believed Ishmael dead or taken captive, along with King Zedekiah. Apparently, he'd fled to the hills with the resistance so he could return and...what?

Slay the Butcher in the streets? Take him captive? Herd Liora into another dark alley? He'd certainly been waiting *here* for her to fling herself out from the fire. A fire likely caused by *his* men. Intentionally, if his readiness to catch her was any clue.

Wheezing, she gaped at him and fumbled for the knife at her waist.

He batted her hand away from the weapon. "Shalom, Liora." The bid for peace effectively disarmed her.

Even so, her fist clenched, and a vicious urge rose within her to claw at his face. Shalom? *Shalom?* Where was peace in this act of violence? Where?

Where was *shalom* in her swollen throat and baked skin? She would certainly not find it in the bloodied street or in the fire that almost ate her alive.

Panting through needy lungs, she could say none of this, which seemed to suit Ishmael just fine. He twisted at the neck for a backwards look. "*Water*, woman. The lady cannot breathe!"

Now he cared for her well-being? Where was that care years ago?

Scrabbling noises answered the command, and Liora's surroundings slowly registered. He'd dragged her into someone's home. To do what exactly with her? Whatever this was, it was no selfless act.

Fingers loosening on her upper arms, he took a bowl of water one-handed from a female figure obscured by his body. "Now get out," he snapped before bringing the dish to Liora's lips. A gift she would not refuse, no matter her aversion to the man or her suspicions of his motives.

The woman scurried out the door just as sweet water poured over Liora's chin and down her throat. She sucked at it greedily before shoving it away and glaring up at him. "What do you want with me?"

His eyes crinkled with a smile she could not see under the mask, but well knew. "Your trials have made you wise."

"Trials *you* began."

"A man cannot disobey his king," he shot back and released her completely.

Her knees wobbled but kept her upright. They would not hold her long. "Tell me what you want, Ishmael, or go back to your hole in the rocks."

He chuckled. "Speaking bluntly, are we? Very well, Liora. I will say it bluntly. Any woman in the Butcher's bed is one I want aiding our cause."

A FAITH UNTAMED

He might as well have called her a harlot. Shame prickled at the implication and at the confirmation of how Jerusalem judged her predicament.

Ishmael held up a hand to stay the protest rising in her tortured throat. "*But* I have justly earned your distrust. Allow me to repair it with a gift."

"I want nothing from you. And Nebuzaradan provides all I need."

"Can he provide Omar the Kenez?"

Liora didn't mean to freeze at the name. Or was it at the thought of capturing the man of her nightmares? Of preventing him from stalking her again? Whatever the cause of her shock, Ishmael caught it, that gleam returning to his eyes.

"Yes, my lady, I have that filth in my power, and I am pleased to give him to you. Although, I imagine your butcher of a lover will be more pleased yet. His revenge will be...thorough." Ishmael's voice went light with pleasure. "I almost pity the Edomite."

The only thing the general and the rebel leader might ever have in common was their hatred of Omar. Ishmael simply because the man was Edomite. Nebuzaradan because that Edomite had dared to harm her.

A swallow convulsed her throat. Ishmael spoke true, as she had when she'd warned Omar that her husband would flay him alive. That gruesome fact did not stop her from saying, "Where is he?"

The thunder of feet echoed down the street. Shouts rang out. Liora's name mixed with oaths and orders.

Ishmael whipped his head toward it, then back to Liora as he edged for the rear door. "Within the hour, you will find him bound and gagged at the ruins of the cloth merchant's hall."

"Cloth merchant's hall?" Her breath snagged on the last word. The name of the place clung like soured dye to the back of her throat. She had not stepped foot near that hall in years. Not since…

She shoved the thought away. This was not the time to remember. Not the place to break. But to let her anger fly. "You are cruel to choose that place." And for being the next man in a line of them to use her as a pawn, a piece on a board moved against her will.

"Not cruel. Intentional." He secured his face covering as he went. "As for your assistance with our cause, I will find you."

Assistance with what? Taking down the entire Babylonian army? Futility!

"I promise you nothing," she said to his back.

"Take the offering of peace. Consider it a gift."

A twisted gift. But one she would not refuse.

"Think on it. The resistance needs you, Liora. Your *people* need you. Do not fail us."

On that pleading note, he slipped out the door, leaving Liora to slide down the wall and wonder how she was going to tell Nebuzaradan, whose fury was sure to ignite.

Or if she even should.

CHAPTER 3

*They have healed also the hurt of the
daughter of my people slightly, saying,
Peace, peace; when there is no peace.*
(Jer. 6:14)

Nebuzaradan never questioned Liora about why he found her sheltered in a stranger's home. Liora never questioned why he promptly escorted her home, set Devorah upon her with a slew of tonics, and went on to Saba Jeremiah's alone.

And Captain Idadu, bless his obedient soldier's heart, did not question why she instructed him to send a contingent of soldiers to the destroyed cloth merchant's hall to retrieve a traitor, then warned him it might be a trap.

Not the first time the place had been used as such. As Ishmael well knew.

A cluster of women had gathered around the inner courtyard's cook fire, preparing the next meal with Liora. Only two were not family: Gittel and Sapir, who had no place to go and received an exemption from Nebuzaradan's order to clear the home. Liora hated to admit she did not miss her hosting responsibilities, much preferring the relative ease of leading the few women working alongside her.

While they split beans, she pitched an ear toward the street, eager for the general's return. The women, meanwhile, pecked at her with an endless stream of inquiries. Each a reminder she'd nearly died that morning, and Nebuzaradan was out there now, walking those dangerous streets. None of the commentary addressed the Edomite rendered unconscious and tied to a column in the atrium. Ishmael's "gift."

"Was the fire frightening?"

"Were the attackers part of the Last Flame, do you think?"

"Did you recognize any of the men?"

"Might Hannah's father have been among them?"

"Did they wound the Butcher?"

That last one, muttered by Hannah herself, popped Liora's gaze off the green pod in her hand. She didn't look at the young woman, one of Abba's new wives, but at Idadu where he stood guard by the door leading into the home.

Face impassive, he did not appear to be aware of the gravity of their discussion. Ignorant of their language, he understood only tone and body tension, the reason Liora kept a carefully relaxed posture. As much as she could through the coughs scraping her tormented throat.

The mark on her palm tingled where she clasped the bowl. Or did she only imagine its perpetual reminder of her bondage?

"Wound the Butcher?" Gittel flung a bean into the bowl seated between herself and Liora. The woman, inspired by the permanent curl of Idadu's lip, had decided it was wiser to busy her hands rather than lounge about, moping. Unfortunately for the home's tenuous peace, she busied her tongue as well. "We can hope they did."

Liora's back went rigid, and Idadu's head came around.

Devorah clacked her mixing spoon on the edge of the bowl cradled by her crossed legs, one firm rap. "Hush, you fool of a cow!"

Sapir startled where she lay napping on the lap of Liora's dearest friend, Zipporah.

They all startled, Idadu included, then stared toward the north when a low rumble, like distant thunder swelled into a bellow that rang over the courtyard wall. Over the entire city, judging by its strength.

The roar dimmed, ushering in a silence that Devorah broke with a nervous laugh. "Was that..." She frowned.

"A lion?" Liora completed the thought, chills crawling over her skin. She'd never heard a lion's roar, but if she were made to describe one, it would be *that*. Booming, majestic, commanding.

Terrifying.

A whimper from Sapir invited the prompt shake of Liora's head. "Impossible. Temple work is all." She shared a questioning glance with Idadu, who gave a little shrug.

If a lion had made its way into the city, they were all safe enough inside the house. Although...
Nebuzaradan was *not* in the house.

Zipporah made soothing noises as she stroked Sapir's thin brown hair. "All's well, child. Finish your sleep." Zipporah met Liora's eyes over the top of the girl's head and smiled. "All's well."

Liora blinked and expelled a breath before nodding. Her friend was right. Rebels and lions were nothing to the general Yahweh had chosen for a task not yet complete.

Sapir settled once again, but her eyelids did not ease back down. Liora's didn't either. They kept darting in the direction of the street.

"Cow I may be," Gittel said on the *snap!* of a pod, not distracted one whit from her bitterness, "but we are *all* thinking it. At least, the loyal of us are." She cast Liora a blatant side-eye.

Liora flinched.

Gittel's words skimmed rather close to evil speech. She had all but named Liora a traitor, which cut to the very heart of her purpose. Wasn't Liora meant to stand as a shield between her people and her general-husband? How could she be an advocate and shield when they refused her any dignity or trust?

Clearly, her trek into the lion's maw hadn't salvaged her character. Had, in fact, affirmed her supposed disloyalty. A true Judahite would have returned headless.

Silence descended on the group. Every gaze weighed on Liora, Idadu's the heaviest.

Anxiety gripped her. Multiply Gittel's hate by a hundred or even a dozen, and Liora might find herself in the street once more, bracing for a stoning.

Where was Nebuzaradan?

A FAITH UNTAMED

A coal in the fire crackled and tumbled. Sapir let out a tremulous whine, and three beans tumbled from Liora's lax fingers onto the pile.

Devorah's face reddened. She rattled like a lidded pot, then exploded. "Out! Out with you!" Beans flying from her lap, she shot to her feet. She stormed around the circle, gray wisps flying about her face, spoon brandished high. "Out of this courtyard, out of this house!"

"Devorah." Liora drew out the handmaid's name, tone mild despite her scratchy voice. The weapon froze above Gittel's ducking head. "Leave her to Yahweh's judgment."

"Or Idadu's." A small, contented smile played about Zipporah's lips, the same that took up residence the previous day when she'd announced to Liora and Devorah that, come spring, there might be a squalling addition to House Ephraim. She'd not yet shared her suspicions with her husband, Liora's father. Wise, considering they'd been wed under a month, and nothing was confirmed.

"Personally, I would take Yahweh's wrath over the captain's." Zipporah juggled a squirming Sapir as the child clung to Zipporah's neck. "Look at him, just waiting for Devorah to have her go before he pounces."

Every eye angled toward the man. He'd turned fully toward them, his taut figure speaking every form of pouncing readiness, his glower speaking of his short patience. Since rushing in from the rebel attack, Liora had bathed and eased her nerves on Devorah's lavender tea. In all that time, per Zipporah's report, the captain hadn't sat once.

Ash darkened his neck, and a smear of blood caked his temple. Not his own, he assured her. He'd spent the ensuing time standing stiff with tension, his attention divided between Liora's every slight cough and any sound coming over the courtyard wall from the street.

Liora suspected he blamed himself for her near roasting. Miraculously, Nebuzaradan did not. The general must have understood that Idadu did everything in his power to keep her safe. Either that or her husband recognized she would not forgive him if he exercised his frustration on her guard. Idadu would punish himself enough as it was. Even more when they learned the leader of the resistance had had her in his possession.

Had her. Let her go. Intended to find her again, to use her.

How, *how* had she come to be in such a predicament, balancing on a blade's edge between love for her people and loyalty to the man Yahweh had placed her under? Tip the slightest way in either direction, and she was bound to grieve.

A sigh shuddered out of her. One hour at a time. For *this* hour, she had only to survive Gittel's contempt and *somehow* help her survive Devorah and Idadu.

A request for action arched the captain's brow. She waved it away, then wrenched her head toward the crisp march of feet in the street. Only soldiers moved with such precision.

A FAITH UNTAMED

She felt the blood drain from her head and sought Zipporah's eyes. Worry creases replaced her friend's smile.

"Your husband comes, Lady Liora." Idadu snapped his fingers at the guard stationed across the patio before ducking into the building, his red cloak whipping behind him.

Expression somber, the guard crossed the space and took a position near Liora. The other women shifted and murmured. Gittel kicked over the bean bowl in her haste to rise. Cursing bloody generals, she fled up the rooftop stairs.

Liora gazed longingly after her. She would dash off, too, if she could avoid Nebuzaradan's wrath upon the Edomite captain. Upon the trust he'd placed in her, should his understanding of her motives for silence prove thin.

"You should not delay." Zipporah's sweet voice at Liora's ear got her moving.

As she entered the atrium, she barely recalled how she'd arrived. Zipporah held her by the crook of her arm, taking an embarrassing amount of her weight. Liora straightened and turned her back on the bloodied, drooling figure slumped before a stone column. Swallowing a bitter wash, she faced the large front door just as it swung open wide.

Several soldiers strode in first. The crossed swords on their chest plates designated them part of Nebuzaradan's house. Gaze down, brow furrowed, he entered next. Rimutu maintained his assigned position, looking somewhat worse for the wear, his bent ears droopier than usual.

Walking at Nebuzaradan's left was a lieutenant Liora remembered only from the mop of dark curls springing out from around his helmet. Presently, he carried the helmet under his arm, and sweat matted the curls to his forehead.

"...work proceeds as ordered," the lieutenant was saying, voice clipped. Red dust clung to his sandals and the thick hair of his calves, and wet stained his tunic under the arms. "The gold from the wine and oil chamber has been stripped and sorted from the brass. We should be finished there by sunset tomorrow. As for the—" His abrupt halt followed Nebuzaradan's.

From five strides off, the general had Liora in his sights. Doubtless no part of her escaped his notice. The anticipation heightening her shoulders, the uncertainty squirming her mouth, the worry knotting her hands together. She unhooked them.

He watched the move, head angled to better see through his good eye. "What is it, my dove?" He shot a questioning look at Idadu.

While they exchanged silent dialogue, Liora ran a quick assessment of Nebuzaradan's form, counting his wounds from the bandaged forearm to the fresh contusion on his jaw and the still-seeping wound on his forehead. He'd not collected any new damage on this outing.

Something inside her released. May Yahweh forgive her this growing dependence on the man.

A FAITH UNTAMED

She lowered her chin. "Welcome, husband. Peace be upon you and this house. How did you find the prophet Jeremiah?"

His kohl-rimmed eyelids narrowed on her. "Blunt. Stubborn. Weepy."

A smile wobbled Liora's mouth. "Yes." She itched to know whether he'd relieved Nebuzaradan of his oath, but dared not broach the topic in front of his men. "His health?"

"Recovering," he said, impatient. Body poised on the edge of action, he darted his eyes about as if in search of an enemy perched on the atrium's roof tiles. There would be no more delaying. "Will you tell me what distresses you? Or must I—"

Liora took one sideways step and exposed the Edomite to his view.

His black eyes shifted, lit on Omar's crumpled form, and went wide. Every muscle in his body seemed to harden at once. Those of his calves, exposed by his thigh-length tunic, corded and strained against his dark skin. His nostrils splayed, and his chest expanded under his armor.

One hand fisted at his side; the other dropped to the handle of his ax. Did he even notice he gripped it? Every form of violence scrolled across his face. Nothing else bled through. No hint of mercy, of awareness others watched, or even memory that she stood before him.

Axe coming out, he moved.

"Arioch!" Liora resorted to his boyhood name. Another slide of the foot put her back between him and his target.

He pulled up hard, stopping so close his smoke and musk scent wrapped about her. Smudges of gray remained on his neck despite his earlier washing. He looked down at her now, eyes sparking anger before recognizing her and fizzling out. His brows meshed. "Liora?"

"Peace in this home, husband." She placed both palms on the etched surface of his molded armor and gazed up at him through eyes still watering with irritation. Blinking her vision clear, she felt a cool streak trail along the side of her face.

Mouth softening, he watched the tear's path until it reached her chin.

In the worst timing, Omar groaned behind her, coming awake.

Nebuzaradan's sword arm jerked, freeing another hand's width of bronze.

Liora pushed back. "Peace, I beg you!"

She flattened her tattooed palm against one of the axes on his breastplate, the symbol of her servitude pressing in stark defiance against the symbol of his power.

He hissed between clenched teeth. "Do *not* ask mercy of me, woman. I will not give it."

A small cough bounced her shoulders, then another. Unable to speak more than "Hear me," she shook her head and felt a sudden rush of weariness. She rested her forehead against the hard leather covering his torso. She stood, catching her breath and staring at Nebuzaradan's whitened knuckles where they wrapped about his axe's handle, finding reprieve only when the blade slid home again.

His chest compressed, and breath feathered across her head covering. "Who knew a dove could be so cruel?" The question emerged low and rough with frustration. "Causing me to falter, demanding I show weakness before my men."

"Wielding mercy is harder than giving in to violence. Only the strongest men can achieve it."

"Bah! Mercy is a woman's tool. As is denying a man blood, then weeping against him when he cannot hold you. Cruelty, I say."

So. The prophet had not disencumbered him of the vow? Was that relief toying with her stomach or...disappointment? Would she mind if Nebuzaradan wrapped his arms about her to reassure her of his...what? Trust? Protection? Affection?

He'd not approached her in the house where they'd found her, but kept himself away, pacing like a caged beast behind Rimutu, his personal guard, as he helped her to her feet. But she hadn't wanted Rimutu's touch. As loyal and noble as he seemed, he was still a man she did not know.

Remarkably, General Nebuzaradan, the man who'd decided to call himself her husband, did not fit into that category. The fright of that pulled her off him and sent her back a step. "As if I had any power over Babylon's highest general."

His chuckle was the quiet, dry sort. "Perhaps I should let you continue believing you are powerless."

Whatever influence he believed she had over him came from Yahweh. She was only His mouthpiece, a weak reflection of His light. But this was not the time to point that out, not with a dangerous traitor stirring to life behind her.

Liora dabbed her wet eyes and nose as she flicked a glance at the Edomite. "Whatever you intend for the man, please, do it far from here. I could not... Cannot bear to hear..." A shudder traveled her shoulders.

"Shah, dove. Do not distress yourself further. I will take him away, so you mustn't witness. He will be dealt with in the camp. And *you*, my poor, ailing wife, will take to bed for the rest of the day." He arched an eyebrow. "Have we an agreement?"

"We have," she replied at once, the guilt of abandoning the other women to their work a meager price to pay for sparing them Omar's inevitable screams. She lifted Nebuzaradan the strongest smile she could muster under the circumstances. "There is much to discuss. Will I see you this evening?"

"Naturally." Spoken like a man with certain privileges. "Who do I have to thank for tracking down this cursed rat?"

Her heart thudded twice hard, once for his assumptions, once for her apprehensions. Both justified. "As I said, we have much to discuss, but it was Captain Idadu who brought him in from the cloth merchant's hall. The rest I will gladly share"—she glanced about, taking in the soldiers who'd not bothered to step back a respectful distance—"in privacy."

Avoiding Nebuzaradan's penetrating gaze, she swallowed, uttered a silent prayer, and continued. "Should you uncover anything between now and then, my lord, consider that I acted on the hope Omar the Kenez might know what became of my faithful guard, Šulmanu."

Nebuzaradan's head leaned to the side. "You fear I will be angry with you."

"Oh, you will undoubtedly be angry. Whether with *me* is not so certain."

"I see..." He clasped his hands behind him and leaned back to assess her from beneath shuttered eyelids. The scar running through his eyebrow wrinkled with his scrutiny.

Her insides squirmed, begged her to break her confident, chin-level pose. She held steady until Nebuzaradan's lips twitched, rippling the whiskers on his upper lip.

"As for what the Kenez may know about your guard," he said, leaning forward again to speak in intimate tones, "I will most gladly learn."

CHAPTER 4

*Then said he unto me, The iniquity of
the house of Israel and Judah is
exceeding great, and the land is full of
blood, and the city full of perverseness:
for they say, The Lord hath forsaken the
earth, and the Lord seeth not.... I will
recompense their way upon their head.*
(Ez. 9:9–10)

The small lamp seated in the wall niche cast flickering shadows along the dark corridor ahead of Liora and the basin of water she carried. The lamp's thin amber arch did little to dispel the chill in Nebuzaradan's voice echoing from her abba's requisitioned chambers.

"You hear the folly she speaks, Captain," Nebuzaradan said.

Folly? The word stopped her cold. The sheathed blade tapped her thigh, and water jostled in her bowl.

How many in the house had overheard his outburst? Her place among her people was already tenuous. The last thing she needed was his public scorn added to their disdain. So long as he stood with her—his power at her back—so long as she had his listening ear, she could bear the people's contempt.

The thought of losing those privileges set her insides to quivering. Would Yahweh demand she stand alone, as He did Jeremiah?

A FAITH UNTAMED

The basin shook, its vinegar water sloshing dangerously close to the rim. Its tangy aroma released into the air. Not an unwelcome change from the ash clinging to her airways. She stared down at the clean cloth draped over her forearm and listened as he carried on in the same exasperated manner.

"She requests mercy on his behalf? Ha! A quick death is *not* in that traitor's future. Mercy! Toward her enemy!" Nebuzaradan's words boomed with pure frustration. "She may as well strip me of my general's tassels, as well as my manhood."

"Her thinking is indeed quite unusual," Captain Idadu replied, tone placid, no hint of indulgence. He would not be encouraging the general's snit.

Her own fault for setting him off. Upon arriving home that evening, the general had come to her room straightaway to tell her Omar was being tight-lipped about Šulmanu, and to check that she was well. A kind gesture, if one ignored the blood speckling Nebuzaradan's armor and darkening the creases of his knuckles.

Granted, the stains could have come from the morning's battle in the street. Had she simply not noticed in the courtyard? Unfortunately, Liora had not been thinking of the clash, but of the Edomite Nebuzaradan had been all too pleased to prod at sword point out the door. None in that party would care if the man arrived in the general's camp with a few holes in his hide.

Flustered by him suddenly *there*, Liora might have spoken hastily. Things to do with the courtesy of washing before entering a lady's presence. She *might* have even requested a swift death for the Edomite. Although as she stood in the corridor now, she could recall only one thing with any clarity: the heat on her cheeks from the general's overwhelming presence in her bedchamber.

Liora huffed and set herself in motion once again, firming her resolve. The man could *boom* all he wanted; he would not persuade her to accept brutality. She entered her abba's old room on silent, bare feet.

His broad back to her, the general stood with one arm lifted, fidgeting and complicating Idadu's attempts to loosen the side buckles of his chest plate.

Where was the armor bearer or Haldi, the general's steward? Haldi had been scarce since the invasion. Banished, she'd assumed, for his part in the unfinished mark on her palm. Liora glanced about for either man but saw only the heavy frame of her abba's elaborately carved bed looming from the darkness.

She looked sharply away to the lamp sputtering on a short-legged table. It stood beside the lounging cushions arranged near the doors leading into the garden. Tonight, they were shut up, as they had been since Nebuzaradan's torches first touched Jerusalem.

"You hear how she speaks to me. The men hear, too." Nebuzaradan plucked the brass helmet from his head and waved it expansively.

"Would the general prefer," Idadu said mildly, "that I not remind him that he appreciates his lady's boldness?"

A FAITH UNTAMED

A loud snort from Nebuzaradan, then, "I should lock her in these chambers lest she inspire notions of insubordination."

Nonsense. The man was full of nonsense. He had set her free from his camp; he would never lock her up. What need for that when she bore his inked chains wherever she went? And Liora, humble servant of Yahweh, the God who'd ordained Babylon's control of Jerusalem, was the least likely person in the city to incite rebellion. Apart, perhaps, from Saba Jeremiah.

Thought of the prophet sent her padding toward the little table by the cushion. Half of her reason for coming to Nebuzaradan was to glean details from his visit to her saba. The other half... Well, it comprised a variety of parts, most of them requiring a lowered posture. Apologies and confessions were best felt through the knees.

The soft thump of her bowl settling down pulled Idadu's attention to her. Their gazes met, and his mouth opened.

Liora shook her head and used the cloth to wave him back to work. When he waffled, gaze flitting to his general, she laid the towel on the table and folded her hands neatly before her. She would reveal her presence in her own time.

The captain cleared his throat and resumed yanking at the leather straps of the general's armor. "Lady Liora has become every soldier's sister."

She had? Liora's brow arched. Was that...good? It did not sound *bad*. But clearly, there were implications, or Idadu would not have brought it up. Nebuzaradan seemed to agree.

"What has that to do with anything? Speak plainly, Captain."

"The men notice her defiance, yes, but they love her for it." The last strap came free, so Idadu moved to his general's opposite side.

The statement stilled Nebuzaradan's hand where he'd been scrubbing his scalp. "That has strains of mutiny in it." He lifted the other arm for Idadu, lowering the first and leaving his black hair standing upright on his head.

"Not at all." Idadu bent to access the bottom-most side buckle. "They love her for it because they know that should they ever be on the receiving end of your wrath, their sister might be present in the form of your wife. They have the comfort that, even should you refuse her pleas for mercy—as is your right, yourself being a just lord—in their last moments a gentle soul will be at their side, acting with tenderness toward them."

"They assume I will expose my beloved's *gentle soul* to the violence of punishment. No, I have swiftly learned the futility of that." Nebuzaradan made a self-deprecating sound. "Since you are in such a sharing mood, what else do the men think of my dove?"

"They will shed blood for her, die for her as they would their own kin."

"As they should. As they have been commanded."

Idadu yanked hard on the top buckle. It sprang free. He took the armor by the shoulder joints and heaved it off the general's stiff frame. "With every respect, General, they would not so readily die for Lady Aralu. And if you—" He snapped his mouth shut and backed up a stride, angling his crisp bow toward her in view of Nebuzaradan.

Liora took the signal as the end of his tolerance and stepped forward. "And if he *what,* Captain?"

Nebuzaradan twisted to peer behind him. His black eyes alighted upon her, and the scowl lines carving his scar deep smoothed away. His whiskers twitched. "You have been spying."

"I understood myself to always be welcome in your bedchamber, even without summons. Did I mishear?"

"You did not. Save for bloodshed, there is nothing I would hide from you. *Nothing.*" Mouth sliding to the side, he grabbed fistfuls of his tunic and made a yanking motion, as if to remove it.

Liora spun on her heel, neck an instant oven. "My lord!" The cry spawned a cough, its rough hack drowned in the bellow of laughter filling the room.

"I tease! I tease, woman. There will be no disrobing. Do not distress your weakened lungs."

Eyes rolling high, Liora spoke to the ceiling beams. "And you accuse *me* of cruelty." Was it his own cruelty—the hours spent tormenting the Edomite— that had him in such good spirits? The notion revived her earlier pique. "Subjected to arrows and fire and the threat of man's flesh all in one day. It is too much!" The exclamation was only part jest.

Nebuzaradan burst out again with laughter, this time joined by Idadu. "Ah, my dear, brave Jerusalem dove. It is true; the day has been exceptionally trying. But the threats are past. Your virginal eyes are quite safe. You may turn back." The humor, much to her chagrin, had not left his voice.

"Once my cheeks have cooled." Voice vinegar tart, she dunked the cloth in the warm water.

He chuckled. "As you like. While I wait upon your good time, the captain will answer your question."

"Yes, Lord General." Unlike his superior, Idadu shed the levity right quick. "As I was saying, if you treat Lady Liora harshly by locking her away, you risk losing the soldiers' loyalty. Treat her firmly but kindly, and they will follow you to the ends of our great kingdom. Let her be seen among the men, my lord. Nowhere else will she be safer."

"As she was safe today in the company of your men?" The swift retort was not quite a snarl, but neither was it free of warning.

It rotated Liora where she stood, water dripping from her hands. Neither man glanced at her, Nebuzaradan occupied with levying his captain a flat-mouthed stare and Idadu with looking back, seemingly unfazed.

"My pardon, General, but I meant to request you allow me to take her beyond these walls into the safety of our host. This city is a constant danger to her. Every time she leaves this enclosure, she will be at risk. The so-called Last Flame is one such risk, but consider also how the ash and smoke distress her health."

Whether from the shock of the suggestion or simply because she was due a cough, her lungs chose

A FAITH UNTAMED

that moment to spasm. Through the jolting cough, she wagged her head at Nebuzaradan. Her leave-taking would come, but so soon? His campaign of dismantling and destruction had only begun, and what of determining the fate of the people? What about establishing a new government? She'd expected to stay in the comfort of her home until the very end, when Babylon's carts began rolling toward the Euphrates. Not *now*.

She would press her case if the coughing would ever let up.

Brow furrowed, Nebuzaradan studied her while giving his helmet a slow turn between his hands. "I have much need of her as liaison, and daily travel between the city and the camp would be equally hazardous. But..." He rubbed his black chin whiskers. "Perhaps it is time I transfer official matters to the camp."

Idadu bowed curtly. "Let them come to *you*, my lord. In the camp."

Patting her chest, she caught a breath and looked back and forth between them.

Nebuzaradan grunted. "Your reasoning has merit."

It did, unfortunately. But wasn't Prince Nergal due in a few days? Surely, he would be taking over most of the "official matters" with whatever system he had in place. After all, when conquering cities, Babylon had plenty of experience to draw on. Reminding Nebuzaradan of the prince's arrival did not seem a wise course of action right before an overdue confession.

"I will consider it." The general tossed his helmet at Idadu, who lurched to catch it. "Now, get out. My wife will assist from here."

Idadu's retreating strides were fading while Nebuzaradan dragged an upholstered bench to the basin's table. It wasn't until he was seated, arms crossed and long legs extended, that Liora's pulse began to wobble.

Your words, Yahweh. Only yours.

Grateful for the task of removing his shin guards, she settled on her knees before him. Doing her best to ignore his penetrating gaze, she set to loosening the broad leather strap wrapped about his thick calf. "My lord husband, my heart is bowed in repentance before you," she began, voice soft. "As it was before Yahweh a short while ago. You came to my chamber in good will, and I repaid it with tart criticism."

A silent moment passed before he spoke. "Would you take it back? Reverse your plea for a traitor's swift death?"

She paused her unwrapping. "I...would not." Having released that bold truth into the air, she resumed, eyes on her work. "Because his offense is mostly against *me*, I should have a voice in his sentencing." Strap removed, she peeled the stiff leather guard off his shin. At his extended silence, a knot twisted in her stomach. "And now, you will charge me again with folly."

"I should, yes," he said, more grumble in the admission than she'd like.

A FAITH UNTAMED

But since he said *should* instead of *would*, she scooted to his opposite leg and pressed on with her folly. "Once Omar has given up any knowledge of Šulmanu's whereabouts, his beheading should be carried out at once."

He heaved a pained sigh, then bent to rub at the red marks left on the thick muscle of his calf. "Captain Idadu could not tell me how you came to learn the Kenez would be found precisely there. Because you did not tell *him*. Why?"

The shift in subject connected their gazes. The obsidian black of his, combined with the fact he'd ignored her request, did not bode well for her chances of escaping this conversation without a sharp rebuke—in the best case. In the worst? If he'd been serious about locking her away, she might soon become exceedingly useless.

He stretched his other leg before her, never releasing her from his demanding gaze.

Her fingers drifted to the ties on the second shin guard as she dug deep for a resonant timbre that portrayed a grasp of military protocols she did not have. "A soldier needs only the information pertinent to a successful mission. Besides,"—she shrugged and plucked at the loosening strap—"he is savvy enough to have figured it out on his own. As are you, I suspect," she ended much quieter than she'd begun.

"I do appreciate," he said, every word bright with false levity, "that I am the first to hear a member of the Last Flame cornered and attempted to manipulate my wife."

Not a member. The leader. Liora was no advocate of resistance and violence, not in this case, but Ishmael was a fellow Judahite. She was not unsympathetic.

"His name?" he demanded, implacable, all brightness quite gone.

Liora's eyelids slid closed. "My lord, please. I am pressed from both sides."

"A pitiable position, certainly. Especially for my tenderhearted dove. But Liora," his voice sharpened, "how do you expect to maintain my confidence if you withhold information?" A quiet shift, then his upturned hand came into her view. It hovered, giving her a moment to study the callouses and abrasions covering its deep creases. She frowned at it until a swift curl of his fingers stirred the air beneath her chin. "Look at me."

She did not. Instead, she took his roughened fingers with both hands and bowed her forehead to the curled line of his knuckles. "*Please*, Arioch." Her grip tightened, and his jagged fingernails pricked her skin. "Can you not trust me implicitly? I made the man no promises."

His hand bent, almost reflexively, around hers and squeezed gently before he pulled out of her light hold. "You accepted his bribe. That is promise enough."

She looked at him then...and wished she hadn't. In the dark pools of his eyes lived a latent power that evoked a quiet dread. Did she fear him? As one did the crash of thunder.

The lamplight flickered shadows across his face, the air between them as unstable as the light.

"I told him I would take Omar, but that it meant nothing in this war," she said. "He has *much* to account for. I accepted his gift for those reasons. No obligation attached."

Eyes hardening around the edges, he propped a hand on his thigh and leaned toward her. "This man is familiar to you."

In protecting her honor, she'd revealed too much. "Y-yes."

"What reasons? How do you know him? Who *is* he?"

Her head was shaking, small strokes of refusal, before she thought to stop it. "You make me a traitor to my people."

"They have resisted the will of your god." His voice graveled. "*They* are the traitors. And *I* am the will of your god."

Liora drew back sharply, angling her weight over her tucked heels. "Your *pride*, my lord. If it becomes overgrown, my Lord God will humble you so that—"

"And what does your lord god say of obedience to authority?" He growled the question, and she could no longer remember why she was protecting the rebel.

Her throat convulsed through a dry swallow, and her eyes stung. "Ishmael." The name was a painful rasp. At Nebuzaradan's arched brow, she added, "Ishmael ben Nethaniah."

He blinked. "Nethaniah... Cousin to King Zedekiah?"

"Correct." The man's intricate knowledge of her kingdom's customs and history had amazed her from the first. It seemed she must add familiarity with Judah's royal lineage to those wonders. Just one more explanation for how this man had risen to the top of his peers, then shot so far beyond them in exploits they were mere specks beneath him.

"And why does this Ishmael, cousin to the puppet king, feel beholden to you?"

Her stomach sank, that dread coming to life. Because, *of course*, Nebuzaradan would not leave it at a name. She began easily enough. "Years ago, at the king's order, he escorted me to the cloth merchant's hall. To one of the back rooms near the old market inn. He surrendered me to the Edomite who, who—"

There, her throat closed up. She touched the spot, startled at its rebellion.

"Liora?"

Waving him off, she wrenched her tunic away from her feet and unfolded herself. When her toes tangled into the strap of the discarded shin guard, she caught herself on the general's bare knee. It may as well have been a red coal. She snatched her hand away and spun from him, face scorching.

The room pressed in on her, as if the Edomite herded her once again into that confined, windowless space, past bales of cloth, through the dye-reeking storeroom behind the inn, into the hay-strewn corner where the proprietress *happened* to find them.

"I understand, dove." Nebuzaradan's voice came from far away.

Could he understand, though? Had he ever been a woman, one used to inflict damage on a man he hated, to barter for a morsel of food, to play the part of a treasure won in battle?

"Say no more," he continued. "Only breathe."

The bitter odor of madder root dye and the pungent scent of sweaty man and decaying hay stuffed up her nose. She coughed hard to clear it. Crossing the chamber, she flung open the garden door, stood at the threshold, and breathed deep. But was it better to smell the ash of her burning city?

Darkness had newly fallen, but that eerie orange, perpetual now in its glow, illuminated the night. Its hot wind funneled through the fig trees, rattling their broad leaves and smacking Liora in the face hard enough to knock the memory back to the recesses of her mind. Her head covering belled about her face before blowing off. She let it fall on her back and listened to Nebuzaradan's quiet tread.

He stopped so close behind her his heat was almost as intense as the fire-scorched wind drying the tears on her cheeks. "So..." he said, tone deceptively soft, as gentle as the movements pulling the veil from her shoulders. "The man absolves his wicked deed by offering another violent Edomite. In the hopes you will forgive him and...what? Pass along clues for how to eliminate me?" He scoffed. "He and his scrabbling cave rats cannot hope to flush mighty Babylon from Judah."

Liora cleared her throat and prayed it obeyed her. "He did not say exactly. Only that I am to assist in his efforts. He will find me."

"If he does," Nebuzaradan growled the threat, "he will greatly regret it. The Kenez for proof." His arm appeared around her, not quite an embrace. The length of her veil dangled from his fist. Even in the poor light, the dark grime on his knuckles reminded her of why she'd brought the basin.

"Let me tend to you." She wrapped her fingers about his wrist, took the veil, and turned to lead him back.

The general followed without a hitch of resistance. The cords of his broad wrist lay slack under her grasp. An image formed in her mind, and she snorted airily at the irony: Arioch, a lion with a roar strong enough to level a city, clipping along behind her as meekly as a lamb.

"What do you find humorous, my dove?"

"I thought briefly of your sketch. The cavorting lambs."

He chuckled, a pleased sound. "You admired that."

"I admired your skill and wit." She did *not* admire the precarious position it had placed her in with Judah's former king. But she had survived, and Zedekiah was in chains awaiting his doomed journey to King Nebuchadnezzar where he would answer for his rebellion.

A shudder traveled her shoulders. If she knew anything of Nebuchadnezzar's wrath, Zedekiah would soon envy the Edomite's relative ease from this world.

At the basin, she tossed the veil aside and sank Nebuzaradan's hand under the water. He hissed and flinched, but she applied her weight and held him under. "Stop wiggling and let the vinegar do its cleaning work." Taking the cloth, she helped it along by rubbing at his knuckles.

He grunted. "Only if you tell me why you delayed informing me of this contact with the rebel."

Yes, it was past time. Idadu would not thank her for forgetting. Using a cloth-wrapped fingernail, she traced the channels around his broad thumb's nail. "In part, I feared for Idadu, how you might blame him. He did all he could. But mostly, I knew you would tear off after one or the other: Ishmael or the Kenez. Probably both. I deemed your appointment with the prophet to be more important."

"My appoint— *What?*" He jerked in her hold, and she clicked her tongue in reproach. "More important than your innocence in my eyes?"

"You had questions, my lord. Urgent ones." She scrubbed on, though it was no easy task wrangling his twitches of irritation. "Jeremiah is the mouthpiece of the God you serve. He is wise in his counsel. Since you are the governor general of my city and the man who determines the fate of those I love, *yes*. Your appointment with the prophet was more important than whatever trust you might lose in me."

Though her earlier trembles attested to her dread, now she was simply indignant. This was the *very last* day men of power would use her to achieve their twisted ends. Zedekiah, Ishmael, her own husband. Even her abba, much as she hated to admit, used her position with the general to preserve his life and the integrity of his household, though she would not wish it otherwise.

"Agh, Liora." Nebuzaradan's chest rumbled against her shoulder, a long, aggrieved sigh. "How did I not surmise that your reasoning had to do with the safety of others? Over your own, no less!" He flung his free arm wide, and water sloshed over the bowl.

It seeped through her tunic and chilled her thigh. She released his tense wrist and, letting it drip as it willed, then fished the other out of the air. She nudged him into a better position and shoved his left hand into the vinegar solution. "Has my safety with you ever been in jeopardy?"

"Not for a single moment. Alas...another truth I should not reveal." A string of incoherent grumbles ensued from him. "At the same rate that you give me strength, you weaken me, woman." She ignored his commentary and set about wiping the red-black lines from his forefinger. Until he asked, tone wry, "Should I fear for my hair, lest you sheer it off while I sleep?"

The rag stilled on his middle finger, and her gaze swung up to him. "You know the story of Samson!"

"And that of all your judges." The curls of his beard shifted around his self-satisfied smirk. "Though the memory is hazy. Come!" He slipped easily from her shocked-lax grip and, shaking off the drips, stalked to the bed. He tossed himself down, stretched out, and plumped a cushion under his head. Comfortable, he patted the space beside him. "*Come*. Tell it to me again, wife."

Not having budged, she wrung the rag over the bowl and eyed the bed speculatively. Deciding—for obvious reasons—not to mention he'd not undressed, she said, "Did the prophet...free you of your vow?"

"He did not, choosing instead to chastise me." Aggravation spat the words into the night.

Liora took her time smoothing, then folding the wet cloth, giving herself ample time to pray forgiveness for the lightness coming into her spirit. A wife had duties. Eventually, she would be obligated to perform them. If she allowed her fears and stubborn will the liberty to roam now, they would be even more difficult to subdue later.

She laid the rag neatly over her palm. "Knowing Elder Jeremiah, it is safe to assume you deserved his censure." How she regretted not being there to speak to him herself! To see with her own eyes he was truly mending.

Nebuzaradan's lips twisted tight. She'd begun to believe he would not respond when he at last heaved a sigh. "It is a minor detail, a thing hardly worth a soothsayer's wagging finger. Nevertheless, he'll not speak to me again of my *most-rash oath*," he drawled as if quoting her saba, "until I've set this thing straight."

"What *thing*?" The fact they'd had no ceremony, exchanged no vows? That was certainly a *thing* Saba Jeremiah would condemn.

"I told him it will rectify itself within days. That fact did not appease him. Nothing I said would persuade him to go before Yahweh on my behalf. But enough of that. Tomorrow will be another trying day."

Enough of what? He'd said nothing. Had not answered her question.

On slow feet, she migrated toward the bedside. "Trying how?"

"Little as I like the idea, you must accompany me to the temple. We'll go quietly before dawn. No one will expect it. You'll be quite safe."

Liora had serious doubts about that. "What business could I have at the destroyed temple?"

The greater question: would he allow her to be about her own business, that of seeing after the ark? Did it remain in the Holy of Holies, or had the priests thought to hide it before Jerusalem's gates fell? Would Yahweh even approve of such a move? Her great Lord could not be hidden, His glory too immense to contain, but they could not simply stand aside for the Babylonians to descend upon the holy vessel.

And who was *she*, a despised woman, to concern herself?

"There's an undeniable urging in my spirit. Here." He thumped his breastbone. "Your god, I presume. He demands I cleanse his holy place, and I trust no other translator but my beautiful wife." Affection entering his eyes, he reached toward her, then withdrew his hand and cursed.

The harsh language startled her, almost as much as the notion of her involvement in *cleansing*, whatever that might entail. Certainly not cleansed of ash. She'd rather face the fire again, for when Yahweh's patience was spent and He purged His people of sin, He did not use half measures.

A FAITH UNTAMED

Would Nebuzaradan demand she enter sacred ground? Did he understand the gravity of such offenses? The Holy Place was not to be trod upon by women or pagans. How utterly terrifying the thought.

"You tremble."

Nebuzaradan's soft rumble informed her of how close she'd come to his side. Close enough to take another step and dab the bloodstains around the wound on his forehead. Her hands did indeed shake. "If Yahweh has commanded, I will obey. He is my strength so that I do not shame Him. Or you."

"Never, my dove. Impossible. You are my greatest pride."

His pride was she? Of all the things she might come to wish herself to be—his joy, his love, his child's mother—pride was not among them. As abundantly as it ran through him, he had no need of more.

Not daring to look him in the eye, she brushed aside a thick black curl to better reach the rusty smear leading to his temple. "I am your servant." Both a prayer to Yahweh and an acceptance of the next day's task.

"Is that all you are?" Sighing, he crossed his arms behind his head and closed his eyes. "Your voice soothes my spirit. Extinguish the lamps and speak me to sleep, dove. Recount for me the story of the man Samson."

CHAPTER 5

The Lord hath trodden under foot all my mighty men in the midst of me: he hath called an assembly against me to crush my young men: the Lord hath trodden the virgin, the daughter of Judah, as in a winepress. (Lam. 1:15)

An only child without a mother, Liora had no experience with the art of helping someone ease into sleep. That might have explained why she fell asleep herself, a development she became aware of when a soft hand shook her by the shoulder and she popped upright in a place she did not belong.

Others could argue that, of course, a woman belonged in her husband's bed, but an uncomfortable writhing in Liora's middle told her otherwise. Whether because he was Babylonian and the Butcher or some other intuition, Liora felt like a thief stealing through the night, robbing another woman of her treasure. Both when she'd obeyed and sat next to Nebuzaradan's reclining form and when she'd woken under his blanket.

As she squinted through the darkness, she discovered that, mercy of mercies, his side of the bed was empty. Rumpled cushions and blankets remained as proof the bed was well used.

"My lady."

A FAITH UNTAMED

The whisper at Liora's back flipped her around. She slapped a hand to her pounding heart. "Devorah. One day, I am going to sew a bell to your tassels."

The servant's shadowed form hovered at the bedside. "Rise. Quickly. I am to dress you." If Devorah's silence hadn't already stirred Liora's worry, the rush in her voice would have.

She slung off the blanket and swung her feet to the floor. "What is it, Devorah? What's wrong? Is it Zipporah? My father?" Had Nebuzaradan acted on his anger?

"No, no. Up!" Devorah pulled Liora upright, yanking at yesterday's tunic before her backside made it fully off the bed. "The Butch— Your lord husband wishes to depart at once. Where, he would not say. But, my lady, the prophet—"

"Depart?" The question hadn't finished curling off her tongue before the answer rushed back in a staccato of facts. The temple. Its cleansing. Her part in it.

Her stomach roiled, but there was no time to coddle it.

"Listen! Your father himself fetched the Burden Bearer. He is *here*." Devorah wrenched the tunic over Liora's head, bending her almost double in her efforts. Her brusque whisper muffled further as the fabric rustled in Liora's ears. "If you wish to speak to the prophet before leaving, you must hurry!"

Only then did the true reason for Devorah's haste sink in.

Saba Jeremiah. The Lord's chief prophet. In her home.

Questions clambered through Liora's mind, but she saved them for after she'd dressed and dashed into her bedchamber—now his, apparently. She dropped to her knees at the old man's bedside and clasped his over-warm, knotted hand between her own.

It was not enough.

She flung herself half over him in a clumsy embrace made more awkward by her tear-garbled flurry of demands. "I thought you were under guard in the palace prison. It is not safe in the streets! The people hate you, Saba. Are you feverish? You are too warm!"

"Sh-shh-shhh. There, child." He patted her back, his whisper raspy but kind. "You will wake Sapir. If you have not already. The girl sleeps on a pallet in the corner. She greeted me with gentleness. So dear. Unlike the woman. Gittel, I believe her name. But then, I am afraid I deserve her censure for taking her bed."

"My bed." Liora sniffled a laugh as she drew back to gaze at him in the gloom. "And you are most welcome to it, dear one. I am so pleased you have come." She gave his hand a light squeeze. "We will put fat back on these bones and pamper you with love and attention until you are drowned in it and begging for peace."

He chuckled, his beard a quaking pale cloud stretching across his upper chest. "Liora, Liora. Ever the light of our eyes. Our wise Lord chose well." He stroked the side of her face, removing some of the dampness. A wet sniff suggested he'd joined her in weeping, but next he spoke, his tone portrayed only contrived haughtiness. "That lion of a general you call husband, only *thinks* he understands what a jewel you are." His face tipped up and back, as if speaking to the man himself.

Nebuzaradan's masculine scent crept up behind her. A flicked glance over her shoulder revealed his broad form blocking the light from the candle flickering down the hall at his back. Had he come for her already? He shifted, crossed his arms, and settled. She had another minute then.

"He is quite blind, that one," Jeremiah said.

"*Saba*," Liora uttered low. "He understands our language."

"Blind, rash, and proud on top of it. Misplaced pride, as all pride is. For he killed a nation already dead, destroyed a sanctuary already destroyed, and ground flour already ground. These things were decreed by the Lord of Hosts and would have happened with or without the great General Nebuzaradan of Babylonia. Yet the man takes pride in the deeds as if they were his own."

"I conquered through strength," Nebuzaradan clipped, that pride of his on full display. "Forged my own legacy through fire and blood long before arriving at the walls of your miserable city."

"Be warned, Arioch." Jeremiah's timbre deepened and chills erupted along Liora's neck. "As He has darkened your eye, the Lord God of Hezekiah can snap the head from your axe and silence your roar."

Yahweh was responsible for the screen over Nebuzaradan's eye?

She shifted to put him within her view.

His face was slack. Had he not known Yahweh was behind his blindness, or did he fear being stripped of power? Perhaps both. "Watch yourself, prophet," he said, taking a forward step. "You live by my grace alone."

"Oi, that pride." Jeremiah elongated the word, threading it with a tragic sigh. "But Yahweh chooses His servants well."

Nebuzaradan eyed him a moment before relaxing into a grunt.

Liora exhaled. "That tongue will get you killed one of these days, Saba."

"Yes, child. When our Lord wills it and not an hour sooner. Until then, my tongue is His instrument. As for the virgin daughter of Judah"—he covered her hand, voice lowering to a solemn level—"she will soon be trodden like a winepress. Taken by—"

"Silence!" Three slapping footfalls loomed Nebuzaradan's towering form over them both. "You dare speak her harm into being?"

"What? No," Liora said. "He does not mean *me*."

"But have courage, dear one," the prophet continued, undaunted. "The Lord our God is ever near."

"Cease your prophecies, old man!" The general's fists shook with restraint. "Or I will—"

"No, Arioch!" She threw herself over Jeremiah in a bodily shield.

Sapir burst into a wail, and Nebuzaradan growled. "Captain, remove my wife."

A FAITH UNTAMED

Idadu clasped Liora under the arms and plucked her off Jeremiah. "Saba!" She clung to his hand, determined to drag him off the bed if it meant saving him from Nebuzaradan's wrathful shadow.

"Go, child." Jeremiah wriggled his bony fingers from her grasp and waved her off. "It is not my time."

Those words alone stilled Liora's fight. Her arms fell back to her sides.

When Idadu relaxed his hold, she shot forward to throw herself at Nebuzaradan. Arms about his tense neck, she drew herself as high up his tall frame as her strength allowed and pressed her face into his beard. "Jerusalem is the daughter of Judah, not me. Jerusalem," she whispered, nose filling with the subtle spiciness of his bergamot beard oil. *"Jerusalem."*

The word ended on a squeak as Nebuzaradan's trembling arms came about her in a crush. Her feet lifted off the floor, and his hot breath poured down her neck. "He will not take you from me, Liora. He will *not*."

"Ah." The prophet drew out the syllable with the sad sigh of one who knows better. "There you are wrong, General. For she belongs to Yahweh and none other."

~~~

APRIL W GARDNER

*And the captain of the guard took
Seraiah the chief priest, and Zephaniah
the second priest, and the three keepers
of the door.* (Jer. 52:24)

After the prophet's startlingly bold statement, Liora extricated herself from Nebuzaradan's hold and made her way toward the front of the house. The word *trodden* spun through her mind like a dust devil, tearing through her calm.

Saba Jeremiah meant Jerusalem...didn't he? If he'd meant Liora, that she had more trials to bear—or perhaps death—how would she fare?

She already felt her seams weakening, felt herself coming apart from the inside. Would her confidence in the Lord bear up? Would *she*?

Facing Nebuzaradan the day she'd walked into his camp had been easier than facing the condemning crowd years before; her legs had carried her more steadily through the burning stable than through the jeering soldiers. Was it cowardice that she'd rather lose her head to King Nebuchadnezzar's Butcher than endure such a trial again?

Hold me together, Yahweh. Sustain my faith, for I am nothing without you.

For the next hour, she could not stop pondering and praying.

And Nebuzaradan, apparently, could not stop glowering. Not when their small party slipped quietly through Jerusalem's desolate streets. Not when they

A FAITH UNTAMED

arrived at the violated temple, laborers entering the gruesome scene with axes, yawns, and sleep-sluggish steps. Not when the sun crested the horizon and those laborers realized who stood among them, then scrambled to appear busy, most of them somewhere out of sight. Not even when a dozen or more Levites, decked in their priestly garbs, began streaming into the half-crumbled courtyard.

Nebuzaradan's summons had gone out the previous day: every priest and elder to the temple at dawn, no exceptions. Whether they'd been informed of the reason, Liora could only guess. Based on their shuffling and uneasy glances at the general, they grasped this was no call to priestly service. Surely, they realized they would not be offering sacrifices that day. They would be answering to Babylon's Butcher. Through him, to Yahweh.

And Liora...Conviction steeled her soul. The general might believe Liora was there to translate, but Liora sensed her purpose in that place was twofold. Behind her, the temple's parapets towered over the concealing courtyard wall. Had the soldiers breached the Holy Place? Was the ark safe? Before she left, she would find a way to be certain.

Tallest in a row of four, the general—with him, Rimutu, Liora, and Idadu—stood with his legs spread powerfully on the top stair leading to the central dividing point of the temple compound. Framed by the broken-open Gate of Nicanor at his back, he directed his impressive scowl into the Women's Courtyard. Out of sight behind the wall at their backs were the Court of the Israelites, the altar, and the Holy Place.

In fearful respect of Yahweh's Dwelling, Liora had quietly but fervently refused to progress into the compound, scarcely daring to cast her eyes toward the Holy Place. Never mind its double doors stood closed and untouched, the covenant ark presumably safe inside.

Though his scowl deepened at her refusal, Nebuzaradan had not pressed but stationed them at the highest point of the Women's Court. Morning sunlight now brightened the polished bronze of his pitted helmet, and his oiled, gray-streaked curls brushed the top of his red tunic, not a snag or wrinkle marring the fabric. The broad iron girdle spanning his trim waist hadn't a speck of dust on the painted sigil of his house, and his beard gleamed against his sinewy neck, completing the picture of Babylonian splendor.

How long had the man taken in his ablutions? And *where* had he done this? She'd heard nothing, but his impeccable state suggested he'd taken great care.

This explained her glimpse of Haldi in the shadows as Nebuzaradan whisked her through the dark house and out the door. He'd certainly had a hand in Nebuzaradan's transformation that morning. Haldi's touch was visible from the polished arm bands down to the buffed leather shin guards, the dust and scratches from the night before entirely absent.

Who was the general trying to impress? The priests with a display of wealth? The elders with his authority? Yahweh with a show of outward gleam? He would not understand that Hashem did not see as man saw. The Lord God peered deep into the heart, and while it was not for Liora to judge, all evidence pointed to Nebuzaradan's heart being riddled with blinding pride, just as her saba said.

Although, in all honesty, he *did* cut a stunning vision. From her vantage point at his side and slightly behind, she studied his crooked profile, that broken nose, accompanied by the scar jagging through his eyebrow, seeming now to compliment him. She could not imagine him otherwise. In fact, smooth features might seem like a lie, a deception.

She much preferred to stare at the evidence of his butchery. So she might never forget with whom she dealt. Even the gold hoop tugging at his earlobe trapped a thin coil of black hair. She sympathized. Stunning the man might be, but he was still her Babylonian overlord, the husband of every Jewish maiden's nightmares.

An irrational urge to free the strands came over her. She clasped her hands before her, sight dropping to the place the priests' and elders' gazes frequented—the head of the axe half hidden under Nebuzaradan's draping hand. How casually it rested there, ready with a single thought to strike.

Cloaked in menace, he did not evoke thoughts of weakness, servitude, or dependence on the Lord's goodwill, but of exactly what he'd claimed: fire and blood. Both of which trembled the air, poised to descend like a hawk, talons spread.

Or was that Liora's shaky breath? She could not steady it for worry. What part did he expect her to play in the judgment? Bile rose to the back of her tongue, and damp heat accumulated behind the veil covering the lower portion of her face.

Strength, my dove. It is but a moment's task, he'd reassured her on the walk up the Temple Mount. *Their lives are in my hand, not yours. You need only speak my words. The guilty will condemn themselves.*

She dearly hoped he was correct.

The priests and elders—twenty-five, more or less, who'd survived the siege and storming of the city—congregated several generous strides from the base of the stairs. Six elders stood out from the priests, their faces gaunt behind their white beards. Their garments hung on starved frames. Fine linen tunics dyed in deep blues and purples announced their wealth. To a man, they wore ornate mantles draped over their tunics.

Her gaze snagged on a familiar face she'd encountered twice before, once in the king's court and once on the road to the Dung Gate and her stoning. The elder stared at her, a swirl of loathing in his mild brown eyes. What did he see? A traitor? A reject of their king? A missed opportunity to rid the Holy City of a fallen woman?

By the sneer bunching his beard, he would correct that at a moment's notice. If not for Babylon's Butcher standing at her side, this man would have her right back on that road, recoiling under the people's hatred, breaking under their stones.

A FAITH UNTAMED

She flinched, an entirely involuntary motion. *You are my shield, my fortress, my rock. I will not fear these men or their judgment,* she prayed even as her stomach twisted with it.

With effort, she focused on a small group of priests who'd stationed themselves apart. Their bodies angled slightly away from the main group. A show of disunity?

The rest were a huddle of sheep, driven together under the threat of a violent storm. Did they notice where they stood, mere paces from the place where Zechariah's life was spilled by their brethren ages ago? A true priest of Yahweh, Zechariah had dared rebuke his peers for their sins. His blood spilled for it.

The thought of blood sent a wave of nausea through her. For years, she hadn't been able to bear the sight of her own. And for as long as she had been alive, the darkened patch on the limestone at the stairway's base was reputed to be the very spot Zechariah died, a bloodstain impossible to wash away. Now, beneath the priests' cowed postures and bare feet, a shadow of righteous vengeance climbed the hems of their robes. Yahweh had not forgotten His loyal servant. Meanwhile, the priests' white garments rustled, a mockery of consecration and purity.

Granted they might not *all* be weak-spined followers of their own wisdom. They might not all be steeped in idolatry, even if they *were* complicit in their silence and their failure to teach and correct. They might not all be responsible for imprisoning Jeremiah, for disregarding his warnings, for burning the scrolls that the prophet Ezekiel sent from Babylon.

Surely, among the lot, one or two remained faithful? For if they were not...

Long, uncomfortable minutes passed wherein the priests shuffled and murmured, Nebuzaradan glared, and Liora sweated through her linen robes. Her insides trembled as if she were the one standing before Yahweh's judgment. And wasn't she? None could stand guiltless before her holy Lord.

As if he sensed her trembling, Nebuzaradan looked down at her. His brow sported rows of creases, put there by an emotion she could not identify. "Do you recognize any among them?"

Liora closed her eyes briefly. She should have known the general would not be happy for her to merely serve as a translator. Praying for strength and forgiveness, she dipped her chin. "The chief priest and his second. And one other." Would he be content with that?

"One other? A man of note, I take it. Who is he?"

Of note and then some. But why must *she* stand as witness? Why could she not translate, then be about inquiring after the ark? "My lord," she whispered, throat tightening, uncertain who exactly she addressed. "You break me in two."

By the flat line of his eyebrows, Nebuzaradan was not repentant. "Has the man defied Yahweh?"

How curious that the general mentioned her God instead of his king. From genuine devotion? Or was he simply learning to speak the language of her heart, all the better to manipulate her?

He *had* said that he had come to cleanse the temple. Either way, she must respond in honesty. "If rumors are true...yes." Gold glittered in the threads of the man's tassels, an outward compliance to the Law of Moses, while reliable witnesses reported that behind the walls of his home, he knelt before shrines of idols. He and every elder standing before her.

The general sighed with impatience. "Well, then?"

Well then, indeed. Yahweh warned the people through Moses and the prophets that He would not tolerate idolatry. Warned and warned again. He would not share His Sanctuary or the hearts of His children with other gods. Though a God of mercy, He was also a God of justice who could not lie.

But why, *why* must he use Liora to accomplish His word? She was no doom-wielding prophet, no righteous warrior.

My Lord God! Is Nebuzaradan not your sword?

Are you not my light? Shed the light of Truth across the darkness.

Truth. That she could do. She glanced toward the North Gate where she'd once seen the elder enter behind King Zedekiah in a procession of royals. "He is...a prince of the people. Pelatiah son of Benaiah."

A slow smile crept up one side of Nebuzaradan's mouth. "Point him out."

She would *not* be pointing. "Dark blue mantle. Matching turban." She whispered the details unable to look anywhere but at the pitted stone at her feet.

"I see him. Excellent." He rocked on his heels. "You are a true servant of Babylon, my dove, for no male of the royal line shall escape with his life. Orders from our most illustrious king."

Our nothing. Nausea swelled, but he did not allow her to dwell on the betrayal.

"We proceed. Speak my words to them now, Liora. Do not deviate by a single one." Not a fleck of give softened his undertones.

"At your will, my lord."

He lifted his chin, gazed down the length of that crooked nose, and launched into his purpose with loud, declarative speech.

Liora startled—at his volume, at the heat in it, at the words themselves. Of all the approaches she'd anticipated, this was not one of them. When he stopped to allow her to translate, she scrambled her mind into marching form.

Thoughts ordered, she swallowed hard, partly at the sour taste in her mouth but mostly to steady herself. A futile effort. Her voice emerged small and scratchy. "The man Jeremiah has prophesied against my interpreter, Liora bat Chesed. This is most displeasing."

The chief priest, the eldest of the lot per the white streaking his thin beard, broke from the group. His whiskered cheeks were rounded with health, a strange sight in a starved city, and his bare feet poked out from beneath the tinkling bells dangling from the hem of his sky-blue robe. A leather thong looped around the back of his neck and disappeared under his tunic. An amulet? Kept close to his idolatrous heart? Many of the priests had publicly, unrepentantly turned to talismans. Would they do so unless the highest among them approved?

"I am Seraiah," he said, bowing. "Chief of priests. My deepest sympathies, General Nebuzaradan."

The priest had not finished drawling the word *sympathies*, tone wheedling, before Liora felt her skin heating with indignation.

Seraiah continued. "The troublemaker of Anathoth is a biting gnat. Little good has ever come from his false mouth. I would not concern myself." Spoken as if Jeremiah were a bug to flick off one's sleeve.

Repressing her own snappish reply, Liora conveyed Seraiah's response to Nebuzaradan.

The general hummed a considering sound that could mean he appreciated the proffered peace of mind...or that he was placating the priests while he plotted their downfall. Liora prayed the latter, then begged forgiveness from Yahweh.

"According to reports," Nebuzaradan said after a moment, "he has also antagonized *you*, the temple priests."

Seraiah spread his hands in a display of comradeship. "Ah, yes. You have heard correctly. The man is a scourge upon this temple. For long and tiresome years, he has sown dissent and bred fear in this place and across our land. The sad truth is that he will continue to do so as long as he draws breath. In times of unrest and change, such as we have, he is the last man any leader would want spreading discord among the people."

Blood whooshing in her ears, Liora converted the lies into Akkadian, volume subdued, voice tight. Whether she was able to hide her repulsion and fury, she did not know, for Nebuzaradan stared blank-faced over the restless priests. More secure now in their safety, they did not hesitate to murmur agreement.

Another went so far as to contribute his unbidden opinion—Zephaniah the Second Priest, if Liora remembered correctly from her days in court. "He is mildew on the wall, General," the priest said. "Persistent, clinging, nearly impossible to remove." Disdain bled from every angry word, and beneath the shadow of his tall, white turban, his skin flushed red.

Heads nodded, so many Liora could not discern if any man among them disagreed. How eagerly they made signs of compliance with Nebuzaradan. For them to be willing to come alongside the Butcher, how vicious must their hatred of Yahweh's most faithful prophet be?

Nebuzaradan jutted his lips in a thoughtful pose, as though absorbing wisdom from aged magi. "This aligns with the stories brought in by my spies."

Even that—mention of spies, a reminder they were enemies, conqueror and conquered—did not distract the fanged lambs from spewing muttered hatred.

"Jeremiah is a prophet of ruin and the greater pestilence," Pelatiah said, tone so precise and logical Liora had no doubt this was no impulsive plot, but a loathing rooted deep in the soul. He raised a scholarly finger. "But his scribe, Baruch, must not be discounted. The little man is almost as vile as his master. With every due respect, General, eliminating one will not suffice."

Liora caught a blurt of laughter before it made an exit. Had Nebuzaradan made any mention at all of *eliminating* Jeremiah?

Chief Priest Seraiah seemed to realize this, as well. Stuttering a laugh, he lowered his head in a humble posture. "If that is what you wish, of course." The gold of his crown glittered, a deceptively happy twinkle. "May we…assist you in some way, Lord General?"

Liora was so busy corralling her shock at their spite, she forgot to translate until Nebuzaradan flicked her a glance. Clearing her throat, she transmitted the last two messages straight into his hardening eyes.

He didn't bother to blink away the emotion before turning back to the priests. "The prophet vanished in the night. You have intimate knowledge of this city. Put it to good use this day by assisting in his capture." He paused there, and as the priests bobbed their heads, his jaw muscle rippled beneath his beard. "Who among you wishes to see him in chains, his head on a pike? Step up and join me."

The group moved as one, striding two paces closer, Seraiah and Zephaniah among them. Their feet stopped directly over that stain of guilt. Did they not *see*? Could they not feel Yahweh's righteous vengeance sweeping down like a tempest?

Nebuzaradan's fingers tightened around the handle of his ax, and Liora jolted forward, one rushed step down the stairway. Her mouth opened and out flew a plea she'd not seen coming. "Think this through, my lords, I beg you! For harming His chief prophet, Yahweh's wrath will fall upon your heads!"

As if they were a single, malicious entity, the priests' faces contorted with bitterness as voices rang out.

"Jeremiah is no prophet of Yahweh!"

"He has betrayed us to these pagans!"

"Let him die with the traitorous defectors!"

Poison spewed at her from every direction, but it was the reserved tones of the nearest man, Pelatiah, the prince not given to rage, that struck hardest. "Still your snake tongue, harlot of Babylon." He kept his words smooth and mild—perhaps, believing Nebuzaradan did not understand—and finished with a gentle smile. "Its hiss reeks of rot."

She jerked back as though slapped. Pelatiah's malice pursued and coiled around her like a constricting serpent, crushing her breath, her dignity, her very sense of self. Flashes of shouting penetrated her mind, and she could not quite find her place in time.

"Captain," Nebuzaradan said, the name a command.

Behind her, the slow *shhh* of metal sliding against leather announced a sword leaving its scabbard. A death knell, not hers. Even so, the urge to escape clawed at her feet. But where might she go that Yahweh's wrath could not follow? She hunched and slapped her hands over her ears, but the general's rumbling voice still reached her.

A FAITH UNTAMED

"Come, my dove. Ease aside lest your pretty robes become spattered."

Liora eased nowhere. She fled.

CHAPTER 6

> *Moreover the spirit lifted me up, and brought me unto the east gate of the Lord's house...behold at the door of the gate five and twenty men; among whom I saw...Pelatiah the son of Benaiah, prince of the people. Thus saith the Lord...I know the things that come into your mind, every one of them." And it came to pass, when I prophesied, that Pelatiah the son of Benaiah died. (Ezekiel 11:1, 5, 13)*

Liora might have stopped in time if she had been looking up instead of hurrying with her head down as she descended the long, shallow Ancient Steps of the Temple Mount, if she hadn't been covering her ears to block the priests' cries of alarm, if her veil hadn't fluttered across her eyes or if tears weren't smearing her vision. She might have noticed the laborers kneeling on every side...as well the Babylonian royal climbing the stairs.

Idadu called out a warning behind her, but she heard too late.

A set of guards leapt into her path, their crossed swords blocking the way.

She pulled up, lurching back so fast from those blades, she stumbled over the step behind her. Just as well. The prince would want her on her knees anyway.

A FAITH UNTAMED

She rearranged her flailing limbs and took a kneeling posture on the broad stair. Heart pounding, she uttered a prayer of forgiveness. Surely, Yahweh had not brought her to His holy mount to bow before a pagan.

Yet there she knelt, facing the base of the stairs and the royal climbing them. Humiliation poured off her lowered head. The fabric of her gown twisted about her calf and bit into her neck where it tugged on one side. The sheer blue of her veil hung over half her face, but she would not raise a hand to straighten herself.

Could she even if she'd dared? Every muscle had locked down.

A single set of footfalls approached from the temple behind her, too light to be Nebuzaradan's. Idadu then, nearing at a cautious pace. Of all the times for Nebuzaradan to give her space!

A royal guard stepped forward to share her stair. He loomed over her from the right. The tip of his sword dug into the flesh under her jaw, and a sharp pressure lifted her head at an awkward angle.

Lashes down, she held the uncomfortable pose and drew a long, steadying breath through her nose. *You are my strength*, she prayed as David HaMelech, the greatest king, had before, as countless thousands had on these very steps. *You are my fortress. I shall not fear.*

Yahweh had not brought her this far, ushered her through famine, siege, and fire, only for her to die on the temple's Ancient Steps. This was *not* her end. In fact, as a dove cooed on the temple parapet at her back and the royal's footsteps tapped deliberately up the staircase toward her, she sensed this might just be a beginning.

Idadu hurried his last few strides and dropped to one knee at her left. "My prince. Your mercy on the lady, I pray. She is under my protection by order of General Nebuzaradan."

Liora's stomach clenched, her fists doing the same about the fabric over her bent knees. She would not stand for it if her hasty actions caused Idadu harm—or moved him to offer himself in her place. As her molars scraped against the sting of the blade, she willed the guard to say no more.

A red robe rustled into her slitted view. The gold tasseling on its hem brushed a brown ankle. A sandaled foot settled on the edge of the tread spanning between her and Idadu. "Mercy? On this creature?" As the prince leaned in, the warm, luxurious scent of amber invaded her nose. It grew stronger with the hand that reached to brush aside her veil. The fabric caressed her nose and tickled hair across her forehead.

She would have gone on staring at the arm he braced on a raised knee if a tap to the bottom of her chin hadn't popped her lashes up.

Cold brown eyes met hers. She might call them soulless but for the indecipherable emotion stirring in their depths. They did not stay on hers long but made a slow circuit of her face. Equally deliberate were the words sliding smoothly through his oil-shined lips. "I see."

She blinked. What? See? What did he see? The sweat dampening her hairline? The tremble of her mouth? He surely did not miss the wet streaks drying to a crust on her cheeks.

The corner of his mouth twitched, drawing attention to his shaved upper lip and jaw. The dark shadow of growth proved he could grow a beard but chose not to, which was...unusual. She did not give herself long to ponder it but swallowed hard around the sword point doing its best to cut off her blood. "Prince Nergal-sharezer?" she asked, voice raspy and throat aching. At the meager dip of his chin, she continued. "Your arrival in the Holy City has been much...anticipated." Another wincing swallow. "I am Liora, daughter of Ephraim Chesed, noble of Jerusalem. Our meeting under such circumstances is unfortunate. I beg your pardon for my careless behavior and for my unsightly appearance."

One of his neatly trimmed black eyebrows quirked with clear amusement. "Yes, I do indeed see."

Had she said something wrong? Forgotten some protocol? She shifted but could not relieve that stinging jab. "Please, Your Highness, allow me to make amends for my lack of decorum."

"My lady," Idadu murmured in warning. "Perhaps, speak first with the general."

Yes, the general. Where *was* he? Too busy slaughtering priests to notice his *beloved* trembling at the point of his prince's sword.

Prince Nergal pushed off his knee and straightened. "The Butcher's input will not be required." He flicked a finger, and the sword vanished.

Cool air sucked down Liora's throat. The shaking fingers she touched to her neck came away clean, but she would not be surprised to later find a bruise added to those fading from Omar's abuse. Only, in this instance, Nebuzaradan would be helpless to avenge or protect her.

Well, there was no use worrying. Yahweh would do as He wished, put those in her path He willed, and Liora would bend her neck in submission.

When the prince settled back, arms crossed, to observe her, she scrubbed the salt from her cheeks and began to straighten her head covering. Not removing his burning gaze from her, he said, "And where, soldier, was your supposed protection while the lady was in flight?"

Liora's hand froze where it arranged fabric over her hair, but Idadu hunched lower. "I was carrying out an execution, Your Highness. The lady is a gentle soul, and the man's death disturbed her. She fled while I—"

The prince bellowed a laugh so loud, so suddenly, the fabric slipped from Liora's fingers. She snatched it mid-fall but was too distracted by the prince's hilarity to replace it.

"The Butcher?" he said, eyes crinkled. "With a gentle woman?" Leaning back, he flattened a palm to his stomach and laughed again. This time, a forced sound. "Now *that* is new. And...is that a *knife* she has there at her side? You do realize, General, you are supposed to *un*arm the enemy? And that Aralu will claw this one to pieces?" His eyes, still tight with mirth, lifted to some place behind Liora.

A FAITH UNTAMED

The general had arrived at last. Or had he been there all along? Either way, the cords of Liora's neck slackened, and breath hit the bottom of her lungs. When it came out again, she had time enough for only one thought—*who is Aralu?*—before Nebuzaradan replied.

"She will try, yes. And Lady Liora is an ally." The direction of his rumbling voice descended and rose, as if he made a brief obeisance. "Prince Nergal, you are most welcome."

Ally. Liora barely refrained from cringing.

Beside her, Idadu wrapped firm fingers around her forearm and drew her up sharply with him. Backing away, he pulled Liora along, extracting them from between the prince and her unnaturally still husband.

Rimutu remained off to the side, kept there by diligent royal guards.

Nebuzaradan's breastplate rose with a deliberate inhale. His gaze flicked to Liora, then pinned the prince like a hawk measuring prey.

If Prince Nergal felt threatened, his rising smirk did not reveal it. Neither did the loose arms he clasped behind his back, exposing the full of his unarmored chest. "You are no more adept at lying than ever you were, dear Butcher. What did I tell you about practicing?" He ambled straight up the steps, forcing Nebuzaradan to move aside. "A man cannot gain a skill, *any* skill, without endless repetition. But I suppose my father employs his beasts of war to dismantle cities, not construct deceit."

Dismantle... The ark! In her haste to flee humiliation, she'd forgotten her determination to ascertain the vessel's safety. She winced at the pinch of guilt.

After he passed, Nebuzaradan swiveled toward Idadu. "Take the lady home. At once."

Idadu ducked his head, but Prince Nergal stopped and twisted back. "No. His Majesty has questions, and I am sent to find answers, as well as secure the ark. Bring the lady. I suspect she will make herself useful to me in my varied inquiries." He doubled that closed-mouth smirk and carried on.

A tremble that screamed of fury coursed over Nebuzaradan's shoulders. A single shudder, then his body relaxed with a control gained only by that repeated practice the prince had lauded. Scar tight and pulling at his cheek, he caught Liora's eyes and held until she mustered a smile. Convincing or not, the expression shifted his attention to Idadu for a silent command that jerked the guard's head with a nod.

Then Nebuzaradan was off, his long stride devouring the broad staircase to catch him up to his prince. Liora's own legs set in motion, spurred by Idadu's pull on her arm. But she could not feel her limbs, could not hear the hushed words tumbling from the guard's mouth. Never mind he spoke close to her ear. Probably advice on how to proceed. Well-intentioned but pointless. Liora would take her cues from the God of Judah.

Her insides quaked at the responsibility. What if she heard Him wrong? If she acted with human wisdom and angered the prince beyond repair, which of her loved ones would suffer? Prince Nergal-sharezer no doubt had the authority in his little finger to still any number of hearts.

Although, currently, by the bounce in his conversational tone, he seemed more focused on loot than on bloodshed. "I stopped by the king's tribute yard on my way here. You have outdone yourself, Butcher. I thought we had collected most of it on our last visit to this stinking city. But I had to shield my eyes against the shine of gold. That axe of yours is good for more than chopping off heads." He laughed, and Nebuzaradan's hand twitched toward that very instrument hooked through his waist sash. The prince didn't seem to notice, only turned left on the terrace at the top of the stairs.

The space served as a transition between the outer spaces and the inner sacred courtyards. Left led to the altar and inner sanctum. Right, to the women's courtyard. Liora halted several steps below the pair, obliging Idadu to the same. She flattened her mouth at the confusion puckering his brow. She would *not* go left.

Yahweh, your guidance, your peace.

Nebuzaradan's head tipped slightly back, catching her in his peripheral gaze. He paused and gestured in the other direction down the terrace. "This way," he called after the royal, "if it pleases my prince."

Prince Nergal spun, robes whirling. "Ah! Yes, yes." He ambled back and patted Nebuzaradan on the cheek as he passed. "It is good I have you, General. I might have stumbled upon the Jews' *holiest vessel* and been struck with leprosy." He barked a laugh, as if such a thing were beyond possibility, instead of a fate Nebuzaradan might have just avoided.

She hoped to intervene for the ark, if the Lord sanctioned it, but she knew without doubt it would not include violating the Law or presuming upon His glory. Liora's tension unwound. One crisis averted, Yahweh be thanked for that and for proving He would go before her.

The retinue—prince and general, Liora and Idadu, plus guards ahead and behind—continued down the passage. Rimutu stayed, as best he could, near Nebuzaradan. Down the Temple Mount, Jerusalem sprawled out below them, scorched and smoking; a limestone wall rose close on their opposite side, gray with ash. But inside Liora's heart stretched a new field of calm, green grasses bowing in waves and expanses of red poppies gazing up at their Creator. She inhaled and could almost smell the sweet, clean air of peace.

Yahweh's work on her spirit. Whatever unfolded in the next hour, she would face in His strength and in the assurance of His will. If she came across a pile of priestly corpses around the corner, she would bless Him. If they lived to taunt and despise her, she would bless Him; though she might do so while hiding her face and weeping. So long as she found an opportunity to inquire after the holy vessel.

"But I suppose," the prince blathered on, grinning like a boy at a game of Chase the Pebble, "someone will have to brave the infamous *box* sooner or later."

A FAITH UNTAMED

Box...the ark? Liora almost stopped in her tracks. The prince's interest in it could mean only trouble.

His smile calcified in place as he gazed at the general. "To my great disappointment, I did not find it among my father's treasures. Afraid of it, Butcher?"

Liora's heart stuttered at the accusation of cowardice, but Nebuzaradan did not flinch or dither in his firm reply.

"I admit, Your Highness, that I have exercised caution. Turn there, soldier," he called ahead to the guards nearing the south entry to the Women's Courtyard. He addressed the prince again. "Reports claim worse than leprosy on any unsanctioned man who touches it or even looks behind its shielding curtain. Any would be a fool who charged in without forethought."

Prince Nergal waved a jeweled hand, splashing colorful sparkles against the dulled stone wall to their left. "Our preeminent Bel Marduk has subdued Judah's god. Otherwise, we would not be here, walking this passage, dismantling this temple, stripping it of wealth. The reports *I* have received claim its gold could trim a throne hall. Is this true?" Prince Nergal passed the question over his shoulder. "What say you, Lady...Liora, was it? Shall we melt it down and find out?"

Idadu's dark eyes flicked to Liora, in them a wariness that twisted her stomach.

What answer did the prince want? Whether it aligned with the one exiting her mouth was soon to be seen. "If you wish, Your Highness. There is none to stop you but Yahweh Most High. I caution against it. Of late, His patience has been sorely tested. In fact, I advise we go no farther than this courtyard."

They were entering it just then. Two steps inside, she drew to a firm halt, vaguely aware she blocked the rear guard from leaving the passage behind her.

The prince chuckled. "What is this? A Jewess concerns herself for my safety? But I forget," he drawled. "She is a *gentle* soul."

Liora proved him correct by requiring several deep breaths before she could lift her eyes. On the third, she forced them to the place Idadu had executed whatever justice his general doled out. A shudder rippled her spine.

Across the expanse, red shone bright and liquid on the worn-smooth stone, but no corpses littered the ground. No temple-destroying laborers milled about. All that remained of Nebuzaradan's interrogation was a puddle of red. The base of the stairs was empty. Guards held the elders and priests at sword point off to the side in the alcove of the Leper's Bath. Quite appropriate, though their lesions were that of the soul.

Another group, these unbound, stood apart directly opposite her before the North Gate. She recognized them as those who'd divorced themselves from the congregation of priests. The faithful few? Four, if Liora counted correctly.

Four. Only four.

Even so, a meager smile bloomed. Was it a coincidence that there were just enough to transport the ark? Liora thought not. In the next few moments,

A FAITH UNTAMED

as Yahweh's true priests stared unafraid at Babylon's prince and fiercest general, Liora had other thoughts, as well. Such as what plans the Lord had for the four and how she might be involved. If at all.

These priests were much better equipped to address the matter of the ark. The four—one aged, three young—appeared free to go, yet they remained, backs straight and their miens open with purpose. Their unintelligible murmurs reached her from afar, as though the stone itself wished her to hear.

"Liora has been a great asset." Nebuzaradan's rumble brought her attention back to him and the prince, both of whom had stopped with her. They formed a loose circle with her and Idadu, who stood slightly behind her. Though the general's rigid posture did not soften, his eyes beamed with pride. "Her faith in this temple's god has not faltered, for in all things, she is loyal to her marrow. But she believes that, as correction, her god orchestrated Jerusalem's defeat, as well as Babylon's occupation. According to Liora, we are here by divine will, and it is futile for her people to resist."

Liora blinked at the man. How well, how succinctly, he put her stance into words.

His beard shifted, and the fine lines about his eyes deepened ever so slightly—a smile not quite hidden. At least, not from Liora, who was growing to recognize the finer shifts in his demeanor.

"Is that so?" The prince angled toward her, eyebrows reaching for his purple turban. "In that case, do advise, great and gentle asset, how should a prince of Babylon go about moving this vessel called *ark*?"

Awe surged through Liora's soul. There stood a collection of priests, seeming eager to be of use, yet the prince sought her opinion. The Lord God did nothing haphazardly. His will was a precisely crafted mosaic, every tile essential to the whole. And for whatever reason, this day, Liora was a small piece.

But *how*? A sense of inadequacy followed swiftly on the heels of awe. "What does a woman know of such? Just there, behind you, Your Highness, are priests who—"

"I am asking you, *woman*." His voice lowered with threat. "Or did my general speak falsely about your ready assistance?"

Fear shot tingles through her blood.

Lord? Your answer?

Silence greeted the request. No stirring of guidance.

The prince waited, that brow of his frozen in its inquisitive arch.

She cleared her throat and said the one thing she knew for certain. "For his own safety, a prince of Babylon should not move the ark."

"Of course, of course. I understand you do your religious duty in the hearing of your priests." Prince Nergal gave an exaggerated wink. Then he straightened, and the playful gesture fell away, replaced by a sternness more appropriate on a chiding father. "Now. Let us be frank about the matter, gentle Liora. The ark *will* be moved. It will be moved at once.

A FAITH UNTAMED

And it will be moved without commotion. So tell me—were I a man who cared for such things as respect for defeated gods," he said, lips rippling with a sneer, "how might I go about transporting the relic?"

Indignation reared up within her, a righteous fury that burned inside the walls of her chest. She had a notion to fabricate some ancient law permitting those of royal blood to touch the holy vessel. Then he'd learn which God was real and which was a pile of soulless stone.

If she had a shekel's weight less conscience, she would do just that and lead him there herself. But no prompt came from the Lord to pronounce the prince's doom, or even to refute his claim.

As if... As if the man spoke truth.

Truth.

Grief welled like a sickness in her belly. Until that moment, she hadn't realized she entertained the vain hope Babylon might leave the ark untouched. She gazed in sorrow at the towering stone wall enclosing the Priests' Court and the temple itself. At its center, the Lord's holiest vessel. For the next little while, anyway. After...

The covenant ark *would* be moved.

But wasn't that for the best? When the temple walls came down, better the ark not be crushed under its rubble.

Trodden like a winepress.

Jerusalem, yes. But Jeremiah's prophecy could not apply to the ark. Yahweh would not permit it. Not *that*.

It galled to think of Yahweh's dwelling place in the hands of the Babylonians, but it would not be the first time God allowed the enemy to believe themselves victors by stealing the ark. After a time, the Philistines grew so distraught over the ravaging plagues of disease and mice, they returned it with a guilt offering. The Babylonians would be no different.

How, then, to reply to the prince?

If the Lord would give her no more, maybe the noble priests? She cast hopeful eyes that way, momentarily distracted by the guards ushering the bound priests from the compound. "Perhaps..."

Movement among the faithful priests drew her back. The foremost, a young man with a short, dark brown beard, stepped forward and lowered his chin in a nod of encouragement.

Had the prince's demand carried across the courtyard? It must have. And this priest must wish her to...what? Speak with the authority of a scholar? His pushing gesture said as much. Unheard of. And yet, exactly her task. When a prince and a priest instructed a woman to speak, she spoke.

Nebuzaradan's bunching eyebrows advised her to hurry up about it, as did the prince's crossed arms.

"Yes, a moment as I..." Liora dug deep into the vault of stories learned at her father's knee. Which ones dealt with moving the ark? King David bringing it from Kiriath-jearim should do.

She smoothed the front of her tunic to delay so she could recall the particulars. "I am not trained in these matters, Prince Nergal, but"—another glance at the

A FAITH UNTAMED

priest, another nod to proceed—"a cautious prince, such as yourself, would assign Levitical priests to carry it upon their shoulders using poles. First, they would consecrate themselves and don unblemished robes. The ark would travel in a newly constructed cart, and trumpets would go before it with singers to raise sounds of—"

The prince burst out laughing and slapped Nebuzaradan on the shoulder. "Leave it to a woman to bring festivity to a simple task. Why not parade the temple harlots, too, hmm? *Trumpets.*" He snickered.

"No! I...no." Liora spluttered. "Harlots? *Harlots?* No! How could you even—"

"Priests and poles will do." Nebuzaradan eased sideways to cut off her line of sight to the prince, perhaps noting the rage heating her face. "My earlier inquisition revealed four priests who remain true to Yahweh. I have ordered the rest be taken before my king for his wise verdict on their fate. Regarding the consecration, I see no reason we should not pander to their fears. Even defeated gods can sting."

"Sting, you say? Tragic." The prince's smirk emphasized the soft cut of his jaw. "How many of our men have been stung, exactly?"

"Twenty-one of my laborers have suffered a troublesome pox," Nebuzaradan said, voice tight. "Eight have fallen from the scaffolds."

"Eight!" The prince's voice exploded across the space, reflecting Liora's own shock.

She'd heard nothing of this—by Nebuzaradan's express design, if Idadu's evasion of her questioning gaze was any sign. "Yahweh's will is clear," she said. "He shows His displeasure." And she wasn't sure whether to cringe at the men's suffering or rejoice at the reassurance her Lord God lived.

Prince Nergal scoffed. "They imbibed too much, lost their sense of balance."

Nebuzaradan cast his eyes down. "The laborers are not allowed strong drink. And at this point in the venture, they have no sense but fear. As Lady Liora said, they believe their misfortune to be a curse from Yahweh. The three who have attempted to open the temple doors have fallen dead."

"Attempted?" The prince tossed up his hands. "As in not yet breached?"

"That is correct, Your Highness. The matter has become quite irritating, and when questioned on it, the chief prophet, Jeremiah, is mulishly silent."

The statement sent Liora back a stride, as though distancing herself from the speaker might spare her the truth sinking through her system. The prophet of the Lord had refused to answer on the matter. And what had Liora done? Paved a path all the way to Babylon.

She'd felt relatively confident in her choice to instruct the prince, had spoken boldly. Now, a chill spread through her veins. Wasn't the way of the fool always right in her own eyes?

No, no. That wasn't entirely correct.

The godly priest had urged her to speak. Hadn't he? Had she misunderstood? Or perhaps he *hadn't* heard the prince's demand.

A FAITH UNTAMED

In David HaMelech's day, a well-intentioned man had tried to catch the falling ark and died when he touched it. Such was the extent of the Lord's holiness.

Liora had been well-intentioned, too. The sickness in her middle swelled.

"My lady." Idadu touched her elbow. "Are you unwell?"

His attention drew Nebuzaradan's concerned gaze. It lingered, unreadable but steady, until the prince's shout startled her.

"Forget the woman!"

Idadu yanked her back several strides, but even in her stumbling, she didn't miss the flash of anger in Nebuzaradan's eyes as he turned to the prince.

He covered it swiftly with lowered lashes and a stiff bow. Elbows locked straight at his sides, he held the pose as the prince's guards stirred, hands settling on the hilts of their swords. Yes, they should fear an angered Butcher. Even Liora, who was relatively certain he would never harm her, held his capacity for calculated violence in wary respect. Blades were sharp, after all, and to be handled with care.

Presently, that *blade* moved air loudly, if methodically, through his nose.

The prince paced before him, agitation in every movement. "Are you telling me, Butcher, you have not so much as looked inside to verify the ark's existence?"

"I have been unable, though I have tried. Twice, on my command, men have—"

"You have not tried!" Prince Nergal sliced the air with a flattened hand. "Others have tried. *You* have stood by and done *nothing!*" He spun and wrenched a short, curved sword from a guard's scabbard. Eyes narrowing on Nebuzaradan, he raised a slow smirk, the expression a forming plot. Nebuzaradan, apparently, was not the only man capable of bloody calculation.

Surely, Prince Nergal would not execute his father's most efficient *beast of war*. Not over an entirely logical caution. But that was neither benevolence nor understanding scrolling like a death sentence across the prince's wicked smile.

Rimutu, who'd blended with the royal guards, stepped forward and matched the general's posture at his side. Idadu's grip firmed on her elbow, his tension a stream of tremors. Liora's knees felt as they had during the worst of her starvation—weak, knobby, unreliable. If Nebuzaradan went down, they all would.

At last, the prince spoke, his tenor once again airy and casual. "Shall we see how the great general holds up against a god's *sting*?" He raised the sword slowly and pointed it at the Nicanor Gate and the stripped temple columns visible beyond. "Open the doors, Butcher. Now."

CHAPTER 7

*But the Lord is with me as a mighty
terrible one: therefore my persecutors
shall stumble, and they shall not
prevail: they shall be greatly ashamed;
for they shall not prosper: their
everlasting confusion shall never be
forgotten.* (Jer. 20:11)

"No." The denial left Liora on a thin breath. She'd seen this strike coming, had presumed the prince was looking for an excuse to eliminate a rival for his father's esteem. And still, she was not prepared. "Please."

Idadu's fingers tightened to a painful level, made worse by Liora's straining toward Nebuzaradan. He'd already angled away, fixed his gaze on the sliver of temple visible through the destroyed gate. Would he not defend his choice to exercise caution? Would he not defend his *life*?

Frustration surged in Liora's breast. "General? You cannot be thinking to—" She cut herself off. He'd explained already, and if she knew the man at all, he would sooner paint an image of the prince on the side of his chariot than contradict a command.

Nebuzaradan did not look back at her. Eyes distant, he'd lost his will to resist whatever ingrained allegiance drove him. Resignation sloped his broad shoulders. Did the double axes of his house mean *nothing*? Where was the fighter in him who spent his morning hours bloodying himself in the sparring ring?

This unquestioned loyalty of his to the Babylonian crown was enough to compel a rational woman to say things she really should not.

"Your Highness, *please*." Her throat clogged with emotion. "Yahweh is unlike other gods. His presence is not to be borne. And that *box* you speak of so lightly is His throne on Earth, the place He dwells among us."

Nebuzaradan twitched, and Idadu hissed warning tones into her ear. The words did not register, her focus now on the prince, on his unequivocal glare and his outstretched sword.

"Mercy, Prince!" She was not above pleading. "If my woman's tears do not move you, consider your father, the king. Would he not wish to judge his general's actions for himself?" A brazen move, advising a prince regarding the king, but if she did not speak reason, who would? Judah's best chance of survival was with this general. "There is a way that does not include death."

"Another way?" Prince Nergal glanced at her, then back at Nebuzaradan. "It appears you were right, Butcher. The lady is of great assistance. What do you say? Shall I have *her* open the doors instead? Peek behind the curtain for us?"

Nebuzaradan twisted back so fast the tassels on his stole took flight. "What?"

Liora stared at the prince, unblinking. She was a daughter of Jerusalem but no more fit to enter the temple than a blood-stained Babylonian soldier. "What of the priests, Your Highness?"

The prince ignored them both. "She does owe me for her... How did she put it? Lack of decorum. A behavior she continues to exhibit." His mouth wrinkled with displeasure, but his sword lowered. He wouldn't need it to send *her* in. A good shove would do.

A sickening weight settled in Liora's gut. Was this her purpose then? Spare Nebuzaradan so he might live and spare her people the worst of Babylon's cruelty? Did Yahweh consider the Butcher that important to His plan? If this was Yahweh's plan, was she truly willing to be crushed for it?

And Liora? Was she only a grape to be trodden? Her own king had believed so, joined eagerly by half the city.

Regardless, the delight swimming in Prince Nergal's eyes promised he meant to collect his due—Idadu's warning fulfilled. But there would be no escaping the prince's schemes. And hadn't King David himself said he would rather fall into the hand of the Lord than that of man? At least, with Yahweh she might find mercy.

She moved her head in a slow nod. "Yes, Prince Nergal. I will serve you in the way. Though a priest—"

"This temple is my burden." Nebuzaradan pushed her back.

Liora spoke around him. "A priest might readily confirm the ark's location."

"Quiet!" He stepped in front of her. "I will bear it as the prince commands."

"Shall I call a priest over?" she finished, ignoring him.

The prince didn't flick a glance at the stirring priests. He seemed more invested in relishing the thought of wounding Nebuzaradan one way or another. Perhaps debating which avenue would damage him most.

She would not stand for it. A strategic wrench of the arm freed her of Idadu's pinching restraint. "If you will not consider the priests, at least spare your general. I will go."

The general snarled. "Silence her!"

Large hands clasped her about the waist. They hauled back, Idadu uttering harsh commands to *be quiet, woman*. He lifted his voice. "Please disregard her impertinence, my prince. She is but a soft heart distraught over the thought of her husband's death."

"Husband?" The prince laughed. "I did not know! What happy news." He spread his arms, as though inviting a congratulatory embrace. "When did this happen, General? Before or after you read the king's correspondence?"

Unease shifted Nebuzaradan's feet. "You have brought correspondence from His Majesty?"

"*Before*, then." Prince Nergal's arms fell. "Ah, to know the king's mind so well. What a gift!"

Liora's gaze darted between the men. Whatever this was about the correspondence, it set Nebuzaradan's jaw muscle twitching. The man looked on the cusp of a defiant glare, the first since they'd begun this ridiculous episode.

A FAITH UNTAMED

The prince clicked his tongue. "This changes nothing, I am afraid. The temple door remains closed, the ark's presence a mystery, and *someone* must do something about it." He tapped the sword against the side of his leg. "But you fear for nothing, Lady Liora. There is no risk. General Nebuzaradan is Yahweh's devoted servant. His *chosen*. He will surely not die." He formed a snake's grin.

Liora froze, Idadu with her. Neither breathed. Who'd told the prince such a thing? However he heard, he did not approve of the rumor.

The man's spite was beginning to make sense. Nebuzaradan had stated he posed a political threat to the prince. Perhaps this was the weakness Nergal had been hunting as an excuse to eliminate him. Did he fear the king would pass him by as heir? Give the throne to his exalted general instead?

"In times past, Yahweh has shown himself to be a formidable god," Nebuzaradan said, each word firm. "Nevertheless, I have breached his city and his temple. For I am a faithful son of Marduk."

"Pity."

Liora agreed on that much. She'd thought Nebuzaradan believed himself a instrument of her Lord. Had hoped one day he might come to embrace Yahweh as his own. But Nebuzaradan's graveled assertion left no room for doubt. He meant those arrogant words.

"This is our farewell then. Unless"—the prince extended an arm to Liora—"you would prefer the

Jewess go in your stead? If you are not Yahweh's favored, perhaps...it would be best?"

"I would *not* prefer it."

Prince Nergal rubbed his chin, affecting a thoughtful pose. "Is it possible the woman has gentled my father's dearest Butcher? I would laugh if I were not so appalled. Imagine. The Butcher halting the hack of his sword at the bat of a woman's lashes or at the wail of a widow or child. What will become of Babylon under the protection of such a weakened general?"

Nebuzaradan dropped to a knee so hard his armor clanked. Head lowered, he said, "I am ever Babylon's sharpest blade. My loyalty is unquestioned."

"Is it?"

"Allow me to prove myself."

"Hmm."

"My life and death belong to Babylon. I ask only to speak privately with my wife before I approach the temple."

"By all means." Prince Nergal flapped an arm. "Say what you must to her."

"My gratitude." A downward jerk of the chin, then Nebuzaradan was up and coming at her.

Idadu released her to his general and reversed so fast she stumbled forward.

Nebuzaradan caught her by the elbow but let go at once. He cast a wary glance at the Holy Temple. The man was a fortress of resolve. But Liora supposed this was not the time to test a vow.

He brushed past her and strode off with a brusque, "Follow."

A FAITH UNTAMED

She did, her mind churning like frothy waters. Inundated in them, she almost slammed into Nebuzaradan when he stopped and turned.

She spoke first. "Do not do thi—"

"Belshazzar told of one who died for touching the covenant chest. Has a man ever died for looking upon it?"

A valid question. She considered it. "Not...that I recall."

He nodded grimly. "If your god slays me and I do not return, you must make yourself useful to the crown. No, *indispensable*." Bent close, he spoke in a rush while darting glances behind her, presumably at his prince. "Because I have shown great interest in you, the king will as well. Perhaps more so than his son." He grimaced. "I fear I have made a target of you."

"Moments from approaching the symbol of Yahweh's presence, and *that* is your concern?" She yanked the covering from her head. "No priest is permitted behind the curtain, save the High Priest once a year. *After* rigorous purification rituals to cleanse body and soul. To say nothing of Babylon's invading general, an idolater and *son of Marduk*." She threw the facts at him like stones shot from a sling and prayed they hit him with wakening force. "Come to your senses, Arioch. Either insist on employing the priests or fall to your face before Yahweh and beg His forgiveness and mercy!"

Emotion swarmed his face, and she hated it. Hated the sight of fear sloshing in his eyes like rising floodwaters. The man beneath the armor peered at her now, no evidence of the hardened butcher about him. Why she pitied an idolater who boasted of his own might, she did not know. And yet...

"Liora," he rasped, fists hard at his sides. "My prince will never relent. And your god will *never* forgive me."

"Hush! You do not know Yahweh at all." As if anyone truly could. "Turn your heart from wickedness. Pray mercy at every step." She ripped a long strip from the veil as she rattled off a list of cautions and prayed silently, fervently that her instructions aligned with Yahweh's will. "Remove your sandals. Touch nothing. Enter with eyes downcast. You can see shapes through the clouded one?"

His chin bobbed a nod.

"Good. Use this to cover your good eye." She wadded the strip and shoved it into his hands.

He stared down at the crumpled ball of blue. "What help is this against the god who slew an army?"

"It is recognition of His power. Do it!" She crouched and worked trembling fingers over the ties of his sandals. A light smack to his ankle stepped him out of them. She rose and used her veil to dab sweat from his forehead. "For this hour of Judah's fate, you *are* Yahweh's chosen. Surrender yourself to Him, Arioch. Tread in fear of His might and knowledge of His goodness." She peered into his unclouded eye. "His ear is always open to the brokenhearted."

"Liora..." He croaked her name, the fear at last subsiding from his countenance. The spray of lines around his eyes shallowed, a softening effect the prince

A FAITH UNTAMED

would pounce upon with mockery. "Has anyone ever cared for me as much as my little courier dove?"

She stepped back. "I— No. That is not— This is not about me!" Had he not listened at all? "And *yes*. Yahweh cares for you far more than I ever could or will." She flipped the head covering over her hair and wrapped the shredded edge around her neck. "Go to Him then, son of Marduk. Face His judgment. If you survive, you will doubtless come back to me as a son of the Lord Most High."

The assurance sounded bold. Certain. Did he know it rode from her on a thread of hope anchored only in reckless faith? She did not stay to find out but rounded his stiff frame. Crisp strides carried her to where she'd left Idadu.

Head tilted, he sought her gaze, but she looked off, too frustrated, too terrified at the situation to attend his curiosity. Was this truly Yahweh's answer to the question of the ark?

Prince Nergal strolled to her side and, smirking down at her, draped an arm across her shoulders. "Well, well. The gentle lady has a bite to her, after all."

Her back went rigid, and only a timely flash of self-preservation kept her from sloughing him off with a demonstration of that bite.

"Ah, she is angry," the prince said to his nearest guard. "Afraid the general will die, perhaps? Shall we observe? Learn his fate?" He turned them both toward the Gate of Nicanor. "Let us see whether the Butcher will live to slay another kingdom in the name of Babylon and her exalted king."

By the time she gathered the courage to lift her gaze, Nebuzaradan was skirting the puddle of blood at the foot of the central stairway leading into the Priests' Court, the court that would lead to the great double doors of the Holy Place. His barefooted stride was sure, but the strip she'd given him hung forgotten from his fist. Would he not follow her counsel? Impossible man!

Rimutu trailed the general, maintaining his faithful position, though his gait shuffled unsteadily.

Liora, too, shook, as she held open palms before her and cast incoherent prayers toward Heaven. Pleas for patience, for mercy, for a bloodless demonstration of His power. *The man understands only power, Lord Above. Show him yours!*

The prince chattered amiably, but she heard none of it. She felt only the suffocating weight of his arm and the drum of her heart against her breastbone.

The blue strip in Nebuzaradan's hand fluttered and lifted on a brisk breeze that did not reach her. How that might be possible in an enclosed courtyard she did not know.

Her stomach churned with dread, even as her breath stuck fast in her throat. Any moment, Yahweh would have His say over this presumption.

Head level, Nebuzaradan waved Rimutu off, then began a slow climb of the stairs. The guard skittered away, gone before the sole of the general's foot touched the third tread. Two steps more and thunder rolled across the bright, cloudless sky, a distant growl that built into a joint-rattling boom.

A FAITH UNTAMED

Did a storm brew? If so, the temple walls concealed its approach.

Pigeons lifted off the parapets.

Prince Nergal's nattering cut off mid-sentence. His arm tensed, then slid off her.

Liora's chest vibrated with the continuous rumble, her soul with trepidation. What *was* this? Nothing natural. The Lord? Making His presence known?

Armor clinked as guards shifted, Idadu among the wary lot.

Nebuzaradan trudged forward. Deaf to the divine display? He could not be.

The ribbon streamed out behind him now. Locks of his hair whipped about his shoulders. Chin tucked, he leaned as if into a stiff gale. At last, he wrapped the binding crosswise over his face, a sloppy eye patch that would surely not hold.

And still, no wind touched Liora. Yahweh's judgment had come. Fear for the general sliced through her.

Cover him, Lord, with your mighty hand, as you covered Moses on the mount.

Heedless of all, Nebuzaradan pressed on.

Was he *mad*? Careless of his life? Or arrogant beyond comprehension?

He trudged forward, entering the tumbled-stone passage of Nicanor Gate. A second wave of thunder shook the foundations. His big frame teetered, and he grasped for a handhold on the nearest stone. Before his fingers landed, he jolted and flung up both arms in a shielding gesture.

Liora saw no more. Her legs buckled, and she went down. The courtyard's broad stone expanse offered no shelter, just wide-open sky above and men who stood about oblivious to the sacred. Quaking, she cowered under the flimsy cover of her veil. Pain radiated up from her knees, a flit of a thought encompassed by a new sound emanating from the temple. Indecipherable, mind-spinning time ambled past before she could put a name to the noise now traveling eastward through the courtyard.

Not thunder. Not wind. But the flutter and flap of a thousand doves' wings. And beneath it, the rumble of wheels against flagstones. Chariots? If so, they were of a size Liora could not fathom.

And they rolled, rolled.

Nearing. *Nearing*.

Messengers of the Lord? No less than a host of angels.

Liora lost all sense of herself. She was nothing. A quivering mass of flesh. Insignificant. Unclean. Any moment, Yahweh would strike. Or had He already? Was she dead? Spiraling into eternity?

The wings beat on, at once fast and incomprehensibly slow. Over her shoulder now, they moved past, each windless *whoosh* a clap of thunder she was certain would end her.

And yet, her lungs continued to pull air. One rapid suck after another until the doves that were not doves passed her by. From where Liora knelt at the courtyard's center, she sensed the unseen procession leave through the shattered doors of the eastern archway. The host descended into the Kidron Valley and the vineyards and olive groves of the mount far below.

Only then did Liora register the hand shaking her shoulder. "Woman. *Woman!*"

Her muscles, stiff and aching, unlocked enough for her to peel back the veil and peer up at the wizened face of the elder priest. "Are you ill, daughter of Chesed?"

"N-no." She sat up and swallowed through a dry throat. "I am...blessedly well."

"Then up! The prince commands you. His patience thins to nothing. Can you not hear?"

A soft, half-crazed laugh rattled out of her. "I hear quite well. Though, apparently, my lord, you do not."

Concern mashed his wiry gray brows over the broad bridge of his nose. She expected rebuke for her impertinence. Instead, the priest rested a light hand on her head. "I am Buzi, son of Joshua and loyal priest of Yahweh. Has he come to you? Speak on, daughter."

Buzi, a name she recognized from years earlier, before her infamous walk through Jerusalem's streets toward her stoning. From the days her abba welcomed Yahweh's faithful into his chamber of scrolls for prayer and to counsel on the state of the people. Armed with the familiar name, she spoke, urgent and low, using the title of teacher as her abba had taught her. "I heard wings, *Moreh* Buzi. As of angels, flying by and wheels and—" She glanced behind her at the East Gate, its shattered wood blurring with her tears. "And perhaps..." The notion clogged her throat, too terrible to voice.

Buzi's fingers pressed lightly into her skull, an anchoring grip. Pallor washed his features. He swayed and the young, brown-bearded priest appeared at his side. "Abba." He wrapped an arm about the elder's frail shoulders. "What is it?"

Tears shimmering in his white lashes, the old priest stared at the East Gate, lost in thought. Or perhaps, simply lost. "And the sound of the cherubim's wings was heard even to the outer court." He muttered as if reciting a passage of scripture, but it was none Liora had ever heard.

"Abba, tell me, please. Has—" The son's voice cracked. "Has the time come?"

Buzi lowered his head, voice lifeless. "I fear so, my son."

The son grabbed a fistful of his hair and bowed over as one did before retching. Nothing spewed from his open mouth but a silent, agonized cry.

Whatever this *time* was, it appeared to have cracked both priests wide open.

Questions backed up in Liora's throat, but the courtyard noises began filtering back into her senses: the priests and elders protesting, wailing; the guards issuing clipped orders; the prince shouting indignant inquiries. Hadn't Buzi said something about the prince calling for her?

With a groan, Buzi bent and gripped her elbow, drawing her up with him. He patted her arm. "We will speak of this later. In your home? Yes, yes. We will come to you, myself and my son with me."

A FAITH UNTAMED

The son rocked where he stood, tears pouring soundlessly from his eyes.

Buzi released her and rested a supportive hand on his son's back, but it was to her he spoke. "Go now to the prince, my child." A sad smile multiplied the crinkles about his eyes. "Your butcher-general, it would seem, has been duly humbled, humbled by Adonai."

"My...what?" Liora looked between the men until time and reality slammed back into place. "Arioch!" A wrench of the head found him seated on the last stair of the Nicanor Gate. He bent over his raised knees, one side of his face buried in his large palm, as if holding an eye in its socket.

Liora flew then, her head covering a flag behind her. "Arioch!" she called, but he did not move.

This was not Babylon's Butcher, the general who so arrogantly boasted of breaching her city's walls. This was a man who'd come face to face with Yahweh and lived to understand his own insignificance.

She arrived, heart wild, hair streaming about her shoulders. Call her a fool, but she ignored the prince, his cluster of guards, and his snap of rebuke at her delay. She crouched before Nebuzaradan. "Arioch, speak. What is wrong?" She took him by the wrist and pulled his hand away.

Kohl stained his cheek in a wet, black smear that bled into his beard. "I am well enough, Liora." He raised his lashes to look at her. "A little burning. Nothing I cannot—"

Her loud intake of breath cut him off, pursued at once by Prince Nergal's vociferous swearing.

Several nearby guards cried out, more than one stumbling backward, away from the general.

The prince turned his ire on them, giving Liora and Nebuzaradan a moment to exchange a private look.

Nebuzaradan's throat wrenched up, then down. "Tell me."

"Your eye..." She checked the other, consoled herself with its bottomless black iris, and took his hand in a fortifying squeeze. "It has turned wholly white."

CHAPTER 8

> *We acknowledge, O LORD, our wickedness, and the iniquity of our fathers: for we have sinned against thee.* (Jer. 14:20)

Princes of Babylon were not supposed to knock at the knees or retreat before *defeated gods*. Liora knew it. Nebuzaradan knew it. Prince Nergal knew it, too. Which was probably the only reason he ordered Nebuzaradan to the healer and took his leave from the courtyard at a brisk walk instead of a frantic dash.

On his prince's orders, Nebuzaradan departed through the North Gate, delaying only long enough to send Liora home with all speed. Idadu stayed at her side, along with five others wearing the crossed axes of Nebuzaradan's House.

"Shall we?" Idadu gestured toward the South Gate, the same direction the prince had taken.

The man was already a stone's throw distant, unable to part company with the temple and its blinded transgressor fast enough.

Liora hurried after him, slowing when a royal guard stepped between. "Your Highness, I beg a moment in your presence." She strained to be heard above the clatter of marching feet and the shout of relayed orders to clear the Temple Mount.

Idadu, silent for once in his insistence she flee trouble, pasted himself to her side. His voiceless support emboldened her.

"A few words only," she persisted. "Regarding how to proceed in light of this unusual development."

The guards shot her a sharp look of warning, but the prince made no reply.

Liora took this as permission to continue—prince could not be seen taking council from a woman. He tramped on, his turban sitting askew on his head and perspiration beading on the back of his neck. Eyes forward, he focused intently on his exit from the temple compound.

Under different circumstances, Liora might struggle to bite back a smile at the Lord's show of strength. Yahweh *lived*, and the prince of Babylon could not deny it.

Defeated? Ha! Where was Nergal's mockery now? Ironically, defeated.

Under *these* circumstances, however, Liora could not afford to waste energy on humor or hubris. Not with Nebuzaradan's position hanging in the balance. Her *people* could not afford it.

Make yourself indispensable, he'd said. His own approach to handling the fickle and demanding Crowns of Babylon?

Shaken, he had not been in a state to defend himself. Liora, then, would champion his worth to the prince. "Dismissing General Nebuzaradan might be detrimental to Your Highness's purpose here," she began as they entered the enclosed South Gate passage.

Its stones echoed the prince's biting reply. "A blind man cannot command an army, woman."

Blind in one eye only, but this was not a time to contradict the prince. "Even a blind lion, having teeth and claws, is a formidable enemy." At a near jog, she coughed, her lungs unappreciative of the effort. Still, she managed to toss her voice ahead through the double row of guards separating her from the prince. "General Nebuzaradan had the respect of his men before his encounter with Yahweh. Imagine, if you will, what they must think of him now. They will whisper among themselves, 'General Nebuzaradan is favored of the gods.'"

"Favored with a ruined eye? As Judah is favored with crumbled walls and streets lined with corpses? Indeed, let them whisper."

Fool of a man! Wishing dissent among his ranks and contempt for a general who'd conquered kingdoms in his king's name. The same whose loyalty was such that, at a word, he would walk toward his own death.

Liora beat that logic down and, gathering her tunic to free her tangled ankles, brought another to the fore. "Ruined eye or not, who else among your soldiers can say he has approached the Holy Dwelling? None. For they are *dead*. Without doubt, report of this wonder is already spreading down the mount, making its way among the ranks."

Prince Nergal's tread hitched. Resuming at once, he turned right at the terrace to retrace their steps.

After a moment, he jutted his chin at the guard to his left.

The man angled back to wave her forward.

Liora did not hesitate to weave through the guards, positioning herself just off the prince's shoulder, trailing to maintain proper distance. "The general is the right man for this task, Your Highness. The *only* man. He has lost sight in one eye, yes. A warning from Adonai. Against approaching the ark, certainly. Perhaps against pride, as well. A tragic loss, the eye. To be sure. But does it not prove he is favored by Yahweh, that he is chosen?" Using the prince's own words against him was perilous but so was pressing the general's case. She'd already descended into the lair of the jackal; if it was going to end in blood, she may as well give it her all.

"If you remove him from service," she continued, "you risk pitting the men against you. To say nothing of reducing your chances of acquiring the covenant ark." She had no notion of him *ever* acquiring it, but Nebuzaradan wasn't the only one who could learn to speak another's language of desire.

A low growl emanated from the prince. Arriving at the Ancient Steps, he increased his pace to a rapid trot.

Liora's chest ached with the effort. If not for Idadu's grasp on her elbow, she might not have kept up. Fortunately, she needn't speak further. She'd said her piece, but she would not leave the prince's company without some sign of his decision. Prayerful, she stayed precisely where she was, in the stream of the prince's amber scent, all the way into the desolate city streets.

Only there did he slow and hike his chin in decree. "Captain Zakarshu, send a soldier to our *favored* general with these words: Rest out the day. Report for regular duty at dawn."

~~~

When Liora arrived home, she bypassed the door guard and his inquiry after the general, ignored Gittel's cutting commentary about Liora's disheveled appearance, and cringed at Devorah's responding rebuke. Dismissing them all, she charged down the corridor toward her childhood room. She'd not yet arrived when its door swung open.

Saba Jeremiah filled the space, mouth a straight line under his scraggly beard. His stained and battered robe hung off his shriveled frame like a gray cocoon a few shrugs from slipping off. If not for the rope tied about his waist in place of a sash, Liora might be concerned for his modesty.

He spread his arms, and she walked straight into his embrace. She embraced his thin shoulders and hung on, as if an enemy had threatened to toss her into a miry pit. "But what are you doing up, Saba? Are you well enough for it?"

"Hush, child, and tell me what has you quaking like a newborn lamb."

Her arms tightened, and a flood she hadn't seen coming released into his rough, woolen garment. "Saba, I fear I have erred." Of everything that had transpired over the last hours—the trial, the execution, the frightening encounter with the prince, the angelic wing beats in the temple courtyard—her own blunder was what burst from her mouth first. "I am a selfish creature."

"Shah, shah, now." He patted her back as her fingers tangled in the knots of gray hair on the back of his neck. "There is no sin that cannot be forgiven. We have only to acknowledge it before Adonai."

Truth and more truth. But that would not undo the thing she'd done.

"Come. Tell me all." He guided her to the chamber's only chair at her painting table.

The sight of its colorful, spattered wood and the stained pots cluttering its surface did nothing to soothe her agitated spirit. Even its linseed oil scent could not touch her fear of wrongdoing.

"Sit." Jeremiah flapped his weathered hands, as one did at a gaggle of wandering geese. "Before those lamb's legs give out and you take me with you."

She almost refused out of respect for his age and condition but changed her mind when Idadu, who'd entered behind, pressed her down into it. Her quaking thighs gave no resistance. She'd been about to thank the guard when Jeremiah shooed him out with another flap of the hands.

Idadu allowed himself to be herded but rotated at the threshold. "I will be just outside, my lady, if you require any—"

"Yes, yes, very good." Jeremiah closed the door in his face.

A FAITH UNTAMED

"Saba, he was only offering help," she said, since Jeremiah did not speak Akkadian. "Idadu is a fine guard with a good heart."

"None is good save our Lord." In response to the mild reproach jutting her lips, the prophet's eyes twinkled. He opened the door again. Idadu's scowl bore down on him, but the prophet paid him no mind, looking instead at Liora. "Hashem, the nations shall come unto Thee from the ends of the earth, and shall say..." He paused, wiry brows raised in that familiar manner.

She'd often been his pupil and understood he meant for her to pick up the recitation—his own prophecy, handed down from the Lord years before. But Liora started over in Akkadian. A clumsy translation, but the message was too important for Idadu to miss. "The prophecy he recites goes this way." She proceeded, speaking straight at the guard, whose expression morphed from surly to open and listening.

Her heart lightened as she quoted Jeremiah, then completed the prophecy. "And the nations shall say, 'Surely our fathers have inherited lies, worthless and unprofitable things.' Will a man make gods for himself, which are not gods? 'Therefore,' Yahweh says, 'I will cause them to know my might; and they shall know that my name is Hashem.'"

She ended the prophecy and added her own words, her tears multiplying and clogging her nose. "Adonai is Lord of all lords. He is Yahweh, the Creator and King."

As if he'd followed along with perfect understanding, the prophet said, "And if this fine guard will swear by Yahweh's name, then he will have a place among our people, and the Lord will have compassion according to the abundance of his steadfast love." He turned to Idadu. "What say you, young fellow?"

Liora translated, and Idadu's broad brow wrinkled pensively. How much of Yahweh had he experienced that day? He'd certainly gotten an irrefutable view of his general's whitened eye—no work of the wind. What might a pagan make of such a transformation? The unnamed thoughts swirling about Idadu's face said he hadn't quite figured it out himself.

Before he could vocalize a single one of those thoughts, Jeremiah shut the door again. "He will think on it. As any man should who has seen the power of the Lord." The prophet shuffled to the shelves lining the wall and began rummaging in one of her small, lidded baskets. "Now. What has got my favorite daughter of Jerusalem in such a snotty-nosed fit of shame? Did something occur with the Babylonian, eh?" Said as if there were only one Babylonian of note.

Where she was concerned, maybe there was. "Well…yes. But not that."

"Here we are." He plucked a white linen kerchief from the basket and waved it like a banner. "Of late, I have frequent use of these myself."

"It is, indeed, a time of weeping. And of mourning one's folly." Her voice went weak on that last word, the extent of that folly sweeping back in to haunt her.

"Quoting the wise king, are we?" Jeremiah approached, kerchief extended.

A FAITH UNTAMED

"If only I had a fraction of Solomon's wisdom." She took the cloth and wiped her nose. As Jeremiah went back to her shelves, she took a breath and began her confession. "The prince—that is, Nergal-sharezer—he demanded instruction on how to transport the ark. Of *me,* Saba. And when Moreh Buzi's son gestured at me, I thought he meant for me to proceed. So I recited details from when King David moved the ark from Kiriath-jearim. Consecrated priests, designated poles, new cart, and so on. But then Arioch said you had remained silent on the matter, and I understood that I had spoken out of turn." Another trickle wet her cheek.

If the Lord's chief mouthpiece was not authorized to speak to conquering pagans on such matters, she certainly was not.

"Eitan son of Buzi, you say?"

"I did, Saba. He and his father will visit later this day."

"Eitan is a shrub in the wasteland. His roots are shallow and weak."

But he did have roots, presumably in the Lord. "Did he lead me wrong, Saba?"

"His younger brother, however, is like a tree which spreads out its roots by the river and does not cease yielding fruit."

Liora stared at the elder as he poked through her scarves and sashes, wracking her mind for the statement's relevance. She came up empty. "A disappointment then that I did not meet the brother."

"The younger was taken in the second deportation." In his digging, a few delicate scarves floated to the ground in a colorful array. "Did you know Nergal is Nebuchadnezzar's son by marriage only?"

"Is he?" She'd believed the man a prince by blood. Did that make him more or less of a threat to Nebuzaradan than she'd believed?

"Recall to me the meaning of his name." He shoved the lid back onto the basket. "Have you no hair combs, girl?"

"Lower." She pointed at a small cedar chest on the next shelf down and thought back to her childhood studies of Babylonia. "Nergal is the god of war and...plague. And of the underworld?"

Jeremiah grunted, possibly in confirmation, or with effort as he bent his crooked back to retrieve the chest. "He believes himself a god." Would the prophet not rebuke her for instructing Babylon in how to remove their most sacred vessel? She would much rather he got it over with.

"He is a tool of the Evil One," she said on a little cough. "And I have fallen prey to him. I wished to honor the covenant ark and instead spoke amiss and made wreckage of your silence. To add to my sins, my husband bid me hold my tongue. I did not heed him, and now, he is fully blind in the eye." Though she was relatively sure the one had not caused the other.

"You give the Babylonian too much esteem, and yourself too much credit if you believe you could upset the Almighty's plan. And what of this cough?" He cupped the top of her head with his knobby fingers and looked ceiling-ward. "Your healing, Adonai, on this child of yours."

A FAITH UNTAMED

Liora bowed her head. "Blessed be your hands, Saba."

"Besides," he went on, "Any one of Nergal's magi could have read the prophet Samuel's record of how David HaMelech moved the ark." He cracked the lid on the chest and passed it to her. The resinous scent of cedar filled her senses, a perfume lacking its usual comfort.

"The magi. Of course, they would..." Abashed that she hadn't considered this, Liora turned the lid over in her hands and let her words peter out. Was it silliness that caused the lapse? Or mental strain? She was loath to think it could be an inflated sense of self. How very important she must be to have the power in her mouth to advance or stay the ark's removal.

Jeremiah's hand emerged from the chest with Liora's ivory comb, a triumphant grin shifting the saggy skin on his face. Given enough time, she would put fat back under that skin.

Urgent knocking shook the door. "Liora dear?" Zipporah's concerned voice filtered through. "Idadu sent for me, but now the big oaf bars the way. Are you unwell?"

Liora rose. "Let her in, Idadu."

Zipporah pushed her way past the guard, her head covering askew. She grabbed Liora by the shoulders for a brisk appraisal. "You do not *look* well." She stroked the side of Liora's head. "This hair is in shambles. Did you tangle with a jackal?"

"That *is* rather close to how—"

"And what is this?" Zipporah picked up the end of Liora's head covering, now draped around her neck. She held up its ragged edge before Liora and wagged it like an accusation. "Who has been tearing at your clothing?"

Liora rubbed at the tattoo on her palm, as the morning swept back through her mind so powerfully, her jaw hung useless. Nebuzaradan gazing down at her with that softness the prince found so amusing. Nebuzaradan striding toward the temple, the scrap of linen dangling from his fist. Nebuzaradan driven to his knees before—

"Might you have a use for this, Zipporah?" Her saba's aged voice broke into the onslaught.

Zipporah plucked the comb from his outstretched hand. "Most definitely." She rounded Liora and began driving the comb through the ends of Liora's hair with short strokes that bobbed her head and pinched her scalp. Zipporah paused to hug her from behind. "My poor dear friend. I cannot tell if you are pale or...radiant."

Jeremiah took the lid from Liora's weak grasp. "They looked unto Him, and were radiant; and their faces were not ashamed."

While he returned the chest to the shelf, Zipporah came back around Liora's front, eying the prophet strangely. She leaned close and spoke in a hush, her eyes dancing with news. "Is it because Gittel has left us?"

"Gittel has left us?" The morning had indeed been eventful.

A FAITH UNTAMED

Before Liora could decide whether the sensation in her chest was relief or sadness, Devorah's crisp voice carried in from the corridor. "The cow has found a position as a handmaid." She waddled through the open doorway. Sapir straddled her hip, her tousled head resting on Devorah's chest and a thumb in her mouth.

"To *whom*?" Incredulity spiked Liora's pitch. She could not fathom a single household in Jerusalem, besides her own, in any financial state to employ service.

"Bah! Who cares?" Devorah rocked in place and applied rhythmic pats to Sapir's backside. "She is gone. Believing it better to empty waste pots than keep company with us."

If that was true, Liora had failed the woman completely, unable to reach through her grief to the wounded heart beneath. A sigh drooped her. "It saddens me she has gone where we cannot guide her from bitterness."

"But who among us," Devorah said on a wry twist of the lips, "can say she will be much missed?"

A loud silence descended upon the chamber. Each looked at the other, but none, not even Saba Jeremiah, replied. Gaze cast at the cloth-covered window, the prophet scratched his cheek through his beard.

Sapir's sleepy-eyed sucking noises seemed to rouse Devorah from her smug observation. "Well! Sapir is due her afternoon nap."

At that, Jeremiah turned from his study of nothing. "She and this old man with her. Too much excitement in one morning for these weak, old bones of mine."

Too much excitement for young, strong bones, as well. Liora still had much to address with the prophet. She'd not even touched on the wind she could not feel or the sounds others could not hear but that rattled her joints. But perhaps it was best to reserve that for when Buzi and Eitan arrived.

A small part of her admitted she hadn't brought it up yet because she wished to speak with Nebuzaradan first. What had *he* experienced? Had it been enough to convince him that Marduk was sun-cracked dung compared with the might of Yahweh?

Please, Lord, may it be so.

After such an extraordinary show of strength, if the man's proud heart was unmoved, unchanged, she feared what it might take to convince him. If anything could...

Liora rubbed her face and heard the broad bed in her abba's old chamber summoning. The night had been too short, the morning far too long. Might she find a little rest before the general returned? Through the call of sleep, she vaguely heard Devorah speaking.

"Shall I place the child on your cushions, Burden Bearer?"

"As you like, Devorah. Zipporah, wake me when Buzi arrives." Jeremiah crossed before Liora, pausing to say, "And Liora, child, if the Babylonian is not too cross about his eye, might he share more of his exquisite, herbed cheese?"

A FAITH UNTAMED

Herbed cheese? She smiled and wrapped him in an impulsive hug. "I will make certain he does, Saba. All the better to fatten these weak, old bones."

And to pull her from her dark, faithless thoughts.

CHAPTER 9

*Know therefore that the LORD thy God,
he is God, the faithful God, which
keepeth covenant and mercy with them
that love him and keep his
commandments to a thousand
generations; and repayeth them that
hate him to their face, to destroy them:
he will not be slack to him that hateth
him, he will repay him to his face.*
(Deut. 7:9–10)

Liora stretched awake from her nap, her thoughts filtering back from hazy dreams of prickly spined poppies littering a field with red. They'd danced under a cheery sun that beamed with promise. She would go back to that happy place but for the tickle at the back of her throat compelling her back to reality. Another tickle, this one becoming a sneeze that sat her upright and brought Nebuzaradan off the bench he occupied in the garden.

The doors leading from her abba's chamber to the enclosure stood wide. They gave her a full view of the general, standing stiff and alert, and of the budding fig trees framing him in vibrant spring green. Hyssop shrubs in full purple bloom congregated about the bench, and morning glories crawled up its legs. If not for the smoke-heavy clouds above and the world's gray hue, she could almost believe life had a chance in Jerusalem.

Then there was Nebuzaradan's grim expression and white-washed eye. Other concerns altogether...

Head foggy from sleep, Liora hardly felt prepared to confront them. She blinked several times to summon moisture to her dry eyes. A sturdy breeze swept in from the garden and rustled the light wool blanket covering her legs. Ash flakes spiraled in with it, the likely culprit for her sneezing. Although, if her stuffy nose was any indication, the tears she'd shed earlier could not have helped.

She patted about for the kerchief, found it under the covers, and cleared her airways before rising and padding across the room. Her loose hair lifted in the hot wind and flew back from her face as she stepped outdoors. Shriveled fig leaves crunched beneath her tread, evidence of her winter gardening neglect.

Nebuzaradan monitored her approach, head tilted to one side as he peered at her through his good eye. How furious was he, exactly, over that blindness? His disheveled state suggested he'd not accepted his lot. Specks of gray perched on his unkempt black curls and dusted the tops of his pleated-leather shoulder guards.

He'd not bothered to reapply the kohl his weeping eye washed down his cheek, so remnants of black still stained the upper edges of his beard, as well as the light blue stole draping his body crosswise. Had he used the costly garment to tidy himself?

A groove made a vertical line between his brows. "Did I not instruct you to guard your health, my dove?

You grow ill." The pure white of that one eye, combined with the rugged scar bisecting it, added a touch of fright to the censure. If only she could bring herself to fear him. Her heart might be less vulnerable.

She said, "The conditions in the city are not ideal for obeying such orders. But...I should have shielded myself with a veil before joining you out of doors."

Idadu might have had a point about her returning to the clearer air outside the city, but she would not mention it. Liora was not the only one who suffered, and soon, they would all be gone anyway. Hustled off to Babylon as the last of Jerusalem floated away on ash—much as the sound of invisible doves flapping away from the temple, the carts rolling along with them.

With the memory of the noise, Liora's mind spun, questions for Nebuzaradan sparking so fast she didn't quite know where to begin. But there was time. First, she would learn his mood, whether she'd kindled his ire with her disobedience and meddling, and how he fared with the full loss of vision in that eye.

Did he realize how he blinked it? Hard and often. It must torment! If not with pain, then with the knowledge he'd tested the Lord of Hosts and been found wanting.

Reaching him, she bent her knees and lowered her head in deference. "But what of you, my lord? Won't you come in? We have much to speak of." Namely, what happened at the Gate of Nicanor.

"Such as your disobedience? Your wild tongue? Your absolute disregard for your own safety?" His volume rose with each reminder of her willfulness. "Did I not say just yesterday how reckless and bold you are? Can I take you nowhere, woman, without fearing your death?"

She met the outburst with a contrite smile. "Recent events would say...*no*. And I truly regret the distress it causes. You have enough of that without me."

A snort jetted from his nose. "I cannot decide what is worse—that you look so pretty and sweet I cannot hold my anger, or that you do it without a hint of conniving." His mouth slid to the side, twisting the scar that ran into his beard. It created an effect that made him almost...attractive. Or was it simply the compliment that tingled heat across her cheeks?

Her gaze flicked away, only to come right back. "But I would not take a word of it back if it meant saving a life. Yours, in this instance."

His chest puffed. "I can save my own life. And this,"—he waved brusquely at his eye—"is nothing. My grandfather slew a wolf with one arm and my father eliminated King Necho's three-man guard at Carchemish using a broken spear."

"And both men died promptly after." Liora had not spent the days between her stint in the Babylonian camp and their invasion lounging on her couch, but in study of the man who'd marked her. "Do not look at me with such affront. My condolences, husband, but isn't it true? Your forebears each died in the service of your king. *You*, however, have a far nobler purpose than spilling blood for greedy royals, and I will not sit idly by while you throw away your life on misguided notions of loyalty."

He spluttered. *"Misguided?"*

"*Yes*, Arioch. They are not gods, your king and princes. They are men, same as you." She sighed at his fury-flared nostrils. "And you are angry with me for sharing my mind. More each moment, I expect. Is that why you are out here, collecting ash like a statue, spoiling Haldi's fine polish? Because you are so indignant you cannot bear my presence?" She dusted his shoulder guard, then showed him the greasy, gray stain on her fingertips.

He scowled down at himself and brushed a coarse hand over his once-gleaming breastplate. "I am beyond furious with you," he grumbled as he smudged ash over the embossed axe heads of his family's sigil. He scrubbed harder, the rough motion knocking the wooden handle of the real axe resting against his hip. The molded wood jutted through the lush red sash wrapping around his waist.

This time, when Liora looked off, her gaze had no interest in returning. "I will not apologize for voicing my truest thoughts. Or for speaking on your behalf to Prince Nergal. There is no man better suited for this odious task than you." From the side of her eye, she noted his head jerk up.

Angled away, she went on. "Yahweh, in His wisdom, chose you, Arioch. And as I told the prince, quite recklessly, I admit, that even blinded, you are a capable leader and a formidable weapon. He is right to fear you. Although, *that*"—she twisted back and almost laughed at his open mouth and bulging eyes—"that last thing I did not say. Aloud."

A great breath left Nebuzaradan. He took one wobbling step backward and dropped hard to the stone bench. He lowered his head and wiped roughly at his hairline. "Truly, if there is any *formidable weapon* in this miserable city, it is you. For I swear on every god beyond the Euphrates, the day will come that either your tongue, your antics, or your beauty will stop my heart dead." He lifted his face and showed her a snarl, the ashy smear across his forehead and nose undermining his ferocity.

Liora rolled her lips in and coughed to cover the laugh bubbling in her chest.

His eyes narrowed without heat. "You find talk of my death humorous?"

She found *something* humorous. On the heels of it came a dart of guilt that drove away every urge to smile. What was this laughter? She should be weeping, hating, plotting this man's demise, as Ishmael the rebel leader would have her do.

Her eyes lowered. "I should, shouldn't I? So Gittel says. Most of Jerusalem with her, most likely. Sound reason tells me they are not wrong." The casual nature of her shrug did not reach her voice. "Are you not my master?" She rubbed the mark on her palm. "My conqueror and enemy?"

Against her will, her gaze traveled to the crossed axes on his armor, then to the weapon at his waist. Leather encased the blade's edge, concealing its true danger. Even so, a shudder rippled Liora's backbone.

"I am all of those things. And none of them." Nebuzaradan wiped his hands on his stole before sliding the weapon from its seat. He stood and hefted it in his fist, as if testing its weight or value. "There is no fear in this blade, dove. Not for you."

But wasn't there? How much of her people's blood had reddened its edge, and whose would wet it next? She eyed it cornerwise. "I do not recall you sporting an axe in the camp." Odd, since it was the symbol of his house.

"Because I'd stored it, and for no small reason." He popped the protector off the weapon and shoved it behind his sash. Not a speck of blood marred the blade's gleaming bronze edge. "My habit has become to set the blade aside until I have taken a city. Only then, when I have broken down every gate and bloodied my hands on my foe am I worthy to raise it again."

Liora didn't know what was more disturbing—that he found his worth in bloodshed or that he'd done it enough to make a habit of it. Her heel edged back, expanding the space between them. "We really should go in."

Neither the movement nor her words registered with him as he spoke on, lost in recollections. "Did you know"—he held the weapon upright between them and spun it slowly—"that over the long months of siege, my soldiers broke a dozen carts of axes against Jerusalem's gates? By the time you walked into my tent, Liora, not one remained in working order. I'd almost come to believe the gates were stone disguised as wood." He smirked, a secret lurking in the backs of his eyes. One she suspected she knew.

"Yahweh has His own time."

"Such a wise creature, my dove. That is, until she left me and flew back to her crumbling cote." The warmth that had doubled in his tone flattened, almost playfully, as if all were forgiven. "The night I returned from my report to the king at Riblah, I woke from a sweat, looked upon a red sunrise, and knew in my soul the day had come. I pulled this beauty from my weapons chest and ordered a call to arms." He twisted the ax, gazing at it as one might a beloved child. "This blade struck the final blow that brought down the eastern gate."

Eastern? The Gate of Mercy, he meant, the one that led to the temple and redemption. The same gate she'd looked toward that very morning as she'd wondered at the sound of those flapping wings heading out over the Mount of Olives.

Liora looked away, hardly seeing the lobed fig leaves dancing about his head. "Then Jerusalem burned, my people bled, and you lost half your sight for daring to tread upon holy ground." On that last, frankly spoken fact, he turned his head sharply away.

He might avoid her by displaying his blind eye, but he could not run from Yahweh. Or from her dogged questions.

She invaded his space and gripped his arm where a broad brass band nestled in the swell of his muscles. "What happened at the temple, Arioch? For you? I heard birds in flight, the turning of wheels. Did you?

The priest, Buzi, and his son, they heard nothing. But *you*, you went down on your knees for a reason. A wind? I could not tell, since I felt nothing."

"Leave it, Liora."

"I cannot." She spoke to the ashy war mask covering his averted face, to the muscle twitching the curled whiskers on his jaw. "Talk to me, Arioch. Did you meet the Lord Most High when He took your sight? For all your swearing on lesser gods, surely, you can no longer deny He is powerful and worthy of worship. Worthiest of all!"

A long, dry laugh tipped his chin up. "Powerful? Oh, indeed. Who could feel a wind that does not touch the skin but cuts through the soul and *not* believe? Who could experience such a shining light, feel its blade sever the inner eye, and deny the power of it? No man in his right mind."

A vigorous nod bobbed Liora's head. "It is as I have said, as the prophets and the history of my people attest. Yahweh is above all gods and worthy of—"

"No. He is not." He turned abruptly to face her, knocking off her hold with a twist of his arm. "He is real. His power beyond description. But I will never worship him."

For long moments, Liora could do no more than stare into his stone-cold eyes, baffled at his stance. "Because... He took your sight? Arioch, for such arrogance, He could have taken your *life*! He is just and merciful and—"

"And *gone*," he said, bending to put the word right in her face. The puff of it blinked her eyes.

A FAITH UNTAMED

"What?"

"Where do you think he was going? When he opened the temple doors without hands and swept past us? I felt a wind, saw a light like the sun. They passed over me. You heard wheels, a flight of birds moving through the courtyard. All evidences of departure. He left the temple, Liora. He destroyed his people, then abandoned them. He abandoned *you*."

He hurled each accusation at her like an arrow. Only, she had no armor to shield her heart. Nothing but a hasty step back and flat denial. "That is untrue. You only suppose that because you do not know Him." There was another explanation for the phenomena they'd witnessed. From the distance came the deep-throated roar of a lion, low and lingering, as if to remind her of Jacob's promise to his son—the scepter would not depart from Judah.

"The children of Avraham are his treasured possession. Every one of us!" Turning about, she flung her arm wide, as if encompassing all of Jerusalem, Judah, and beyond. The back of her hand struck Nebuzaradan, but she turned again and swept her arm the other direction, intent on covering every hill of their ancient land and every child born on them since Yitzchak pushed from Sarah's womb. "He is *ever* faithful, keeping his covenant of love to a thousand generations!"

Moses's Law continued from there, but Liora's throat closed up tight. Whether from emotion or that denial she entertained. Her eyelids squeezed together, but she could not unsee the remainder of the text laid out in neat lines on the scroll, the words Moses spoke to all Israel. The warning that followed the promise. The condition that the Lord's commandments be kept.

Those who hated Him would be destroyed. But abandonment?

"No." Opening her eyes, she hiked her chin in abject refusal of the notion. "No."

"That." Nebuzaradan jabbed a finger at her face. "Right there. The wound in your eyes. My reason for refusing your god the worship he demands."

"I am not wounded. There is no wound!" Palms out, she shielded herself from his advance, backing away as he pursued, each of his words milled between the teeth.

"I could forgive Judah's god many things, including my stolen vision. But I cannot, *will* not forgive him for turning his back on Jerusalem's purest soul, his most faithful daughter, and the woman I—" His teeth clicked shut as he stared at her raised hands.

Chin jerking in, he eyed the axe still fisted low before him, then fumbled for the leather case tucked into his sash. He stepped aside and nodded sideways at the bench. "Sit." Fingers unsteady, he slipped the covering over the blade's edge and drove the handle behind his belt. "*Sit*. Before you tumble."

"Why would I—?" The sting registered then, a low-burning fire on the back of her hand. Sensations collided—the warmth dripping down her wrist, the wet patter on the dead foliage at her feet, the woody scent of hyssop underscored by the tang of blood.

A FAITH UNTAMED

She knew better than to look, but the eyes often had a mind of their own. Hers shot to the back of her hand and a triangular puncture in the precise shape of the upper tip of an axe's blade. The wound discharged an unreasonable amount of blood, but then any amount of leaking from Liora's body was enough to turn her stomach. The mere sight could spin her head—the exact thing that happened next.

Her head went light, her tongue thick. The garden tipped, and she stumbled sideways before catching herself. "I'm well, I am well." And they were not done speaking.

"You are not. Sit *down*. Captain!"

"Why call for the captain?" She waved off the order, careful to avoid seeing red. "If Yahweh no longer dwells in Jerusalem, He cannot see what you do." Vaguely, she was aware of her tilted stance and slurring words. "Your vow is obsolete, General. Carry me, as you did before. It is surely safe now." She raised her arms in invitation.

He backed away. "Stop this nonsense. Captain Idadu, you will come at once!"

"Have you changed your mind about Him? Has Yahweh not"—she swallowed hard against nausea—"abandoned me, after all?"

Running footsteps sounded from behind, deep within her abba's chamber.

Shrieking pierced Liora's ears, a discordant mix of whistling and jeering. Echoes of another day. The captain would not arrive in time. Her first step toward the bench buckled her knees. Shadows crowded her vision.

When they cleared, she blinked up at the paneled ceiling above her abba's bed. Dull pain radiated through her knuckles and up her forearm. Someone manipulated her hand, binding it tenderly. Devorah, by the angry mutterings filtering into Liora's awareness.

Idadu's face moved in, blocking the view, his dark brow a terrain of worry. He stared into her slow-blinking eyes and answered the question opening her mouth. "The prophet summoned my lord general. Your guests have arrived. The priests. They bring scrolls and downcast faces and—"

"Did he let me fall?" she asked, voice cut to less than a whisper.

"My lady?" Idadu tilted his ear toward her.

She cleared her throat and did not think of the blood wetting her bandage or of its red stain. There were other more important issues to address. "Did the general let me fall?"

When Idadu's eyes darted off, Liora had her answer, and she didn't know whether to rejoice that Nebuzaradan recognized Yahweh watched on despite His "abandonment." Or cry because she hadn't known until now that she expected him to always catch her.

CHAPTER 10

*Cut off thine hair, O Jerusalem, and
cast it away, and take up a lamentation
on high places; for the Lord hath
rejected and forsaken the generation of
his wrath.* (Jer. 7:29)

The sounds of droll conversation guided Liora down the short corridor leading from her abba's bedchamber toward his chamber of scrolls.

Echoes distorted Saba Jeremiah's hoarse voice, but Liora's familiarity with his tone helped her pick out his words. "This would go more quickly if Chesed were allowed to join us. It is his library."

"His organization system is admirable," another man said, an aged one. Priest Buzi, perhaps. "We will find it soon enough without Chesed."

"For shunning my wife, that man is not permitted here." *That* near growl belonged indisputably to her husband, and he hadn't bothered speaking Hebrew.

Had he ever? Certainly not with her abba, who would not be greeting her in the chamber, apparently. Liora sighed and barely refrained from looking back to share a roll of the eyes with Idadu padding silently behind her. Honoring her bullheaded husband did not include belittling his decisions before his captain.

She and Idadu had already shared an awkward moment that hour. He'd been unwilling to speak a single word on the matter of Nebuzaradan's reaction to her faint—how he'd let her fall. The captain could not even look her in the eye. Had it been absolute discretion that clamped his lips, or shame at his general's behavior? Even a butcher-general would be expected to prevent injury to his wife. A tender spot had developed on her elbow, leading her to believe it was the latter.

She could conjecture all day. Or she could ask Nebuzaradan at the next opportunity. The man's refusal to bend his heart toward Yahweh would have to be addressed soon anyway. She would *not* allow herself to be used as an excuse for idol worship. If he wished to place her above Yahweh in importance, he would do so with an earful from her.

As she stepped into the chamber's open doorway, the perfumes of beeswax, lemon oil, and decaying parchment embraced her but were no replacement for her abba. He should be there, seated at the low writing table occupying the room's center. He should be going through his ritual of ordering the table's supply of tablets, reed pens, and seals. A king's collection of writing implements.

The chamber of scrolls in their home was a rarity among men. But then Chesed ben Ephraim, merchant, vintner, and dealer in fine wines, was no regular man. At least, he hadn't been before he'd chosen loyalty to Elohim over their former king. Blessedly, the room's contents was one of the few treasures King Zedekiah had overlooked in his vendetta. Tucked into the farthest corner of her grand home and surrounded by thick stone walls, the scroll room remained untouched by king or fire, its chill perpetual, even on a warm spring evening as this.

Liora pulled her head covering close about her arms and stepped inside. Her entry went unnoticed.

Saba Jeremiah faced away, poking through a stack of scrolls in one of the dozens of cubbies lining the far wall. Matted and dark with grime, his gray hair protruded at angles from under his faded black turban. Zipporah should have used the comb on him instead of Liora. Before the day was through, Liora would see it done. That and a much-earned scrub in the bathing tub.

To his left, Priest Buzi, who'd exchanged the garb of his office for ordinary robes, explored another compartment, its wood dark and smooth from generations of burnishing. He removed a stack of clay tablets to reach farther into the space, but he would find nothing there.

His son, Eitan, stood behind a lectern in the corner nearest his abba. His robe glowed a rich brown in the broad beam of late afternoon sunlight streaming through the window on the west wall. The amber rays fell across the scroll rolled open before him. Head bent, he slid a thin, silver stylus evenly across the text and didn't stir at Liora's movement in the doorway.

The men hadn't delayed making themselves at home in her abba's chamber of scrolls. Never mind the host himself was absent. And how he would love to see it! How many years since the men of the city had gathered in this room to read the sacred texts, deliberate over matters of governance, and share news from abroad? Too many. And her abba was missing it.

An insane urge came over her to back up and march across the street to retrieve him from the abandoned home he'd taken as temporary shelter. What a stir that would create. The selfish sort. The foolish sort.

The general hadn't sounded the least softened in his position regarding her abba, but Liora wasn't without other tools, those that did not include disobedience. How badly did he feel about her wound? She fingered its bandage and promptly felt the sting of guilt. Manipulation had never been one of her recourses. She would not start using it now, even if intuition told her Arioch was more lamb at the moment than lion—scowl notwithstanding.

Mouth in a pinch, he leaned his left shoulder against the paneled south wall. Arms crossed over his broad chest, he managed to look both uninterested and menacing. The tension straining the cords of his neck, however, told Liora his boredom was a ruse, leaving only the menace. His arms bulged, that brass band cutting into stiff muscle, and his weapons gleamed. He hadn't bothered to remove them out of respect for a house of knowledge. Menace, indeed.

But where was the threat? Or was it vulnerability that had the general so on edge? Rimutu gazed at her now, arms clasped loosely at his lower back, but Nebuzaradan hadn't so much as twitched in recognition of her presence. That white eye to blame. It blinded him to any activity at the door.

A FAITH UNTAMED

What was the man thinking putting himself in such a position? Was he that distracted by the priests' interpretation of the temple incident, or did he trust Rimutu so implicitly?

The guard nodded at her, a deep plunge of the chin. "General," he said, ear tips blazing red. "Your wife, the Lady Liora."

Nebuzaradan shoved off the wall and looked around his guard. Head cocked at that odd angle, he raked her with his good eye. Assessing, cataloging. Frowning.

If her appearance mirrored how she felt—clammy, heart rate shallow and fast—she probably looked pale and less than composed. She should have rinsed her face and tidied her garments before rushing to greet her guests. Ignoring Nebuzaradan's disapproving look, she turned to Idadu behind her, almost expecting to see Šulmanu with him. A twang of sadness struck her heart.

Protect him, Lord. Wherever he is, she prayed, then issued quiet orders. "Remain here, Captain. We are not to be disturbed. No one enters, save the prince himself."

"As you say." Idadu saluted and closed the door.

That settled, she strode partway in and stopped to bend her knees and head. "*Shalom aleichem.* Welcome, Priests Buzi and Eitan. In my abba's absence, I greet you warmly."

Stylus frozen, Eitan stared at her, brows drawn in confusion, as if she were a donkey in a throne room.

Buzi turned, squinting through rheumy eyes toward Liora. "The daughter of Chesed has arrived?"

Saba Jeremiah kept rummaging. "Liora, child! Be my Baruch this day. Help an old man with ailing sight."

Mention of the prophet's scribe begged questions about his travel to Anathoth, but they would have to wait. Prince Nergal had given Nebuzaradan the evening to recover and adjust, but she didn't trust him not to back out or add conditions. Time was short, and they needed guidance. Yahweh could heal an eye as easily as he could blind one, and there had to be an explanation for the wind she hadn't felt and the mysterious sounds whooshing in her ears.

At the temple, Priests Buzi and Eitan had seemed to have one, if their ominous *the time has come* statement was anything to go on. Considering how she'd come upon them—both men deep in search—perhaps her certainty in their expertise was unfounded.

"Saba Jeremiah, I trust you rested well. What do you seek here?"

"Letters from Babylon." He shuffled back to allow her to approach the shelving, but she moved instead to the other end of the unit.

"Correspondence with crown officials would be here." She gestured broadly over the last two rows of compartments rising to the ceiling.

Nebuzaradan came to stand over her shoulder, a shadow radiating heat.

A FAITH UNTAMED

"Crown, you say? Not with the royals." Buzi followed her but stopped a few strides off to cast a wary gaze up at the general.

"Do not fear him," Liora said. "He is our Lord's instrument."

"Of death," Eitan muttered, the solid wood lectern between him and the general whose gaze he avoided.

"Have you done something worthy of death?" Liora arched a brow at him.

"Does the Butcher's axe consider *worthiness* when it comes crashing down? Again and again."

"Another nitwit," Nebuzaradan drawled in Akkadian, "who does not realize I understand his language. Shall we keep it that way, my dove?"

Liora glanced back to twist her lips at him and nearly snorted at the devilish grin shining down on her. "Play your games if you wish, but these men passed your test at the temple and are to be spared *cleansing*. There will be no bloodshed in this home."

His grin faltered. "Too late for that." He leaned in so close his breath tickled her forehead. "Does your hand hurt very much?"

The intimacy of his volume, the tenderness in it, pattered her heart and made her keenly aware of the other three men in the room. What must they think of her? What words crept through their minds?

Coward. Traitor. Harlot. She'd heard them all and had no doubt they were making new rounds.

She picked at the bandage. "A little only. My own clumsiness." When protest built behind his eyes, she took a small step away and returned her attention to

Buzi. "Please, go on, Moreh Buzi. What of these letters?"

Buzi cleared his throat and spoke to the shelf at his right. "They are from my eldest, Ezekiel. A record of his visions from the Lord."

"Ezekiel the prophet? He is your son?"

"He is both. The Lord's messenger and my son." Buzi beamed, and Eitan sniffed.

In the years before the siege, Ezekiel sent a written record of his visions while in exile in Babylon. His warnings of impending judgment, read outside the temple, had been received as well as Jeremiah's, which was to say with stones and rotten vegetables. She'd had no idea she addressed the prophet's father.

She looked to Jeremiah, who'd joined their small circle. Not a hint of surprise at the familial connection shifted the wrinkles on his face.

"Ezekiel is a great servant of the Lord." Eyes alight, the elder priest rubbed his knobby knuckles, seeming to have forgotten the general staring down at him. "Today's events are strikingly similar to a passage Eitan and I recall from one of Ezekiel's visions. We must confirm."

"And the prophet's letters are...*here*?" Doubt arced her pitch. "My abba told me nothing of this."

"Upon my request." Buzi's nod unseated his turban. He caught its wobble, not pausing as he rushed on. "After the last reading, wherein the people burned the scroll, I hid a copy of the visions here. These last years, Chesed has graciously safeguarded them."

A FAITH UNTAMED

"As guided by the Lord, no doubt," Eitan added, daring at last to set eyes on the general. "Since *someone* set a torch upon our home. Turned every sacred prophecy to cinders."

"Oh." Liora rested a hand on her chest, though in a city whose wealthiest homes had been targeted by fire, it defied logic to be shocked. "You are without a place?"

Before either could answer, Nebuzaradan took a firm step toward Eitan. "If they are so sacred, these prophecies, a little fire should not matter. Unless your god's words must be written on parchment to come to pass?" The question, given in a tone of irony, did not demand an answer. Though why he should mock when Nabû, the god he was named for, was a scribe who wrote down the fates of men so they might come to pass.

When Liora chose not to translate, he looked back at her. "Well? Tell him."

She struggled again to contain a smile. "If I do, your game will be spoiled."

He grunted and waved her on.

After she'd conveyed his message, Saba Jeremiah raised both arms to the heavens. "The Word of our Lord is enduring. It cannot be destroyed. Even the evil ones"—he nodded to Nebuzaradan—"know the Almighty's great power and tremble."

Nebuzaradan gave him a flat look. "Do you see me trembling, prophet?"

Unable to resist, Liora replied in Akkadian, "Are you calling yourself evil?"

"Who among the kingdoms calls the Butcher anything better?" His grin was back, double in breadth and devilry. Combined with his scar and cursed eye, his visage was one that would send most men retreating a few steps.

Liora raised a challenging eyebrow. "The woman at your side." She did not pause to parse out the emotion erasing the wicked grin. Later, she would ponder the hitch of his breath and the fear-tinged warmth widening his eyes. She nudged him in the side. "Move away from the wall. My abba does not store delicate materials with the rest, but here."

Still staring at her, Nebuzaradan edged away, unspeaking, until she began trailing her fingers over a smooth cedar panel. "In the wall?"

"Behind one of these panels. This one, I believe. If we remove this molding," she said running her fingers along the vertical seam, "the panel should be free. Will you help?"

She needn't have asked. Nebuzaradan was already there, leaning over her, crowding her with his turmeric scent, knocking on the wood, making sounds of wonder at the responding hollow echo. "Extraordinary." He pulled the knife from the sheath at her waist and held it away from her. "Stand back, dove. Soldier, hold the panel in case it slips."

Happy to leave them to it, Liora did as told.

Rimutu moved in, and within moments, the two had the molding off and the panel sliding away. A large niche opened in the stone. Rimutu carried the panel off while Nebuzaradan poked around inside the hollow.

A FAITH UNTAMED

The first document he removed was short, rolled tight, and sickeningly familiar.

Her contract of betrothal. Signed when she was little more than a child. Broken long ago. "So this is where it went," she said, unable to disguise her bitterness.

"This is Zedekiah's seal." Nebuzaradan's regard sat heavy on her face.

She would not look at that blob of red wax, or at him. "What it is, is rubbish." She snatched the scroll from him and shoved it back inside.

Five larger rolls occupied the remaining space. Ezekiel's prophecies? Likely. There lay the Word of the Lord, and Liora was fuming over a long-ago betrayal.

Forgive me. She breathed out to regain composure, then piled the five in her arms and carried them to the table, only just remembering to handle them with care.

Buzi chattered, excitement pouring off him, and Saba Jeremiah wiped a tear from his eye. Liora shared Eitan's sentiment. The man paced, seeming almost afraid to approach.

She remained at the edge of the room as the elders bent over the treasure, their voices rising in awe as they confirmed the scrolls were Ezekiel's letters. "That one, son." Buzi wagged a crooked finger, directing Eitan who seemed to have overcome whatever fears held him back. "Open midway, yes? Or farther down. The passage should begin with the glory of the Lord rising above the cherubim."

"I remember." Eitan crossed his legs on a cushion and began unrolling. "It goes, 'Then the glory of the

Lord rose from above the cherubim and departed from—'"

"Not there." Buzi cut in. "First, the Lord of Hosts moves to the threshold of the temple."

Nebuzaradan joined Liora against the wall, his presence a solid weight beside her. Tension poured off his stiff frame. He watched the priests fuss over the scroll, but his distant gaze said he was elsewhere. Was he remembering the light that severed his vision, the wind that drove him to his knees? Her own ears howled again with those impossible wings and wheels, the memory so vivid her tight muscles trembled. Whatever they'd experienced—no, *endured*—it hadn't been for others to see or hear or feel.

Why them? The question burned through her chest. Why would God reveal such mysteries to a pagan general and a woman marked by shame, while His prophet and priests remained in the dark? Was it a warning? An impending judgment? Had they displeased her Lord?

Saba Jeremiah had reassured her she'd not erred in sharing David HaMelech's method of moving the ark, but Jeremiah could not see into her heart. Had the Lord found her wanting? Detected pride? Questions and possibilities tangled inside her. The priests were not moving fast enough.

When her fingers curled in, she startled. At some point, she'd grabbed Nebuzaradan's hand. Long enough ago that his warmth had chased away the chill from her fingers. She didn't look at him—couldn't—but felt his steadiness in her bones.

A FAITH UNTAMED

The callouses on his palm scraped her finger pads as he tightened his grip. Had he abandoned his vow after all? Or was this evidence he believed Yahweh had abandoned Jerusalem? Perhaps, like her, he didn't realize they clung to one another. Why *that* might be, she did not dare to guess.

"Here!" Eitan's voice jerked Nebuzaradan's fingers within her grip. "And I read: 'Then the glory of the Lord departed from over the threshold of the temple and stopped above the cherubim.'"

He read on, his voice rising and falling in pitch, but Liora's hearing went in and out, catching only segments as her mind snagged on words and phrases.

Departed... whirling wheels... departed... glory... wings... east gate....

"Wait." Liora found herself standing at the table's edge, her heart pounding a path up her throat. "Did you say cherubim?

Eitan looked up at her, his mouth a downward curve inside his beard. "I did."

"The wings I heard, they were...*cherubim*?"

"Departing cherubim," Nebuzaradan stepped up to her left, his tone grim. "And according to this vision, they did not depart from the temple alone. Yahweh went with them. Which would account for the bright light and the power I sensed passing by."

He left the temple, Liora, he'd said not an hour before. *He destroyed his people, then abandoned them. He abandoned* you.

All that remained was for Nebuzaradan to lean in with a smug look and say, *Did I not tell you?*

When Liora translated Nebuzaradan's observation, Jeremiah replied. "You speak true, Babylonian." Seated beside Eitan, he rained tears into his whiskers. "The cherubim escorted the glory of the Lord out of the temple."

Throat knotted and aching, Liora shook her head. They'd misinterpreted the vision. Nebuzaradan was wrong. He was a pagan, after all. The Lord would not abandon them. "He has not left," she croaked still shaking her head in denial. "He *can* not. He is Creator and Almighty King. There is no place He cannot be. The world is His, the cattle, the hills, the seas!"

A dull roar sounded in her ears, and for unknown time, she heard nothing but those wings, felt nothing but encroaching despair. Somehow, Saba Jeremiah came to be at her side, an arm wrapped about her quaking shoulders. He tried to guide her toward a seat cushion, but she resisted and glanced at Nebuzaradan.

He stood now before the open door, scowling at a royal guard. The soldier did not look at him as he spoke, but at her. Nebuzaradan sidestepped to block his view.

"Yahweh has hidden Himself from us, my son." Buzi's cry turned her back to the table and the truths unfolding against the wishes of all present. "In His anger, He has concealed His glory from His children and revealed it to a pagan butcher!" The priest covered his face with his hands and wailed, rocking where he stood.

His glory. The Lord's shekhinah. Liora blinked at the priest who'd voiced the very thought trying to take a foothold in her mind. She had little context for Yahweh's glory. Stories only from the Sacred Scrolls. Moses on Sinai. The pillar of fire, another of cloud. But could anything else explain the awe that had melted her bones, the light and power that had blinded Nebuzaradan?

Her mind whirled like the wheels from the vision, even as her knees bent at Jeremiah's urging. As she began to sit, the guard pushed past Nebuzaradan into the chamber.

"Lady Liora, do not sit."

She bolted upright again. "What?"

The man came to a crisp halt before her and spared a moment to sneer at the weeping elders before focusing on her. "At the command of Prince Nergal-sharezer, son-by-marriage to our king, you are to come at once. You have been summoned to the role of interpreter and will now reside in the royal quarters."

CHAPTER 11

> *Woe be unto the pastors that destroy*
> *and scatter the sheep of my pasture!*
> *saith the Lord.* (Jer. 23:1)

The last person Liora expected to see in Prince Nergal's audience hall was Gittel. And the last garment she would have expected the woman to be wearing was the dingy white of a servant's tunic, belted with a gray cord.

This was the employment Gittel had found? After hissing and spitting at every mention of Babylonians, after sneering at Liora for having the gall to catch the interest of their highest general, the woman then bustled off to serve them? Hands folded at the waist and face a blank tablet of emotion, she stood off to the side, last in a row of waiting servants.

The peculiarity of the sight nearly stopped Liora's trek across the polished stone floor. The columned chamber was large enough, its timbered ceiling high enough, for the tap of her sandals to echo, quiet enough for heads to turn when she halted. The only head that didn't angle her way belonged to Prince Nergal who sprawled on a sea of colorful cushions center-dais.

Even Gittel raised her eyes at Liora's halt, the flash of recognition in them stark enough to reveal she was equally surprised at the encounter. The second flash, that of disdain, said *nothing* had changed. Gittel might be wearing Babylonian garb, but she had not suddenly sold out to Jerusalem's conquerors.

A FAITH UNTAMED

Why, then, was she there? Had Captain Idadu made good on his promise to banish her? Perhaps he'd taken inspiration from his general, who'd shown her abba the door and slammed it closed behind him.

Liora would certainly be finding out. Right after she inquired about the six unrighteous priests lined up against the opposite wall, armed guards stationed around them. Undoubtedly, the priests were of some use to Prince Nergal, even if only for a chuckle as their heads rolled down the thick wool runner leading Liora to the dais.

The chamber's wide-open space yawned about her, returning memories she'd rather not claim. Shoulders chilled, she walked on alone, abandoned at the hall's rear doors by the royal guard who'd escorted her from the gate and through the compound. A guide she hadn't needed. This was not her first visit.

The walled residence had been Zedekiah's before King Nebuchadnezzar took Jeconiah, his uncle-king, captive and installed Zedekiah as a puppet on the throne. A child in those days, she'd stared in wonder at the rich fabrics draping the windows, the tapestries covering the walls, the gold trimming the sconces. Unable to fully comprehend that the press of Zedekiah's ring on wax had sealed her future, set her life on a devastating course.

A woman grown, she was determined to walk with her eyes fully open this time. She focused them on the royal lounging on the low dais, colorful pillows supporting his sprawl.

At Prince Nergal's elbow stood a teetering stack of clay tablets. He held one close and rubbed his smooth chin while reading. A single vertical groove sat precisely between his trimmed-thin eyebrows, and his mouth tipped at the perfect contemplative angle. An act? The visual did not fit with Nebuzaradan's "indolent royal" description or that of a man unconcerned with management or politics.

Or was he after those answers King Nebuchadnezzar sent him to collect?

Liora had plenty of time to ponder this as she stopped five strides distant and bent at the waist, knees slightly flexed. She held the position for a three-count, appropriate obeisance for a prince, then straightened and waited.

Time ticked away as Prince Nergal perused his tablet, very scholarly, and Liora grieved Nebuzaradan's absence. He'd been stopped outside the gates to the compound and had no issue showing his displeasure over it. "What is this?" he'd demanded as he moved his imposing form into the guard's space. Close enough to count the freckles dotting the man's nose. "Am I not permitted entry?"

Spear upright and held two-handed, the guard shuffled nearer his companion, tightening the line of men who blocked the closed wooden gate. "His Highness Prince Nergal instructed me to tell you to return to your rest. He requires you here at sunset for the evening meal and advises you not to be late."

"I am never late!" Nebuzaradan shouted into the man's face.

A FAITH UNTAMED

The guard's shoulders bounced, and Liora pitied him, wondered if he found the general's choice of argument as irrational as she.

But then, they'd just traversed a city rife with tension for the third time that day. Liora's skin still burned from the glares coming at her from all directions. Her heart still smarted from the curses. Though uttered quietly and with trepidation, they bruised like hurled stones. Hebrew, all of them. None meant for the general who kept her so close his shadow blocked the sun from her eyes. If only he were as efficient a deterrent for the spite.

It had taken every bit of Liora's cunning to talk Nebuzaradan into restraining his sword. He'd complied with her wishes but not without dislike curling his lips. And now, patience spent, he would give the soldier the brunt of it.

"Lady Liora is under my care," he snapped. "And I have no desire to waste the day res—"

From behind, she laid fingers on his elbow where it strained from clutching the head of his ax.

Heat radiated off his skin and off the scowl he swiveled back at her. "What?"

"You are exhausted, Arioch."

"And you are ill." He jabbed a finger at the damp kerchief she clutched.

The cloth tied about the lower half of her face did little to filter the ash. She cleared a croak from her throat. "I am well enough to stand before the prince." Although, if he required extensive translating, her voice might not hold out. "You did not sleep last night, husband, and you have had an extraordinary morning. His Highness is wise to send you to rest. I second the order," she said, even though she would much rather enter the jackal's lair with the general's shadow blocking any heat coming her way.

Not relinquishing his scowl, he turned back to the gate and cut every guard with a glare teeming with menace. Liora might have snickered at his overprotective behavior if his skills at flushing out and defeating the enemy hadn't won him kingdoms. The man had not earned his name by ignoring threats. She eased forward, not releasing her touch, but would trust where his instincts led.

At last, the tendons beneath her fingers relaxed as his frame sank into a conceding posture. He looked back at Idadu, who stood at Liora's side, and smirked. "Who is the Butcher to question his fearsome wife? I entrust her to your care, Captain."

"None—" The guard's voice broke, its volume shrinking as Nebuzaradan's gaze jerked to him. "None may enter but the lady."

Liora alone? And unarmed. Nebuzaradan had already removed her weapon, reluctance in every move. Neither had any choice in the matter. One did not appear before any royal bearing arms. Unless that *one* was the kingdom's exalted general.

Trepidation wobbled Liora's heart. No Nebuzaradan. No Idadu. Why? Did the prince want no witnesses outside of his loyal guards? Or was this a power move against his rival that had nothing to do with her?

A FAITH UNTAMED

The exchange devolved again, with Nebuzaradan snarling, the guard flinching, and Liora murmuring reassurances. "I am ever in Yahweh's hands, Arioch. Go in peace. No harm will come to me." She parted from him then, slipping between the guards and through the gate they cracked open.

It closed behind her with a bang that startled a bounce out of her. She shook it off and removed her mask. This was no corpse-strewn valley with a committee of piked heads and a butcher-general at its end. This was a courtyard decked in fountains and potted flowers with a lazy prince through the doors at its end, gold glinting in his eyes.

The wait for him to finish feigning study—a test, a show of power, both?—became interminable. But Liora had likely pushed this prince further and harder and more boldly than any woman before her. For fear of her God, he'd allowed it or been too distracted and distraught to address it. Now that he'd distanced himself from Yahweh's fearsome temple, he'd regained composure and seemed determined to reestablish control. And perhaps punish her along the way.

Well, Liora hadn't made it through the Butcher's tent without a lesson or two tucked beneath her sash. She could wait the prince out, even if her knees threatened to unhinge while doing it. *Elohim*, she prayed, falling into the Miktam David composed when the Philistines seized him at Gath. *What time I am afraid, I will trust in Thee. In Elohim I will praise His Word. In Elohim I have put my trust; I will not fear what man can do to me.*

She'd meant what she said to Nebuzaradan outside the gate. Yahweh held her in His tender care. And yet her heart raced like a dove's when snatched from the cote. How many times had she felt a bird's little heart tapping frantically through downy feathers and grieved its impending death? *I will not fear, I will not fear. Guide me in my fear, oh Lord. May it not overcome my faith in you.*

At last, the prince set aside the tablet, announced by the clatter when it landed on the messy stack at his elbow. "Lady Liora," he drawled. "The renowned beauty of Jerusalem."

She did not look up, barely kept from wincing at the old epithet, now more a mockery among the people than a compliment. Although, the prince's use of it seemed pure curiosity, his pitch rising with genuine interest. "Or should I say, *infamous* beauty?"

He'd heard then. Or read? Was that what he'd been doing? Reviewing the royal decrees? There'd been the one in which Zedekiah dissolved their betrothal under accusations of indecency. Another in which he'd publicly absolved her of death by stoning. But no, those would be written in Hebrew. Unless, like Nebuzaradan, the prince requested her translation services under the pretense of ignorance, he did not understand her native tongue.

"But where has the beautiful lady's boldness gone?" he asked. "Do not be coy."

Coy? Liora was anything but. Lifting her lashes, she looked him straight in the eyes and flexed her knees in a second bow. "Your Highness," she said, grateful for the strength in her voice. "I trust you are well recovered after your frightful morning at the Almighty's house of worship."

His eyes widened an instant before he laughed, the bellow accompanied by the tinkle of his dangling earrings. "There it is, that carefully groomed defiance. What a bizarre pleasure you are, Lady Liora. Part of the draw, I suppose. The captivation."

Liora gazed at him, mind a blank refusal. This prince was *not* interested in her—not in that way. He toyed with her, yes, but he'd shown no sign of attraction beyond that of amusement.

Still chuckling, he tipped his head back and spoke in an aside to the manservant stationed at his shoulder. "The woman has the audacity to appear confused."

Face impassive, the servant stared at his folded hands.

"Let me enlighten you then, Lady Liora," the prince began in the engaging tone of a storyteller. "Never, in all the Butcher's years of service, has he shown the least care for any woman save his mother. Not even his wife. But *you* come along, and suddenly he is on his knees before the throne, spurning the king's own sister and refusing every war trophy but you." He shoved the stack of tablets and, wearing a little smile, watched them tumble. "What a god-cursed *fool* he is."

Anger shot like lightning down Liora's center. That *fool* had willingly walked toward his death just that morning, an admittedly foolish act in Liora's estimation. But shouldn't it have earned him more respect than the derision pouring from Nergal's throat? Nebuzaradan would walk through a fiery furnace for this pampered prince, and what did he get in return? Conniving and envy. Did any royal exist in any kingdom who was not a spoiled child demanding his own way?

Clenching her teeth, Liora made a careful study of the crouching manservant and the tablets he collected from the floor. She would have shut her ears to the prince if it were possible. This slander could not be why he'd called her there.

Prince Nergal snapped his fingers at the servant who hastily produced a white cloth. "The general has the authority to take any captive he wishes." The prince daintily wiped his fingers, as if to rid himself of the degradation of work, then swept his arm wide. "Any woman. Save the royals, naturally. And yet!" He tossed the cloth back to the servant. "He goes to the king to *formally request* the one he most wants." He burst out with an incredulous laugh. "The Butcher may as well have stood you on the archery range, painted a circle on your forehead for good measure. Why would he do such a fool thing?"

He paused there, true confusion warbling his pitch. Leaned forward, waiting, the man expected an answer.

Liora had none. She wasn't even sure she could believe the story he'd woven.

Nebuzaradan kneeling? Difficult to picture. Kneeling before the man he'd called "exalted ruler who is the beloved of the god Nabû"? Yes, and yes again. At every opportunity, she imagined. But to do so for her? *That* she could not imagine.

A FAITH UNTAMED

As for spurning the king's sister, she could not believe he would refuse anything his *exalted ruler* offered. Unless... Was his unfaithful wife related to the king? Aralu, the prince called the woman. In Liora's research, she'd not come across Aralu's ancestry, but if she was indeed the king's sister, Liora supposed the request for a divorce, which he'd admitted to, was as good as *spurning*.

Then there was the claim that Nebuzaradan refused trophies for conquering Jerusalem. Hadn't he boasted he'd recently come into substantial wealth? Of course, by *recently* he might have meant the plundering of Lachish. The Babylonian king would have surely lavished treasures upon his general for such a feat.

In short, unless she heard it from Nebuzaradan's lips, Liora would hesitate to believe a word of the prince's speech. But she did agree on one count. It was outlandish for the Butcher to request, to *kneel*, for something he had every right to possess. Which was why he'd stamped his House symbol on her palm—or tried—then forged a contract her father had no choice but to sign.

Prince Nergal's lips puckered, as though he saw her inner turmoil and savored its bitter taste. A carefully laid trap coming to fruition. While he sat there "reading," he'd been spinning a tale designed to provoke her. Why, she could only guess. To unbalance her? To tease out a stammered revelation about his rival, the general? Something he might later wield as a weapon?

It could also be nothing more than a game to him, a way to pass the time. Well, if he wanted to dance with words and make believe, she would lead their steps.

On a sideways glance, she took in his posture, his trimmed and buffed nails, his oiled hair curling just so around his ears and under his jeweled turban. The man was in love with himself and fascinated with the idea of his reliable butcher-general having lost his mind to a woman. A romantic, then. The sort who might happily be swept away by a tale of conquest in love.

"I might have an answer to that," she said, then put a harmless twinkle in her voice when she redirected his own words back at him. "Let me enlighten you." His grin and slight bow told her she'd chosen her approach well. On a prayer of gratitude, she went on in that vein. "Perhaps a man goes to such lengths, putting in a formal request with the king, as you say, because he knows if he *took* the woman, he would lose her."

The prince tipped his head toward one shoulder, the red gem on his turban sliding with the motion. "How so?"

Head jutting back, she feigned shock. "I would have thought a prince of Babylon, especially one wed to the king's daughter, would be well-versed in the art of winning a woman's heart."

The prince gazed at her rapt with interest, but as before, in the temple courtyard, he did not reply to the challenge to his royal impeccability. And, as before, Liora took it as permission to proceed. "The walls of a woman's heart cannot be conquered, Your Highness. They cannot be battered down with siege engines. They must be scaled, one hard-earned grip at a time. This one led by trust," she said, miming a climbing motion. "The next by respect. Yet others by sacrifice and vows of protection and provision. And then—"

Prince Nergal lurched to his feet and grinned like a boy with his finger in the honey jar. "And *then*, he leaps to the other side and claims the treasure within."

Her brows arched. Naturally, a prince of Babylon would make that assumption, take the short route, that of entitled brutes. "And then," she replied, elongating the word, a reproving nursemaid setting the jar of treats out of reach, "if the man is diligent and true, and if Yahweh so leads, she will open the gates of her heart and entrust him with the key to the treasury. To *guard* it. To prevent theft and all harm."

Blue robes billowing, the prince took the two broad stairs off the dais in long-legged strides. "What an absolutely ridiculous notion." He stopped next to a sober-faced guard stationed at the platform's left corner. "Have you ever scaled a woman's *walls*?"

Eyes straight ahead, the guard had time only to blink before Nergal charged on.

"Neither have I. At least not the sort she speaks of." With a salacious laugh, he spun back toward her. "So tell us, Lady Liora. Where is the Butcher on your heart's wall?"

A little cough scraped her throat. "Pardon?"

"Feigned ignorance does not become you, *dove*." He clicked his tongue. "Terrible name for you, that. You are no gentle bird but a lioness. Almost a match for my Ashara," he said with a snicker, amused at the comparison, whoever Ashara was.

He fluffed his robe, its sapphire sheen catching the muted sunlight from the chamber's latticed windows. "But never mind that. Come, tell us. How goes our dear Butcher's climb? Does he cling by his fingernails while the *beauty of Jerusalem* glares haughtily down at him? Or has he reached the top and now hangs with a leg over the edge while awaiting the king's leave to plunder?"

Which insult to address first? The accusation she pretended stupidity? The idea that Nebuzaradan would lower his mighty self to *climb* for any woman?

Neither. The last, the insinuation their marriage had yet to receive the king's approval, was too grievous an affront to let pass—an affront and a lie. Hadn't the prince said, only moments before, that Nebuzaradan was authorized to have any woman he wished, free and clear?

She straightened her spine and faced him fully. "On that last matter I *must* defend myself, Your Highness. With such blithe comments, you make me into...into a class of woman I cannot even contemplate without blushing." As evidence, her heating cheeks.

The prince made a study of something over her shoulder. He rubbed his jaw, that vertical groove etched perfectly again between his eyebrows. "What motivates the man, I wonder?" he said, as if he'd heard not a word of her defense. "Perhaps you dangle the treasury key like a scrap of meat before a hungry dog?" Fingers pinching the air, he waggled his hand.

A FAITH UNTAMED

A bolt of anger heated her chest. She strove to weed it from her tone but feared she failed. "General Nebuzaradan is no dog, Prince Nergal. And I speak in generalities. In the longings of women, in the things we dream but rarely voice." She'd been telling a *story*, not confessing her feelings. Though as far as most women were concerned, the image she'd drawn of the surest way to their hearts was true enough.

How had the conversation turned so swiftly? She'd been leading the tale, spinning it expertly, the prince enthralled and distracted from his anger. And now, they spoke of...what? Nebuzaradan panting after her like a dog. Liora wielding power, holding him at bay. Teasing him.

"In other words,"—grinning, Nergal angled back toward the silent guard—"the Butcher is already inside, guarding her jewels. Whatever will my father say?"

Liora's head began shaking before he'd even finished speaking. "That is not... I did not say that. General Nebuzaradan is the man burning my city. Killing my people. There is no *winning of hearts* where he is concerned. Such imagery does not even apply to us."

The prince vested her with a flat, almost pitying look. "Then why use it?"

"I... Well, it..." Faltering, Liora wiped the kerchief under her nose. The question was valid. Why *had* she gone from the prince's taunt of Nebuzaradan kneeling before the king on her behalf to the story of a man winning a woman's heart? Why had she jumped to his defense with such a tale? Why did she continue to jump to his defense at all? The general was more than capable of defending himself.

She squeezed her eyes shut. None of that mattered. It couldn't. Not while Jerusalem burned and her people starved, hovered on the brink of deportation. Not while the ark hung in the balance, absent the Lord's Shekinah. My, but she was selfish.

"Great Marduk, she is flustered." Muttering again to the guard, Prince Nergal crossed his arms and stared at her, settling in like a spider at the edge of its web. "Does the woman not realize she has already given him her keys?"

Had she? Could the prince, even in mockery, have struck on the truth of the matter?

Preposterous. A forceful swallow washed down the bitter taste at the back of her tongue. Liora was reasonably certain she was familiar with the look of a woman's surrendered heart. When it came to her heart before the Lord, surrender had the appearance of sacrifice, obedience, defense against all contempt. When it came to men?

General Nebuzaradan is no dog.

Her own words came flying back at her, each a blow to her denial.

Even a blind lion, having teeth and claws, is a formidable enemy.

And again, *The general is the right man for this task, Your Highness. The only man.*

Exactly how many times in the last days had she stood up for the man, risked her safety to spare his honor and position? Sacrificed her own scant reputation to stand beside him in obedience?

Her lips parted to answer the prince, to reject the notion, but no words came out. Another question blocked their exit. If the general was no dog, then what *was* he?

What is he to me?

A set of shackles. A foreboding future. A godless man who scoffed at the Lord's might. And yet he'd shielded her from violence. Fed her, sheltered her.

No. No, no, no. She denied, refused.

And still, deep in the hidden places of her soul, a truth whispered, *He is more than he should be...*

Her tongue clung to the roof of her dry mouth, every rebuttal too weak to move it.

Stay your snake tongue, harlot of Babylon. Its hiss reeks of rot. The words of the slain priest lived again to slither cold and true down her spine. Had she survived a stoning over an Edomite only to make the false accusations come true with a Babylonian?

A quake began inside her, small, invisible, utterly terrifying.

Or could the prince see? Another moment passed of his blatant staring, wherein the guard shifted on his feet, Liora trembled, and Nergal rumpled his brow in crafted thought. A smile climbed one side of his mouth. "*There.* Now, she understands her own conquered heart. How very tragic a revelation. All the more because—" He halted, mouth open, before waving away the thought. "Ah, but we shall save that for later.

I've not summoned Lady Liora to discuss a woman's *walls* and *treasures*."

But hadn't he? He'd dug and goaded until he'd found evidence, shallow as it was, to prove...what? That she'd fallen in love with Nebuzaradan? Wasn't that what he alluded to? She almost laughed out loud, released the derisive sound. As if any woman could love the man who'd destroyed her life, stamped himself onto her flesh, manipulated her loved ones, *banished* them.

Sacrifice. Obedience. Defense. Before Yahweh, these were acts of love. Under the threat of an ax, they were survival. She clutched her bandaged hand—one side marred with ink, the other with blood—and relished the wound's burn. Never mind Nebuzaradan had sworn he would never harm her, he had. Many times over, and he would continue to do so as long as it benefited him.

With every crash of the axe against Jerusalem's gates, he'd struck her. With every possessive look, word, drop of ink, he violated her, denied her the right to consent. With every theft of the temple vessels, he'd done more than defile the sanctuary; he'd stripped away another piece of her soul, left her as bereft as the ark. To him, she was little better than the gem glinting in garish display on Nergal's turban, sliding with every tip of his head.

No, Liora did not love Nebuzaradan. Could not.

But would anyone believe her? If Jerusalem got a whiff of the prince's accusation, what bitter oaths might the people add to their medley of hate? It was

A FAITH UNTAMED

one thing to be married against her will. Another completely to embrace the role, to hold affection and loyalty for the man.

If it ever circulated she loved the Butcher of Babylon, she would lose any chance she might have at redeeming herself in their eyes. Then she would be without recourse to help them. They would reject any offer of aid coming from a traitor. She could not allow it.

Prince Nergal swept back across the floor, snapping his fingers in rapid succession toward the priests along the wall. "Bring him." The priests' assigned guards burst into motion, prodding the men about, searching.

Liora had become so absorbed in her exchange with the prince, she'd forgotten the priests stood behind her. Gittel, too, was there. Silent, but her downcast gaze was every bit as sharp as the curses and insults that pelted Liora on the walk over. The prince's interest alone was enough to stoke the woman's ire. But their wordplay? One needn't understand Akkadian to catch the ease in their tone. That alone was enough to feed suspicion that she'd sold herself to the enemy.

Of course, if Gittel had caught the banter, she had surely caught the prince's sly attack. A true skulking jackal, he was. Worse, she wouldn't have missed the quiver in Liora's voice, the uncertainty, the loss of footing. Gittel would be reveling in Liora's humiliation.

And if the prince's accusation held even the smallest grain of truth...

Perhaps, Liora deserved disdain. A full shudder rocked her. She made no effort to hide it as the chief priest approached. Why bother? The man had already stamped her with a harlot's brand.

Belled robe jangling, Chief Priest Seraiah approached her with his back straight and his arrogance on full display: nose tipped high, lashes lowered as he gazed at her as he might a mud-crusted pig. Did he not notice the blood staining the hem of his once-pristine white robes, or was this self-assurance another piece of his pious act?

She would issue a second warning to repent if she felt it would serve any purpose. Her first had been a pointless use of breath. Pelatiah's blood crept up Seraiah's hem, but it may as well have been Zechariah's leeched off the ancient temple stones, his murder at last avenged. Seraiah would be next; although, from the tilt of his nose, he believed himself spared of Yahweh's wrath.

"I see you two have met." The prince sidled up to her and wagged a finger at Seraiah. "This one is the high priest, yes?"

"He was, Your Highness, yes." The elder might still wear the ephod, but per Ezekiel's prophecy, the Lord had already marked him for death.

Prince Nergal rocked on his heels, nodding. "Your recommendations for moving the ark from the temple were well received, Lady Liora."

The ark. Shame nipped at her. She'd been so focused on fending off the prince's jabs, so intent on self-preservation, she'd lost sight of what mattered most—the ark and its safekeeping.

"Tomorrow, at first light, these priests will remove the ark from its place and carry it down the mount. My carpenters construct a new wagon as we speak. Inform this priest he has the night to purify himself for this task."

Liora bowed her head. "I will, but first, might you permit me an observation, Your Highness?" At the impatient wave of his hand, she continued. "According to the prophecy that foretold today's events, these men are marked, condemned for disloyalty to Yahweh, whose sacred vessel you wish moved."

Nergal frowned at Seraiah. "Unfaithful in his role, is he? What proof have you?"

"Yahweh strictly prohibits the use of amulets. If you withdraw that leather thong from the priest's robes, I suspect we will find evidence of his infidelity."

The prince flicked a gesture at a guard, who bore down on Seraiah.

Eyes large, the old priest backed away. He flailed and cried out as the guard wrestled the thong out from under his clothes and tore it from his neck with a fierce yank. The force of it threw Seraiah to the floor. He landed in a heap of tinkling vestments, the crimson stain prominent across his calves.

Tears pricking, Liora looked away, could not even glance at Prince Nergal as he identified the amulet as a tiny clay tablet inscribed with a prayer to Marduk.

"And this disqualifies the priest from service?"

"It does, Your Highness," she said over Seraiah's vicious oaths. "These men are not fit to touch Yahweh's throne on Earth." His presence might no longer dwell there, but it remained His throne.

Compelled to his knees, Seraiah summoned not a shred of repentance but glowered at her from beneath his lashes.

She swallowed hard, but it did nothing to clear the rasp from her voice. "The priests who transport the ark must be in right standing with Yahweh, and they will require a full day for proper purification. If you allow me freedom to move about the city, I will select them." She had four in mind already, the only four who might be remotely qualified.

Nergal grunted and grumbled, likely peeved at the delay, until at last, he said, "I will allow it."

Liora bowed her head. "My thanks." Whether the Lord would actually allow them to move the ark, Liora could not say, but she felt a boost of elation at this small return of influence. Saba Jeremiah, perhaps even Moreh Buzi, would know how to proceed from this victory.

"Tomorrow," the prince said, "the priests you select will perform their rituals. On the morning following, either the ark will be removed or heads will." Grinning, he showed her his sharpest teeth. "Starting, *dove*, with yours."

CHAPTER 12

> *If thou hast run with the footmen, and they have wearied thee, then how canst thou contend with horses? and if in the land of peace, wherein thou trustedst, they wearied thee, then how wilt thou do in the swelling of Jordan?* (Jer. 12:5)

Liora stifled a groan of annoyance as she exited the audience hall behind her assigned chambermaid. The woman's gait, just shy of a sashay, told Liora everything she needed to know about their impending interactions. Although what Gittel had to be smug about, Liora hadn't a clue.

Of all the servants Prince Nergal could have chosen! Was he aware of their connection? The man was both informed and perceptive. Perhaps he could feel the hate radiating off Gittel like heat from a baking stone and leaped at the hope of a clash. The prince had made no secret of his mission to antagonize Liora, amusement his singular goal, and shoving Gittel into her affairs was sure to provide just that.

The assignment could also be Yahweh's doing. To test Liora's mercy and grace? To reach Gittel's hard, baking-stone heart? The latter was almost humorous in its seeming impossibility. If any scrap of a heart remained in the woman's chest, she had laid it entirely on the altar of spite and revenge. As far as Liora had seen, anyway.

Yahweh, of course, looked deeper, saw farther, hoped longer. What did He detect that Liora could not?

Fit me with your eyes, Lord God, for my own fail me, she prayed as she turned a corner behind Gittel.

"This wing houses King Zedekiah's queen and consorts." Gittel spoke in the curt tones of an escort, no hint of the submissive servant about her.

Her abrupt manner almost distracted from her startling revelation. When the guard said Liora would be residing in the royal quarters, he hadn't meant Prince Nergal's but her own queen's. Her sandal caught on the lip of a stone, and she lurched before steadying herself. Call her a dumb rock, but she'd rather face Nergal's sly smirk again than her own leering past.

"Down there, Queen Hodaya and the princesses." Gittel jabbed a thumb at the guard standing before an arched entry to a narrow corridor, then swept on past.

Liora breathed hard at her heels.

"And here,"—another poke of Gittel's finger, this time at a door on the left—"the first and second consorts with their daughters."

More stern-faced guards. Another swift bypass.

Hand to her chest, Liora hurried along after her. "This cannot be where Prince Nergal wishes me to sleep."

"Bit of a step down for you?" Gittel replied, tone dry.

For Liora, no. This hall was grand beyond her own considerable wealth. But the women behind the doors

A FAITH UNTAMED

had to be chafing in the confines of Zedekiah's former residence.

The harem once lived in the sprawling palace built by King David, the one whose exquisite cedar beams and panels now swirled in gray, ashy cyclones across the city. This place, a secondary residence, had been preserved, perhaps for this very purpose: to temporarily house the captive queen and consorts and any Babylonian princes who chose lodging in Jerusalem over the encampment.

General Nebuzaradan's destruction of their city was nothing, if not methodical. And he would *not* appreciate her being lumped into the midst of Zedekiah's women. One of the reasons she could not be there.

Liora looked back the way they'd come and considered the wisdom in returning to request alternate arrangements.

The guard at the end of the sconce-lined hall shook his head, the indigo plume atop his conical helmet swaying with the slow movement.

Sighing, she abandoned the idea and skipped a step to catch up to Gittel. "But I have my own bed not far from here." Her own comforts, her own people. Those who loved her.

Unlike Gittel, whose mouth pinched in smug satisfaction, as though she relished Liora's displacement and the uncertainty warbling her pitch.

"At the evening meal, I will request a return to my own place, for I cannot fathom why I must be here in this—"

Gittel stopped and twisted back so fast, Liora almost slammed into her. "Truly, Liora?" She sneered, her disregard of Liora's title a pointed indication of how their relationship would proceed. "You *cannot fathom*?"

Well, she *could* but would rather not. "Because...he wants his translator near at all times."

Gittel loosed a ringing cackle that turned more than one guard's head. "Considering you are the purest daughter of Zion, this dishonesty is truly refreshing." She dabbed at the corner of her eye, feigning the wipe of a laugh-tear. "But I suppose an argument could be made for the prince not wanting to risk your life in the streets while you go to and fro, *translating*. Who in the city is not aware that every time you leave your home, you risk an impromptu stoning?"

Liora flinched, her gaze flitting off the smile thinning Gittel's lips. The wound stung exactly as she'd intended, but the greater likelihood was that Prince Nergal was aware of the rebel attack that nearly took Liora's life. "That may well be," she said, voice shamefully weak. "But there must be other accommodations better suited to me." Did he do it just to unsettle her? She feared not. "Why this wing?"

And *why* did Liora care? Cared so much, she had actually asked for Gittel's opinion—*Gittel's*—knowing full well she would receive nothing but vitriol for an answer. But maybe, just maybe, the woman could supply a logical reason, one that had nothing to do with the dread curdling Liora's insides—or with the conclusion she refused to acknowledge.

A FAITH UNTAMED

There was one compelling reason Nergal would house her with the king's women. But that would mean he'd been digging into her history, and he couldn't be *that* determined to destroy Nebuzaradan. Could he? It would mean Nergal believed Nebuzaradan cared enough about Liora's welfare that wounding her, wounded him. Which would mean Liora was more than a pawn in their private battle. She was the battlefield itself.

Sweat broke out as memories flashed of the pitted ground she'd traversed beyond the wall. Of arrows and broken axes littering the field. Of carrion birds perched on rocks, too sated to take flight. Of stinking, bloated corpses and heads on pikes. The ground wavered beneath her feet, the pitch of that path and the sharpness of its stones fresh in her knees and soles.

"You will recall"—Gittel's voice wrenched Liora back to the present, her head light—"that at first I could not decide if you are the most fortunate of women or the most cruelly cursed." She shrugged and walked on. "I no longer wonder." The satisfaction in the smirk bunching her cheek left no doubt which option she'd landed on.

Crushed, Saba Jeremiah had prophesied. The virgin daughter of Jerusalem, crushed.

The temple or Liora? Gittel had her opinion, and Liora was beginning to form her own.

But which was truth? The Holy Temple was stripped to stone, Liora of home and dignity. Soon, the stone would be rubble, the rubble blackened with fire.

But hadn't Liora passed through the fire? The film in her throat still tasted of it.

No denying the prophet could have meant them both—the temple *and* Liora.

But whereas the Lord had left the ark, His earthly throne, He had *not* left Liora. Even in that desolate hall, with memories hounding and fear creeping about the corners of her mind, she understood He weaved a plan the breadths of which she could not comprehend.

She swallowed the lingering taste of ash. "And as I said, there is no luck. Only Yahweh's hand moving in the lives of men and women. Whatever my circumstances," she said, strength barreling back into her voice, "I intend to serve our Lord. Whether by using my connections to provide the people with food and shelter or by saving the ark from destruction, I am willing to lay down my life for Him."

Gittel's stride hitched, her head whipping toward Liora. "*Die* for the ark? Appears to me you'd as soon hand it over to the enemy."

So Gittel understood Akkadian after all. Liora had wondered more than once. This enemy comment confirmed it. Gittel had followed every word Liora exchanged with the prince. Later, she would have to parse out what complications might arise from it. At present, she wished only to sink into whatever quiet she might find in her assigned chamber. She and Yahweh had much speaking to do on all this—her role in the ark's fate, how to go about secreting it away, whether He even wished that of her. The only clear direction she had so far was which priests to recruit.

A FAITH UNTAMED

Liora gestured absently. "A delay tactic." That she, perhaps, should not be allowing into this woman's eager ears.

But...no. Gittel's hatred for Liora was rooted in her fierce loyalty to their people, not just because she'd become a wife to the Butcher of Babylon. Gittel believed Liora had succumbed too easily, hadn't fought hard enough. Liora suspected any resistance she showed would be met with approval.

The impressed arch of Gittel's brow confirmed that assumption. "Delay for what?"

"I..." Liora shook her head. "I trust the Lord will reveal it in His time. He has not led me astray yet."

Unless one considered putting her in the company of the queen and consorts *astray*. Even at this loose association with her former betrothed, the foolish "puppet king" who'd ruined her, Nebuzaradan would be furious. Which would probably make Nergal absolutely giddy.

"Good plan," Gittel muttered, and Liora honestly could not tell whether she meant it in jest. "Third and fourth consorts that way." Gittel didn't bother pointing at the last silent hall before stopping before a closed door and rapping against the etched wood. "Gittel again, Mehetabel! May I enter?" She didn't wait for a reply before releasing the latch and pushing inside.

Mehetabel, an Edomite name belonging to the king's fifth consort.

Liora's throat cinched as she minced forward into the eerily quiet room, her eyes darting for the woman who'd replaced her.

She spotted the consort slumped against the post of an open balcony door. The narrow balcony clung to the building, its low, wooden railing poor protection from the drop. Beyond, the valley's opposite hillside stretched far. Flowering shrubs vied for space between boulders, the colors vibrant, but Mehetabel's blank gaze angled high at the unnatural, black cloud of smoke crowding the blue from the sky.

She stood statue-still, not even a twitch of the eyelashes at Gittel's noisy entry. Her only movement, the wind-blown strands of hair that had come free of her disheveled, golden braid. They danced with the mild breeze that ushered in the dim clangor of the Babylonian encampment.

In the distance, row upon row of tiny army tents lined the landscape. Directly below the balcony, nothing but space. Liora hadn't realized the home merged with the city wall or that it perched so high up the hill. So high, so precipitous, in fact, it might be the safest place in Jerusalem—as far as storming enemies went. No general, not even the brazen Butcher of Babylon, would be insane enough to point his army at this steep incline.

"Mehetabel." Gittel stopped halfway in and spoke loudly, as if the woman were hard of hearing. "I brought you a companion. Mehetabel!" When the consort did not turn, Gittel tossed her arms in an angry gesture. "Useless Edomite."

Useless? Or broken? A rip in her dark brown tunic exposed skin at her shoulder, and stiff red patches stained the fabric around her thighs. Her bedraggled

A FAITH UNTAMED

hair covered a portion of her face but could not hide the gash running down her cheek. The work of a defiling blade, and of a man's theft.

Pity seeped through Liora's heart. She glanced about again, this time reading the room differently.

Of immediate interest—and repulsion—was a mural of the goddess Ishtar. The supposed Queen of Heaven was depicted radiant, arms outstretched and holding stars. Cracked and crumbling, as if from a blow, Ishtar gazed benevolently at Liora, the promise of fertility in the rose she held.

Liora jerked her eyes away. Her attention landed on the opposite wall where faint outlines of dust were all that remained of the decorations. A small table lay on its side, one of its three legs splintered and crooked. Beneath it were scattered shards of a clay jug. In the room's center, a wooden chest sat open and empty. Several richly colorful tunics draped its edges as if they'd died trying to crawl out.

Other items strewn about: a sandal with a broken strap, a cushion with a slash across an embroidered purple iris, a gilded cup entirely out of place in the ravished chamber, and an overturned pot of turmeric staining the floor orange and scenting the room with a mild zest. On the floor beside the sleeping mat, a single oil lamp sat cold and dark, almost useless against the smoke-dimmed space.

Liora shuddered to think what evil had transpired in this place.

Gittel, however, persisted in shouting Mehetabel to attention.

"Leave her be." Liora nudged Gittel in the arm. "She has suffered much. Does she even speak Hebrew?"

"I care not either way." Gittel spun without being dismissed and made for the exit. "She is your problem now."

Liora gazed again at Mehetabel. The woman rocked now, fingers digging into her ruined hair. A truly pitiful sight.

Had Nergal placed Liora in this chamber to see what might be done for the woman? Or was it to tease Liora with her own fate? Both had been violated—Mehetabel in reality, Liora in rumor—making them "useless" in the eyes of men. Why should Liora not end up in this state of abuse? Without a shred of doubt, she knew Nebuzaradan would fight for her against any man. So long as that man was not of the royal house...

Her breath picked up speed, the jeers of a hateful crowd echoing through her mind. But *no*. She would not succumb to fear.

Hearing hinges squeak, Liora spun and called Gittel's name, stopping the woman before she drew the door closed behind her.

Gittel stared at her, expectant, impatient. "What do you want?"

What was it Liora needed? She blinked away the mockery and twisted her fingers into the fabric at her waist. "Might you bring me another tunic for the evening meal?" The one she wore was beginning to stink of anxiety.

A FAITH UNTAMED

Gittel snorted. "Do I look like Devorah? If you want fresh clothing, wear one of those." She nodded toward the chest. "Mehetabel did not appreciate them, but maybe you will?" She released another cackle.

"Very well." Frowning at the chest, Liora could not grasp the woman's humor. "Before you go, I must know. Did the general banish you from my home?" In fairness, Idadu had also voiced concern over the woman's bitter, sidelong stares. Either man could be responsible. Neither would be safe from a scolding. Liora knew what it was to be unwanted. "He can be...protective." To state the fact mildly. "But I will speak with—"

Something she said slashed a scowl across Gittel's mouth and snapped Liora's mouth shut.

"Believe it or not, Liora," Gittel fumed through her teeth, "things are not always about *you*." She slammed the door.

Liora's shoulders bounced.

Mehetabel turned her head and stared at Liora through dead eyes. An uncleaned gash bisected one cheek but could not detract from her beauty. It was easy to imagine why King Zedekiah chose her.

"Shalom, Mehetabel." The greeting savored of ash, but she constructed a smile anyway. "I am Liora."

The consort's gaze dragged to the chest. Her lashes batted slowly once before she looked back toward the billowing smoke, an admittedly hypnotic view.

Sighing, Liora trudged to the chest and picked up the first garment her fingers brushed. Of lighter weight than she'd expected, the deep purple fabric brushed silky against her skin. She manipulated the garment and lifted it upright before her. Light shone through the thin fabric, and gold embroidery adorned a low-cut neckline. A slash rose from the ankle up to the thigh, creating an opening that stumped Liora's mind.

Head cocked, she stared at the slit. "Is this an undergarm—"

Her breath snagged. This was no undergarment.

This was a harlot's raiment. The braided red sash that coiled snake-like at the bottom of the chest sealed it.

Fingers springing open, she leapt back. The beautiful fabric floated into a pile, and Mehetabel released a strangled sound, that of a bird crushed in the hand.

Crushed, crushed.

The prophet's words struck Liora again, and she understood she'd not been placed there to witness devastation but to brace for it.

CHAPTER 13

*Thus saith the Lord, Let not the wise
man glory in his wisdom... But let him
that glorieth glory in this, that he
understandeth and knoweth me, that I
am the Lord which exercise
lovingkindness, judgment, and
righteousness, in the earth: for in these
things I delight, saith the Lord.*
(Jeremiah 9:23–24)

A lioness. A pacing, chain-rattling *lioness*.

Ashara, Liora presumed.

Tethered to a pillar in the audience hall, the animal looked about as pleased with her attendance at the celebratory gathering as Queen Hodaya. The dethroned queen of Judah lingered in the farthest corner beyond the long, low table stretching the chamber's length. Regal in her finery and glaring heat, she all but spat at any who neared.

Similarly, the lioness growled over the lutes and lyres. She did not appear to care for their warbling sounds, for the singers praising Babylonian deities, or for the chamber's hubbub, which grew in proportion to the flow of wine. She did not appear to care for sweating translators either.

Liora edged farther away from those yellow, pinning eyes, putting Prince Nergal directly between herself and the beast. Her skills did not include translating snarls and nerve-shattering roars. Let *him* interpret the beast's keen-eyed, plotting stares.

Oblivious to her maneuvering, he wiggled jeweled fingers as he selected another morsel of roasted lamb from a tray trembling between a slave's hands. The prince cooed at the animal and tossed the meat, then broke into a cheer when she snatched it midair, a string of drool flying off her snapping teeth.

Why Liora was surprised at this addition to Nergal's feast, she could not say. Except that perhaps, she'd not given the man's greed for power enough credit. What said *I represent the conquering Babylonian throne* better than a living symbol of the kingdom itself? Only a male of the species with a shaggy crowning mane could improve on the image, instill greater awe in the military officials mingling in the chamber.

That, and a chained, dull-faced Judean concubine.

The prince had ordered Mehetabel to be positioned so close to Ashara her dirty tunic received a beating from a swiping paw. A moment later, a thin crimson stream twined about her brown ankle. More slashes to blend in with the rest. None had bothered to tidy the woman before prodding her into the audience hall. Tangles of dirty-gold hair hung about her downcast face, and dried blood streaked her neck. The puffy, red cut on her cheek seeped fluid that made Liora's stomach pitch with sympathy.

Gittel had stationed herself against the nearest wall, her foot tapping to the rhythm of the hand drum.

A FAITH UNTAMED

Should Liora send her to attend Mehetabel? Perhaps not. Gittel never did anything without fuss.

Liora resisted the urge to leave Nergal's side and try again to approach the woman herself. Mehetabel hadn't allowed it in the bedchamber, batting and shrieking and proving her voice did, in fact, work. Liora skittered back, giving the woman space and time to trust. Hours later, when Liora was venturing through the halls, knocking on doors in search of a clean tunic, she finally admitted to herself she'd given up because looking at Mehetabel was akin to looking a prophecy dead in the eye.

Crushed, crushed.

Even now, Liora angled away, unable to bear sight of the woman Liora should be but, by the grace of God, was not. The woman she *could be* if He so allowed, if Nergal became a trifle less amused with her bold tongue. If he grew weary of using her to toy with Nebuzaradan.

Make yourself indispensable.

Sage advice from her general.

Her general? Liora's eyes slid closed. *Right your thinking, Liora!*

The man was not *her* anything. She was his. Plain and simple.

Calling him husband on occasion had clearly altered how she appraised him. All thanks to Prince Nergal for shedding light on that change.

Liora could be an obedient wife to an enemy general appointed by Yahweh. She could stand in his defense before a furious, terrified prince, but she could *not* allow herself to grow attached—to give him her keys.

Her people would never forgive her. Then what use would she be?

None, she reminded herself, then said it again and again, while darting glances at the doors every time they opened to admit another guest.

Nebuzaradan was late. A subtle rebellion?

If so, Nergal didn't seem to have noticed. He teased the lioness between non-committal grunts at the official addressing him about city affairs.

Liora sighed out her disappointment when another group of military officers strode into the chamber, their pale-yellow stoles indicating lower rank. Immediately behind came a group of Edomites warriors, distinguished by their rugged attire, bead-adorned beards, and tattooed features.

Their duke, wearing a rich brown mantle with blue and ochre trimming, strutted into the royal residence with a smug satisfaction that stabbed Liora through with grief. How glutted they must feel for having gorged themselves on violence and pride. Centuries the Edomites had waited to watch Judah fall.

Chief Priest Seraiah entered next. He wore a fresh white tunic, his tall, matching turban glaringly absent its gold crown. The accessory probably rested somewhere in the pile of treasures growing in the Babylonian encampment—Nebuchadnezzar's tribute yard. Strolling inside as if a guard didn't trail him, the priest glanced her direction, his plump, rosy cheeks visible across the span.

A FAITH UNTAMED

Her gaze darted off him and back to the lioness, a preferable subject by far. *Where* was Nebuzaradan?

Nervous energy tingled through her limbs. She shook out her hands, the air refreshing against her hot, damp palms. What was *wrong* with her? If only she could blame her anxiety on the beast, though Ashara did give cause for concern.

With only the twitch of a tail for warning, she leaped toward them. The chain stretched taut one swipe-length shy of Nergal. The copper links gouged the pillar's plaster and yanked Ashara back by her neck. Her scream swallowed Liora's bleat of alarm.

Nergal backed up a step, laughing.

Straight-faced, the official beside him surreptitiously wiped at a line of sweat trailing from the gray-black hair at his temple. "As I was saying. Yes, the grain will hold another seven days but at reduced measures." Introduced earlier as Nebo-Sarsekim, *rab-saris* by title, or chief chamberlain, he seemed the quiet, sensible sort, his words carefully weighed before meeting the air.

While Nergal turned to deliberate again over the meat tray, Sarsekim closed his mouth and waited. The pause gave his statement time to sink through Liora's hearing.

Had he said reduced grain? For whom? She sidled closer, head cocked, and caught Sarsekim's sidelong attention.

A good three-score years had etched themselves into his features, but no scars marred his skin, a true man of ink and tablets. Carriage erect, he observed her with neutral interest before dipping his chin in acknowledgment of her presence and resuming his report. "Your Highness, with every respect, extending our stay in Jerusalem will require diminishing rations by a third to prevent supplies running dry before we reach Riblah. If you wish a decent number to arrive in health, I do not recommend it. We would also be wise to withhold further celebrations until we may rejoice in the presence of our noble king. As wondrous as it is, this feast has taxed our royal reserves to the point of concern."

Liora's spine straightened as the details settled in. Seven days in Jerusalem. Then Riblah. Rations reduced by a third.

Sarsekim had followed the rationing statement with a comment on the royal larder, but she was not fool enough to believe he meant any princes would be feeling the cut of that nourishment.

Prince Nergal showed the chamberlain a feigned pout. "You and your caution, Sarsekim. Next, you will advise I deprive Ashara her share." He threw a small piece of meat high in the air. His pout turned genuine when the beast watched the meat splat to the stone and swiveled to give him her swishing tail.

"As always,"—Sarsekim folded his hands before him, his tone even, logical—"you may do as you wish, Your Highness. I only report and advise and leave the decisions in your capable hands."

Prince Nergal capable? If he severed his captives' rations—by a third!—Sarsekim might have to recant the compliment. For a people already siege-starved,

A FAITH UNTAMED

such a blow to their diet would be crippling. Would travel be possible at all? For any ill or wounded, it could be a death sentence.

More disturbing yet, Liora realized Yahweh had not placed her there, in *that* spot to hear the news and do nothing.

Lord? Your guidance?

Liora wasn't sure what she expected from Him, but no light shed across her mind. No brilliant plan to prevent the deprivation. She rubbed her sweating palms down the fronts of her thighs. The rough texture of the servant's garb she'd chosen bunched her bandage. The strip pressed against her wound, but the twinge of pain was no distraction from the urge to fidget.

"But please consider," Sarsekim continued, a patient father schooling a son, "the more for the beast's belly, the less for yours."

"Such a bore. Must you always ruin my pleasure?" Nergal heaved a sigh worthy of a man told to roll a boulder. "But I do appreciate a contented stomach. Perhaps,"—his gaze slinked left to Mehetabel—"we should find my Ashara's meals elsewhere."

Liora's hands spasmed into fists, collecting handfuls of fabric. He would *not*.

Lips slack, the concubine stared straight ahead at a spot on the floor, but Sarsekim's bland expression wavered.

"That...should not be necessary, Your Highness," the chamberlain said. "The king has vested me with the responsibility to keep you fed as you usher us safely from this disease-infested city. I shall do so without the need to sacrifice any concubines to the jaws of savage beasts." Sarsekim laid a palm across the gold sun-disc on his chest, a vow to the sun god, Shamash. "I do, however, advise the temple work advance more quickly."

Temple work. Said as if it were a noble labor. Indignation festered in her gut, but what use was there in stomping one's feet. The temple belonged to the Lord, and He'd chosen its cleansing and destruction. Chosen which axe would hew it down, too.

General Nebuzaradan of the House of Axes.

Both men, prince and chamberlain, whipped their gazes toward her.

Taken aback, she returned their stares. Warmth bled into her cheeks. Had she said the general's name out loud?

"Yes, that is correct, my irrepressible translator. The temple is General Nebuzaradan's field of interest. And as I have been informed," the prince said, smirking at her, "the Butcher is the *very best* for the task. But perhaps he should consult with your priests? I see at least one here who still carries himself with the arrogance of divine authority."

True enough. Seraiah grazed from a table laden with heaping platters, as if he were the host instead of the entertainment. His cheek bulged as he chewed.

Liora narrowed her eyes at him, the seed of a thought burrowing into her mind.

A FAITH UNTAMED

"Why is the dish empty?" Nergal snapped at his quaking slave. "Can you not see my Ashara is still hungry?"

The slave ducked his head low over the juice-smeared tray and, uttering apologies, backed away on fumbling feet. At the last second, he veered out of Ashara's path, then all but ran toward the servants' entry. He would be back with meat heaped on that dish.

More for the beast. None for those who truly needed it. Seraiah not included.

The seed took root, and a knot of tension released in Liora's chest. It tightened right back up as a familiar stride reached her ear. Crisp and steady, the footsteps neared from behind. Could any but King Nebuchadnezzar's Butcher enter the royal presence with such unwavering confidence?

"There he is now," Nergal said, all farce, "our god-blessed general." He extended an elegant arm toward the imposing figure appropriating Liora's peripheral vision.

The scent of spice, uniquely Nebuzaradan, pervaded her next inhale. Her heart flopped like a fish on the deck of a boat. She did not turn toward him.

Rimutu maintained his post a distance off, not far from Gittel.

"Your Highness, congratulations on a most engaging occasion." Nebuzaradan made obeisance to his prince. Rising, he sidled nearer to her, the heat of him touching her skin even through her thick-threaded tunic.

No, that was her own body flushing with heat. *Stop it, Liora! He is nothing.*

If she could, she'd kick the prince in the shins for setting her off kilter, for feeding her preposterous ideas when her thoughts were required elsewhere.

"Should I return the bow?" The prince snickered, but Sarsekim did as he suggested, recognizing the higher authority in the leader of their armies.

"General Nebuzaradan, my condolences on the loss of your eye," the chamberlain said, not a shred of mockery on him. "One does not have an audience with the gods and walk away unchanged."

"Well observed, Rab-saris Nebo-Sarsekim," Nebuzaradan replied. "The stories of Yahweh's power appear to have a grain of truth, after all. I am grateful to still be in possession of my life."

Nergal twirled the end of his purple stole. "So you may devote it to Babylon and her king?"

Nebuzaradan dipped his chin. "As ever I have done, my prince."

"As ever you should. So, tell me, my faithful Butcher, with so many of Babylon's spoils passing through your hands, how will you part with your choicest treasure?"

Liora's heart thudded. The prince did *not* mean the covenant ark.

Or did he? Nebuzaradan did have a history with the holy vessel, though not of his own choosing.

She glanced at him. Whether he gleaned any double meaning, she could not tell. His tensing posture could stem from the reference to any treasure being *his*.

As he dipped into a shallow bow, Liora latched her sight to the lioness testing the length of her tether. Could the beast feel the plaster crumbling under the bite of the chain? Did she believe liberty to be a few hard leaps away?

"All treasure belongs to our king," Nebuzaradan said over the animal's low growl, the thunder of it rolling in. "It is none of mine."

Grinning, Nergal extended his arms out to the sides, as if exhibiting the spoils themselves. "Well spoken. Well spoken, indeed!"

A paused followed, and Liora could practically see the questions filtering through Nebuzaradan's mind. He was too perceptive to believe the exchange to be innocuous, too uninformed to understand its fullest meaning. "I speak but truth, my prince. May I inquire of Lady Liora?" He waited for Nergal's acquiescing gesture before he angled toward her. "Are you well?" he said, his voice an intimate rumble. "You appear...feverish. Has the wound—"

"Perfectly well, my lord." Under his penetrating gaze, she straightened her head covering, ascertaining it crossed neatly under her chin to hide any blush. If its side edge hid her from his scrutiny, all the better.

"Look how she pretties herself for you, Butcher." The prince's eyes twinkled with mischief.

Liora dropped her arms. Was she prettying herself?

No, she was becoming distracted from her task. Huffing softly, she let another *irrepressible* observation pop off her tongue. "In answer to your earlier concern regarding food, may I point out the chief priest has an abundance of flesh on his bones?" She nodded across the hall to where Seraiah picked at a large roasted fowl. Grease shone on his lips.

Prince Nergal's eyes lit with a mixture of shock and delight. "*Vicious*, Lady Liora. There, see? You are no dove, but a lioness. Ashara approves and thanks you for your care of her stomach. Shall we set the Butcher on him?"

Liora blinked at the prince. "The Butcher on... Pardon?"

"I do not believe," Nebuzaradan said, wry humor lightening his voice, "that my wife meant to suggest feeding the priest to your lioness."

She released an abrupt, incredulous laugh. "Forgive me, Your Highness, no. I sadden at any living being suffering hunger, Ashara no exception. But Arioch is correct."

"Arioch, is it?" The prince quirked an eyebrow at Nebuzaradan.

Liora plowed on, eager to correct the horrid assumption. "I wish merely to alert you to the possibility you might find the priestly quarters have hidden grain untouched by the fires. To assist with the rations. My own stores have already been exhausted, or I would offer them. But Seraiah there..." She let the thought dangle as she joined the men in examining the priest. "How likely is it he has horded grain barrels somewhere in the city?"

A FAITH UNTAMED

Nergal snorted. "As likely as a scorpion under a desert rock."

Sarsekim nodded, eyes tight on the chief priest, but Nebuzaradan's gaze swung back to her. The weight of it, almost too heavy to resist, burned into her.

She blinked repeatedly, her eyes on the priest but her every thought on the general raking her with his attention. If she knew him at all, he was scowling at her servant's attire, at her uncombed hair, at her rumpled bandage and deliberate avoidance of his gaze. At her death grip on her *keys*.

Well, he could frown all he wished. She had other more important matters to attend.

Clearing her throat, she tilted her head to block him from view. "If I am correct, the supply might extend the rations without sacrificing Babylon's stockpiles and without depriving the people of food. They have already suffered so much want, Your Highness." How much more would the Lord allow? "Whatever you recover from the unrighteous priest might be offered as incentive to those who labor hardest to ready the city for travel. Two goals met at once. And you may continue to feed Ashara without resorting to"—she glanced at the animal, now lying down licking the space between two dagger-sharp claws—"other measures."

Slow clapping sounded from Nergal, but it was Nebuzaradan's grunt of approval that pulled her attention from the feline. Admiration shone in his eyes so brightly she could not hold his gaze.

The idea had not been her own. Could he not understand she was as much of an instrument as he? She had prayed, and the Lord had granted.

Sarsekim spoke to the prince, drawing him away. Something to do with interrogations and searches.

She heard none of it, only the general murmuring, "Do not lie to me, dove. You are unwell."

She tucked her chin and fiddled with her bandage, straightening its creases. "Disjointed is all. This place..." Prince Nergal insisted he required her presence at his side for her services, but she had yet to translate a single word. Eyes downcast, she leaned in to whisper. "It has the feel of a snarl about the ankle." Threatening to tighten, to yank her up and dangle her from the nearest column for their amusement. Perhaps she *was* the lioness, pacing, plotting, for she would be no dead-eyed Mehetabel.

"Yes. I do not like you here." Nebuzaradan bent near, arms behind his back, but that was no casual pose. Tension rode his frame, the volume of his voice fluctuating slightly as though following a gaze that roved the hall. "But you continue to handle yourself remarkably. Every man present has taken notice of you. Even in that humble garb, you outshine the queen."

Of all comments, *that* was the one to tear her eyes off the ground. Fortunately, the general's head was turned, his glowering attention invested in a group of captains. They blatantly stared at her, not yet aware her husband targeted them. "That is not my intent," she hurried to say just as the foremost officer's eyes drifted off her, landed on his general, and flew wide.

"The men confuse you for a common maid." The snap in Nebuzaradan's reply was not meant for her. He sidestepped and effectively blocked her from every view, save the lioness's. "Why did you dress so lowly?"

"Because I prefer it to harlot's raiment." The reply shot off her tongue so tart it startled her. Apparently, she harbored a load of bitterness. Or was it fear?

Nebuzaradan went utterly still. "The prince provided you with the garment of a harlot?" His timbre dropped to the depth of the barrel drum booming across the room to mark the arrival of a roasted boar. "Why?"

She shook her head, reluctant to release the emotion clenching her heart. "I lay blame at no one's feet. But in whose eyes am I anything better?"

"In my own!"

Liora flinched but raised a defiant chin, daring at last to meet Nebuzaradan's sparking, half-white eyes. "Am I?" Had he respected her enough to give her a proper ceremony? Honored her name? Her family? Her desire to speak vows before Yahweh? To all these questions, she clamped her lips shut. There would be an occasion to address them, but this was not it.

For long moments, they exchanged stares—Nebuzaradan's flinty and probing, Liora's undaunted and entirely unbowed. The space between them crackled with a tension that pressed against her ribs with an ache borne not of fear but of self-reproach.

What was she doing? Alienating her only shield in this wretched place. All because the prince had filled her head with ideas of walls and keys and giving one's heart to the enemy. What a foolish, pliant pawn she was! Tears sprang to her eyes, hot with regret.

Through their blur, Nebuzaradan's stone veneer melted away, leaving only a furrowed brow and something resembling concern. "Liora, dove," he whispered roughly, reaching a hand that stopped shy of touching her arm. "What has he done to you in my absence?"

Done? Nothing but terrify her with her own heart.

But that was no answer she could give. Before she could conjure another, a trumpet blew, summoning the guests to dine.

Nebuzaradan exhaled a low, irritated growl, then gestured toward the table. "The prince will expect you at his side. But do not think we are done with this matter."

CHAPTER 14

But the Lord is with me as a mighty terrible one: therefore my persecutors shall stumble, and they shall not prevail. (Jer. 20:11a)

Hours into the feast, a thin layer of smoke from the torches lined the ceiling, and the weary musicians were twanging wrong notes. Liora doubted any present heard the mishaps, since the wine flowed. Its cloying scent mingled with the smoky tang of cedar-wood incense and the prince's warm amber perfume.

From her kneeling position at his elbow, Liora had a prime view of his descent into his cups and his cushions. Sweat glistened at his hairline, the locks of his oiled black hair limp about his shoulders. Whiskers shadowed his jaw, and inebriation glossed his eyes, though his mind had been clear enough to follow Liora's reasoning about Mehetabel being a bore and dampening the spirit of his celebration.

Playing to his ego proved remarkably effective. He ordered Mehetabel returned to her chamber at once, then threatened the musicians with dismemberment if they continued their slackened pace. Another remarkably effective tactic.

Liora sipped tea, more at ease with Mehetabel removed from the path of the lioness—and men's roving gazes. Her nose persisted in its dampness, but the lemon-honey tea provided merciful relief to her sore throat. The padding beneath her did little to ease the ache in her knees, and she worried her numb feet would give out when the prince at last tired of her and waved her away. So far, he'd had no use for her. Since the chamberlain had vanished with Seraiah, the only person present who might not understand Akkadian was Queen Hodaya, and she sat at the table's opposite end. Beside Nebuzaradan.

What the prince had meant as an insult, the general embraced as an honored role. "I shall guard one of our king's greatest spoils from filthy, grasping hands," he'd said at a booming volume, a rogue's twinkle in his teeth-baring grin.

The men hooted and cheered and bowed out of his way as he stalked to his assigned place, the handle of his axe swaying at his thigh. Several slapped him on the back as he passed, the gestures of support morphing his stalk into a swagger.

Liora stared. She'd only ever seen trembling respect from his men. This was something other. Something she imagined she might witness in the sparring yard where ranks blurred and respect was not granted by command.

The only variant, the Edomites who quieted their carousing to watch him. Their duke dipped his chin as Nebuzaradan passed, the gesture neither friendly nor hostile. Merely a measure of the man who had stolen command of the hall.

Nebuzaradan dropped onto his cushions, sprawled out beside Hodaya, and a made of show of raising his goblet to her, as though she were the honored guest.

A FAITH UNTAMED

Bellows of laughter rose with the crimson splotching the queen's face, but Nebuzaradan remained true to his word. When clipped warnings to rowdy men lost their power, a blow to the temple got his message across.

On that single occasion, the general tossed the dregs of his wine onto the unconscious official, then turned his back on him. "Show wisdom, men. She belongs to our king."

When heads lowered, as if bowing to him, Prince Nergal snatched up his goblet. A muscle twitched over his jaw as he glared over the cup's rim. Envy always looked most childish on a royal.

As for Liora, she imagined she bore a similarly notable look, hers one of surprise. If anyone had told her, while she was marched across the Babylonian camp, that the Butcher would one day defend Queen Hodaya's honor, she would have laughed them into the refuse heaps of Gehenna.

Nebuzaradan, of course, might counter he was only defending his king's spoils while redeeming his own honor for being seated at the table's end. And he was. But a niggling curiosity questioned if he understood she would abide nothing less from a man she called husband.

Such an assumption would mean he took her feelings into consideration. An improbability for the Butcher? Or was the wall-scaling imagery she'd given the prince more than imagery after all?

The walls of a woman's heart cannot be conquered, she'd said, never actually connecting the romantic notion to Nebuzaradan.

Now, as she gazed down the table's length and, for the dozenth time, met Nebuzaradan's focused, watchful eyes, she allowed herself to ponder whether he was, in his own brutish way, scaling her walls one tenuous grip at a time. A clutter of dirty dishes, picked bones, and olive stones lay between them—to say nothing of three dozen burping, reveling men—but she felt the questions in his piercing mien like a stylus pressed into her skin.

Are you well? those black eyes asked. *How do you fare? Have you made yourself invaluable?*

She passed him a discreet, reassuring smile she prayed didn't convey her truest feelings.

The prince had seemed to value the idea the Lord had given her about searching Seraiah's residence for grain, but she'd served no purpose since. Twice, Queen Hodaya had sent her maid toward the table's head. Twice, Prince Nergal sent her back before she could voice the queen's request—for an audience, Liora presumed.

Sharp-eyed and perfectly erect, Hodaya maintained her poise without flaw. The woman was undaunted. A quality that would serve her well through her coming trial. An audience with Prince Nergal was nothing next to prostrating before King Nebuchadnezzar, begging the sovereign for her life and that of her daughters. Her sons' lives were all but forfeit.

Liora, as the Butcher's wife, would find herself in a similar position. Although, her pleading would be for the lives of her people, a surety she doubted

A FAITH UNTAMED

Nebuzaradan had considered. Invaluable? Yes, she planned to be.

Nerves assaulted her stomach, but Yahweh had stood at her side before a general. He did so now before a prince. He would again before a king. And between this place and that, He would strengthen and sustain her.

A commotion at the end of the table brought the instruments to a discordant halt and snapped Liora from her reverie. Queen Hodaya stood hunched, halfway to her feet. She did not struggle, merely speared Nebuzaradan with a beautiful glare. "Take your hand off me, Butcher."

He clutched her by the forearm, not bothering to rise with her. "You have not been granted permission to stand before His Highness. *Sit*, woman. Before I drag you down." He spoke in Akkadian, then darted a glance at Liora.

She was already up, needle pricks tormenting the soles of her feet. "My queen, please. This is not the way." Her Hebrew rang loud in the death-silent chamber.

Only Nergal's crunching could be heard. He stretched for the bowl heaped with roasted almonds and tossed another between his chomping molars. "At last. Something interesting."

"I *will* be heard." Dark skin glistening, chestnut hair coiffed high and draped with a diaphanous blue covering, Hodaya was undeniably stunning. The absence of her usual jewels did nothing to dim her grace. Expression icy calm, she exuded dignity, her royal bearing clear even in her stooped posture.

Feeling Nebuzaradan's prompting gaze, Liora rushed to reply. "You must obey and remain seated. He threatens to use force."

Nebuzaradan pulled on her arm, a slow, deliberate tug that bent Hodaya almost double.

Undeterred, she lifted her countenance and directed her next demand at Prince Nergal. "A conquered queen has the right to stand before the one who holds her fate."

"Prince Nergal has no say over your fate," Liora responded, drawing Nebuzaradan's hiked brow. Until someone silenced her, she would speak. "In seven days, we travel to King Nebuchadnezzar in Riblah where you will surely be granted the audience you demand."

Ashara snarled, her claws clicking the stone, and Hodaya's inflexible expression cracked. Grief commandeered her poise. "News of my husband and sons?"

Leaning back into his mound of cushions, Nergal stretched out his legs and clasped his hands behind his head. "Am I to be allowed into the conversation, little lioness? Or shall I name you vizier? Pass you the royal seal?"

Bending at the waist, Liora faced him fully. "Your pardon, Prince Nergal. I have taken the liberty of reasoning with her. Now, she inquires of the dethroned king and his princes."

A FAITH UNTAMED

"Does she! If I were the queen of ashes, I would leap at the chance to disassociate myself from that mule of a puppet."

As Liora herself had done. With all haste. A response she could not give without opening a chest of curiosity and questions, none of which this prince had any likelihood of leaving unasked.

Chin down, she waited for him to go on, but after long moments, the only input she received was a man's snicker from somewhere at the table. Hodaya remained as she'd been, stubbornly resisting Nebuzaradan's all-too-patient clasp on her.

Liora shifted on her tingling feet while one of Nergal's eyebrows peaked high.

He expected *her* to respond? But of course. She was half the entertainment. And he was ready to be entertained, there where he reclined, elbows jutting out from the sides of his head. Circles of sweat darkened the blue silk under his arms, the work of the fanning slave boy serving better to blow body odor toward Liora than to cool the prince.

Anger brewing, she could use a little cooling herself. But who was she, a prize and a piece in his game, to become indignant at her lot?

Very well. She would open her mouth and speak her heart, a choice that had yet to fail her. Abandoning her submissive posture, she hiked her own brow. "A woman wed, whether a washer of rags or a *queen of ash*, has no such privilege as choosing disassociation. In Judah, until the bonds of marriage are severed by death or law, her life is tied to that of her husband.

Hodaya wishes only to know whether hers yet lives. May I answer that he does? I assume he has been imprisoned until his hour before the king."

Liora wouldn't have thought it possible, but the room's hush thickened.

On a lazy roll of the head, Nergal put the fan boy in his sights. "The woman assumes much," he said, uncaring of the boy's pallor or of the new tremble in the fan's ostrich feathers. "One day, such *liberties* will cost her that pretty tongue."

Wisely, the boy kept his lashes down and his mouth shut.

On a long groan, Nergal curled up to sitting, then hooked an arm around an upraised knee. His attention turned toward the man on his left, a high official she'd overlooked in favor of vigilance toward the jackal in the room. "She would instruct me?" The prince affected a snort, the sound of a brewing scheme. "*Me*, a student of the laws of every land, in the ways of marriage?"

Lips skewing sideways, the official produced a curved dagger and extended it toward Nergal, handle first. "For collecting that pretty tongue?"

Liora's pulse tripped, but Nergal never looked at the blade.

He swiveled those scheming eyes on her. "*You*, a woman despised, rejected. By a king, no less," he said, every light, carefree word the pierce of a dart. "You, a woman paraded through the streets in shame, then tossed like a sack of blood-stained gold at the feet of a brutal general."

A FAITH UNTAMED

With the deep resonance of a balag-drum, the prince's plot came into full focus. He would drag her through the past, humiliate her. And Liora wanted nothing to do with it.

Body in agreement, her ears whined, an echo of the booing masses. Head turning, she instinctively sought the exit. Her heel slid backward. The sole of her sandal scraped the stone, betraying her preparation for flight. Her hips were twisting when Nebuzaradan's voice penetrated her distress.

"My prince." He was standing now, facing the lounging jackal. Whatever expression he wore was lost in the blur of Liora's vision, but his words cut through the clangor in her head. "If my wife was despised, it was for her virtue in a palace of conniving vipers. If she was rejected, it was by the king you call a fool. If she was exhibited and shamed, it was no fault of her own but that of a spiteful city too eager to crush the one who shed light on their corrupt souls."

Crushed, indeed. They had broken her skin, her bones. Phantom pains jagged down her arm where the first stone landed. She clutched it close to her body and startled at the prince's burst of laughter.

"Who knew our Butcher was also a poet? Ah..." He drew out the sound, as one does after a refreshing drink. "And such perfect poetry. Scribe! Put it in your book." Arm raised, he snapped his fingers. The man was all drama and spectacle, and Liora and Nebuzaradan stood center-stage. "Record this too. Is it not also perfect poetry that of all those you listed just now—the fool king, the denizens of his foul city—*you*, Butcher, are the one who has most harmed her?"

Nebuzaradan stepped back from the table, as though to distance himself from the accusation. "Your pardon?" The question emerged rather weakly.

Weaker than Liora would like. Her senses pricked, each one tuned to Nebuzaradan. To the slow descent of his shoulders and the smoothing of his brow on an expression too blank not to be deliberate—the demeanor of a man tamping embers beneath his sandal.

Liora would like to believe he worried the prince would hold him accountable for her brush with the Last Flame, but the devilish pleasure teeming in the prince's smirk told her to brace for far worse. She pulled her arm closer, an embrace that did nothing to comfort.

"Are you not curious," he said, wielding that smirk at Nebuzaradan like a scorpion's tail, "what the king has to say about all this? About his best general smitten with a reputedly faithless Jewess? And *that* after flinging accusations that his own wife in Babylon lets other men warm his bed? The irony."

Put that way, who could blame any at the table—soldier, prince, queen—for wondering?

Someone far down the table murmured a sound of agreement, but Nebuzaradan's only reply was to engage in a stare far too close to defiance. A clear *no*, contrary to Liora's own response.

She would like to know. Had the king granted Nebuzaradan the divorce he'd requested, or would

A FAITH UNTAMED

Liora be forever subject to the first wife's claws? Judging by the knowing tilt to Nergal's lips, he had the answer. Hadn't he mentioned he'd brought correspondence from the king for Nebuzaradan? Until that moment, with everything else that had come between, Liora had put the memory from her mind.

Prince Nergal raised his groomed eyebrows at Nebuzaradan. "No? Not curious at all?"

Curious or not, the prince *would* reveal whatever news he harbored. The only choice she and Nebuzaradan had was whether they would allow him to make them yoked captives trailing the rear of the parade. Or whether they would walk proudly at the front, conquerors of their own humiliation.

"I am curious," Liora heard herself say.

Murmurs exploded around the room, and true delight opened Nergal's expression, making him almost handsome. Tragic that it came at her expense, but it was not the first occasion a man used her to prop himself up before others.

"*Liora.*" Nebuzaradan took several brisk strides toward her before catching himself. Warning flashed in his eyes. "This is a matter to be addressed privately."

"Are the matters of the nobility ever private, my lord?" she countered.

"Well said! The scroll." A second snap of Nergal's fingers sent a servant from the room, robes flaring. "While we wait for my steward, I have a curiosity of my own. Perhaps the disgraced queen can satisfy it?" The prince directed the question not at Hodaya, who remained standing, but at Liora.

She genuflected. "I give voice to your will."

"A story, then. Humor us, queen of ashes. Is it true Lady Liora survived a stoning?" He stared at Liora through wine-heavy eyelids, clicking his signet ring against his silver goblet.

Liora's heart sank. She should have known he would grant no reprieve, not until he'd drawn blood. Metaphorically. *Lord, please.*

But no, her worry about violence was misplaced. Nebuzaradan was too much the soldier, too much the crown's servant to lash out at the prince's taunts. Had he not, upon command, faced his own death without hesitation? The general might pound the skull of a disrespectful subordinate, but the only blood spilled that night would be from Liora's shredded reputation.

A glimpse of his clamped lips confirmed it. Fear might swim in those bi-colored eyes as they burrowed into her, but he would not intervene. The man was a roaring, axe-swinging lion who willingly chained himself to a pillar of loyalty.

But Liora could not judge. She had done the same, albeit to an invisible, so-called defeated God instead of a king lauded for his might. Which of them, in man's view, showed greater lunacy?

But where he'd shackled himself to power, she'd bound herself to a faithful hope. Although, in that moment, she heard only the echoing beat of cherub wings—Yahweh leaving His house—rather than the shelter of His voice.

You are my buttress. Lord of Hosts, you are my shield.

A FAITH UNTAMED

She swallowed uselessly at a bulge forming in her throat and angled toward Hodaya. "My queen," she began, unable to look higher than the loose clasp of the woman's hands, quite regal compared to Liora's twisting fingers. "His Highness Prince Nergal asks you to confirm whether your husband put a halt to my...execution."

"He did." Hodaya's voice rang out.

Perhaps gleaning the queen's answer from her tone, Nergal said, "Exceptional!"

The response was boisterous enough to startle the fellow refilling the goblet the prince held aloft. Wine sloshed over the rim, but Nergal didn't quit his study of Liora, even when wine dripped off his fingers.

"Exceptional, indeed." The official who'd offered the dagger now bobbed his head like flotsam caught in a rippling current.

"Imagine the pain. The distress. Yet there she stands." Nergal waggled the cup at her. "Intact in both body and mind. Oh, I do like her." He gushed this to the nodding official. "Enough with the glowers, Butcher. My meaning is entirely honorable. The lady is quite safe...from *me*." The fanged grin he turned on Nebuzaradan was a match to that of the lioness still pacing the length of her chain.

His guests responded with the expected laughter, some lewd. Others obligatory. All placating.

All save Hodaya, who gazed at Liora with unvoiced questions. And Nebuzaradan, who'd directed his glower to the wall.

"But I am unsatisfied with the tale," the prince said. "Speak on, ash queen. I require details of this forestalled stoning. What crime did the lady commit, how was she caught, and why would the puppet king change his mind? Come, tell us the whole tale."

A weight settled on Liora's shoulders, but she held firm against the onslaught of humiliation and translated as required.

If the queen was put out by recalling her husband's plan of marriage to another woman, she gave no indication. Carriage erect, tone steady and firm, if clipped, she began. "Lady Liora was contracted to my husband as fifth concubine. Before the day appointed for their marriage, she was caught lying with an Edomite. Our law demands such infidelity be met with a stoning."

She spoke without pause, challenging Liora's skill. One ear on the woman, the other on her own quivering voice, she translated word for word. "My husband, however, was struck by an unexpected bout of mercy. He sent runners. Before they could halt the execution, she lay torn and bloodied. By some miracle, she recovered. Some say she now suffers a strange abhorrence to her own blood. At the sight of it, she... I..."

Red flashed before Liora's eyes, and a metallic taste coated her tongue. Liora blinked fast, her heart faster. "I..." She gave her head a tiny shake before lowering it. "I faint dead away. Is that enough detail for you, Prince?" she continued, tongue fumbling. "Or should I add that her…her father, Chesed ben Ephraim, sent me from his house to live in poverty?"

"Poverty was it?" the prince demanded.

"Your Highness, pity the lady." That was Nebuzaradan's deep rumble. Close by. Not a pace behind her right shoulder. The earthy scent of turmeric rode his words. "She appears close to fainting now."

Indeed, her knees wobbled, half boneless.

The prince groaned a deep sigh. "First, Nebo-Sarsekim spoils my joy. Now, the Butcher. But very well. It would hardly serve my purpose to have her lying unawares on the floor while you read the king's missive."

"Sit," Nebuzaradan murmured.

While Liora descended less than gracefully to her knees, the prince received a scroll case from a bowing servant.

Without warning, he tossed it to Nebuzaradan. The wooden case flipped end over end, passing over Liora's head.

A smacking sound, as of wood on skin, promised the general caught it.

She snatched her breath and in the collective silence listened to the crack of wax and the squeak of wood-on-wood, as of a lid being wriggled off. The crinkle of parchment and a pause. An intake of breath.

Then a shout. It came from behind her deep within the palace. Running feet smacked stone.

Men scrambled up from the table, exchanging confused glances. All of them soldiers, none bearing weapons per the custom. Except their general.

Liora twisted where she knelt just as his axe emerged from its seat on his belt in a flourish of gleaming bronze.

She tried to rise, but he shoved her back to the cushion with an order to, *"Remain there."*

A short sidestep moved his bulk to cover her from whoever tore toward them.

View blocked, she did not see the fellow who ran into the hall. Only heard him screaming, "Murder!"

~~~

When the prince strode from the banquet hall, Liora planned to disappear into her assigned chamber and shut her ears to whatever evil Nebuzaradan and his soldiers discovered on their hunt. That hope had lasted the few minutes it took him to learn the location of the violence.

Now, she gripped the wooden rail of her bedchamber's balcony, her veil whipping in the smoke-tainted breeze, and tried not to be sick as she peered over the edge into the darkness below.

At the escarpment's base, four shadowy figures carrying torches moved along goat trails, all aimed toward one spot. Several had already arrived, the yellow of their stoles identifying them as foot soldiers. They surrounded a crumpled female form, their torchlight rippling over the long stretch of a distinctive golden braid.

"Mehetabel," Liora whispered, her throat clenching on grief and sickness.

Beside her, Nebuzaradan leaned over the rail and spat a foul word. "His Majesty will not be pleased." He followed that callous observation with a murmured, "Pitiful wretch. Perhaps in death, she has found peace."

A hopeful thought and gentler than Liora might have expected from the Butcher. Whether there was any truth to it, only Yahweh could say.

"I pray so." Liora palmed her uneasy stomach and told herself not to look away. That *pitiful wretch* deserved better than a glance. She deserved better than Prince Nergal's whining, too.

"My dinner, spoiled," he said from within the chamber at Liora's back. "Over a concubine. A *fifth* concubine, no less. Are we even certain it is she? Have you confirmed, Liora?"

"Yes," she said, unable to blame her damp eyes entirely on the smoke. "She is Mehetabel."

From this distance, the concubine's face was a pale blur in the moonlight, but that beautiful braid was unmistakable. It wrapped around her neck like a noose. Combined with the awkward tilt to her head, she appeared almost as if hung by her own hair. But no, any could see her death came on the rocks. A patch of glistening red haloed her. No skull could survive such a fall.

A waste. Such a grievous waste.

Wind gusted into Liora's face, cooling the tears on her cheeks and tickling her throat. She caught her flying veil and coughed into it. When she recovered her breath, she found Nebuzaradan had straightened and regarded her from his grand height.

Angled away from the chamber's lamplight, his face was a mask of darkness. His only clear feature, the frowning slash of his black eyebrows and that one white eye, catching faint moonbeams.

"Do not look at me so, Arioch." She dabbed her wet face with the veil. "I am well. Let it go." They had other, more important matters to attend than his obsession with her sensitivity to the smoke. Such as Mehetabel's needless death. And the charge against Gittel.

Earlier, when Liora entered the chamber, the handmaid had been on her knees before a guard. Even while confronted with a sword point, she'd worn defiance like a living curse, directing it at any who glanced her way, Liora included. The only fear she'd shown came when she hurled a demand at Liora. "My hands are clean, Liora. Make them understand."

Liora gave the woman no promises, not that she'd had much of a chance since Nebuzaradan had been ushering her swiftly toward the balcony.

Now, as he stared down at her, he seemed poised to make a few promises of his own. Such as vowing to banish her to cleaner country air. "Not well enough." He clipped the statement. "This day has been too much for you."

In an hour, he might be correct. But for the moment, Yahweh gave her the strength to stand and speak on behalf of those whose voices had been silenced. Liora looked back at Mehetabel's sprawled figure and gritted her teeth against the rise of anger. "Do you see me wilting? I am no fragile poppy."

"I see you trembling."

A FAITH UNTAMED

Glancing at her hands, Liora could not argue. She curled them into fists, relishing the sting of her wound, and fought a growing urge to pound his chest.

Mehetabel might have been from Edom, Judah's longtime antagonist. She might have been the woman to replace Liora in the harem. But she had not deserved to be violated, abused, despised, her brokenness put on display. If not for Babylon, if not for Nebuzaradan himself directing his army of unruly soldiers at the palace, Mehetabel would not be a collection of broken bones at the base of a cliff.

He leaned close, startling her. "Strike me before the prince," he warned in hissing tones, "and I cannot save you."

The fathomless hollows of his eyes bore into her until she pulled a breath, restarting her frozen lungs. She let it out on a gust. Taking her fury out on Nebuzaradan was not the answer. And, truly, how much of it could be traced back to Mehetabel's death?

Her fists relaxed, and her arms lowered to her sides. "Forgive me, Arioch. I... I am uncertain why I feel so..." She bit off the lie and picked at her bandage.

Long moments of silence passed. Indecipherable voices filtered up from below, carried on the warm breeze. The soldiers gathered Mehetabel into a blanket, handling her with enough care to please Liora. She'd almost forgotten Nebuzaradan when he spoke again.

"You are no wilting poppy, my dove," he said, his voice a rumbling caress that did her drying eyes no favors. He pointed a stiff finger into the abyss below. "You are not *her*."

The lump in Liora's throat seemed to double, but after a moment, she nodded.

No, Liora was not Mehetabel, not in the strictest terms, the most obvious being she was alive. But she, too, had been assaulted, despised, stoned. The only difference between them? Liora's hope lay in Yahweh, a lifeline that could snap, given the right circumstances. What would it take for Liora to lose trust in her Lord?

"And now you shudder." He clicked his tongue. "This day has been a trial for even the strongest among us. My night has only begun, as I will likely be assigned to investigate. But you may rest after answering to His Highness." He pointed toward the balcony door.

"Yes, my lord." She left the rail and stepped into the chamber.

His back to the room, Prince Nergal stood picking the broken plaster of a ruined mural of flowers. Crumbles fell from the wall, adding to the pile accumulating at his feet. "The maid purses her lips in the most stubborn manner. It is *irritating*."

Liora stopped just inside, sidestepping to allow Nebuzaradan to pass into the room.

Gittel had not moved from her spot. She knelt low, hands flat on the floor, eyes straight ahead, presumably on the gilded cup resting on the floor nearby.

"You have gleaned nothing from her?" Nebuzaradan asked.

A FAITH UNTAMED

"If she were a lovely creature," the prince said, tone conversational, "my patience might not have run out so quickly. I do consider myself a reasonable man. As it stands, I am one question away from removing those ugly lips to see if it gets her talking."

Would he do that? Liora took a quick step forward before Nebuzaradan's raised hand halted her. She gave him a look stubborn enough to match the maid's. "Gittel spoke to me before. She claims innocence, Your Highness."

"They all do." Nergal flicked a finger, and a large chunk of plaster sailed through the air.

"Your Highness." Nebuzaradan stopped before the prince and assumed a casual pose, his thumb hooked in his weapons belt. "The day has been long, and you are surely weary. Allow me to handle the matter so you may rest."

Liora's head tipped to the side. What was this excessive concern for their rest? What was she not seeing?

"There you go again, being terrible at deceit." Nergal leaned a shoulder against the mural, dislodging more plaster. He folded his arms over his chest and shook his head in disappointment. "If this is what you call practicing deception, I suggest another approach."

Clearly, the prince saw what Liora did not.

Nebuzaradan's thumb unhooked to let his arm hang. His posture straightened, but he stared at Nergal another beat before responding, tone impassive. "If I may, which part of what I said do you perceive as a deception?"

Chuckling, Nergal pushed off the wall. "The unspoken part." He crossed to the cup and bent to pick it out of a mess of white cosmetic powders. Dusting it off with his sleeve, he spun back to Nebuzaradan. "What do you *really* want, Butcher?"

Nebuzaradan blinked, then gave a conceding nod. "If it pleases Your Highness, allow Lady Liora to return home for the night, so my men might investigate unrestricted. Sleeping in this place of violence is much to ask of a lady who suffers distress from what she has witnessed."

Eyebrows on a slow rise, Nergal assessed Liora from top to bottom. "I see no evidence of distress. But...very well, Butcher. To spare her the maid's interrogation on the concubine's murder, she may return to her home."

Nebuzaradan dipped into a bow, but he stilled when Liora neared.

"My gratitude, Your Highness." She curtsied. "For your leave to enjoy the comfort of my home. But Mehetabel was not murdered. She took her own life."

The men exchanged a questioning glance, and from the side of Liora's eye, Gittel slumped.

Before any could question her further, Liora went on. "Mehetabel had been despicably used. She was a broken woman with no hope of any respectable future. That, assuming King Nebuchadnezzar allowed her to live. I also suspect..." Liora paused, uncertain whether she should risk completing the trail of her logic.

"Finish," Prince Nergal said, removing the option. "What else do you suspect?"

"That she understood your threat to feed her to Ashara and, believing herself worthless and Your Highness capable, chose her own end."

Nebuzaradan's head jerked back, but the prince's mouth skidded to the side as though he'd expected just such a revelation. "If so, she was not wrong. Although...in this instance, I spoke in jest." His gaze drifted off Liora to form an expression she dared not call remorseful. In the next instant, he shrugged. "One less trouble for our king to attend. If you are certain, Lady Liora, I will call this matter settled. Consider carefully that His Majesty might question you on it." He showed her an arched brow.

Liora spared a moment to glance at the doorway where an after-image of the concubine stood gazing at the sky, as if longing to fly away. "Mehetabel was gone before I ever stepped into this room," she said, voice as dead as the corpse in the valley.

Finally, that weariness Nebuzaradan predicted came over Liora. Her shoulders fell with the weight of it as she nodded. "I am certain." On that affirmation, she brought her attention back to the prince.

He gazed out the open door, eyes haunted. From somewhere in the residence, Ashara roared. Nergal stared on, unmoving, but flinched when Liora spoke.

"Rest well, Your Highness."

CHAPTER 15

In that I command thee this day to love the Lord thy God, to walk in his ways, and to keep his commandments and his statutes and his judgments, that thou mayest live and multiply: and the Lord thy God shall bless thee in the land whither thou goest to possess it. But if thine heart turn away, so that thou wilt not hear, but shalt be drawn away, and worship other gods, and serve them; I denounce unto you this day, that ye shall surely perish. (Deut. 30:16–18a)

Liora did *not* rest well, but she did rest. Unlike Captain Idadu, who'd rushed to her side the moment she stepped foot outside the prince's residence. He'd then sworn to keep watch by her door while she slept.

And unlike Nebuzaradan, whose tread clomped down the corridor at a predawn hour.

She bolted upright in bed, the blanket held at the base of her throat, right over her tripping pulse.

The rumble of his voice, though low, penetrated the closed door and the chillingly silent night. "The lady is in?"

Idadu responded in a murmur.

"She is well? Sleeping?"

Whatever Idadu said next extracted a heavy sigh from the general. Moments slogged past before he spoke again, slow and dim. "Have you ever wished, Captain, that you were not a man of honor?"

The blanket slipped from Liora's fingers to puddle on her lap. Nebuzaradan thought himself a man of honor? In what capacity?

Toward his rulers, certainly. To her knowledge, none could find fault in his loyalty. He carried out his king's commands with flawless diligence, but he did so unconcerned with those he hacked down in the process. Liora herself might have been among the dead if Yahweh had not seen fit to send her into the general's camp. The destruction the man wrought was without compare.

A man of honor?

What kind of honor did a general such as the Butcher believe in? His own twisted sense of justice? Certainly not purity or righteousness—her own notion of the concept, taken from the Holy Scriptures.

His idea of it, perhaps, involved obedience to vows and to bloody rulers, to meting out punishment until his inferiors quaked in fear. Liora understood that fear, having been driven to her knees before the general's volatile anger once before. No, Nebuzaradan did not have the sort of honor her abba raised her to seek in a husband. And yet...

The question he'd posed said something about him—that honor was important. Even if his perception of it was as contrary to hers as a dove's coo to the whistle of a falling axe.

Idadu made no verbal reply, and Nebuzaradan remained unspeaking for so long, Liora wondered whether he'd taken up guard duty with his captain. At last, he said, "When she wakes, she may find me in her former bedchamber."

Liora frowned at the night-black door. What of Saba Jeremiah? Would her husband wrench the elder from his sleep and steal his bed?

For three heartbeats, she considered jumping from the bed to object. On the next, it occurred to her a midnight chat with the prophet might be his truest aim.

Unwilling to interfere with that possibility, she eased back down to the pillow, turned to face the door, and tried to expel her concern for her future as his wife. Or rather...concubine? The shock she'd heard as Nebuzaradan read the king's missive replayed endlessly in her memory. What news could make the Butcher of Babylon catch his breath? Anger over being denied permission to set aside his unfaithful wife, certainly. A likelihood that boded ill for any peaceful existence Liora might have hoped for in Babylon.

An age trailed past before she closed her eyes again. But even there, behind closed lids, his worried gaze flashed intermittently with that splash of red framing Mehetabel's blond head.

She dozed some before female voices floated down the hall, Jeremiah's gruff intonations among them. But the sound that coaxed Liora fully into the day was the flurry of flapping wings in the doves' morning rituals. Her mind flew straight to the temple where her soul dropped again to its knees, partly in worshipful awe, mostly in grief.

A FAITH UNTAMED

Yahweh's glory had, inconceivably, departed the temple, leaving the building to the whims of pagans. Did He not care what became of the ark and the sacred items within? Granted, without His holy presence, the ark's value amounted to a chest of wood prettied with gold. The Tablets of the Law inside were but a stone memorial. They could turn to dust and God's law would remain.

Your word is true from the beginning, Liora prayed, then finished the psalm as she rose from her bed. "Every one of your righteous judgments endures forever." She repeated it as she splashed water on her face and again as she strapped on her closed-toe sandals and donned her thickest linen robe against the chill air.

The psalm carried her through the house, past Devorah's urgings to break her fast, and into her old bedchamber. The only occupant, the sunlight that brightened the space and made her paints glow in invitation. Shutters open wide, the cheery window invited her to the painting table standing beneath it.

In the middle of the clutter of brushes, paint pots, and dirty rags sat the plate she'd begun for Zipporah and the baby she'd sworn grew within her. Unfinished, its poppy red verse of scripture danced down its white center. Liora hadn't touched it since Nebuzaradan interrupted her work days before.

Where *was* the man? The bed appeared untouched, its woven blanket folded and resting at the foot. Either no one had slept there, or Devorah had already been in to tidy up. Jeremiah, too, was absent, his cloak missing from its hook on the wall. If Nebuzaradan banished him for whatever reason, Liora would be setting him straight before the hour was up.

Of course, the prophet might have gone into the city to preach. King Zedekiah's threatening presence had never stopped him. She doubted Prince Nergal's would.

Thought of the prince led to thought of the ark's removal, which led to thought of its preservation—all of which sapped her mental strength. She pulled the chair out from the table and dropped into it, telling herself that keeping the covenant ark out of Babylon's clutches was not her responsibility. Who was she but a woman with grand illusions of service to Yahweh? Wife to the Butcher. Pawn to a prince. Stripped of every right and little better than a vassal to both. And still...her heart wept and yearned and could not let go.

The Lord might have withdrawn His glory, as prophesied—turned His face from the wickedness unfolding in His house—but He would not shield Himself forever. That, too, the prophet Ezekiel foretold. When souls repented and righteousness returned, so too would the Shekinah.

Was it not left to the faithful to ensure that when that blessed day arrived, the holy vessels would be in their proper places? A sign of His enduring faithfulness. If the people saw Yahweh had not cast away His ark, they might more readily believe He had not cast them away either.

Seventy, the number of years Jeremiah prophesied would pass before the remnant would return from

A FAITH UNTAMED

Babylon and Judah would be restored. By then, Liora would likely be dust in her tomb. "But can I not play a part, Lord?" she asked the strip of sky beyond the window. Its blue shone rare and beautiful. A gift.

"What has you smiling this morning, my friend?" Zipporah's arms came around her from behind for a tight embrace. She propped her chin on Liora's shoulder. "Could it have to do with the fact I have yet to see my monthly?"

"That was it. My very thought." Liora leaned her head into her friend's and rocked side to side, making her knife in its sheath tap at her hip. "How do you feel?"

"Wonderful. The blessings of a sated stomach. And"—the click of teeth sounded in Liora's ear—"my molars are no longer loose."

Liora laughed and pulled away to twist and view her friend full on. "You look wonderful. Cheeks rosy and plump again. And there's a certain shine to your eyes."

Grinning, Zipporah straightened and laid her fingers over the pink patches. "That would be...Chesed's doing. He is quite the—"

"Agh! Say no more. I beg you." Liora plugged her ears and sang "La-la-la-la-la!" until Zipporah bubbled a laugh. A charming sound, both for its source and its purity.

Liora grinned at her, a prayer of thanks in her heart for this moment with her dear friend. How many more would they have? How long until their laughter ran out again? Nine days according to Prince Nergal. Then flames and chains and a months-long trek through the wilderness to a foreign land.

Now *there* was a sobering thought.

Silliness put away, Liora dropped her hands into her lap. "My abba, how is he?"

The smile faded a bit on Zipporah's face. "He misses you. But he is well. Your Nebuzaradan has supplied us with ample provisions. We want for nothing."

Ample? From where? The waning stores?

If so, when it came to her loved ones, Liora found it difficult to object. That Nebuzaradan had thought to provide for them at all...

Liora picked at a flaw in the chair's wooden back rest. "That is unexpected."

"Mm." Zipporah glanced behind her to peer back at Idadu standing guard in the hall. Though aware the captain spoke no Hebrew, she reduced her volume to a discrete level. "Even more unusual, he stopped in yesterday on his way to the banquet. To stalk into the home and glare, naturally." Zipporah snickered as if he were a stray cat instead of a lion with a dangerously heightened sense of *honor* where Liora was concerned. "I served him watered wine," Zipporah said, humor lightening her voice, "while he sat king-like on our sole cushion and terrorized your abba with his brooding silence."

Liora huffed. "The very man I know." Control by intimidation.

A FAITH UNTAMED

At times, with threatening silence. At times, with brutality. Of that, Šulmanu could speak at length. Thought of the missing guard twinged her heart.

She was devolving into new worry over him when Zipporah quipped, "You *would* know." Her eyes twinkled. She patted Liora's arm. "Your husband meant us no harm, Liora. Otherwise, Chesed would not have spent the hour regaling him with stories of your youth. Of your *pure and intrepid soul*, as he called it. On the chance praising you would endear him to the general." She rolled her eyes in a good-natured spirit. "As for myself, I believe Nebuzaradan came to personally see we are well. He understands what we are to you and, perhaps, decided to have a ready answer for the next time you asked how your abba fared."

Blinking, Liora stared at Zipporah, on the hunt for even a hint of jest. "That is...gracious of you."

Far more so than Liora whose first thought had been disparaging. But then, of the two, Zipporah had always been the type to offer her oil lamp to a stranger in the night, while Liora monitored them and weighed the risk of ambush.

"Is it?" Zipporah asked. "Or is it simply true?"

If it was, if Nebuzaradan had visited their home to put Liora's mind at ease, then the one being endeared would be Liora.

Conjecture.

Pure conjecture. She and her abba had just as much of a chance of being correct in their assumptions as

Zipporah. Better Liora not credit the man unduly. Her heart could not afford the charitable thoughts.

Unable to look her friend in the eye, Liora scored the wood with her fingernail and shrugged. "What is the point of caring one way or the other?"

Nebuzaradan would be who Nebuzaradan would be—their conqueror and the man who'd denied her a marriage ceremony before kin and Yahweh.

Zipporah grunted, quite unladylike, but restored her tenderness with a kiss placed on Liora's head. "Better to care, dear friend, than to live in misery. Or self-pity." She clicked her tongue in reproach. "You should eat." She didn't wait for a reply before leaving as quietly as she'd come.

Outside the window, the mourning doves began their love songs, and down the hall, the soft tap of Zipporah's tread was soon replaced with the general's clomp.

Liora sighed, uncertain whether the release of breath was from relief or dread. She stood, and hands clasped before her, waited for his commanding stride to carry him into the chamber. He ducked under the doorway. "Dismissed."

Idadu saluted smartly at his back and left them in privacy.

"My lord." Liora bent her knees in deference but wobbled out of the pose when Nebuzaradan strode on, coming in fast and close. She quick-stepped backward until the backs of her legs hit the chair, shoving it back under the table and rattling the pots.

A FAITH UNTAMED

Her head jutted back as he loomed over her, reaching around, grabbing for...the chair. Heat dashed up her neck. "P-pardon, my lord." She scuttled out of the way. "Please. Sit."

He did, his armored weight crashing to the seat. On a great breath, he leaned forward and scrubbed both hands over his face then through his hair. "Nergal's men will be arriving shortly to escort you through the city on his order."

"Nergal?" What happened to the prince's title? Had Ashara, the lioness, eaten it? Or perhaps Nebuzaradan's own waning respect had devoured it—assuming he'd ever had any to begin with.

"The prince," he replied, mistaking her question. "I tried in vain to provide my own men, those with whom you've become familiar. He would not hear of it, claiming those of the House of Axes were too *infatuated with the lady* to do a thorough job of it. Whatever that means," he added on a grumble.

"My thanks for trying. But I will fare well enough."

He jerked upright, eyes flashing. "I do not trust them, Liora. Not to control themselves. Not to protect you. And certainly not to care for anything other than garnering favor with their master. One whiff of betrayal to this task, and they will report you." He gripped her arm and pulled her close, their gazes level. His issued warnings chilled her blood and made her remember that moment at his feet with her forehead pressed to the carpet. "Whatever schemes you've got forming in that head of yours, *forget them*."

Her arm smarted where his fingers pinched. She wiggled, but he did not release her. "I— I have no schemes."

His eyes tightened on hers, fierce and penetrating, the one so white not a fleck of color shone through. After an uncomfortably long study, he said, "You disappoint me, dove. I did not believe you capable of deceit."

"N-no. I do not lie to you."

"Then why do you stammer?"

"Because you startled me! And what became of your vow?" She tugged against his hold.

Blinking, he released her.

She rubbed the spot and took a moment to smooth the stutter from her delivery. "I have no schemes, Arioch." Not a single one. Not yet. She raised her chin. "But when I do, I will rely on the Lord of Hosts to protect me, not you."

Nebuzaradan stared at her, lips parted. Then leaned back and laughed. He carried on until the leather joints of his armor squeaked. "Not capable of deceit, indeed!"

Huffing, Liora backed up a pace, folded her arms, and watched.

He laughed on, an arm wrapped about his shaking stomach. Tears coursed into his whiskers, but it wasn't until he bowed over and groaned his laughter to death that it occurred to her he was no longer amused. He groaned again and rested his head in his hands, elbows propped on his knees.

A FAITH UNTAMED

"Arioch? Are you well?" When he groaned again and shuddered, she reached out a tentative hand and rested it on the fingers he'd threaded through the mussed coils of his hair. "You asked for the truth. Does my honesty so disturb you?"

"I cannot protect you from him." The downward angle of his head muffled his voice but could not dim the bitterness of it.

The intensity of the emotion took her aback, almost frightened her. Liora had always found fault in his mindless, unadulterated devotion to the House of Nebuchadnezzar. But if a man who controlled the armies went down the path of bitterness, she feared where it might lead.

And wasn't his worry premature? Perhaps even unfounded.

She stroked down the length of his fingers until she had a light grip on the thick bones of his wrist. "Will there be a need for that? From what I understand, Prince Nergal hasn't the authority to—"

He stood so fast, she skipped back a step, then cranked her neck to meet the fear peering down at her. "Not *him*," he said on a strident whisper.

"Then who? The king?"

His gaze darted out the window, as if checking for eavesdroppers, and back to land on the plate she'd painted. Swearing softly, he plucked the veil from her head and dropped it onto the plate's surface, hiding the Scripture. Bearing his teeth, he pointed at the blue bundle of fabric. "Him."

Understanding seeped through her more slowly than Nebuzaradan apparently had the patience for. With another leery glance at the plate, he paced off, then back, his lips curling in a snarl directed at the window. At the sky beyond?

"Elohim," Liora breathed The Name, garnering a grunt from her agitated husband. "Do you believe covering words on a plate, as holy as they are, might hide you from His presence? Have you heard nothing I have said?" She wrenched the fabric from the plate. "Yahweh cannot be *contained*. He is all-seeing, all-hearing."

Nebuzaradan spun back around, fury scored into his hardened features. "Then let him hear! May he know I am no fool. I see his plans for his most faithful daughter."

Now, that could not be true. "What is this anger, Arioch?" Her eyebrows flew up. "Did Jeremiah tell you something? Where is he?" She whipped the veil toward his vacant corner of the chamber. "Did you send him away too? After he told you something unpleasant?"

"The god of Judah will kill you, Liora! He will use you and slay you for thanks!" He snapped the covering from her grasp and ripped it in two. The pieces fluttered to the floor.

Staring at the veil's tattered edges, Liora nodded, her voice as sluggish as her nod. "Possibly, yes. Or He could close the lion's mouth and deliver me from destruction." He'd handled foreign royals before, and quite expertly. Had Nebuzaradan so soon forgotten how efficiently the Lord of Hosts dispatched Pharaoh's chariots? Sennacherib's armies? Compared to those swarms of locusts, Nebuzaradan's spoiled prince was a grasshopper crawling about on the nose.

"Such *risk* you take. And for what?" He stalked across the small chamber, petulant in the pound of his stride, and flung an arm at the plate. "For a god who has abandoned you!"

Liora choked out an incredulous laugh. "Which is it, Nebuzaradan? Has he abandoned me, or does He use me? It cannot be both ways."

His chest heaved with gusts of breath, increasing in frequency even as his volume lowered. "I felt the wind of his passing, Liora."

"And I heard it." The memory of those wings so vivid in her ears, she suspected it might be embedded forever. Might forever weaken her legs, tempt her knees to bend. She gripped the table's edge and met Nebuzaradan's hushed tone. "So then, Arioch, what is there to bother you? If He is gone, as you say?"

"Because...I cannot... I cannot be certain. Can a god capable of this"—he jabbed his index finger toward his white eye—"be truly gone? If He is the creator of *all*, as your holy writings claim, He could be..." Another glance out the window finished his unspoken thought.

"Anywhere? Everywhere?" Liora couldn't help the little smile, completely unrepentant. Even while facing the Butcher's scowl. "You have been in court, High General, so tell me—when a king rises off his throne, does he cease to be king? When he walks from the audience hall where supplicants make their requests, does he resign his kingdom?"

Nebuzaradan's derisive snort couldn't halt the flurry of questions.

"When a king is betrayed, and the enemy invades, storms the palace, does a good king abandon his people, or does he withdraw, seek out the faithful, and regroup?" She went to him and, reaching over his folded arms, cupped his bearded cheek. Undeterred by the grinding of his teeth or the stare he directed over her head.

"You are a man of vows, so tell me this, too. If a God makes a vow of blessing and protection for listening to His voice and keeping His commandments, should He keep it?"

"What a question!" As He spoke, His beard scratched the sensitive skin of her palm. "A vow is not a vow if it is broken."

"And if he makes another vow that He will remove that blessing and protection should His people turn their backs and betray Him, should He keep that one, as well?"

He rolled his eyes high, his patience thin enough to see through.

She had heartbeats, at best, to reach him. "It is written in the Book of the Law, 'I command thee this day to love the Lord thy God, to walk in his ways, and to keep his commandments and his statutes and his judgments, that you may live and multiply. And the Lord your God shall bless you. But if your heart turns away and is drawn to worship other gods and to serve them, you will surely perish.'"

A FAITH UNTAMED

His lashes beat twice fast, the muscle of his jaw softening beneath her touch.

Encouraged, she rushed on. "In Mehetabel's chamber, did you see the shrine to Asherah? What of the altars to Molech in the groves and high places outside the city? What of the shrine your king dedicated to Nabû last he was in Jerusalem? The same shrine *my people* worship at? Each an evidence of hearts drawn away in false worship. Look at me!" She gripped his whiskers on both cheeks.

Startled, he allowed her to redirect the haughty tilt of his chin so his face angled down at her. His arms loosened and fell, opening himself to her more fully.

"Yahweh has done no more than keep His vow, Arioch! And He has not *gone*. He has merely turned his holy face from the wickedness and betrayal while sending *servants*"—she pounded his chest with a flat palm—"to separate the goats from the sheep. At the same time, He gathers the faithful to preserve them."

"In Babylon?" His sneer obliterated the grain of vulnerability. "The land of your enemy?"

"Yes!" Not ideal. But just as the Lord guided His children from Egypt, He would one day guide them from Babylon. "And in that land, we will worship and grow in number and faith until our return."

One black eyebrow curved up, stretching his scar. "Should I be concerned?"

Stepping back, she waved that off. "Not in *our* time. That of our children or grandchildren."

That eyebrow had yet to descend, though his sight slid sideways to the bed.

Heat bloomed in Liora's chest. She hadn't meant to send his thoughts *there*.

He stepped around her to tap a fingernail on the plate's edge, likely recalling she'd painted it for the child Zipporah carried. "But will you give me children, dove?"

She might have expected such a question to carry a tease or a lascivious grin. Instead, it fell flat, devoid of emotion. Almost as if he held no hope of such an eventuality. Did he believe her incapable of bearing children? Unwilling?

"I would like children. Very much. As many as, well, as Yahweh wills."

"Always Yahweh's will." There it was again, that bitterness. He twisted to pin her with a demand. "What of my king's will?"

Her mind dashed back to that royal scroll case and the general's angry hiss of shock. "He denied your request to put away your wife, Aralu." No sense asking when she was certain of the answer.

A low, dry laugh emerged from him on a crackle of heat. "My dove is astute. What else do you perceive?"

Her brow tightened. There was more? "That...he has tied you to him through his sister." Political maneuvering through marriage was common in court. A ruler with a keen understanding of his general's strict adherence to oaths would be wise to use it to his full advantage.

"His *dearest sister*. Aralu, the faithless snake." His lip curled with disgust. "Only death will separate me from her. Preferably hers."

A FAITH UNTAMED

"Arioch." Further reprimand was on Liora's lips, but before she could voice it, Idadu marched down the corridor.

"My lord general." The captain saluted curtly in the doorway. "The prince's escort approaches. Shall I take the lady to them?"

Nebuzaradan sank into a glower. "Better you than I."

Rummaging for a smile, Liora squeezed his hard knuckles where they clutched his axe's head. "The king's heart is in the hand of the Lord. How much more that of a city humbled by His rebuke? Do not fear for me, General."

He grunted. "Impossible."

"Try." Another squeeze of the knuckles, then she left him for the basket at the bed's foot and chose a new head covering. She was draping it over her hair and walking toward Idadu when Nebuzaradan called her name. She halted and glanced back. "My lord?"

His gaze dropped. "There is an important matter we must discuss upon your return."

"Regarding my father's banishment?"

"No."

"The prophet's?"

He huffed. "I granted the prophet leave to enter the city for some *godly* task or other." He swatted at the air. "After, he will travel to his village."

"Anathoth?" Her volume spiked. "In his condition?"

Nebuzaradan smirked. "Can Yahweh not imbue his messenger with strength?"

Not a terrible point. Liora quirked her lips at him to hide a smile. "The great general can be taught." Turning from his affected frown, she swept out of the chamber. "And if Yahweh wishes it, the prophet can fly!"

A sound suspiciously like a chuckle followed her down the passage, but her good humor was fast fading under the reminder of the task ahead: recruit righteous priests willing to transport the ark.

Devorah met her in the atrium as the courtyard gate swung open to Nergal's guards. She twisted her hands. "They have come for you, child."

A stern-faced soldier stepped into the courtyard. He wore the purple-trimmed black tunic of the royal guard. A younger fellow, bald beneath his black turban, accompanied him.

A two-man escort?

Nebuzaradan would be furious. And for sound reason. Better she went alone than make herself a target with an escort nearly powerless to protect.

"So they have." Liora embraced the handmaid, the grip of her arms tight enough to surprise even her. The general's fear of the streets must have gotten to her. Or was it that *matter* he'd alluded to?

"There, there," Devorah stroked her back and attempted a laugh. "The priests do not bite."

No. But the Lord's wrath did. And what if, in her desperation to preserve His sacred vessel, she acted outside His will and crossed a forbidden line?

"Pray for me, Devorah," she said, hating the quiver in her voice.

A FAITH UNTAMED

As she pulled away and stepped toward the guards, the roar of the lioness ripped across the city and merged with distant thunder.

CHAPTER 16

When he uttereth his voice, there is a multitude of waters in the heavens, and he causeth the vapours to ascend from the ends of the earth; he maketh lightnings with rain, and bringeth forth the wind out of his treasures.
(Jer. 10:13)

A strange, hot wind twisted Liora's tunic about her ankles as she scurried to reach her first destination, the temporary home where Priest Buzi and his son sheltered as the city awaited deportation.

The guards flanked her, their gazes flashing intermittently toward the dark clouds amassing on the horizon. The captain swore and hurried them along. "I do not like the weather's looks, Rim-sin."

"Nor I, Captain," the subordinate said.

Liora agreed. The sky had been a beautiful, striking blue. Then it had not.

Signs and wonders were the arena of prophets, but the encroaching weather had the feel of a warning.

Or a wrathful God.

And sometimes, a storm was just a storm.

She picked up her pace, eager to bring the matter before an anointed man of God. "What would you have me do, Lord?" she said in Hebrew, unconcerned her guards would understand her whispered prayers.

A FAITH UNTAMED

Thunder rolled, and Ashara screamed, as agitated as Liora.

Face tipped up, she eyed the billowing black clouds and blinked at the cold splash of a raindrop on her cheek. *Do you speak through the heavens, Lord God?* "Would you have me walk the ark into Babylonia without a protest?" As ludicrous a notion as the first time she'd considered it. "But is that your will?" The question slowed her steps.

The senior guard stopped two strides ahead and looked back, impatience in his aspect. "What is it? What have you been muttering about?"

She set back into motion, relieved they approached the last turn before arriving. "Prayers to my God. Nothing that concerns you, Captain."

"Ah, yes. The invisible God of Judah." In the loud wind, Rim-sin's snort lost some of its derisive effect. "The easiest we have conquered yet."

"Shut up, you fool." The captain smacked the man's helmet. "You speak of the god who blinded the Butcher."

"At last, a little wisdom from Babylon." This time, Liora's mutters *did* concern him.

She skirted the officer and jogged the remaining steps around the street corner. A gust of howling wind smacked her hard in the face. She barely caught her flying veil. It trailed her like a brown flag as she counted doors.

The first two were nothing but tattered slats leading to dark interiors. Third down on the right, she banged her fist against the intact wood. "Moreh Buzi! It is I, Liora! I have come with—"

The door opened wide. Priest Eitan stood in the narrow entry. "Shalom to you." The scowl on his bearded face contradicted the peace he'd wished upon his visitors. "We were expecting your arrival. Do enter."

"And shalom to you, Priest Eitan." She wasted no time stepping past him in the narrow space.

The guards crowded in behind her.

Spluttering, Eitan stumbled against the wall. "What are they—"

"Move or be moved, Jew." The captain angled sideways to make room for his armored shoulders. Or to give better access to the sword pommel he gripped.

"Let them pass, Eitan." She waved the guards inside, not that they'd slowed their forward push. "They cannot stay outdoors. A storm approaches."

"In case you were unaware, young woman, the *storm* arrived some time ago." Eitan avoided eye contact with the Babylonians as he squeezed past them to lead the party. He jerked his turbaned head. "This way."

Liora hesitated in the entry. "My lord captain..."

"What now?"

She met his demanding eyes. "Only Hebrew will be spoken in this home, Captain. Nothing you will understand. And the priests will be more comfortable planning the ark's removal if you remain out of sight."

A FAITH UNTAMED

Shuffling with impatience, the captain removed his helmet and used his sleeve to wipe rainwater from his face. "See that they hurry."

"You have my thanks." She bowed her head and followed Eitan into a small, windowless chamber where no less than five priests and her Saba Jeremiah stood in silence. "Saba!"

He held out his arms to her, and she rushed into them without a thought. Inside his embrace, she released a sigh. She would have lingered, but they hadn't the time. And questions cluttered her mind. She pulled back and took in the tears shining on his weathered cheeks.

"I thought you had left for Anathoth!"

Smiling, he patted her cheek. "And abandon the brightest light in Jerusalem to these thick-skulled old crows?"

Her saba might have been speaking of the ark. Just the same, she ducked her head. Brown strands fell to sway before her downcast sight, reminding her of her uncovered head.

"Bah! Who is the old crow?" Priest Buzi came up behind her saba, footwear scuffing the hard-packed dirt. "I take offense, Elder Jeremiah."

Saba Jeremiah shared a secret smile with her as she rearranged her head covering, then turned to Buzi. "Take it up with the Almighty. It is He who robbed me of sleep as He impressed an urgency upon me."

Liora used the end of her covering to dab at the wet on the elder's cheek. "And what urgency is that, Saba?"

"To recruit the ark bearers, of course." He swept an upturned hand toward the small congregation. "The Lord, He is ever the God of Israel."

Liora's dabbing motions froze, her voice small from emotion when she said, "You gathered the bearers for me?"

She and Jeremiah had exchanged brief words the night before when she'd arrived from the banquet weepy and exhausted. Never in her sweetest dreams would she have expected the ailing prophet to take it upon himself to organize the ark's transport. Tears might be threatening, but she would not complain.

Neither would the prince. He had tasked her with the effort, but he hadn't said she must do it alone. And how comforting to have a loved one at her side for such momentous business.

She gripped his hands and peered at the tear-streaked faces of those behind him. "And you have all agreed?"

"The storm rolls in, child." Priest Buzi raised a finger in a teacherly pose. "As my Ezekiel saw—clouds, fire, and the glory of the Lord! We are honored to labor for Him. And to die for him, if we must."

"If the Almighty has called you to this task, He will surely not *smite* you for it," Liora said, aghast.

Saba Jeremiah squeezed her fingers. "They are true men of our just God and will follow wherever He leads."

~~~

The next hour passed in a flurry of plans and bursts of thunder. Purification rites were planned, the bearers anointed, the location of the poles confirmed. No hand would defile the holy vessel.

Liora waited in the entry with the captain and his subordinate. Whether awed by the priests' somber tones or unnerved by the storm, both were inordinately silent. Almost reverent. When the storm died, Saba Jeremiah announced he must be on his way to Anathoth. In the confines of the entry, the captain left ahead of Jeremiah and joined Rim-sin in the soggy outdoors.

Liora walked her saba down the street, surprised when the guards didn't call her back. How far would they let her go? She clung to Saba Jeremiah's arm until they reached the first turn.

He peeled her off him, chuckling. "We will see one another again, child."

Would they? Anathoth was a great distance for an elder with a staff. And Liora was due to be crushed.

Heart pounding in her throat, she said none of this to the man of God, only kissed his white-whiskered cheek and thanked him for delaying his journey to help her.

Shrugging, she spoke through a painful knot. "I would go with you farther but..." A glance back at the captain standing in the lane finished the statement for her.

The man had fixed his attention elsewhere, but if she vanished, he would be on her before the pigeons sheltering in the eaves could take flight.

"Your burden is here in the city." Saba Jeremiah's smile rose too sad for her comfort, and that word—burden—settled like an ember in the chest.

She pressed the spot. "Does that burden not include preserving the ark? I had so thought it did! I am in a unique position of influence. Surely, the Lord can use me to...to...do *something*. Mustn't we have faith God can do anything to preserve the ark, to work a miracle, even?"

"Is it faith you have," the prophet came right back at her, voice stern, "or something less noble?"

She recoiled. What did he accuse her of? Her instinct was to deny any sin of the heart. No, her pride urged denial. If the messenger of God rebuked, she must listen. Though it burned, she plunged her chin.

"Do not confuse the covenant ark with the covenant itself," he continued, no longer her saba, but the preacher. "Without the Shekinah, the ark is merely an earthly symbol, but the Lord of Hosts is not earthly. He is far above arks and temples and cities. And His covenant, His Words will endure forever."

A message shamefully like the one she'd given Nebuzaradan. Repeatedly.

Still, she voiced the question that had been pestering only an hour before. "Does He truly mean for us to carry the covenant ark into Babylon?"

"He has seen fit to walk His sanctified people there, with more soon to join them. Why not His holiest vessel, too? In the days of Moses, he rescued our ancestors from Egypt, reducing the great city and its chariot army to drowned splinters. And in seventy years?"

At his pause, she supplied, "He will do it again."

"May He be praised forever, *omain*!"

"Omain." She repeated the amen but fidgeted with the tassels of her sash.

"If you believe it, why do you limit His power and elevate your own in believing you must interfere?"

Indeed, who was she to carve the Almighty's path for Him? How did He even bear to look on her arrogance? And she'd accused the Butcher of pride...

"What of the symbol, you ask? I ask, what of the *souls*?" Jeremiah stamped his staff into the dirt.

Flinching, Liora took the chastisements like a willow switch to the back of the thighs. Had she been so wrapped up in the ark that she'd lost sight of those around her?

How thoroughly you reproach me, Lord.

"Concern yourself with Gittel and Sapir, your missing guard and your arrogant general." Jeremiah laid a cold hand along her cheek. "Let the Lord concern Himself with His sacred vessel."

Reach Gittel's stone heart? And Šulmanu... How long since she'd prayed for the man, wondered at his safety? She could not raise her head.

Forgive me, Lord God. Cleanse me of pride.

"Be of great courage, my child."

For what? She dearly wished to ask, yet could not bring herself to it.

The anemic nod and smile she formed were likely of little encouragement, so she brought one of his old sermons to her tongue. "In Yahweh's strength, I shall stand like a tree by the water that does not fear the heat." The words of the Lord as spoken by His prophet lifted her chin.

Jeremiah's eyes crinkled. "Just so." Then he was patting her cheek, walking away, and leaving her for Anathoth and whatever task the Lord had for him there.

"Take care, Saba," Liora called after him, her voice a croak of emotion. "The stones are slippery when wet!"

He raised his staff and waggled it in the air.

Sighing through fresh tears, Liora watched his hunched figure until he disappeared around the corner. Water dripped from overhanging roof tiles and hit on Liora's nose. She sniffed and wiped it clear, then turned to find the captain still standing alert, his gaze fast upon the shadows of an abandoned doorway. His hand moved toward his sheathed sword.

Liora's ears perked for danger, but the heavens' incessant grumbling obscured whatever noise might have drawn the captain's attention.

Priest Buzi stepped outside his dwelling, and the captain twisted toward him. Behind the officer, a scrawny rat ambled from the doorway and trotted brazenly up the street. The captain spun back. Swearing loud enough for Liora to catch his curse on every rodent, he rammed the sword home.

Oblivious, Buzi shook a finger at her. "What do you there, child? The prophet has gone, and the day follows fast. Come, come!" He scooped air toward himself in a broad wave. "Your Akkadian is much in demand. These brutes haven't a word of our blessed tongue!"

Liora spent the next short while under the rumbling sky translating, explaining, helping to straighten out the particulars of the day. After much fussing, many requests by the priests, and even more refusals by the captain, they settled on the entire party migrating to the temple. The priests *heartily* requested clearing the Lord's House of laborers so they could pray and prepare in peace. Whether they would succeed was a matter for His Royal Highness Prince Nergal.

"It is not for me to decide." The captain sliced an unyielding hand through the air.

The trek up the hill through the charred warrens was a challenge to Liora's sandals, their thin soles not equipped for the march. To say nothing of her stamina. The guard strode ahead, sights on a constant swivel, while behind her, Priest Buzi lagged. His son served as a crutch, but the elder still wheezed. The others struggled in a loose line between her and Buzi. They managed better, but none, not even Liora, were in any condition to keep up with the captain's brutal pace.

Not that she wished to drag out their time in the streets. En route to the temple, the destroyed city offered passage through only a few streets. Even those were a maze of wreckage and tested the sturdiness of her ankles. Another peril, the corpses cluttering the way. The bones and rotting flesh forced the priests to raise the hems of their robes and pick their way carefully through. To touch them was to be defiled, and the restoration from that impurity would require days of separation and ritual washing.

Nothing to be done about the stench of death wafting from the gaping holes of ruined doorways but cover the nose and hurry along. Half of the cave-black homes they passed were no better than tombs. Jerusalem had long ago ceased carrying out their dead. Law prohibited burial inside the city walls, and what purpose was there in tombs when all would burn in short order?

A soul-wringing reminder of how far the Holy City had fallen. As was the eerily empty market square. Where life once thrived with food stalls, vendor carts, and the bleat of lambs, the dead now resided. Murmurs echoed off the stone. Ghosts of her memory? No, the voices of those unwilling to show themselves.

Ahead, several figures darted into the shadowy alcoves where buildings met, their walls coming together at odd angles. Avoiding the royal guard or...something else?

Prickles broke out across the back of Liora's neck, and the spitting clouds were not to blame. Lungs heaving, she picked up her gown and pace and left the square fast on the captain's heels. Her speed hitched when she realized tumbled buildings and blocked streets would compel their path through Pottery Row.

Really, Lord?

Why would He impose this street upon her? To remind her of...what? How He'd redeemed her broken life? Made something beautiful of it, then destroyed it all over again?

A FAITH UNTAMED

A bulge grew in her throat, but she forged ahead and entered Pottery Row with a prayer on her lips. *Open my eyes to what you wish me to see.*

The cramped lane had once belonged to the best potters' shops in the city, Liora's own shop *not* among them. What remained of Potter's House was in the Lower City. An almshouse for rejected women, she'd run the place with the love of a mother and the savvy of a merchant's daughter.

In it, Liora had found bottomless joy. Her abba donated funds, and Yahweh blessed. None of it mattered where Pottery Row was concerned. She'd been welcomed on the street at the precise weight of her coin purse. The weekly visit had been so consistently upsetting that Liora refused it to any other. She would have shunned the row altogether but for her need of pigments and glaze.

The lingering mineral scent of that pigment greeted her now. Shattered vessels littered the ground: handle-less cups, incense burners, a cracked plate with an idolatrous image, that of a winged sun disk split down the center. Revulsion burning her stomach, she stomped a bull-shaped figurine. Satisfaction curved her lips when the bull sank into mud. So much for Baal.

Above, thunder rolled across the sky. Wind funneled down the passage, having the vague sound of flapping wings.

I hear you, Elohim, Mighty Creator. And I see it.

The strength of pagan gods amounted to shattered clay.

What might Nebuzaradan see if he were at her side, peering with his one eye at the scattering of abandoned gods? The curiosity had Liora's every thought straining for home. Excitement grew in her breast. She would tell him of this, of how Marduk and his cohorts lay in the mud while the Lord of Hosts reminded her of His holy might.

A clatter, as of disturbed debris, jerked her thoughts from her husband. Her heart stopped, then took off at a sprint. The noise had come from deep within a shop's dark hollow.

The captain's head wrenched left, then back as pebbles fell onto the path ahead. More followed, rolling off a rooftop. He raised a halting fist. His sword rasped from its scabbard. "Rim-sin, to me. At once."

Within moments, the younger man trotted up, posture tight. He gripped his sword in one hand, a dagger in the other. "Here, Captain."

Their halt allowed the priests to catch up. Panting, they shuffled onto the lane and congregated near Liora, seeming grateful to catch their breath.

"We are not alone," the captain replied, voice a tense hush. His eyes flicked side to side, calculating. He spread his legs in a fighting stance.

Only then did Liora spot the figures crouching in doorways. Two left, one right. Another crept across a low roof, the outline of a blade held low at his side. Still two more materialized from behind a kiln.

Before Rim-sin could respond, several leaped down from low roofs ahead and behind.

A FAITH UNTAMED

Priest Buzi bleated in alarm. The other priests added their cries.

Liora's own voice stuck in her throat, her mind too busy assessing their attackers.

She was no expert in matters of battle and weaponry, but she knew a scrappy rebel band when she saw one. Armed with crude weapons, they stalked on swift feet, closing in before Liora could do more than trip over her own sandals.

She caught her balance, her head whipping about for a gap in the net they drew. Finding none, she edged closer to the captain, who'd gone back-to-back with Rim-sin.

He brandished his sword at the nearest leering rebel. "In the name of Babylon, stand down!"

The man was of a height that cranked the neck and a muscular breadth that rivaled Nebuzaradan's. His robust figure told tales of a life of sparring outside the walls. Most of the resistors had not suffered the ravages of the siege. This one wore the smug, bloodthirsty expression of a fighter aware he was one slash of his sword from victory.

He laughed, a low-pitched deadly sound, not a hitch in his deliberate stride. He hefted a long-handled hammer—a tool she'd seen applied to the temple walls. Now, as he tested its weight against his palm, he seemed keen to apply it to the guard's skull. Though by the gleam in his eyes, he'd be content to let the violence begin another way.

But surely these rebels hadn't come merely for revenge. They had a *cause*. Demands.

"Wait. *Wait.*" Her Hebrew warbled as she edged between the men, arms spread. "You are the Last Flame, yes? I speak their language. What do you want? I will tell him."

Behind her, the captain said, "These are not the speaking sort, my lady. Move before you are hurt."

As if in confirmation, the rebel snarled. "I am Keshet son of Hoshayah," he said in the deepest voice she'd ever heard, "and I will not trust a woman in league with Babylon."

Despite the sting, Liora marshaled her patience. "I am foremost a daughter of Jerusalem. And you, Keshet bar Hoshayah, are in opposition to Yahweh's will according to the prophets."

He sniffed, unimpressed, and swung his hammer in a wide arc.

"Easy, Liora," Eitan murmured from a few paces behind her. "They are here for the soldiers and have no cause to harm us."

"Listen to the priest and stand aside," Keshet said. "The time for words ended with Babylon's first arrow."

"Nonsense," she shot back. Judah's king had simply refused to listen. "Where is your leader? Is he not a man of reason? Bring out Ishmael."

Flattery. A man of reason would have seen the idiocy in serving his cousin Zedekiah, a weak-spined king who ignored the Law of Moses as given to them by the Lord God. But what other weapon did Liora have but her wits and her nimble tongue? If she wielded them properly, she might avoid bloodshed. "Let us reason together as the prophet Isaiah—"

A FAITH UNTAMED

"Reason?" The rebel rumbled a laugh. "Will you reason with Babylon's fires, too? Or with the disease they brought with their war machines and their siege berm?"

She certainly would not reason with this man. "Ishmael! Show yourself!" The call echoed through the street. "Where are you, Prince of Rebels?" And *where* were the thousand soldiers supposedly patrolling the city? Sheltering from the few drops of rain? "Have we no hope for backup?" She directed the Akkadian question behind her.

"Unlikely," the captain replied, voice grim. "There was a skirmish near the eastern gate. Forces were redirected there."

"No question why," Liora muttered.

"You must step away." The captain tapped her arm with the flat of his sword. "*Go.*"

"Enough!" Keshet jutted his chin at someone outside her view. "Get the priests out of here. And *you*, take the woman."

Several masked rebels herded the priests back the way they'd come. Another came at her.

"Liora!" Priest Eitan's voice rang through the street.

"Just go! I am under no threat." She waited only long enough to catch Eitan's nod before turning back to Keshet. "I can negotiate on your behalf." She held a trembling hand before her, as if she might block the swing of that hammer.

"Can you then? Very well. We shall negotiate." Lowering his hammer, the rebel grinned, showing broken teeth. "I have orders to let one of these Babylonian swine run off squealing to your Butcher. If you smile at me pretty enough, I will let you decide which. So, fallen *beauty of Jerusalem*, have you got a smile for me?"

Liora stared at him, dragging heavy breaths through her open mouth. She would not be giving this rebel anything, and she would certainly not decide the fate of any man. "That is... That is not a decent—"

"Move, woman!" The captain grabbed her by the arm and flung her aside.

She spun sideways and, stumbling, slammed into a man's chest. Before she could lift her face for a look at him, he seized her suffocatingly close.

"Hurry it up!" he said.

Neck at an awkward angle, she thrashed and tried to speak. Ribs aching, she couldn't expand her lungs for a breath or a question.

Someone from behind yanked off her head covering and shoved a gagging wad of fabric into her mouth. With a fierce yank, another cut the thong binding her knife to her sash. She kicked and spat, but harsh fingers held it in place. A moment later, he secured the gag with rope that burned her lips and pinched her scalp.

She loosed a muffled scream. The ring of weapons told her no rescue was coming from her escort.

Nebuzaradan.

Yes, he would come. Whether she lived or died, these men had summoned their deaths.

A FAITH UNTAMED

Pinned in place, Liora saw nothing but her captor's tunic until a dark fabric fell over head and cinched at the throat, turning the world black.

CHAPTER 17

One of the rebels bound Liora's hands behind her with a blood-pinching rope. Another flung her over his shoulder and took off. She thrashed and released a muffled scream.

He was too strong, his arm a binding clamp around her legs. His shoulder slammed into her gut with every jarring stride, jetting bile in a scorching path up her throat. He didn't seem to care she might vomit into her gag. A true possibility if he didn't stop running soon.

In moments, congestion filled her nose, clogging her only airway. Panic set it. Built. Another thrash had her nearly tipping off the man's shoulder.

Air. She must have air!

Eyes watering, she kicked against his hold, but he clamped down harder. She shifted focus to her hands and yanked furiously at the rope, heedless of the burn of ripping skin.

Breath eked into her lungs in snuffling gasps. Every flail increased the demand. Still, panic drove her on until strength bled from her muscles. Heartbeats later, she was down to twitches. Control all but gone, her chin hammered his hipbone with vision-blurring force. Her head drooped, then hung, jostled at the mercy of her captor's race through the streets.

Unconsciousness came in a series of waves. Her mind dimmed and blanked. A flash of pain in her ribs slapped her awake and forced a trickle of air into her aching lungs. Too soon, blackness returned, disrupted again when the world tipped—her captor swinging her down. He caught her in his arms and laid her on a cold surface, his hand cradling her lolling head.

Next she knew, he was smacking her cheek. The sting revived her enough to realize the gag was gone, her mouth now empty.

Her lungs spasmed to life. She sucked in a breath and, rolling onto her side, coughed a burn into her throat. Her ribs throbbed, and salty mucus coated her lips. Convulsing, she blinked watering eyes to assess her surroundings, but all her blurred vision gathered was the dim light of indoors.

The musty scent of old grain registered thick in her nose. Where had they brought her? Someplace old and forgotten.

Tense male voices filtered through her ringing ears. Someone laid a few stinging smacks to her back before manipulating her into a sitting position. Too focused on restocking her lungs and stilling her spinning head, she could not protest.

A brusque hand swatted a curtain of hair from her soaked eyes. "There you are. Not looking so fresh, but you will recover."

"This will wake her up," a woman said, then the man was wiping a wet cloth over Liora's face.

Fight returning, she gasped at the shock of cold and swiped an arm to bat him off. "S-stop." The command emerged weak and raspy.

"Unfortunately,"—he gripped the back of her head as she sat and shook—"we haven't the luxury of delicacy." He shoved the wet cloth into her shaking hand and shoved out of his crouch.

"She should be thankful she is alive." The woman's voice, droll and edged with bitterness, snapped Liora back into herself.

She cleaned the mucus running into her mouth and glimpsed Gittel's sharp-nosed profile before the woman spun away.

So. She'd joined up with the Last Flame.

Gittel, Gittel. What have you done?

After this, could there be hope for her? Saba Jeremiah would believe so.

And the priests huddled in the back, prayer shawls covering their heads and voices low? What would they say?

She blinked hard to clear the blur from her eyes. Little light reached the rear corner of the old granary, hampering her view. But the priests appeared unharmed. The Last Flame, it would appear, was not heathen enough to abuse the Lord's anointed.

"If she wants coddling," Gittel went on, "she can get it by the barrel from the Butcher." She returned with a cup in her grasp. Reaching Liora, she held it out, not a hint of pity on her harshly cut features.

"Shalom, Gittel," Liora said, hoarse. She took the cup, choosing to view the water as an offer of peace—probably the closest to humility Gittel would ever come.

The woman rolled her eyes and walked away, making room for another familiar face.

Water slid down Liora's throat as the rebel leader dropped to a squat beside her sprawled legs. She cleared film from her throat and set the cup on her

A FAITH UNTAMED

thigh. "Ishmael ben Nethaniah." She laid his name out between them like a proclamation of death.

"I heard you called for me." He grinned as if it were all a game—terrifying priests, kidnapping women, killing men. Or *man*, if the prince's captain meant what he'd said about leaving one of her guards alive.

"So I did." Assuming his flippant demeanor, she glanced about, taking in her surroundings as she did.

The place was a graveyard of mud-brick storage bins, some cracked, some cloaked in cobwebs. All blanketed in a thick layer of dust that dulled every color. Not a stray kernel of desiccated grain remained. Those would have been swept up and eaten long ago. A rusty hand sickle leaned against a dirt wall and a stack of reed winnowing baskets slumped beside the door where shafts of sunlight streamed through its wide-set slats.

In the chamber's center loomed a great stone gristmill. Its round base half-sunken into the ground, with a leaning beam and arm rising from its center. A torn tether still hung from the arm's end where a mule would've walked in endless circles.

The rear of the room vanished into shadow, no windows to break the gloom. In the dimness, the cluster of priests gathered near the back wall, huddled in prayer.

Where had Ishmael brought them? She rifled her memory for granaries near Pottery Row and came up with only one. They were near the temple mount.

Grimacing at the ache in her wrists and ribs, she leaned against the mill's cold stone and looked Ishmael square in his dark eyes. "You do realize General Nebuzaradan is going to find you."

"That is the hope." His grin skewed, begging her to inquire about his vague statement.

"And butcher you."

"A man must live up to his name." Ishmael shrugged but didn't quite disguise the flicker of uncertainty in his eyes.

She pressed into that fear, leaning toward him when she said, "When he mounts your head on a pike, would you like it to be with or without your turban? I am happy to let him know your preference."

Ishmael released a chesty laugh. "The Butcher's savagery has rubbed off on you, Lady Liora." He looked to Gittel and jabbed a thumb toward Liora. "And not a glimmer of shame on her anywhere."

"A false front." Gittel folded her arms over her thin chest and stared down at Liora, her head bared to the world. Had the Babylonians taken her modesty along with her conscience? "She is only a hissing kitten. Hoping her puffed fur will make her seem frightening."

As Ishmael studied Liora, he stroked his shaggy brown beard. "The woman survived our king, the Butcher, and Nergal-sharezer. Make no mistake. She is frightening." He broke out again in that devilish grin. "Which is why it pleases me so to have her on our side."

"What?" Liora blurted the word.

Forearms propped on his knees, he angled toward her in the manner of one sharing a secret. "And I thought having Gittel in the prince's house was a boon.

But *this*." He popped Liora on the arm as he might another fellow.

Liora stared at him, trying to recall anything she'd said or done to make him believe she'd joined his bloody cause. The threat of losing his head couldn't have been it. Concluding he was insane, she shifted her attention to Gittel. "*That* was why you left my home?" The woman's strange choices were beginning to make sense.

She was frowning at something beyond the mill Liora propped against. "And to get away from you." A snort bobbed her shoulders. "Now here you are, sickening me again with your sanctimonious... everything."

Liora's jaw eased open. Were they both insane? "That sanctimonious *everything* saved your life." Had Liora's intervention with the prince meant nothing to the woman? "Should I have been callous and cold-hearted and let you die for all the senseless hate you've shown me?"

"A smarter woman would have." Whatever Gittel glared at made noises of scratching and muted speech. A man, likely gagged as she'd been.

Liora sat up straight. "You have another hostage?"

Gittel flicked her an annoyed look before stomping to the other side of the mill. "You. Stop that!" The dull thud of a kick, followed by a groan, made Liora flinch.

The priests' muttered prayers hitched. As she gathered her feet under her, Eitan lowered his upturned hands, looked across the chamber's rear toward the noise, and frowned deeply.

"What have you done, Ishmael?" She used the mill to pull herself up, its stone frigid against her trembling hand.

"Only what is necessary to preserve what remains." He stood to give her room, his broad chest blocking her view of the other captive. All she saw were a man's curled limbs, his leg wrappings giving away his heritage.

"You have a Babylonian?" She circled Ishmael to see and stopped fast. "Šulmanu!"

The soldier lay on his side, facing her in a wide patch of red dirt. His knees were drawn close in a protective measure, and his hands were bound behind him. Shallow gashes covered his bare chest and arms, in the way of pagan priests calling down favor of their idols. Fresh blood oozed over caked blood, and deep bruising patched his abdomen.

Gittel stood over him, so close the tips of her sandals touched the black hair sprawled in the dirt around his head. Liora's own short blade protruded from her white-knuckled fist.

"Get away from him!" The earth tilted beneath Liora's feet. That didn't stop her from stumbling forward.

Ishmael caught her by the arm. "Easy. The lady said back away, Gittel. If he dies, he is no use to us."

Liora tugged against Ishmael's iron grip, and Šulmanu vocalized a long, pain-filled, *Mmph*.

As suspected, a tight gag opened his mouth wide and strained his lips. Snot streamed from his nose, and a purple contusion swelled his cheekbone. His head rested at an awkward angle, and his eyelids hung heavy, as if he fought to remain conscious. Even so, his eyes locked on her, hope and pleading rife in their depths. The prideful youth she'd nursed in the camp was nowhere about, and her heart twisted in her chest.

She held his gaze long enough to convey fury and determination and to note the tear forming at the inner crook of his lid.

Then his tight muscles eased and went lax. His lashes fell.

That fury shook her from the inside out. Only the slow movement of Šulmanu's ribs kept her from whirling on Ishmael.

Šulmanu lived. He *lived*.

Barely. And for some foul purpose.

A lump cramped her throat. The need for violence coursed through her veins. She would like to think it righteous indignation, but her conscience told her otherwise. This was hateful vengeance burning inside her, nothing less.

Maybe Ishmael was right. Maybe the Butcher's bloodthirsty ways were tainting her mind.

She squeezed her eyes shut to rid herself of the red hazing her sight. Vengeance belonged to Yahweh, and pitting Ishmael against her would probably thwart any effort she made to be free of him. Relaxing her stance, she pulled several deep breaths.

She must have been convincing because Ishmael released her.

He said, "I allowed Gittel to release pent rage on him last night. But when we took him from the Kenez, most of those marks were already on him."

And she was supposed to believe him? She rubbed the aching spot where he'd grasped her and forced calm into her voice. "Omar had him?"

"Then we had Omar. Now the Butcher does. And you have your soldier back."

She narrowed her eyes at him. "Do I?" He could have returned Šulmanu with Omar. This timing was deliberate. Why? She had yet to learn whatever plan had driven him to abduct a woman and a group of priests off the street. But for now, she cared only for Šulmanu.

He gestured magnanimously at the unconscious man. "We shall call him a second gift. Or a first threat, if you give us trouble." There it was, his true motive.

Liora refused to bite. She nudged him out of the way and strode resolutely toward Šulmanu.

"Liora, here." Hurried steps and a tap at her back paused her rush.

She twisted back to find Eitan holding a full cup.

He used it to indicate Šulmanu. "For him."

Liora blinked at the priest. From the start, he'd been nothing but abrupt. What were the odds the disturbing day had altered his perspective of her?

Before she could question him on it, he pressed the cup into her hand. "Show him Yahweh's tenderness. Come, I will help." He left her and crouched behind Šulmanu.

A FAITH UNTAMED

Too grateful for the help, Liora followed but veered off to confront Gittel. "Do you see the evil you have done?" She pointed at Šulmanu.

When Gittel's eyes flicked that way, Liora plucked her knife from the woman's grasp. "My thanks." Ignoring the woman's protests, she carried on toward Šulmanu. The leather of the blade's handle felt comforting against her palm—Nebuzaradan protecting her even in his absence.

Ishmael laughed. "I knew every effort to win you to our cause would be worth it. Any woman who walks away from a stoning and retains the fight to survive an enemy general has the spirit of a rebel."

I am no rebel! Liora caught the denial a second before it exploded from her mouth.

"We cannot let her have a knife." Gittel, with her balled hands and flashing eyes, looked ready to tackle Liora for the weapon.

"She has earned it." Ishmael propped his backside on the mill's top grinding stone and settled in to watch. "And look at her, Gittel. The woman is a healer, not a killer."

He would think otherwise if he'd had a peek inside Liora's mind. But yes, at present, she wished only to make Šulmanu more comfortable. She set the cup aside and, while Eitan worked on the gag's knot tangled with Šulmanu's hair, she carefully wedged the knife's dull tip under the rope at his torn wrists.

"Why did you bring me here, Ishmael?" She sawed in tiny strokes. "And what do you want with the priests?" Ishmael had to know the general would not be the only one coming after his rebel hide. Prince Nergal would not stand for his plan being thwarted. Every royal guard, common soldier, and man of the House of Axes would be scouring the area for them.

Judging by Ishmael's earlier comment, that was precisely what he wanted. But why?

The man did not make her wait long for the answer. "Our missions are aligned, my lady."

She peered at him from the tops of her eyes. "You seek to use my position in the general's company to aid our people in this difficult time?" A few rope fibers snapped, drawing her focus down.

"To prevent the ark from falling into Babylonian hands, of course. Gittel told me of your fierce determination to act on its behalf."

A rash and foolish determination. And more detrimental than she could have known. But she sensed this was not the time to reveal her altered stance on the matter.

The blade's edge tore through the last fibers, and the rope gave way. Šulmanu's arms released with an audible pop in the joints. He didn't stir.

"Turn him onto his back, Eitan." Liora eased Šulmanu's free arm across his chest. "Watch his other shoulder there. It might be out of socket."

Eitan manipulated him into a better position and eased him to the ground with surprising gentleness. He probed the joint. "Appears in place."

"Blessed are you, Lord." She massaged the guard's fingers in an effort to return blood to their blue tips. "What is your plan, Ishmael?"

A FAITH UNTAMED

Shaking his head, Eitan gave up on the rope securing the gag. "This is useless. The knot is too tight."

Liora passed him the knife. "With care."

"I am no brute," he snapped, already bending over Šulmanu, testing for any gap between rope and skin.

Her lips twitched, tempted to smile at the return of Eitan's blunt manner. It was almost comforting.

"The plan," Ishmael said, crossing his extended legs at the ankles, "is to lure the guards from the temple, to clear it for my men to get in and remove the ark. There is an entrance near to the tunnels under the city. The one accessed through the wine merchant's cellar. Bigvai was his name. A friendly sort. He would be honored to know the covenant ark found refuge in his home."

"Idiot," Eitan muttered under his breath. He finagled the blade under a space he found near Šulmanu's ear and set to work nipping at the rope one thread at a time.

"In short, you have sent your men on a mission of death." Liora sat back on her heels and gave Ishmael a drab look.

"What do you know of it, harlot?" Gittel paced on the chamber's opposite side, near the priests. She'd found another knife and taken it upon herself to guard the old men and, apparently, to prod at Liora's old wounds.

"Stay back, priest." The woman made good use of her flashing blade and her well-practiced glower to attempt corralling the elders.

They ignored her as one did a circling fly. Having finished their prayers, they watched Eitan and Liora work. Priest Buzi shuffled nearer, the tassels of his prayer shawl swaying with his hobbled steps. He blinked hard in the gloom. "My son, are you well?" His ancient voice wobbled and scratched. "Are you safe there by that heathen?" Sweat stood out on his forehead, and his breathing was labored. If this day did not kill the elder, worry for his son might.

Bent over Šulmanu, Eitan did not look up. "The soldier is unconscious, Abba."

"I meant the rebel."

Ishmael's eyebrows shot high.

Gittel laughed and pointed her knife at Ishmael. "The holy man has sketched your soul, noble leader. Should we be worried?"

"Yes," Liora said. "Do you truly believe Yahweh will bless your task when it opposes the one he gave the prophet and these priests? The men you have in place to remove the ark have not been sanctioned."

"You want a word from the prophet?" Ishmael shoved off the mill and swiveled toward Buzi. "The Shekinah has left the temple. Is that not so, priest? Your son, the prophet, predicted the occasion. Per my able informant,"—he indicated Gittel—"it has come to pass."

Occasion, he said, as if the Divine presence leaving the sanctuary were no more significant than threshing wheat, no more commonplace than shelling peas. Liora turned her gaze from the man, preferring Šulmanu's slack features. She stroked his bruised knuckles and longed for simpler days when she'd occupied Omar's tent and wondered whether the Butcher would keep her or kill her.

No, that wasn't entirely accurate. In that tent, she'd feared her death for an hour, perhaps two all told. Never a full day. From those first moments together, she'd known her life was safe from his infamous brutality. All it had taken was for his gaze to fall on her broken lip, then cast about for whom to hurt.

The man whose hand she now held had borne that punishment, deserved or otherwise. Let it not be said Omar the Kenez had a minah's worth of integrity in any matter, certainly not where saving his own skin was concerned. With the Butcher sharpening his axe, Omar would have been swift to find a man to blame for the infraction. Any man would do.

Once Šulmanu was up and bickering with her again over his bathing habits, she would question him more thoroughly. Later. After Nebuzaradan arrived, got his hands on Ishmael, and...and...

She squeezed her eyes shut to bar images of the blood he would demand for this. For all her bluff about heads on pikes, she was still a weak-stomached female and not the least apologetic for it.

Regardless of the bloodshed he would bring, thought of her husband squeezed her chest with longing. She'd never wanted his overbearing presence more than in that moment. The sooner he put an end to this idiocy the better. And the clearer she made her part of the rebellion, the safer from Prince Nergal she would be. She and her loved ones. A stew of fear and anger made it an effort to hold Šulmanu's fingers in a gentle grasp.

Eitan mirrored the sentiment, if his mutterings could be interpreted as anger rather than frustration over his slow progress. His abba, perhaps tempered by age and wisdom, skipped the anger and hung his head. Thin shoulders shaking, he covered his face and wept.

Ishmael, the unsympathetic bull, prodded the priest with questions until Buzi admitted the prophecy had unfolded as told. The Lord's glory had departed the temple. "As I thought!" Ishmael thrashed an arm high. "Until the Lord God blesses us again with His presence, the covenant ark is little better than a symbol. It is a torch without flame. But worth preserving for posterity, for the day Yahweh descends once again and lives among us."

Regrettably, Liora could not disagree with Ishmael, not in full. Saba Jeremiah had said the same.

That did not cancel the fact this approach, forceful and flat out violent, could not be in Yahweh's plan. Jeremiah hadn't told her what that was, exactly. But he had gathered these priests, blessed them, prayed over them, anointed their heads. For what? To huddle in a rotting granary and weep about their state while rebels invaded the Holy of Holies? Hardly.

But what could Liora do about it? Leave Šulmanu in his vulnerable condition and take on the rebels with a rusty sickle? Nebuzaradan would lock her away with a twenty-man squad of guards if he learned she even considered it. His pleasure in her "reckless and bold" nature had its limits. Just the same, Liora eyed the instrument. Pits gouged its curved blade, but it would incapacitate. With enough force. Grimacing, she turned her back to it.

"Almost, almost..." Eitan grimaced as he sawed at the fraying rope. Another moment of careful wiggling and the binding broke. He swiped his sleeve across his sweaty brow and sat back on his rump. "Done."

Liora patted his shoulder. "And not a nick to his cheek. He will thank you." She fished the stinking, wet gag from Šulmanu's mouth and tossed it aside. She dipped the bottom edge of her head covering into the cup and wiped the cracks on his dry lips. *When will the violence end, Lord? How long?* How many more men would she clean of blood before the day was through? "I agree with you, Ishmael. In part, at least. But why now? Why not before the walls fell?"

Ishmael threw his arms up. "Because my fool cousin, the king, would not act! Until he chose to flee, of course. Then he could not act fast enough." His upper lip curled. "And now he is fodder for another king's wrath."

Ishmael swiped the turban from his head and raked fingers through his oily hair. He exhaled so miserably, Liora almost pitied him. It could not have been easy following orders from such a ruler, and Liora knew from personal experience that Ishmael, much like Nebuzaradan, did not question his kin and king. He obeyed without objection, without hesitation. Even when those orders ruined an innocent woman's reputation, setting the stage for her stoning.

"With Zedekiah taken, along with his sons," Ishmael said, touching the crumpled turban to his chest, "it falls upon me as the next in the line of David to shepherd our people until the Lord's reappearance. That includes a sacred duty to ensure the ark's safety by any means."

Liora stared at him. Did he believe that slight bow and downward sweep of the lashes conveyed humility? How important and wise he must sound to his own ears. If Gittel wanted *sanctimonious*, there it was. But the woman was not listening. She was peering outside through a crack in the door.

To Liora, he sounded as ignorant as the Butcher, the pagan who believed Yahweh was limited to a landscape. "Who appointed you a priest of Israel?" she said in a voice of challenge. "Have you forgotten you are of the House of Judah, not Levi?"

Ishmael's eyes sparked. His shoulders squared, and his mouth opened on a sharp inhale.

Liora cut him off. "Ah, yes, you said the line of David. Were you anointed as king? Did I miss it while I was trapped inside the walls?" While Ishmael enjoyed freedom in the hills, he and his band of rebels.

Tensing, Ishmael took a menacing step toward her.

Eitan gripped her arm as if to yank her back.

"Keshet comes, my lord," Gittel said from her post, halting her leader. "There's a hurry about him."

Ishmael didn't turn but narrowed his eyes at Liora. "We have entered a new era of judges, of which I am the first. Like Samson before me, who wielded the jawbone of a donkey, I will slay a thousand Chaldeans!"

A FAITH UNTAMED

"In this scenario," Eitan said, tone droll, "are you the lust-addled judge or the dead donkey?"

A laugh blurted out of Liora, strikingly similar to Priest Buzi's.

The rebel-judge did not laugh. Nostrils wide, he clenched a fist and glared darts into Eitan. Perhaps not daring to strike a man of the Lord, he spun and strode for the door. He pressed an eye to one of the gaps. "Took him long enough."

Eitan, who hadn't released her elbow, hauled her close. "Promise me you will care for my abba," he whispered into her ear, his breath hot and harsh. "That you will take him with you to Babylon, reunite him with Ezekiel."

She pulled back to look into his wide, intense eyes. Was this why he'd volunteered his help with Šulmanu? Because he felt the urge to entrust his abba to her care? She glanced to where the elder now stood speaking in low tones with his fellow priests, then back to Ishmael. "Why?" she whispered. "Do you have something planned for—"

He yanked her arm and mouthed, *"Promise me."*

"Y-yes. If I am able." If the journey allowed. Babylonia was no small kingdom. "But where will you be?"

The door creaked open just as the skies opened for a downpour. Keshet squeezed his bulk and his hammer through the space. Had he been running ahead of the rain? Its arrival sounded through the thatching above, a muffled rattle of reeds. Sweat coated his face and patched the underarms of his tunic. He breathed hard, but he grinned. "They have entered the quarter." He spoke above the pound of rain. "A squad of ten wearing the Butcher's sigil. He leads the charge, and a charge it is. It won't take him long to enter the miller's square."

"Have they spread out?" Ishmael asked.

"Not last I saw. They come with purpose," he said with a pointed look at Liora, "straight as an arrow flies."

"All the better to encircle them."

Liora was on her feet before Ishmael finished speaking. "You've used me to lure the general?" And he'd come with only ten to his aid. So swiftly! Which made her wonder whether he'd had her followed, or had followed her himself...

The Butcher also came with his ruthlessness and his reputation, neither of which should be discounted as weapons themselves. She'd watched his own men cower before his disapproving glares. How much more his enemy? If these three were a reliable answer to that question, not much. Even Gittel sneered.

"Always assuming you're the center of every plot," the woman said, then nodded at the priests. "We have them too. The prince wants the ark, and he needs them for it."

Again, Liora could find no fault with the rebels' logic—Prince Nergal had his own orders to accomplish—apart from the small detail of the slaughter it invited.

"Or so you informed him." Whatever sting Gittel intended with that jab was absent.

A FAITH UNTAMED

Liora ignored her and addressed Keshet. "And when the soldiers arrive?"

"When they arrive,"—his grin skewed wicked as he drew a short sword from his belt—"they will discover we are not as paltry as they believe. We are a force to contend with, a people who will not be so easily subdued."

And there was the trouble. Though it went contrary to Judah's pride, subjection was precisely what the Lord intended for them. Even now, those in leadership could not conceive of it. Could not understand their predicament was meant to purge and correct.

"We fight the Lord's battle," he said, so vehement spittle dotted his beard.

The Lord's battle included ignoring His messenger? Taking priests hostage? Twisted logic. The man was all misguided passions.

She said, "You will die."

"Can you think of a nobler cause?" Keshet rotated his wrist to swing the hammer in threatening arcs. It whistled in the air.

"Ishmael ben Nethaniah!" Nebuzaradan's voice boomed from outside, clear even above the rain.

Every head in the mill swiveled toward the wind-shaken door.

"Fool cousin to a fool puppet king!" His roughly accented Hebrew cascaded goosebumps down Liora's arms. "I am General Nebuzaradan of great and glorious Babylon, and I am here for your head! Send it out now in the lady's care, and I might let her convince me to spare some of your men. Defy me, and your fool head will be the last part of you I remove!"

CHAPTER 18

And I will make thee unto this people a fenced brasen wall: and they shall fight against thee, but they shall not prevail against thee: for I am with thee to save thee and to deliver thee, saith the Lord.
(Jer. 15:20)

"The Butcher speaks our language?" Eitan stared at the door. His question overlapped with last strains of the ultimatum Nebuzaradan shouted through the storm. "Or was that even him?"

The one that chilled even Liora's blood. "None would dare impersonate the man." She stroked hair back from Šulmanu's forehead but directed her next statement at a paling Gittel. "Or act against me without incurring the wrath you have just heard."

"How is he already here?" Eitan asked.

"Not important." Keshet, hammer firm and held at the ready, clutched the door's latch and watched Ishmael. "On your signal, my lord."

Ishmael raised a staying hand. He stood with his back to the earthen wall beside the door, thoughts galloping across his rumpled brow. Was he, like Eitan, wondering how her general-husband had arrived with such speed?

Liora was not confused, and she was not shy about it. "Nebuzaradan did not become Babylon's greatest general through stupidity. He expected this."

Ishmael cut her a scathing look, but Gittel slid a little farther back from the door.

Liora continued, not entirely certain she was correct, but appreciating the strength it sapped from Gittel's fight. There was still time to repent of her choices. "He would have assigned my guard to follow me while he gathered forces." She slid a hand under Šulmanu's lolling head and cradled it protectively on her lap, but there would be no shielding him should the oncoming fight burst out of the rain and through that door.

"In that case, he took forever." Eitan's grumble didn't sway Liora from her growing conviction in the general's stratagem.

Nebuzaradan answered to the prince and would have been unable to move until the rebels took action. Then it would have been a matter of Idadu sending a runner with her location and waiting for the general and his axe-swinging reputation to arrive to cut the rebels to pieces. How hard must it have been for Idadu not to interfere in her captivity?

Probably about as hard as it was for Liora to pretend she wasn't terrified. And for Gittel to realize she'd gotten in too deep and that if the Butcher didn't kill her, Idadu would. The woman looked to be merging with the shadows beside the empty grain bins. What had she expected would happen? Was Ishmael that good at persuasion, or had her hate blinded her to the fact Judah's plight was irreparable?

For the prophesied seventy years, at any rate. Between then and now, any resistance was folly.

A FAITH UNTAMED

"What do we do, my lord?" Gittel's uneven question was a shadow of her former self, too.

"Let go that blade, child, and come to us." Buzi motioned her to join the somber priests.

Gathered close, the men did not weep or tremble but accepted their lot with a calm found only in full trust in the Lord. Jeremiah had selected well. Which reminded Liora that none of this had taken Yahweh by surprise. Which reminded her that she, too, had a task to carry out.

She shifted nearer Eitan and spoke for his hearing alone. "The men Ishmael assigned to remove the ark must be stopped." If for no other reason than the possibility they might die. "The elders," she said, tipping her head toward the priests, "would intervene, would they not?"

"Without doubt."

"Then we must get them free of this place."

"At all costs," he returned at once, not a flicker of fear in the daring statement.

It struck her that the man was a warrior-priest, likely having taken his turn guarding the wall or gates. An unusual role for a priest, but times were not the usual sort.

Liora understood all about unusual roles. She'd been destined for the king's harem, not the Potter's House or the general's tent or the prince's table. Certainly not the rebels' hideaway.

Thunder rumbled overhead as she and Eitan exchanged a weighty look. His deep brown eyes were as hard and unflinching as at their first meeting. This time, they reflected her own determination. A strange warmth bubbled under her ribs, an unexpected camaraderie that had her echoing his vow. "At all costs," she said, then prayed those costs were low on the scale of life and death.

Perhaps Gittel was coming to the same realization. She gazed down at the knife laid across her palm.

"Gittel." Keshet snapped her name like a whip. A seasoned soldier, the man had lost none of his nerve. He looked over his shoulder and glared Gittel into firming her grip on the weapon's handle.

"Rebel cur!" Nebuzaradan's loud call could only mean he'd drawn dangerously close. "Why do you not answer? Has your courage deserted you? Or did you find a modicum of intelligence and spare me the hassle of removing your head?"

Ishmael straightened, resolve falling over his expression. "I am willing to sacrifice my life, Butcher!" His reply carried spitting hate. "But are you willing to sacrifice hers?"

"So," Liora muttered. "I am to be his shield *and* his bait."

"And he is the dead donkey." Eitan *tsk*ed as he reached for the water cup Liora had tucked against Šulmanu's side. "A true disappointment. I'd so hoped for a righteous judge."

"Shut your mouth, priest." Stance wide, Ishmael adjusted his grip on his sword, sight fixed on the closed door. "I cannot speak for the others, but this day, I do not die."

A FAITH UNTAMED

The roach of a royal was probably right. The Last Flame had a knack for escaping Nebuzaradan's soldiers.

Such a profound silence followed his bold statement that the wind singing through the door slats was as loud as the swallow convulsing Liora's throat. It rustled Keshet's robes and whisked up dust that floated across the chamber. She tracked the cloud to the rear and squinted into the gloom.

Where does the wind go?

Arrows thumped into the thin wood from the opposite side, whipping her attention to the front. Two brass arrowheads protruded from the door. A third found a gap in the slats and flew straight through, over Keshet's outstretched arm, and into the mill's central beam. The shaft quivered, dripping rainwater and mirroring Liora's pulse.

The rebels didn't twitch, but Gittel loosed an abrupt shriek.

Nebuzaradan's angry rebuke set Ishmael to cackling.

"Or perhaps," Ishmael said through his laughter, "your rogue soldiers have killed her already!"

"Liora! Tell me you are unharmed!" Nebuzaradan's bellow, so like his demanding self, triggered an almost manic urge to laugh.

Ishmael inhaled and raised two fingers to his puckering lips, a battle-call in the making.

The ill-timed humor transformed into another, more pressing urge. "It is a trap, Arioch!" Liora rushed to get the warning out. "He has you surroun—"

Ishmael's shrill two-blast whistle startled her mouth shut.

Breath stormed through her nose. In, out. Then roars erupted in the street.

Nebuzaradan's hollered order of "Rally to me!" rose above the noise. An instant later, the clash of blades rang out, their report loud against the stones.

Keshet waited for Ishmael's nod, then threw the door open. A cacophony of clashing swords and agonized screams stormed in as they dashed into the fray, hollering a war cry.

Liora slapped her hands over her ears, poor shields against the pounding chaos and the blood-curdling sounds of death. Outside or in, there would be no escaping it. At least, not for her, not while Šulmanu lay like the dead.

Swearing like a pagan, Gittel slammed the door shut behind them. She fumbled with a barring plank, finally slamming it into place. Entry secure, she darted back and stared wide-eyed at the door as if it were a crouching jackal, ready to spring an attack. Not an unfounded fear.

Liora highly doubted any more Babylonian arrows would fly toward them. But at first opportunity, the general—or any one of those bearing his crest—would be kicking down that rickety door. Arioch would come for her. A few threadbare resistors would surely not take him down. She told herself this. Told herself again.

Just the same, her hands refused to steady.

Surrounded, Ishmael had said.

A FAITH UNTAMED

And Nebuzaradan brought ten. How many Last Flame resistors had rallied for the opportunity to slay Yahweh's instrument of wrath? Odds were strong the butcher-general had considered ambush before closing in. Surely, he had not come oblivious, unprepared.

Which meant the tattered rebels would soon be lying in their own blood—a stomach-sickening likelihood.

Those tattered men were wrong in their reasoning, but they were her people. And they were outside that door, bleeding, dying. And for what? To prove Judah would not be *so easily subdued*? As if surviving the two-year siege, the demolished wall, and the burned-out city had been easy.

She tore her gaze from the snippets of roaring, battling men flashing through the door slats. Šulmanu's head sat at an awkward angle on her lap. She adjusted it, fingers trembling as the clangor of metal meeting metal pressed in around her.

Grime and sweat from his hair coated her fingers, and she welcomed the distraction. "I look forward to squabbling with you over bathing," she told Šulmanu in Akkadian, then switched to her own tongue. "Until then, shall we get water into you, my friend?" She tipped his head back and to the side and ignored Eitan's penetrating look.

"You are too good to our enemies, Liora."

Swords clashed at the door, and Liora flinched. Then exhaled through tight lips. "I am too good. The Last Flame is too horrid. I suppose that puts you in the exact center of Yahweh's will." Her mouth twitched, the closest she would come to a tease in such a grave situation.

Eitan's chest bounced with a curt, humorless laugh. "Hardly." He set the cup against Šulmanu's mouth and drizzled water over his lips.

A man's death scream rose above the din, and shudders ran across Liora's shoulders. A sudden gust rattled the door and kicked up dust from the floor. The dust swirled through the space, moving toward the back.

She glanced again at the priests, who'd resumed their prayers, then to the chamber's dark rear. That wind was going somewhere.

"What are you thinking?" Eitan asked.

She swallowed the bitterness of dust and anger and used the water dribbling from the corner of Šulmanu's lips to clean dried blood from his cheek. "I am thinking that being a pawn is a terrible, disagreeable thing. And it *infuriates* me that Ishmael has dragged our revered elders into it."

Lips pressed tight, Eitan rocked his head in a sage nod. "How he will go before our Lord to account for this, I do not know."

"On his face in fear and trembling, that is how. We must get you away from these misguided resistors. You and the others have a task to accomplish at the temple." Liora eased Šulmanu's head to the ground. "I noticed wind passing through the chamber to the rear." She explained no further before climbing to her feet.

Ribs aching, she jogged around the giant millstones.

A FAITH UNTAMED

Crushed. Crushed.

The prophet's warning pursued her. She shoved it away, along with the torn mule tether dangling in her path.

The chamber was not large, but the gloom was thick—worse behind the light-blocking mill. It pressed down on her with the weight of impending doom. Her heart thudded against her breastbone, even as her pace slowed.

She progressed on careful, shuffling feet, following the breeze that tickled her cheek on its way past. When her eyes adjusted to the dimness, forms emerged: sleeping pallets, rumpled blankets, a stash of clay water jugs, and a pile of woven baskets. Those were not the features to snag her attention.

A shallow wooden chute ran the chamber's length, raised off the ground by a rickety framework of beams. It sloped downward from a square hole in the rear wall—positioned about shoulder height—straight to the grinding stones in the center of the room. Likely once used to feed grain into the mill from outside.

"What do you see?" Eitan's voice was faint behind her, struggling to cut through the battle din and the rain hitting the reeds above.

"A chute," she called back. "Long and narrow. For grain, I think. It starts at a wall opening. There's a little light coming through it."

Faint gray lines glowed around the deep-set hole, painting its edges in a dusty haze. Hope flickered in her chest.

Sharp clanging echoed from the front of the granary—close to the door. A brutal reminder the fight raged on.

She crouched beside the chute's mouth, inspecting the size and angle. Could a man's shoulders fit through? Assuming, of course, the passage led somewhere useful. Rain pattered from the cracked reed-and-mud ceiling above, tapping her shoulder and spotting the packed dirt floor near her hem.

The rain would hinder the fighting. Bring it to a halt? By the nerve-rattling ring of it, not yet. Would Nebuzaradan fight as well in the slippery wet? She scoffed at her own worry. The man was a battle-hardened war machine. And he fought rebels who had spent the last years hiding in sunless caves.

Gittel appeared from the gloom on the chute's opposite side.

Liora startled and slapped a palm to her chest. "What do you want?"

"Is it a way out?"

Liora openly stared at the woman. "Do you mean for yourself?" Perhaps there was a bed on the other side with a blanket she could hide under while Liora straightened her mess.

Gittel merely stared back. Too proud to admit she'd cast her lot in with the weaker party? Regret must have nipped her hard since the Butcher's axe arrived.

Though tempted to do a little nipping herself, Liora shook her head. "I am not yet sure." She leaned over the old chute. It complained under her slight weight as she squinted into the opening. The square opening in the thick wall stretched back the length of her arm, and at the end, the thinnest strips of light outlined the shapes of bricks. "Someone has blocked off the entry, Eitan!"

Before she could pull back, the priest was beside her, peering over her shoulder into the hole. He grunted close to her ear. "It does not seem mortared. Scoot away, both of you."

On their respective sides, Liora and Gittel skittered back, while Eitan hiked his robes to his knees, pitched his weight back, and slammed his heel into the channel.

Wood splintered, and shards went flying. The chute's head crashed to the ground.

Liora raised a blocking arm, but Eitan bent and grabbed a plank. Without warning, he rammed an end through the hole. One blow. Two. On the third, the sound of clattering preceded two bricks tumbling into the chamber. A similar clatter sounded from the opposite side as bricks fell to the ground outside.

The noise of rain came through, and diffuse light illuminated billowing dust. Liora inhaled the fine cloud and coughed in harmony with Eitan.

Gittel seemed to have no such troubles. She clamored over the debris, pushed past Eitan, and scrambled through the opening.

"Oi, you!" He snatched at her ankle, but she kicked and swore.

"Let her go." Liora's next inhale sucked in dust. It triggered a wheeze that brought to mind Nebuzaradan's scowl and his *Do not fall ill.*

The man would slay an illness as he did the resistors. A burst of hilarity left her mouth, followed at once by a swamp of blurring tears. She sniffed them into a swift death and turned from Eitan's flat, judging eyebrows.

She swiped a dusty sleeve over her face and waved at the other priests. "We have an escape!"

Cheers and praise erupted in morbid contrast to the shrieks of pain coming from the street. The priests hurried over, one of them aiding Priest Buzi with an arm about his waist.

She eased back to allow them room. "Be warned. The way is tight, and the drop on the other side might be jarring." She cleared her scratchy throat. "Who goes first?"

"Besides the angry one?" Buzi pointed a crooked finger at the vacant opening.

Liora sighed, soul weary. Gittel would always think of Gittel first. No matter Liora's best efforts to reach her with the Lord's light.

Taking over, Eitan waved the priests toward him. One by one, they stepped forward, Eitan hoisting, until only he and his abba remained. He reached for the elder. "Come, Abba. It will be cold and wet but not too bad."

"Not too bad, my son says!" The old priest, still catching his breath from the race to the mill, leaned heavily into Liora and wagged a finger at Eitan. "Good or bad is not the issue. In the words of Samuel, I ask: Am I not eighty years of age? Why should I, your servant, be an added burden? And in the words of myself, I say, be about the Lord's business, my boy. I remain here."

Instead of protesting, Eitan shot Liora a speaking look. He'd foreseen this and would now call in her promise.

"I have no plans to leave my injured guard," she said. "You may entrust your abba to me."

Eitan didn't waste time replying. He swept in, taking Buzi from her arms and wrapping him in an embrace.

The men clung to one another until Buzi broke away and patted Eitan's chest with warped fingers. "Go, my son. The Lord has not left me. Neither will this strong young woman." Grinning through a tear-drenched smile, he shuffled back into the circle of Liora's arm.

"Yes, Abba," Eitan said, voice thick. "May the Lord bless you and keep you." Without another word, he spun and climbed through the opening.

Liora and Buzi gazed at the spot until his shadow disappeared and weak light once again penetrated the opening. "May the Lord make His face to shine upon you." Buzi's broken prayer clashed poignantly with the noise of battle reaching from the front.

"Omain." Liora whispered the amen, then ushered Priest Buzi back to where Šulmanu lay.

Buzi chose a spot against the mill and, with Liora's help, lowered to sitting.

She went to crouch at Šulmanu's side. He had not moved, but the shallow line between his eyebrows was new, the look of a man in pain even in sleep. His fingers trembled where they rested on his chest. She did not envy him the climb from unconsciousness.

"Poor boy, beaten so." Buzi clicked his tongue, and Liora rubbed her forehead.

"And just when I'd gotten him well from a prior beating." She squeezed his hand, sharing her warmth and strength.

His chest rose with a greater draw of breath. He let it out, and the pain-groove smoothed from his brow. Maybe he wasn't ready to climb, after all. But he would. For that, she was thankful.

"The general will be angry that I chose to stay with him. With you. But it will be all roars." Similar to those exchanged between the men battling in the rain.

"Lions do not frighten old men waiting for death."

"This lion will not touch you," she said with conviction. "He will escort you safely to your son, Ezekiel, in Babylon, who will weep at the sight of his dear abba."

Buzi lifted hands in praise. "A beautiful thought, yes?"

"It is, Moreh Buzi." Minus everything unspoken in the word *escort*—departure from Jerusalem, months of barren travel, unfamiliar lands.

She smiled at Buzi, but his milky eyes did not point precisely at her. For the best. The gesture was too sad to offer much comfort. She released it as her ribs expanded, a match to Šulmanu's next deep inhale.

"You have the look of weariness."

A dry laugh escaped her. "Because I *am* weary." Weary of the blood-chilling sounds of blade on shield, and of pain and death. She straightened to standing and removed her head covering. Angling away from Šulmanu, she shook it out. Dirt particles rained to the ground.

"How long since you observed Shabbat?"

She blinked. When had she last *thought* of Shabbat? "What day is it?"

"It is First day."

The sadness returned, engulfed her, set her to pacing the stretch of floor beside Šulmanu. "I spent Shabbat dining with a Babylonian prince." Not that she'd put a morsel to her mouth.

"I fear the coming days will allow no rest or reflection on the goodness of God."

"As do I, Moreh Buzi." The coming days, meaning dividing the people, traveling to Riblah, standing before the king...

Between *coming days* and *escort*, Liora did not see her life finding any normalcy, much less rest, for a long while. But stranger than all that? Her first thought had not been whether she would survive *this* day. Was she a fool in faith? Or simply a fool?

Hugging the veil to her chest, she eyed the door. While she'd been preoccupied with talk of Shabbat, the clamor had lessened. "Did the downpour at last force a retreat?"

A peek through the door should give an answer. Liora rose and was one step from her goal when she registered a large moving figure through the wide gaps.

He ran full tilt toward the mill, as a man did when fleeing his death. Water splashed high with every pounding stride. And he was not slowing.

Too late, she realized he would *not* slow. She torqued at the waist and flung her arms up to shield her face just as he rammed a shoulder into the door.

The bar snapped in two. The door crashed open and into her elbow. Pain slammed her as she flew backwards. The opposite arm broke her fall, but her forehead collided with the dirt. Stunned, breath shocked from her lungs, she slumped. Gasped.

Something struck her hip—the man taking a stumbling leap over her.

Disoriented, she watched him land in a flop behind her, her mind scrambling for *who*.

Enormous frame.

Drenched, coarse robes. Brown.

Filthy sandals. Kicking for purchase.

Rebel.

She pushed up on her stinging palm, eyes darting.

Šulmanu. Unchanged.

Buzi. Tottering toward Šulmanu.

Keshet. Mouth an open pant, he glanced at the same two occupants.

She'd have preferred Ishmael. Or any other resistor. This man was cold as flint.

And Nebuzaradan?

Liora's glance darted past the remnants of the still-swinging door. In a set of ragged breaths, she took in the situation.

A FAITH UNTAMED

Beyond the entry, sheets of rains fell on a gray-cast battleground, not quite drowning the cries of the dying. Lightning streaked horizontal across black clouds and outlined the carnage.

Corpses littering the ground. Muddy puddles. Rivers of red.

Men floundering, dying. Every one of them wearing the drab colors of her people.

A mix of soldiers milled about—the yellow stoles of House of Axes, the black of the royal guard. Was that Rimutu's lithe frame? Some soldiers trotted for cover. Several wandered the bodies, running javelins through rebel hearts.

Last Flame, extinguished. It was done.

Except for the general who stalked through the watery curtain straight toward her. The axe he held low chopped the air with his long-legged strides. Water poured off its blade. Blood off his brow. Rage twisted his features, that white eye a beacon in the gloom.

Death walked her way.

Her heart lurched, but she caught her recoil. That death was not meant for her.

Scrambling noises at her back foretold more bloodshed.

"Arioch, wait!" She stretched out her hand, flashed him her palm. "Wait! I can talk to—"

A stony clasp on her bracing wrist yanked her down, then up, dragging her to her feet.

She screamed—part startle, part outrage—and wrenched against the unyielding clasp. She strained and scratched about for anything to use against

Keshet. Her fingers curled around a winnowing basket. She swiveled at the waist and swung. The strike landed true, splintering against the side of his head.

The man didn't balk for a second.

"Know when you are finished!" She hit him again. The basket's rim knocked his skull. And did nothing.

He growled. "Be still!"

The slap came from nowhere, a blow to her temple.

Liora's neck rotated so hard it burned. Her fingers loosened. The basket fell, the ringing in her ears not loud enough to cover Arioch's bellow.

This lion would not be all roar.

Keshet had to be aware. Had to be desperate. He gripped her around the ribs and hauled her against him. Her cheek mashed against his heaving chest. "Stop there or she dies!" He punctuated the command with the point of a blade to the base of her skull.

She blinked into the folds of his soaking tunic. Each labored breath sucked in his body odor. She beat a weak fist against his side.

How, *how* was she in this position again? Only days ago, Omar had her by the throat on her rooftop. In that instance, she'd had her knife, her own little surprise for the fiend. This time? A basket.

And breath. Keshet did not pinch her windpipe. A blessing. And a convenience for him, since he likely wanted her voice, her persuasion.

Yes, she could breathe. Which meant she could think.

Think. *Think*. While she tried, her feet dangled.

A FAITH UNTAMED

He panted in her ear, breath sour. "There is a rumor that says the Butcher would carve out his own black heart if his harlot but asked." He spoke at normal volume, for her as much as for his stalking death. "The bewitched butcher, they call him in the street. So, woman, bewitch him. Your life hangs on it."

There it was, the expectation she would save him from this sinkhole.

Despite her roiling nausea, Liora chuckled darkly. "They are wrong, whoever *they* are. Only the king controls that man."

"And the Delilah who tames him." Keshet jostled her into a better position. A deep ache throbbed the ribs he'd bruised earlier, but the movement freed her neck and opened her view of Arioch.

Blinking hard and fast, she latched her gaze to him. The rebel had not lied.

Just outside the structure, Arioch stood frozen mid-stride, feet planted wide. He breathed so hard rainwater sprayed from his lips with every exhale. His lashes beat to fend off the downpour, his helmet gone the way of his sword. His gaze flickered between her and Keshet. The fire that blazed in them before fizzled now to a wary spark that fought valiantly against a wash of fear.

Did Keshet see it as plainly as she? Arioch's fear of her death, his willingness to do everything in his power to prevent it. According to the soft chuckle bouncing his chest, Keshet saw. "As I thought."

With painstaking motions, Arioch brought his rear leg forward and held his arms out to his sides.

"The axe, put it down!" Keshet's shout pushed the knife's point into her skin. A warm trickle traced a path from the sting.

Hissing, she arched as far from the threat as allowed. Hadn't she just been expressing confidence in the day's outcome? How presumptuous she'd been!

This man would kill her, then trample her body on his way out.

The general had clearly come to the same conclusion. He dipped his chin and, speaking Hebrew, crouched to drop his weapon. Water splashed his ankles. "The woman has always had a way of disarming me."

Ah, but a lion was never disarmed. Liora's mouth curved into a shallow smile.

He stayed there, lowered, as if to make himself small, inconsequential, harmless. As if such a thing were possible.

Forearms propped on his bent knees, he spread flipped-up, empty hands. "See? I am a reasonable fellow. Even where it concerns my dove. What use is a man's life if he cannot spend it on love? The rumors are wrong only in that she need not ask for my heart. I give it willingly and regret only that it is black and unworthy of her. So, rebel, what do you want? Your life, I presume. What else? The quarter? The city?" He smirked, having regained his cocky poise. "The prince's head on a charger?"

The knife's tip eased up, Keshet's arm muscles softening. He shifted in place, and she could almost hear the thoughts whirring through his stupid brain.

A FAITH UNTAMED

For her, Arioch the lion, might sheath his claws. But Nebuzaradan the butcher-general, would *never* let Keshet go.

"What do you want?" Arioch continued, the question a velvet cloth hiding a whetted edge. "Ask it of me, then let her go, and I swear on the House of Axes I will give it to you."

Keshet's laugh was a throaty, crazed thing.

Breath exploded from her as she fought the urge to join in. What a merry set of lies the general wove. But then, he was Babylon's best strategist. This was a ploy. Where would he go with his pretty lies?

"You laugh, rebel? You think me a liar?" He snarled, lip curling. "The woman will attest. I am a man of vows."

Liora dared not nod and rock that blade into her skull. "He would die before breaking his word."

"May it be so," he replied in Akkadian, a switch that wormed unease through her. He *had* sworn on his house.

Her heart hardened against the notion. No, he was not serious. Could not be.

Arioch said, "Your terms, rebel?"

Keshet's breath came shorter. Excitement building? Strength depleting?

"Do not negotiate with him," Liora said for them both.

"But I must. I have sworn it." Arioch's stance relaxed, his gaze wandering—over Keshet, behind him, covering everything but her. A soldier's assessment. Did Keshet see that too?

"Well?" Arioch swiped a hand down his face and flung water off his hand. "I would like to get out of this rain."

Keshet shifted her to one side but followed the move with the knife. It never left her skin. "I want my life, naturally. And, and—"

"Give him *only* his life." Liora strained to see better and felt the blade dig in. She winced and stilled.

"Hold there, dove," Arioch said in Akkadian, voice smooth and warm, even as a vicious smile curved his mouth, contorting his scar. A terrifying visage, no doubt. For Keshet. "Hold very, very still."

His gaze at last returned, gripped her with a strength that eased the breath from her stiff frame. Water streamed over his face, down the channel of his scar, off his beard. His chest expanded, contracted.

She matched it, and when he held on his next inhale, prickles erupted across her body.

A whistling sound came from behind. *Hissss-thwack*.

Keshet jolted, grunted loud in her ear. His arm slackened, and she slid down his front.

Her feet hit down, but her knees betrayed her. She crumpled at his legs.

He gurgled a liquid choke, and his feet jerked.

Another *thwack!*

Warm liquid sprayed over her like red rain.

She screamed, hunched, her raised arms doing nothing to stop his fall or block the crush of his weight.

CHAPTER 19

Keshet's head rocked to a stop a short reach from Liora's nose. His shocked-wide, sightless eyes stared her down.

A scream ripped from her throat. Wild, shrieking. Senseless. A sound made by other women. The hysterical sort. Not Liora. Some detached part of her mind informed her of this, while the rest raced with a single thought. "Get away, get away!"

Her from him. Him from her.

Plastered to the ground, she thrashed under the man's draping bulk as another horror flashed before her memory's eye, a long row of decaying heads mounted on pikes, her own rapid breath, her stumbling feet, and the taste of fear coating her tongue like poison. *This* was Babylon.

And she was crushed. Her ribs strained to feed her air.

If someone was speaking to her, she didn't hear. Didn't care.

One of her arms was trapped beneath her chest. The other broke free, her wrist smacking Keshet's nose. The head wobbled on its ear. She gasped out another scream, as every horrid, bloodied thing from the last weeks assailed her.

Mehetabel's lifeless eyes, her broken body.

Someone shouted. A booted foot kicked the head out of her sight.

Ashara licking her maw, the beast's pacing, the clicking claws.

The corpse's weight jostled, eased up. Disappeared.

The sensation of Omar's hand around her throat.

Panic surged. Liora scrambled to her knees but tangled in her robe and slipped in a warm puddle. She fell forward, the smack of her chin cutting her scream to a grunt. Pain sliced the side of her tongue. She tasted blood, but it was Keshet's that coated her hands, dripped down her cheek, soaked her tunic.

The horror of it left her on a jagged cry.

Again, that commanding voice, unable to penetrate the noise of her mind.

The stained ground fell away as Liora climbed to unsteady legs. Long locks of her hair dangled over her eyes. Wet, dripping.

She felt half rabid. Must look it, too, with her arms held away from her body and with blood weighing down her robe. A deep quaking inside her worked its way to the surface until she shook.

"Liora, child?" That was Buzi's voice, emerging from the rear.

Her head tottered on her neck as she tried to look behind her. When she lost her balance, she thought better of it. Something was wrong. Seconds passed like minutes. Her body moved sluggishly, her mind in concert as it slogged through the process of reorienting her to the now.

Same dark chamber. Same large millstone. Same deluge buffeting the street at her back. Cleansing. Tempting.

Was Arioch still out there?

A FAITH UNTAMED

Šulmanu was awake, on his feet again. Water poured in through the leaking roof near where he stood, staring at her. The old sickle dangled from his hand.

He dropped it, and Liora flinched.

The shadows to her left moved, and she jumped again.

"Ari?" She squeaked his name, but his muscular, armor-clad shape, even in darkened silhouette, was unmistakable.

He dropped Keshet's ankle where he'd finished dragging the man. "Yes, dove. It is only I. He is gone."

Arioch. Just Arioch.

Not Omar. Not Keshet. Not Ishmael or Nergal or Ashara.

Stepping over the corpse, he strode toward her. Was he growling, or was that the skies? Lightning flashed, illuminating his white eye and the fury etched into his features.

No man had ever looked sweeter, more alive. The battle had not taken him from her.

Yahweh be thanked.

Relief poured through her, and the shoulder-shaking tears began all over again. Here was safety. Here was a man who wouldn't look at her like a creature from the deep.

Even dripping wet and weaponless, he looked at her as if he would take down the world one sovereign at a time to make it all go away.

She would run to him, eliminate the rapidly closing distance if she could trust her legs not to drop her back into the puddle beneath her.

No matter. In the next heartbeat, he'd reached her anyway. He bent and scooped her straight up and flat against him, never pausing his stride.

She flung her arms about his neck, buried her face in the warm place under his ear, and sobbed. "I c-cannot keep on this way, Ari! It-it is too much!"

Too much fear. Too much violence. Too much responsibility.

"Foolish talk. You are the daughter of a god." He held her tight, one large hand on the back of her head, the other wrapped about her hips. Ducking, he walked them straight into the rain.

She gasped, soaked through before she'd finished hauling in a breath. Warmer than expected, rainwater poured down her face, dragging hair with it. Her feet touched down, sank her to the ankles in the river rushing down the hill.

Then Arioch's hands were on her, scrubbing her scalp, her cheeks, her neck. Arms next, he rubbed up and down, scouring her sleeves and the skin beneath. It burned. She welcomed the sensation. Stood there and shook. Gulped air around the flood streaming over her face and let him kneel before her and scrub it all gone.

Gone. Keshet. His blood.

Her tears. They'd been shocked clean away. In their place, a growing steadiness.

Daughter of a god?

A FAITH UNTAMED

Daughter of *the* God. The Most High. A present help in trouble, a shelter for the weary.

And Liora was that, weary in body and soul. Horrified, too, and a little out of her mind with it. But as Arioch and the rain washed away the grime and blood, she found a renewed sense of footing. Her sandals might wobble in the watery street, but her soul stood on the Rock. If He chose to welcome her into eternity that hour, that day, or the next, she would walk there with strength and purpose.

Bless her pagan husband for reminding her.

She put her hands on his shoulders and gripped his armor as he scoured the robe at her hip and thigh, moving down. Better to have peeled the thing off, but even in her frazzled state, she understood how it would expose her. And with the return of her senses, she felt bare enough already.

And Arioch?

The rain contoured his clothes to his body, highlighting every corded muscle. From his straining neck to the bulging muscle of his squatting thighs, little was hidden. In some distant, objective corner of her mind, Liora recognized her husband was handsome.

And fearsome.

This was the brawn Keshet had fled—just as the rain beading on Arioch's oiled armor ran over the sides, keen to be away from him. Only the rebel's blood remained, and it too fled Arioch's relentless pursuit.

With the expertise of a washerwoman, he rubbed fistfuls of fabric together until the dark patches released. Shifting, he checked her opposite side.

Satisfied, he pulled her hands off him to check her fingers and nails. First one hand, then the other.

Nothing. Not a speck of blood or dirt.

He nodded and rubbed her fingers anyway, then inspected the torn flesh on her wrists. He said nothing but lowered his forehead to the tops of her fingers, as if she were a queen and he beseeched a favor. His hair tickled her forearms, and her fingers twitched, tempted to pull away. Before she could, he flipped her hand and laid his mouth on the flame tattoo on her palm.

His hot breath puffed against it in spurts that came in time with the rumble of his voice. Was he talking...to her hand?

"Arioch, what are you doing?" The question vanished under a roll of thunder. She shivered at the sting of rain on her shoulders. They should be under shelter.

She gazed down at the top of his bare head. The water flattened his black curls, its darkening effect highlighting the peppering of gray, the difference in their ages never more stark.

How many battles would a general of his years have survived? In how many would he have contended with the terror of the enemy reaching Aralu?

Liora's best guess—none. Babylon took its wars beyond its borders, met opposing kings on their own soil. Unwittingly, Liora had subjected Arioch to a new burden. A new fear. Likely, she was not the only one in need of comfort there in that washing rain.

A FAITH UNTAMED

She flipped her hand back over and squeezed his fingers, appreciating their rough breadth. These were the hands that killed men to reach her. Was it wrong to thank him for that bloodshed? She had her life, and for *that,* she was certainly thankful. With her free hand, she stroked his head, all the invitation he needed to tip forward and press his face flat to her stomach.

He wrapped his arms around her hips, pulled her closer, and locked her in place.

No sense resisting. Not that she wanted to. The man had earned a moment to touch his wife, to draw comfort from—

Realization like a drum's resonant *boom* struck her mind.

Arioch was touching her. *Touching* her.

She stared into the blinding curtain of rain. Pain throbbed at her temple where she'd been struck. She ignored it as she blinked against the deluge pouring over her lashes. Had he forsaken his oath? Deemed it complete? Something had changed since the previous night when he chose to sleep in the prophet's chamber. Had he spoken with Jeremiah that morning, been released from his promise to Yahweh?

Either that or this was what he would consider an illicit touch. A broken vow. But was he even capable? What of his speech to Keshet? Her confirmation of it?

When Arioch rose, climbing her front, and saying, "Forgive me, forgive me," she concluded her last assumption was correct.

The man could break a vow after all. Should she stop him?

He burrowed his face into her neck, much as she'd done to him, and straightened fully. Bringing her up with him, he squeezed her aching ribs and held her so fast to his body, she wondered ironically whether *this* was the crush Jeremiah had meant. She would take this one any day over the one Arioch freed her from minutes ago. Or any other the Lord intended to send her way.

The strength of Arioch's embrace, the possessiveness in it, was precisely as expected. But it was not so terrible as she'd feared, his touch less dreadful than she'd imagined.

He went on begging forgiveness, his beard scratching the sensitive skin under her jaw. The discomfort barely registered, as his lips climbed her neck and rested gently on the place that throbbed at her temple.

"There is nothing to forgive, Ari." He'd arrived in spectacular fashion and eliminated the threat with a speed and efficiency she doubted any other man could have managed.

"Forgiveness. Please."

Had he even heard her? Later, they would sort it out. For now, she would relish the security of his arms, the wall that he was between her and a brutal world.

Where is the Butcher on your heart's wall? Nergal's question came back at her with the force of a gale.

Butcher? Indeed, he'd done well enough hacking at her resolve to perceive him only as the man who burned her city, killed her people. Liora had spouted

A FAITH UNTAMED

that the way to a woman's heart was not through siege or by battering down walls. A man must earn a woman's respect. Make sacrifices and vows of protection. He must guard her from all harm.

Which part of that had Arioch *not* done?

No denying, he'd laid siege to her freedom—detained her in his camp, claimed her as wife without a ceremony. And didn't her people lay sprawled at her feet like rubbish on a dunghill? In her heart, she'd thanked the Butcher who was her husband. She'd held his hands and blessed them for protecting her. The same hands that palmed her back and cupped her hip.

Where is the Butcher on your heart's walls?

Or had she already opened the gate to him? *There* was a thought for another hour.

Through the torrent, she squirmed as the world bled into her awareness. Idadu stood in the mill's doorway, seeming a few seconds from dashing into the rain to save her from her own husband. And all around them, the forms of the dead rose in accusation of their callous behavior.

Another bout of shivers coursed over her, and Arioch's face lifted.

He blinked fast against the rain, or a daze.

She held his bearded cheeks between her hands, looked straight into his bloodshot eyes, and shouted above the storm. "Take me inside."

A few disoriented blinks more, then he nodded. He turned toward the mill.

Idadu backed out of their path. "Your orders, General?"

Arioch stepped over the threshold, took two steps inside, and stopped. "Search for a more comfortable place for the lady to wait out this weather."

Liora didn't hear Idadu's reply, but when she looked back, the doorway was empty.

They remained there a moment, dripping, catching their breath. Her eyes grew accustomed to the darkness. When Šulmanu and Buzi's forms materialized, Liora couldn't tell who was leaning on whom.

Šulmanu with pain, Buzi with age. The grooves of his craggy face collected shadows that pierced her with regret.

"I am unharmed, Moreh Buzi," she said. "Forgive me for upsetting you."

"Praise be!" The priest tapped Šulmanu's chest. "Did I not tell you, young man? She is well! Are you not glad?"

"The old one thinks I understand him." Šulmanu scowled at Liora as if it were her fault he didn't speak Hebrew. "But...I am glad to see you are well."

Liora shocked herself with a light laugh. "You and the *old one* understand each other perfectly."

Arioch frowned as he gazed about. "Where are the other priests?" Droplets from his hair shook loose onto his nose.

Liora resisted wiping them off and instead fidgeted to be let down. "At the temple, I would hope."

"Hope? How do you not know? Captain Idadu said you were brought in here all together."

Lightning flashed, making her squint.

A FAITH UNTAMED

She rapped his shoulder and squirmed. "We were, but when you arrived with your soldiers—"

A clap of thunder shook the building.

Arioch released the lock on her dangling legs only to flip her sideways, swing her body up, and catch her under the knees. Her stomach flipped before he settled her again in his arms. "What were you saying?"

Good question. Heat flamed in her cheeks. It was one thing for a man to carry a woman when her limbs were unreliable, another for him to carry her because...because... Well, for no reason at all.

She shot a glance at Šulmanu and Buzi. The guard regarded them intently but showed not a wrinkle of shock at his general's unseemly attentions.

Buzi's unfocused gaze was elsewhere entirely. Lack of clear sight—or of a willing participant—did not stop him from rattling on in the nodding, deliberate manner of a learned teacher.

"We sons of Israel do not despair, young fellow. Ezekiel speaks of a time when the covenant will be fruitful and our cities restored. These hardships shall pass."

Šulmanu ignored him in favor of hanging on his general's every move.

Their disinterest in Liora's predicament didn't soothe her embarrassment one bit. She leaned in and whispered, "Ari, my legs are steady again. I can—"

"The priests, dove. Where did they go?" Gaze roving, he seemed not at all interested in letting her use her own two feet.

And Liora wasn't interested in fighting him over it, not with Šulmanu tracking their interaction. She sighed and pointed toward the back of the chamber. "I found an old grain chute that opens to the outside. Eitan and I helped them through."

His head jutted back and tipped sideways as he studied her. "Did you? Why?"

"Because we have a task to accomplish. Rather...they do. Mine is finished, I suppose." Sadness threatened to spill into her soul, but she banished it. She would entrust the covenant ark to Yahweh and His dedicated men. "The Lord surely has other things for me to do." And she would be little good to Him if she lost herself in despair. "All but Priest Buzi have gone to do as instructed." She pushed a reserved smile onto her face.

Arioch met her attempt at joy with the same cocked head and analyzing expression. He held it so long she began squirming again. Her lips were parting to protest his awkward staring when he said, "You are a light to my soul, Liora. Your father named you well. He may rejoin your household."

Mouth still open, Liora stared at him. Just that simple? After all his talk of well-deserved banishment, he would allow her abba back because he *named her well*? Her molars clicked closed. "The lord general is ever gracious."

Laughter rumbled from the depths of his chest. "Why did I ever encourage your boldness, little dove?"

"The way I have experienced it, General," Šulmanu said, rather boldly himself, since he both inserted himself into their conversation and interrupted the rambling priest, "the lady has never needed encouragement to speak her mind. And I will be forever grateful."

Arioch turned sharply at the waist, seeming to put Šulmanu in line with his good eye. "Indeed, you should be," he said, not the least abashed at the reminder he'd ordered the man's death—over a kiss. Or that Liora had outwitted him in front of his men, all but forcing him to stand down and surrender Šulmanu's life to her.

"And as Isaiah proclaimed," Buzi said in a preacher's droning voice, "'Babylon is fallen, is fallen! All the carved images of her gods lie shattered on the ground' And so, it shall be as the Lord has spoken."

"Omain," Liora said on reflex.

Arioch's arms tightened about her, but his eyes narrowed on Buzi, then slid to Šulmanu. "I suspect the lady has taken yet another yowling stray into her care. How appropriate that you and he are on friendly terms. Consider him in your charge, soldier. From now until I tell you otherwise."

"But I promised Eitan to do it myself," Liora said, while Šulmanu's eyes grew large with barely concealed horror.

A new roof leak dribbled water onto his shoulder. He gave no sign he noticed. "How do you mean, General?"

Arioch's huff ruffled a wisp of hair hanging over Liora's eyes. "I mean stash the man someplace safe. Protect him from dust and damp. Use your imagination, man."

As Šulmanu formed a hasty, if halfhearted, salute, she bowed back as far as Arioch's tight hold allowed so she could cock an eyebrow at him. "Teacher Buzi is a revered elder, not a sack of grain. And Šulmanu could use stashing himself. He is in no condition to play chambermaid."

"Chambermaid is little punishment for leaving you unguarded on the roof, and he well knows it. Besides,"—Arioch's shrug bounced her in his arms—"how much effort can it take to guard an old man?"

"Though we walk through the valley of dry bones," the priest was saying to a withering Šulmanu, "remember Ezekiel's vision!"

Her eyebrow arched higher.

Arioch smirked, then dropped it and directed a commander's glare at Šulmanu. "The lady's strays have a habit of surviving. Try not to break her pattern."

Captain Idadu jogged into the mill, appearing out of nowhere through the rain. He stopped just inside and, breathing hard, wiped water from his eyes. "There is an abandoned home across the street and five doors downhill. No food but I found several blankets that will serve my lady."

"Well done, Captain." Arioch strode toward the door. "The rain is a drowning one, dove. Catch a breath."

Liora pulled her chin close and tucked her face against Arioch's neck. She filled her lungs just in time for him to plunge them back into the stinging rain.

At the abandoned, single-chamber home, Arioch stood outside under the eaves while Liora used the dusty blankets to dry off, even found a set of moth-eaten clothes Idadu had overlooked at the bottom of a chest—the remnants of some poor woman's life. Thankful to her, Liora changed, rubbed her hair on a blanket, and succumbed to sleep on the chamber's narrow cot.

Until the simultaneous flash of lightning and ground-shaking thunder wrenched her eyes open to an unnaturally bright room. It shot her straight off the cot.

Arioch banged the door open and leaped inside.

Eyes readjusting, she saw only a chest-heaving silhouette filling the doorway, his arms stretched across it as though to bar entry. She blinked several times and finally made him out.

He was scanning her head to foot, as if the lightning might have gotten past him and split her down the center.

She didn't realize she was doing the same until she said, "Are you all right?" at the same time as he.

They paused, then chuckled nervously.

Arioch breathed as if he'd raced in from the hills. "That was..." He looked over his shoulder into the deafening rain.

"Divine?" Liora meant it in jest, but when Arioch looked back, his eyes held a light she couldn't have foreseen, that white orb almost glowing.

"Perhaps?" The vulnerability in the question, in the softening of his rigid posture, slowed Liora's galloping heart.

She palmed it and smiled. "Praise the Lord from the earth. Fire and hail, snow and mist and stormy winds fulfill His word."

"A quote from your sacred scriptures?"

"It is."

Nodding, he let go the door's edge and picked at the top of his axe head where it sat tucked behind his belt. He gazed back into the storm, speaking so low she wasn't sure he meant for her to hear. "He is angry." Did he realize he touched his ruined eye?

"Most often, a storm is simply a storm. But if I were to attribute it to God, I would call the rain His tears and the lightning, the sound of His breaking heart." Liora joined Arioch at the doorway, her cheeks instantly damp from the torrent's spray.

"Angry and grieved...." He didn't acknowledge her presence but stared into the gray sheets of rain. "Because Babylon tramples his city and his people. And because..." His throat bobbed, but he said no more.

But what he *had* said was insightful enough. And heartening because he spoke of Yahweh as though He was real and powerful enough to control the heavens, to display His wrath any way He pleased. As though Babylon was deserving of that wrath. Clearly, he believed it of himself—he had yet to lower his fingers from where they'd frozen on his cheekbone just below that cursed eye.

No surprise he could not comprehend a God of provision, forgiveness, and grace—the God of the desert who fed and watered, liberated and guided. The

A FAITH UNTAMED

God who rejoiced in hearts devoted to the pursuit of holiness.

Of Yahweh, Arioch had witnessed nothing but judgment and righteous cleansing.

In time, she would show him the many beautiful facets of Hashem. "And because His people reject Him," she said. "Because *you* reject him." Hesitating, pulse tripping, she wrapped an arm around his waist and leaned against him. His vow did not stipulate she could not touch *him*.

He stiffened. His ribs expanded and held. "Liora..." Her own name rumbled against her cheek, a different sort of ominous thunder. "It was a moment of weakness. I... I should not have touched you...cannot."

Before she could do more than unclasp her arms, he straightened, pulled away, and stepped beyond the overhang, all the way into the beating rain.

CHAPTER 20

*O Lord, thou knowest: remember me,
and visit me, and revenge me of my
persecutors; take me not away in thy
longsuffering: know that for thy sake I
have suffered rebuke.* (Jer. 15:15)

When the storm quit, Liora, Arioch, and their retinue made tracks for her home.

Rimutu had appeared from another shelter and, as was his nature, silently slid into place beside his general.

Arioch never glanced at the man, but Liora leaned around her husband to pass the guard a smile. "You live, Rimutu. I am glad for it."

Rimutu ducked his head but couldn't hide the tops of his flaming ears.

Liora eased back and sent Arioch a questioning look.

"Go easy on him, dove. Your charm is too potent for the average man." Puffing his chest ever so slightly, he flashed her a roguish grin, and she sighed with relief at the return of his more amiable side. Even if it came in the form of ridiculous statements.

They were still half a street away from her front door when it burst open. Devorah flew past the guard, calling Liora's name and waving her cleaning cloth like a victory flag. Upon spotting Šulmanu, she halted short, then rushed in and swatted at him with her rag.

A FAITH UNTAMED

Not even Buzi's presence or his little cry of shock could stay her ranting at Šulmanu for disappearing, for nearly dying, for giving her mistress a terrible fright and heartache.

Arioch backed up, edging them away from the onslaught. Chuckling, Liora let him. Let Devorah expend her pent emotion, too.

Head bent, the young guard took it as his due. But he was so weak, his voice so slurred with the wine Liora had found for his pain, she doubted he would remember in the morning that he'd subdued the chambermaid with a sudden, teary embrace. Devorah would probably be happy to remind him—while denying that she, too, wiped a stray tear.

Zipporah and Abba, likely hearing the commotion, emerged from their temporary home across the lane, though they held back, uncertain of their welcome.

Arioch scowled in their direction until Liora elbowed him in the ribs hard enough to make him grunt. When Devorah and the others went inside, she took his hand and dragged him to her Abba where he grumbled a reversal of his banishment.

Zipporah hugged her, then exclaimed over the abominable disrepair of Liora's hair and "beggar's garb."

Meanwhile, Abba bent himself almost double in a scraping bow. "Humble thanks to my gracious lord, the husband of my dearest light. Your rebuke was just and wise and well received. Your mercy beyond my deserving."

Her abba gushed so profusely and shamefacedly Liora's cheeks flushed. She bit her tongue against the urge to interrupt as Arioch regarded Abba through barely tolerant, half-lidded eyes.

Sharing a sidelong look with Zipporah, Liora squeezed her friend's hand and said nothing. Arioch would not go back on his word, and as the general, he could handle himself.

He promptly did so, declining to join them at the table for an evening repast. Apparently, duty in the camp suddenly required his attention. Liora walked him back into the street where he paused and gazed long in the direction of the East Gate.

Low, black clouds rolled across the darkening sky, moving off into the horizon as if gathered in by a mighty hand. Dim thunder rumbled a departing word, and Arioch's mouth went flat as it did when his jaw tensed. "This city is not the same without him."

Liora's brow tightened. "Without whom?"

His nostrils sprawled wide. "While we are on poor terms, I will not speak his name."

She stood on the side of his bad eye and stared at its thick white film. Was Arioch thinking of that blinding light or of the holy wind sweeping out of the temple and into the hills? He hadn't heard the flapping wings or the roll of wheels, but he'd somehow known which direction the Shekinah took as it departed Jerusalem.

But shouldn't the man be happy to see Yahweh, the God who'd half blinded him, step away from His earthly throne and relinquish the city to him? Or did

A FAITH UNTAMED

she misinterpret? Perhaps it was not bitterness she saw on Arioch, but fear. On that wild assumption, she said, "Those terms can be corrected."

He gave a firm shake of the head. "Not while my obedience is yet incomplete. Surviving Judah-ites remain in the city. I must determine their fate. Whether they stay in the land or go. And the walls have not all come down."

Liora's gaze fell to the mud caking her sandals. *Correcting poor terms* was as close as he'd ever come to humbling himself before Yahweh. But not until he'd completed his calling. "Samson repented," she said, "*then* executed judgment. Not the other way around."

"Samson was one of you."

Her head lifted. "As you could be. If not by blood, then by vow."

His shoulders pulled back. "I am Nebuzaradan, High General of the armies of Babylonia, servant to His Majesty Nebuchadnezzar, ruler of the world."

And he would cling to *that* vow foremost. "You are stubborn is what you are."

He said nothing, and she sighed and watched the mass of clouds grow smaller.

Seven days, Prince Nergal had said, until the army left Jerusalem and the city marched to Riblah and King Nebuchadnezzar. Seven, now six. She would not hasten that dreadful day, but she could not lie to herself by denying a tiny thrill at this glimmer of hope. At imagining how the people of Judah might benefit from a proselytized Butcher.

Questions pecked at her, most to do with what led to this turn of his heart.

She had dozens of her own questions regarding her Lord. Namely, when His glory would return to dwell on the holy mount. Seventy years as prophesied for the people's return? More? There was every chance the Shekinah would remain absent until the arrival of the Great Light Isaiah foretold, the male child who would be called wonderful and mighty and who would reign on David HaMelech's throne.

Whenever that may be…

"How long, oh Lord?" She murmured the prayer, drawing Arioch's gaze. "Will you be angry forever? Let your compassion come soon because we are brought very low."

Tears pricked, always ready of late. They welled up as she pulled a lungful of air made cool and fresh by the rain. Not a whiff of fire or ash to wrinkle her nose or make her sneeze. Only pure restorative breath, threaded through with the promise of repentance and redemption. And small prayer from Jeremiah to make her well.

"I would hold you now." Arioch's rumble tugged her attention off the retreating storm. He'd stepped near enough to brush her head covering with the leather fringe of his shoulder armor. Near enough that his heat penetrated the sleeve of her robe and warmed her arm. And she hadn't noticed. Not his nearness. Not his gaze. She'd grown so accustomed to his presence, it no longer announced itself. It simply was.

A FAITH UNTAMED

Now that she did notice, she almost backed away, as a wise woman should. As she'd done from the lioness who'd tracked her with eyes tight from hunger.

Arioch *was* a lion, after all. So said his name, the strength of his axe, and the rule of his men.

The same *zing* of alarm she'd felt in Ashara's presence now traveled around her ribs, up her neck, and straight into her lips. She hugged herself. "Hold me...if?" There'd been more to his statement, thoughts she didn't like left unspoken.

"If I could be certain the storm would not reverse its course and come back to strike my other eye." His mouth tugged up on one side. "I do enjoy looking at you, dove."

"You might enjoy touching me, too," she quipped, "if you were not so stubborn."

Arioch's eyebrows took flight, pulling his scar so taut it tugged his cheek and whiskers. "Liora bat Chesed, I do believe there was disappointment in that observation. Did you enjoy our embraces? Do you *wish* to be touched?"

She gave a soft, refuting snort. "I see you do not deny your stubbornness."

"As you do not deny your wishes. Which affirms your attraction."

"Attraction? Please." She let her eyes roll. "To the Butcher?"

"To the Butcher."

"To the man destroying my city?"

"Yes."

He was insane. "You are an overgrown brute."

"I am a talented painter. You said so."

Liora dispensed a drab look. Clever of him to draw on their mutual love of paints. "Rimutu, Idadu," she said to the soldiers who kept a discrete distance down the street. "Tell your general he is an overgrown brute."

Rimutu wagged his head so hard his helmet teetered on his bent ears, but the captain replied straight-faced. "As my lady says."

Arioch spluttered, but she would not relent, driven by an urge to stomp all over his notion of *attraction*. "You are an overgrown brute who banishes fathers—"

"Who *un*-banishes."

"Who breaks precious pottery." Her volume was on the rise, and she was not sure why.

"That was *once*."

"And who kicks heads across the ground!"

Arioch threw his arms wide. "To spare the woman he loves the sight of it!"

Her head bobbed back. "The woman he *what*?" He couldn't have meant it. The Butcher, per the children's ghost stories, was not capable of love. Only of spewing flame from his throat and hissing with his snake's tongue.

The Butcher took. He *possessed*. He did not love.

Rimutu found something to investigate in the other direction, but Idadu cleared his throat. "He said *loves*."

Arioch pursed his lips as if to belatedly withhold the sentiment. "Very helpful, Captain. I should flog you for impertinence. And for making the lady blush."

No lie there. Liora's neck radiated heat. She could not look at the man. Could not bear to peer into his eyes to see whether there was any truth to the slip. "Brute," she muttered.

"The blush would be your doing, my lord general," Idadu said. "Shall we grant you privacy to properly confess your love?"

"This is not the place for such powerful sentiment." Arioch raised his bearded chin and tugged on the lower edge of his chest plate. "I take my leave now. And *you* are not to wander from Lady Liora's side."

Idadu beat his chest in a salute.

"My love." Arioch bowed crisply. "Eat. Rest."

Her lips hung parted.

A last few glances flicked from the side of his eye, then he snapped his fingers at Rimutu to follow and left her.

Left her staring. Left her reeling.

She had not seen this conversation coming—the two near confessions, repentance and love. He rounded the corner and with him out of sight, she could almost convince herself she'd imagined the whole thing.

Ignoring Idadu's poorly concealed grin, she trudged on numb feet into her home.

Eat. Rest.

How? After all that, *how* exactly was she to put food in her mouth and actually swallow?

My love...

The Butcher of Babylon had not only spared her and married her, he'd loved her in the process. Or so he said.

Abba and Zipporah chattered her back into the house, Zipporah insistent Liora have a warm meal and head straight to bed. Liora listened, responded when appropriate, and sat down to eat when instructed.

But she had scarcely taken a mouthful when twenty royal guards entered uninvited, pushing straight past her powerless guards. The black-clad soldiers escorted her right back out, not a whisper of explanation among them.

"But I cannot go before the prince in these clothes." She shook her dusty, hole-speckled robe.

Deaf to her pleas, the captain refused any delay, but when Idadu gripped his sword's handle and threatened trouble should he not be allowed to accompany her, the prince's captain huffed impatience. "Very well. Considering the rebel activity, you may come." He nudged Liora along until Idadu shoved between them, spouting more threats.

Robe gathered in her fists, Liora bustled down the street on weary legs. So much for rest and Devorah's restorative fussing and tea. The maid would be bereft, but she would make do with Šulmanu.

Zipporah and Abba trotted after them a ways. "But why?" Zipporah asked. "What could the prince want with her at this hour?"

"Translating," Abba replied, out of breath. "We must let her go, my heart. Without trouble or it could be worse for her." He was not wrong, even though it stung he was not the one demanding answers.

"Do not wait for me," Liora said over her shoulder as the guards ushered her around the same corner

A FAITH UNTAMED

Arioch used a short while before. She raised her voice to send it back to her family. "The evening grows late. Dine without me!"

"God go with you, dear one!" Zipporah called, her voice catching.

If Liora were the type to use foul names, she would be using them on the guards for leaving her friend confused and in tears.

"What does the prince need from me?" She peered around Idadu to address a stern-faced guard. "Will I be able to return before the night is through?"

"They will not answer, my lady," Captain Idadu muttered, eyes cutting back and forth across their path.

By the time she and her clamp-jawed escorts reached the second street over, she stopped asking.

As commanded, Idadu did not leave her side. Not when they reached the prince's gate and not when they entered his eerily quiet audience hall. Inside the large doors, their escort forced him to separate and remain at the back while Liora proceeded with the captain of the royal guard across the columned expanse. She passed back a smile too wobbly to reassure Idadu. At least the tap of her footfalls echoed crisp and steady.

Directly ahead, Nergal stood before the dais, looking at an unrolled parchment. A studious wrinkle bore into the brown flesh between his trimmed black brows. To the right, the lioness snoozed on her side, the scraggly tip of her tail twitching, and on the left—

Liora's stride faltered.

"Kneel." The guardsman took a pinching grip of the back of her neck and forced her down to her knees.

She flailed for balance, barely catching it before he was shoving her farther. Gasping, she slapped the floor to save her forehead from crashing against stone. Locks of hair tumbled forward and narrowed her view to the stains beneath her nose.

All the better to spare her the sight of the corpses piled at the end of a long bloody smear. The other end of the broad red stripe began under her stinging palms. The spilled blood was old enough to have dried around the edges, fresh enough to feel tacky.

She stared at the gore and breathed through her mouth to avoid the smell.

Who? *Who?*

Two people, at least. They'd been dragged to the wall and dumped one atop the other. Someone had tossed a blanket over the lot, but their brown robes and worn sandals protruded at odd angles. And they were not Babylonian.

Liora's next swallow stuck in her dry throat. *Not the priests, not the priests.* She couldn't stomach the thought of those dear elders, but would the waste of their lives be any better if they were rebels?

She blinked furiously at the strands of hair sitting in the blood, mind spinning. What message was Nergal trying to send, and what could Liora have to do with it?

His footsteps passed in a lazy cadence from left to right at the base of the dais, then back again. The pitted stone was biting into her knees by the time he deigned to speak. "Liora, Liora. Lady Liora, daughter of a disgraced nobleman. The beauty of Jerusalem who snared the heart of a general, caught the eye of one king, and the attention of another. I find this infinitely fascinating. But I do have a question." Crinkles of parchment indicated he still held the scroll. "More than one, actually."

She locked her molars. The man could ask his questions, or he could stuff that scroll down his throat. But Liora would not say one word beyond necessary to get herself and Idadu out of there—and *not* in a cart destined for the Dung Gate.

"I shall begin with the easiest." The tap-tap of Nergal's sandals was too slow, too casual to portray him as anything but lethal. "Where, *dove*, is the ark?"

The ark? That was not the way she'd expected the conversation to go. And why ask *her*? She frowned down at the dull red spatters. "Is it not in the temple, my lord?"

Nergal clicked his tongue. "I believed you smarter than to ask such a stupid question."

He was right. If the ark were in its proper place, he would not be interrogating her.

She had to *think*, not spout the first thought to enter her head. The problem was, her first thought on the subject had been her last. Her mind blanked. Heart pattering, she shifted to relieve her aching knees. "If the holy ark is not in the temple and it is not in your possession, then...I do not know."

"Hmm."

She squeezed her eyes shut. *Lord! Wisdom, guidance. Anything.*

Low, sleepy growling came from Ashara's quarter. The beast grunted, even that small noise a deep rumble that made Liora's blood run cold. She was rising, her claws clicking and scratching at the stone floor.

"What *do* you know?" How was it Nergal spoke with such calm? Never mind the rousing beast, with the king's order to secure the ark hovering like an axe above his neck, the man had to be anxious. Furious. Was this a ploy? A false sense of security to put her at ease? Snakes could be still as stone before striking a death blow. Had the men under the blanket seen their death coming?

Ishmael had not. *This day, I do not die.* Braying donkey of a fool.

The rebel's red-trimmed turban flashed behind her lids, popping them open. "The rebel leader said he anticipated the general would withdraw the guards posted at the temple. To give aid in the ambush. Ishmael's men were to remove the ark and hide it once the area had been cleared. Might they have succeeded?"

"*Someone* succeeded. Whether the resistance or the four priests you selected."

Liora did not miss the slight emphasis on the word *you*. As sure as the blood pasting to her skin, Nergal would pin this on her. Then Arioch would retaliate and either be slain in the attempt or executed after. Either way, he would be out of Nergal's path to the king's highest favor.

Or perhaps his path to the kingdom itself? The prince was no military leader, but a cunning mind was as likely to win a throne as a mighty arm, as likely as idiocy was to lose it.

She said, "The priests would not have touched the ark without the appropriate preparations, and there was no time for such rituals."

"The priest avowed the same." His pacing halted. "Right before I ran him through."

"Pardon?" Instinctively, she made to sit up, but a foot pressed down on the back of her neck—hard, unexpected. Her elbows buckled, and her forehead clunked against the floor. Not so hard it knocked the confusion from her mind. "Ran...through?"

"With a sword, woman. Did the thunder rattle you witless? He resisted. Fought to distract from the others."

Sword. Through.

Liora's stomach clenched so fierce and fast vomit stormed her throat. Her body convulsed, but she caught the gag on a cough.

Nergal killed a holy man of God. "Which...which priest?"

Nergal huffed impatiently, and the parchment rustled. "Captain."

"He called himself Eitan, Your Highness." The man replied in monotone. "Eitan son of Buzi."

Molars clenched, Liora choked down a knot of grief. He'd known. Somehow. Had Jeremiah warned him? Or the Lord?

Whatever the case, he had willingly answered the call. Volunteered to transport the ark despite the outcome. Fought to make a way for the others. Fought for Yahweh.

For all her talk of sacrificing her life, could she have done the same? Honestly...she could not say. Not as she was, kneeling in the evidence of his sacrifice.

"And...the other priests?" she ventured, dreading the answer.

"Missing. Conveniently," the prince said, tone drab. "Along with the ark."

Missing! Had the elders done the impossible? Moved the ark and hidden it in the storm?

She could hope. While Nergal fumed.

Someone succeeded.

Rebels. Priests. Nergal clearly assumed the latter. What other reason might he have for slaying Eitan?

"Why? *Why* would you..." A sob jolted her.

"More stupid questions. Why do you think?" the prince snapped. "No, do not answer that. I haven't the patience today for your *gentle soul*. I killed him because we are short on rations. As you well know. And because he was violent and, as such, a threat to Babylon. And, by Marduk, woman, because I *felt like it*."

He laughed. *Laughed.*

While Liora's nails scraped the stone, and she imagined sharpening them. Better yet, she'd unchain the lioness and stand back. The Almighty had once used bears to avenge his prophet. Why not a lioness?

"And now," the prince said on a long laugh-ridding exhale. "I feel better. You should thank him, really. For the sacrifice. Thank your mole of a maid while you are at it. She cleared your name of the whole gods-forsaken debacle."

Gittel? He could mean no other.

How? Had he stationed more soldiers in the area than he'd let on? To have arrested Eitan and Gittel in the middle of a skirmish and a raging storm...

Prince Nergal-sharezer played an expert hand.

A political beast, Arioch called the man. Despite the caution, Nergal's indolent-prince act had deceived her. A cunning front, indeed, for an ambitious, far too sly schemer.

Meanwhile, Ishmael and Gittel had believed themselves terribly clever for placing her in Nergal's employ.

Mole of a maid. Had the prince *ever* been oblivious to their plotting. For even a moment?

"Where is she?" Liora asked in a dead tone, dread pooling in her center.

"Under the priest, I believe." Nergal fell silent. The pause dragged out, expectant. He wanted her to rail at him over the slain maid?

Liora bore down on her molars, dripped fresh tears, and inwardly railed at the maid instead. She had told Gittel, *told* her what would happen!

"I'll admit," Nergal continued at last, conversing like an old friend. "I wondered whether she was lying, speaking on your behalf because you intervened over the concubine's death. In the end, I decided her hate toward you was of the purest form. No, it was only her last shred of honor that obligated her to repay the debt. Which made her the most reliable witness of the lot.

Quite convenient for you since your innocence is clear."

Convenient, yes. Except for the blood seeping into the stone's pores, into her own.

"But enough about dusty artifacts and dead handmaids. I have a second, more pressing curiosity. At least in regard to your life."

No surprise Nergal would step right over Gittel's death, but the manner in which he dismissed the ark left her blinking as stupidly as he'd accused her of. Was the covenant ark not the coveted plunder she'd understood it to be?

Destroying another kingdom's idols hampered their gods, weakened them to the point of no retaliation. So the pagans believed. No conquering king would ignore the gods of the defeated. They either broke the idols to pieces, made sacrifices to appease them, or carted them off and absorbed them into their own pantheon.

The ark was as close to a physical representation of Yahweh as any enemy would find. Apprehending it should be at the top of Nergal's priorities. As it had seemed to be until this moment.

Something nagged at her, a thought she must pursue.

But the prince was speaking again about that *pressing curiosity*. "Is it customary in Judah for a woman to join one man in marriage while betrothed to another?"

What a question! "No, my lord. Such a thing is unthinkable." Reprehensible. Paramount to adultery.

A FAITH UNTAMED

"As I thought." A pause. "Why then, have you done it?"

"What?" she blurted.

"Why then," he repeated, slowly as if to the stupid side of her she'd brought into this hall, "have you done it?"

Done...what? Three sluggish heartbeats passed before she connected his last question to his first. He thought she'd married Arioch while betrothed to another?

Liora sat upright so quickly the room spun around her. "My lord?"

The guard made no move to force her back down.

She closed her eyes to set the world straight, though it helped her riotous thoughts not one bit. *Where* had Nergal gotten such notions as Liora bound to two men at once? Could Gittel have spread such poison? Vengeance before being *run through?*

"There is that look of shock I'd so hoped for." Nergal stood several long strides off. A red, sleeveless robe fell elegantly about his trim figure, and not a speck of blood marred the ringed fingers tapping at his smoothly shaved chin. The parchment dangled forgotten from his other hand. He wore a smirk, his amber-brown eyes almost a match for Ashara's.

The lioness paced, her astute golden eyes never leaving the prince. Break that taut chain, and Nergal's bowels would be the first to spill.

Commotion sounded from beyond the closed doors. Shouting. A single man. The clatter of striking shields or armor. Liora did not dare turn.

"Otherwise," Nergal said, frowning toward the disturbance, "I would be obligated to send a bad report to the king. Which would not bode well for your odds of living beyond the hour." He fluffed his robe, and the rich scent of his perfume wafted over, a brief respite from the stink of blood. "You see, in spite of your connection to my greatest rival, the very one hassling my men," he said with a significant look at the doors, "I find you agreeable."

He shifted focus to the guard at her side. "She is likable, is she not?" The man's feet shuffled, perhaps considering another stomp on her neck, but Nergal pressed on, already back to addressing Liora. "In truth, I cannot conceive of a situation that might produce the chambermaid's hatred. Apart from one of her own making. But that is aside. *This* matter"—he rapped the parchment, rings glittering in the braziers' light—"is not."

A furious, roared demand to "stand aside"—distinctly Arioch—hiked Liora's shoulders a fraction. The man would earn himself a beheading. She cleared the desert from her throat but not the tremble. "And what matter, exactly, is that?"

The doors rattled on their hinges, and Ashara chuffed.

Nergal raised his voice. "The matter of your betrothal to King Zedekiah remaining intact and— Oh, let him in!" He flung a gesture at the chamber's rear.

"Yes, Your High—"

The doors banged open and crashed against the scrambling inner guards.

A FAITH UNTAMED

Liora's shoulders bounced, then bounced again at Ashara's high-pitched snarl.

Marching strides slapped their way into the chamber. "Your Highness." Arioch barked the title like a reproach. "Respectfully, it is unlawful to interrogate a woman without her husband's—"

He halted abruptly at the commanding lift of Prince Nergal's hand.

"Husband." Chuckling darkly, the prince never removed his eyes from Liora, and Liora's whirring mind never left that other ridiculous thing he'd said.

"Betrothal?" Her head shook, rapid wags that exacerbated the lightheadedness. "No, it...it cannot be."

"Your Highness, please," Arioch said, not a hint of *plea* in the word. Only deep-throated threat. "Though falsely accused, the lady carried out her sentence. Bringing it up now is—"

"If you value her life, Butcher,"—Nergal slid his eyes to Arioch, his smile leonine—"you will utter not another word." Unfazed by Arioch's loud, furious breaths, he rolled his arm at Liora. "Go on."

She must, to clear her name. But her lips had gone numb, her tongue a shriveled piece of meat left too long in the sun. "The day"—her throat lurched with a swallow—"he accused me of...of..." There, her voice croaked to a stop, refusing to air the hideous lies. Bringing them to light now could not help the prince's opinion of her.

"Of dallying with an Edomite?" He arched a black eyebrow, and her jaw slackened. "More shock, *dove*?"

he said, ignoring Arioch's huff. "It is all here in the records. I told you I had come to Jerusalem to investigate." He pointed vaguely behind him, presumably at a short stack of tablets sitting on the dais. "But do continue. The day he accused you..."

What use was there to continue? If he'd gotten his twisted facts from King Zedekiah, she was already doomed to whatever judgment entertained the prince most. Her skin went clammy. "He burned the contract. Publicly. Before the court. Then, then he sent me out to be..."

Her ears filled with phantom shouting. Hateful, vulgar names hurled at her with as much force as the projectiles cracking her bones.

Breath rushed in and out of her open mouth, serenaded by Arioch's snarling.

"To be stoned." Nergal filled in, his flippant reference to the king's betrayal and to the terror of a stoning sparking enough anger to straighten the hunch from her spine.

"Yes." She licked her lips, tried to think past worry Arioch's mounting fury would grow into something more deadly. "My arm was broken before Ishmael arrived to call a halt."

Arioch's growling cut off.

"Ishmael?" Nergal sucked a tooth as if to free a chunk of meat. "The rebel leader."

She dipped her chin. "The same, Your Highness." Wiping her filthy palms on her robe, she felt a modicum of steadiness returning to her. So long as Arioch stayed put. Kept his words behind those gnashing teeth. "The king's cousin. I spotted him after the fight today. Dead."

"Our bloody Butcher to thank for it." The prince left off fussing with that tooth to slide his lips into a smirk. "Ashara and I approve."

The lioness shook her massive body, rattling her chain, then dropped to her haunches and curled her tail about her forelegs in an innocent pose.

Nergal asked, "Did you read the contract Zedekiah burned?"

"I did not." Hadn't even considered it, as terrified and humiliated as she'd been.

"Your father?"

"He was not present. It...it all happened very fast and was..." A blur of stinging accusations, the dart of betrayal a blinding, physical pain in her chest. She rubbed the spot. "Confusing."

"Per the puppet king's orchestration, no doubt." For once, Nergal's voice softened with what might pass as pity. "But whatever he burned, it was *not* your betrothal contract. That remains intact, complete with signatures, seals, and so forth." He pinched the wrinkled parchment and extended it as one might a soiled undergarment.

Liora agreed with the sentiment. And yet, she held out her hand. "May I read it."

In the quiet, Arioch exhaled loudly, the sound of relief.

"She learns!" Nergal's few steps put the document into her unsteady hands.

A skim of it confirmed the prince did not exaggerate. It was longer than she recalled, but she'd been a child then and didn't remember a word of it. Now, as a woman, she recognized the precise script of the royal scribe as well as her abba's signature and seal, that of her king beside it.

Her betrothed. Because, as she'd reassured the queen, Zedekiah was not dead. And because, as she'd so blithely told Nergal, in Judah, until the marriage was severed by death or law, her life was tied to her husband's.

Any person could set this document beside the one binding her to Arioch and accuse her of the very thing she'd been refuting for years—deceit, unfaithfulness, treachery.

And both held her abba's name.

The memory of his agony over Arioch's ultimatum returned with new perspective. After an hour of consideration and prayer, he'd emerged from his chamber pale and shaken, her marriage contract to Arioch still wet with his seal.

Abba, what have you done to me?

Saliva filled her mouth, precursor to the bile once again climbing her throat. She swallowed the bitterness. "The contract is in order. Although, I cannot... I do not know how...*why*." Her gaze flickered to the flames dancing in the nearest brazier.

Two quick strides and a hasty toss would undo it all.

"Ah-ah-ah." Nergal shook a raised finger. "This issue now falls before my king—and yours, seeing you

A FAITH UNTAMED

are now his subject. Although..." He tapped the same finger against his chin, eyes widening, as if struck by a sudden thought. "No, in fact, this elevates you *beyond* mere subject to King Nebuchadnezzar. Does it not?"

"Beyond?" she asked, her head in a continuous shake of denial.

Beyond combined with Nergal's all-too-pleased expression could mean only one thing.

No. *No, no, no.*

"Ah. You are unfamiliar with the Law of Conquest." Smiling like a benevolent father, Nergal extended an arm toward Arioch. "Dear Butcher. As His Majesty's conquering general, this is your area of expertise. Would you do us the honor of explaining?"

Slowly, a boulder of dread weighing her sick stomach, she turned, lifted her eyes.

The devastation on Arioch's face was everything Nergal could wish for. Everything she'd feared. His arms hung limp at his sides. Jaw moving, he said nothing.

She would be ill. Right there before those powerful men, she would spew the contents of her stomach all down her robes. "Ari?"

He groaned. "Your Highness, please." This time, the appropriate pleading and deference filled the request.

"Oh, very well. *I* will have the honor of educating the woman." Nergal heaved a long-suffering breath. "According to royal decree, all wives, consorts, and concubines of a defeated monarch become the legal property of the conqueror. Which means, Lady Liora," he said, snatching the document from her senseless fingers, "you now belong to Nebuchadnezzar, King of Babylon, Sovereign of the Four Quarters of the Earth, Chosen of Marduk, and most recently,"—he swept a low, flourishing mocking bow—"collector of discarded Judean brides."

CHAPTER 21

Behold, I am the Lord, the God of all flesh: is there anything too hard for me?

For I know the thoughts that I think toward you, saith the Lord, thoughts of peace, and not of evil, to give you an expected end. (Jer. 32:27, 29:11)

Half of Babylon knew that Prince Nergal was a lying, fork-tongued snake. Nebuzaradan held this as fact. How many times had Nergal mocked him for his inability to concoct a believable deception? Had urged him to practice the skill as one did swordplay?

Indeed, Prince Nergal was a supreme liar.

And yet, as Nebuzaradan worked alongside his soldiers inside Jerusalem's eastern wall, he could not banish from his mind Liora's shocked expression. She'd gripped that contract, read its contents, and gone as pale as a winter sky. Schooled in her father's script and seal, she would recognize an authentic document. A forgery would not easily deceive her. Even one crafted by a prince with a tongue split down the middle. Which gave that pallor of hers a level of meaning Nebuzaradan could barely stomach.

"Heave, *heave!*" He put his own order into action. Hitched mule-like to a crumbling section of the wall, he bore into the rope biting his shoulder and *pulled*.

Down the line, men grunted and shouted out their effort. Beside him, Idadu made not a sound, though sweat pasted his tunic to his chest, and drops fell from the hair dangling over his forehead. In Nebuzaradan's blind spot, Rimutu groaned with the best of them.

"Heave, you motherless wretches!" Thighs burning, molars grinding through grit, Nebuzaradan canted forward to add his weight to the force. The hunk of stones at their backs rocked in position but refused to tumble down with the rest of the rubble.

They'd been at this section for the last hour, hacking at the mortar and picking away smaller stones. As blood pounded in his temples and his knees wobbled, he entertained the notion he'd chosen too large a portion to remove at once.

On a bark of fury, he relented. Ribs laboring at double-speed, he raised an arm. "Halt!"

Men crashed to their knees. Several took advantage of the reprieve to flop out on their backs and pant up at the bold blue sky.

Anger flared in Nebuzaradan's gut. He stormed around Idadu to jam the toe of his boot against the nearest man's quivering thigh. "Get your miserable carcass off the ground!"

The soldier's eyes flew open. Stuttering apologies, he scrambled upright. As did the fellow just past him. Those farther away took their time climbing up from the dirt.

"If your general is not down, neither are you," he bellowed and tasted the salt of sweat. He spat and swiped a forearm across his mouth. Dust scoured his lips, and he spat again, a curse on Jerusalem and its impenetrable walls held on a short leash inside his throat. Even if he was mostly certain the god was gone.

This was Yahweh's territory. Nebuzaradan would not be heard praying damnation on any part of it. Not until he was safely beyond the river in the land of Marduk. Until then, it was buckets of sweat and backbreaking labor. He was, after all, a slave to the Jewish god, under orders to destroy the city.

If his blinded eye told him anything, it was this: Do as told. Tread carefully upon holy ground. Guard the god's most precious daughter.

He'd failed at all three.

An agony shot through his chest. He wheezed and gripped the spot. With the way his heart spent the last days aching like a bruised muscle, he might say it was dying. If he didn't know better.

If he weren't fully aware it was simply not in residence.

Torn from its mooring, his heart now beat inside the Jewish harem somewhere in the black hole of the prince's snake-pit residence.

All that was left to Nebuzaradan was a bleeding, gaping chasm. There was some comfort in knowing his heart was in tender hands. Liora would care for it well Even as she clicked her tongue at his current behavior.

"Back to it!" he shouted. "But shift those ropes there. Forget that section. Not *that* one!"

While he bellowed and berated and went down the line shaming his men into new placement, he imagined her carrying water to each one. The same he'd worked to within three panted breaths of passing out in the heat. Never mind they were not her people but the very soldiers who'd heckled her on her way into his camp.

She would pass around the water skin, not leaving until she'd conjured a smile from each fellow. Not a difficult feat for such a woman. She had a habit of inspiring blushes and smiles.

Liora, his dove, his light. The stunning ray of goodness who'd banished a sliver of darkness from his butchering soul, enough to persuade him it might be worth salvaging. To convince him redemption was perhaps not a forgone loss.

Liora. His spirit groaned as wretchedly as his body. Anger, the surest distraction.

He pointed to two men where they struggled in their awkward positioning in the rubble. "Tighten the gap there! And for the love of every accursed god in—"

Captain Idadu stepped into his path and gripped his shoulder, drawing close.

Armor-less and shirtless, Nebuzaradan snarled at the hot, unwelcome touch. But he'd seen it coming and hadn't prevented it. Why, he didn't care to explore. Though he didn't prevent that either.

When Idadu met Nebuzaradan straight in the eye and murmured, "We will *all* think more clearly after a rest," Nebuzaradan admitted to himself he *wanted* someone to moderate him, to control this relentless drive to demolish the wall. Because he could not do it himself. Could not rest. Could not stop.

Three days he'd been at it. Tearing at the last standing segment. Beating away its parapet. Opening a

A FAITH UNTAMED

breach to prevent future entrenchment in a siege. No more festering resistance behind these hateful stones.

Yahweh had ordered him to disassemble this city. So he would.

No more defiance. No more distractions.

If he must, Nebuzaradan would take it apart himself, stone by bloody stone. With his very teeth.

The sooner the task was done, the sooner they could march for Riblah and Nebuzaradan's laid-bare soul—his desperate plea face down before the king. He would humiliate himself if King Nebuchadnezzar required it.

And he would. At a minimum.

One look at Liora, one hour in her presence, and the king would understand. It would all make sense, the reason Nebuzaradan had left his post and arrived with the all-too-transparent excuse of reporting in person. Followed promptly by a request to wed a captive Jewess.

Babylon's Butcher *never* left his post. Unless it was to march home in pomp and victory, a conquered enemy king fumbling behind in chains.

His king might have let it pass with mere cheek-scratching curiosity if Nebuzaradan had not also requested a divorce.

Nebuzaradan had known better, of course. Had calculated the risk. But he also knew Liora. Or thought he did...

Instead of being relieved she might become First Wife instead of Second, she'd scolded him about the request for a divorce. Her worry over Aralu, the straying heifer, still flabbergasted him. But then, unpredictability was part of Liora's irresistible charm. Unlike Aralu who was a squat stool, standing on the three legs of jewels, parties, and dalliances, Liora was a net of fluttering, mesmerizing butterflies. No pattern to her behavior apart from complete devotion to a god not bound by stone.

Yes, King Nebuchadnezzar would understand why Nebuzaradan had wanted Liora wed to him before his sovereign had a chance to meet her.

He would understand all too well. And he would be smitten.

Had any man, in one form or fashion, met the beauty of Jerusalem and *not* been? Even ancient Buzi was taken with her, referring to her as *chamanit* when Nebuzaradan stumbled into the house the night of Nergal's gut-punching revelation.

Chamanit—little sunflower. An appropriate endearment. Sunflowers stood tall, bright, and cheery, their wide-open faces always pointing up. They lightened the spirit and blanketed the fields in colors of sunlight.

Although, when the king laid eyes on that chamanit, when he learned she was untouched by any man, the only *blankets* he would be thinking of would be those covering his kingly bed.

When he claimed her, she would protest. With dignity. With weeping. Neither would move him. But if any woman could survive Nebuchadnezzar's bed with her spirit intact, it was Liora bat Chesed.

A FAITH UNTAMED

The thought of it, though... The thought of any man invading her against her wishes...

Nebuzaradan's next inhale cut off, his chest bound by that aching vice of emptiness.

Yahweh, where is your army slaying might? Intervene for your daughter!

Abdomen contracting, he hunched slightly forward into Idadu's space.

The captain's sweaty brow puckered with concern, his fingers pinching hard. "Have you injured yourself?"

Nebuzaradan gave his head a swift, firm shake, not trusting his thickening throat not to shame him.

Idadu's mouth flattened into a line. He was not convinced. Were any of them? Had any *not* heard of Lady Liora's predicament, not passed gossip behind their hands like empty-headed biddies?

Sweat seeped into his eyes. He let it sting. "What do the men say about her?" He spoke low through his teeth.

Idadu pulled back, his head tilted. "Nothing bad. Not about her, at any rate."

"About whom?"

"The father. And the puppet king. Some of the men talk of..." Idadu looked off, indecision trailing his voice.

Nebuzaradan was keen to let him work it out, but—blast his ruined eye—someone spoke up outside his limited view. "We will kill him for you if you wish it, General."

Twisting, Nebuzaradan searched for the speaker in the crowd, but each man looked the same as the next. Sweaty, filthy, exhausted but determined. Same as he, most likely. With the way he'd worked them at the wall, he did not deserve their loyalty.

But they wanted the task finished as much as he. Apparently, they wanted Zedekiah's blood on their hands, too. Or had the soldier meant Chesed, the father? The man was in the camp guarded by men under firm orders to keep Nebuzaradan away. He could not trust himself. Apparently, he could not trust his soldiers either. Or should he say Liora's soldiers?

She is every man's sister, Idadu had said. And what did an honorable man do to avenge his sister's dishonor? *Shed blood for her, die for her as they would their own kin.*

"Let it be known," Nebuzaradan said as he turned a slow circle, voice ringing, "the lady's father will render account to the king." He paused to let that—as well as the unspoken consequences of interfering—sink in. "And when the time comes, the dog Zedekiah is *mine*."

King Nebuchadnezzar would grant him that much at least. Even should Nebuzaradan be out of favor, his title of Chief Executioner should ensure the puppet king's suffering would fall to his pleasure.

"But," he added, with a nasty grin, "if you have any suggestions for how it should be done, I am happy to entertain them."

A chorus of hoots and laughter greeted the invitation, and Idadu's eyes twinkled, a true exhibition of emotion for the reserved captain. The man would cheerfully hold Zedekiah down for punishment, his dedication to Liora unmatched by all but

A FAITH UNTAMED

Nebuzaradan. And perhaps the irritatingly likable worm Šulmanu.

"Back to work!" Idadu's order scattered the men just in time for another call to come from behind Nebuzaradan.

"General! My lord general!" Haldi trudged up on strides that dragged and might have once been a run. The steward—recently reinstated from his banishment over the tattoo incident—was as sweaty and winded as the men who'd spent half the day hauling stone. He stopped before Nebuzaradan, angled forward in what looked to be the beginnings of a bow but ended up with an arm wrapped around his lower ribs. Holding up a hand, he grimaced and gasped for breath. "A...moment."

Nebuzaradan frowned at the man's rumpled tunic and skewed turban. What had him in such a state? Was it— Fear zinged through his veins. That morning, Haldi had determined to take a change of clothing to Liora.

He grabbed the steward's arm in a locking grip. "Is it Liora?"

Haldi jerked his head up and down.

Nebuzaradan felt the blood drain from his face. *Bring her back to me Yahweh, and I promise you this. I will tear up that sham of a marriage contract.* He would wed her properly.

As she'd begged of him. As the prophet had demanded of him. As he'd almost proposed in her bedchamber before Nergal's accursed guards arrived to escort her away.

Even as he vowed his second vow to the foreign god, he passed a beseeching look to Idadu, who then snapped at Haldi.

"Breathe later, man. Speak!"

"I bring"—Haldi gulped air—"a message. From your wi— From Lady Liora. But I cannot make sense of it."

Because the clever woman didn't mean for him to. Nebuzaradan clenched his muscles to keep from rattling the steward's brains in his skull. "What did she say? *Exact* words."

"She said." Haldi hauled another draught of breath. "Look behind the panel for a way out."

Way out...way out... Of Jerusalem? Nebuzaradan shook his head. "And? What else?"

"And that is all, my lord." He produced a kerchief from his sash and mopped his brow. "I asked her twice. She only smiled and repeated herself. So I came here straightaway trusting my lord would—"

"Way out," Nebuzaradan blurted. Of her betrothal. Through the scroll he'd come across behind that panel. He whipped a glance at Idadu.

The captain's wide eyes said he'd unraveled it, too. "The father's study." He stretched an arm in the direction of Liora's home. "I am with you."

Nebuzaradan turned to peg Rimutu with a commanding tone. "Bring this wall down."

The soldier's spine straightened so fast his helmet teetered on his ears.

If he responded, Nebuzaradan didn't hear. He was already marching off, the whistling wind muffling his

A FAITH UNTAMED

hearing, his mind stretching forward to that panel. Three streets from the house, he abandoned the pretense of dignity and broke into a run.

True to his word, Idadu stuck to his side, even shouted ahead. "Open for the general!"

The guard swung the massive door inward and jumped out of Nebuzaradan's way.

Inside the home was a blur. Devorah bustled in from somewhere, Šulmanu not far behind. Neither spoke but plastered their backs to the wall when Nebuzaradan barreled past. His hands were shaking when he wrenched the panel off the wall in the study. He tossed it aside.

Only one scroll remained inside the dark stone niche, a roll of parchment eerily similar in cut to the one Nergal had flaunted like a victory flag. Nebuzaradan snatched it out and spun to find Idadu by the table with an oil lamp. Its flame lit such a bright-eyed look of hope on the captain's face, Nebuzaradan's stomach flipped.

Had Yahweh actually heard his prayer? Intervened so quickly? The god *was* powerful. But would he use that power in this manner? Only one way to find out.

Nebuzaradan strode for the table and nearly tripped over the panel's edge where it hid on his blind side. He kicked it out of his path. "Lamp."

When Idadu shoved the flame nearer, Nebuzaradan rotated the scroll to shed light on the unmistakable seal of Zedekiah, an unbroken dab of clay impressed with a circular image. Two clasped hands. Zedekiah's attempt to convince the world he stood in alliance with his master, Babylon.

Idadu's swallow was audible. "Should we wait to open it until we stand before—"

Nebuzaradan cracked the seal. Clay crumbled to the floor. He bent over the table and unrolled the sheet on its top.

"Very well, then." Idadu brought the lamp close, and golden light flickered across the horizontal rows of text. "Can you...read that?"

Nebuzaradan's eyes skipped to the left to read, then remembered the symbols ran backwards. He traced the jagged marks with a finger, right to left, leaving a dirty trail and frowning at how the words ran together. "I told Liora I could read Hebrew as well as she." The upper edge began rolling up. Nebuzaradan slapped a hand over it.

"And?"

"And I might have been exaggerating."

The flame wavered under Idadu's breathy laugh. "The things we say to impress a female."

Grunting, Nebuzaradan tried the next line but only picked out a word here and there. "One would think me impressive enough already." His gaze hopped to the bottom of the document to confirm both Zedekiah's and Chesed's marks occupied the space. He began again but stalled out a few words in.

"What is this? Vines?" A bolt of anger exploded in his gut. "I cannot read this scrawl!" He shot a glare at the door and the puffing sounds coming from the hall. "Haldi!"

A FAITH UNTAMED

The steward jogged, feet shuffling, into the chamber. His sweat-shined cheeks flamed red. "At your exalted service...my lord."

"Read." Nebuzaradan thrust the document at him, and Idadu provided light.

Haldi skimmed, brow furrowing. "A duplicate of the betrothal contract."

"Yes, yes." Nebuzaradan waved impatiently. "Is there any inconsistency with the one Nergal described?"

Over the last days, he had discussed the matter at length with his closest advisors—strangely, the men in the room. Nebuzaradan had never been one to require counsel of any person. He did as he wished and either suffered the consequences or basked in the praise alone. But this thing with Liora—King Nebuchadnezzar's curiosity with her history and Nergal's zeal with using her as a plaything and a weapon—had left him at a loss, paralyzed with indecision.

Idadu's candid wisdom and seeming immunity to trembling in Nebuzaradan's presence had proven invaluable. While Liora was escorted away in the prince's residence, it had been Idadu who'd physically restrained Nebuzaradan. And again when he'd gotten it into his mind the next day to storm the harem.

Haldi proved his worth by savvy in the law and his unflinching faithfulness to the House of Axes.

They stared at him now as he panted garlic breath all over the sheet, his expression growing grimmer by the second. "The same, the same," he muttered, gaze speeding across the text. "That too. Yes, and that."

This was bad. Very bad. Confirmation of everything the prince had claimed unfolding right before Nebuzaradan.

That fast-becoming-familiar agony in his chest climbed his throat, tightened it painfully. He would weep. Before his subordinates, he would humiliate himself with woman's tears. Jaw clenched, he held the emotion at bay, clinging to dignity by the edges of his fingernails.

Haldi raised a finger. "Wait."

Air burst from Nebuzaradan's lips, the breath he hadn't realized he'd been holding. "What is it? Something different? Tell me it is different." Something they could work with. Any minor detail might be useful in the correct hands. And Nebuzaradan had a set of those.

"Here. This passage crammed in above the king's mark." Haldi tapped the bottom segment. "Almost as an afterthought. Indeed, the cramped script would say so."

"What is it?" Nebuzaradan boomed.

Idadu sighed, a long-suffering sound, but Haldi's shoulders jumped high.

When they came down, the steward had the audacity to huff. "A clause, my lord," he said, nose lifting with scholarly hauteur. The man was in his element, and Nebuzaradan never appreciated it more. Especially when a gleam came into his eyes. "A condition, if you will. If the prince's copy contains the passage, he said nothing of it."

Nebuzaradan would strangle him. "Of what!"

This time, Haldi did not flinch; he grinned. "Of vineyards. Zedekiah's. His choicest. A plot on the ridge above the Kidron Valley. It shall pass to Chesed ben Ephraim should Zedekiah strike his daughter, Liora, a death blow."

Silence fell over them.

"But...he *did*." Idadu's brow rumpled. "He condemned her to a stoning."

The reminder flushed raging heat through Nebuzaradan's chest. He breathed methodically through his nose to allay the urge to destroy something. When he was at last given permission to make the Jerusalem king pay, he would take his time at it. Make the man understand exactly how Nebuzaradan earned the name Butcher.

Then he would take an axe to that *despicable* vineyard above the Kidron and—

Nebuzaradan froze, his hand reaching reflexively to grip his axe's head. "Above the Kidron, you say? On the mount with the olive grove?"

Haldi scanned the document once more. "There is nothing about an olive grove but—"

"It is the same."

"The same as *what*?" Haldi asked.

"Devorah!" Nebuzaradan shouted, hope springing his heart in his chest.

The maid appeared so fast she had to have been waiting just out of sight. She stood in the doorway and wrung her hands in the rag that never left her possession, her sun-browned complexion as drawn as he'd ever seen it. "You wish to know about the vineyards, my lord?"

"I do." Later, he would address the spying. "Go ask...Zipporah"—the woman's name almost eluded him—"if Chesed ever acquired the lands and vineyards mentioned in this document. They are called *the king's choicest* and are located on the Mount of Olives. Go!"

Devorah vanished without so much as a bob of the knee.

Nebuzaradan whipped his attention back to Haldi. "What else?"

"At first glance, nothing. But allow me to read more thoroughly." The steward set about the task as Nebuzaradan paced.

They'd found that *something different* he needed. *She* needed.

A triumphant laugh belted past Nebuzaradan's teeth, startling the steward.

Snorting indignation, Haldi went back to his study while Idadu grew a subdued smile and watched Nebuzaradan stalk, content to let his general share when he was ready.

He wasn't, too afraid to voice his hope lest it vanish like a mist.

Yes, Nebuzaradan the great Butcher was afraid. He feared like he never had before, the power of it enough to choke a man. But hope...now *that* was stronger. And infinitely more terrifying.

A FAITH UNTAMED

If the vineyards had changed hands, his argument was a golden scepter. King Nebuchadnezzar could not dispute the worthlessness of a contract founded on collateral that did not actually belong to the obligated party.

Because that vineyard, the one with the shrine dedicated to Nabû, patron god of the king himself, was not Zedekiah's, but Nebuchadnezzar's. Zedekiah had the keeping of it but no authority beyond hiring workers to dress it. Did Chesed not know? Nebuzaradan intended to learn the answer.

But first, the vineyard's fate. If it had *not* changed hands, he still had leverage, though it would be weaker. He might be forced to rely on his ability to sway King Nebuchadnezzar into giving up his prize. The odds of that were...far from encouraging. Breaching Jerusalem's walls was a less-daunting task.

After shackled kings, King Nebuchadnezzar most enjoyed parading his most beautiful concubines. Of that collection, Liora would undoubtedly be the crown.

Fury propelled Nebuzaradan's strides through the chamber's confines. Chesed did this. He signed away his daughter. No, Yahweh's daughter. To a dirt-eating grub. Then sent her to *him*, a merciless Butcher. A pagan, as Liora would call him.

She also called him husband. His heart squeezed painfully, a beautiful ache.

As much as he wanted to, he could not harm his love's father. Apparently, could not even speak of *not* harming him. The memory of her sparking eyes and lashing tongue almost made him smile. Until he thought of Zedekiah.

Unfortunately, Nebuzaradan could not conceive a world where he was allowed to kill Zedekiah. One of King Nebuchadnezzar's greatest pleasures was collecting conquered lords and kings, caging them as Nergal did his lioness, then bringing them out in chains at banquets to humiliate them before his guests.

Liora would detest it. One more reason to remove her from King Nebuchadnezzar's clutches. One of dozens.

"She is here, General." Devorah's heavily accented voice startled Nebuzaradan from his bloody imaginings. The friend, Zipporah, new wife of the scoundrel Chesed, stood straight-backed beside the maid. Not a shred of fear about her, only indignation. She clipped out a few sentences, and the maid translated. "To her knowledge, House Chesed has not acquired new lands since her husband's marriage to his first wife, Liora's mother."

"None. Not one plot?"

The women exchanged words before Devorah shook her head. "Not a one."

Nebuzaradan's flagging knees forced him to drop his weight to the tabletop. He bent and buried his fingers in his hair, breath shuddering out of him.

"What does this mean?" Idadu asked.

"If it is the vineyard I recall, nothing for certain," Haldi stated, too hasty to cast the discovery in shades of caution.

A FAITH UNTAMED

"It is everything," Nebuzaradan snapped, pushing to his feet. He strode to Idadu and clasped the man on the shoulder. "It means we have a weapon." One with a dull edge, to be sure, but what was Nebuzaradan if not a soldier who knew how to sharpen a blade?

A grin formed on Idadu's thin face, then grew. "Nebuchadnezzar might be king of Babylon," he said, voice dim enough to carry nowhere but to Nebuzaradan's ears, "but you are its greatest conqueror. In the realm of women, of course." His eyes twinkled.

A lie if ever Nebuzaradan heard one, but he appreciated the sentiment. He squeezed the man's shoulder and returned the grin. "Careful, Captain. That is treason with which you flirt."

The humor faded from Idadu's expression. Resolve squared his shoulders. He locked eyes with Nebuzaradan in a silent repeat of his earlier promise. *I am with you.* But when he opened his mouth again, it was not his own loyalty he spoke. "This vineyard detail is no coincidence. The god of this land, *her* god, is with you."

Nebuzaradan's fingers migrated to his cursed eye.

Yahweh *with* Nebuzaradan? Perhaps the way a master was *with* his slave when he applied the whip. For his defiance, for his deplorable care of the god's daughter and loss of his sacred artifact, no slave deserved it more.

But this find... Perhaps the captain had a point. Judah's god had made a way. *A way out.* For the sake of his most deserving daughter.

Nebuzaradan had much work to do. His brain whirred.

He blinked and found himself traversing the halls of Liora's home, mind stuffed full with questions and possibilities. Blinked again and he was seated at her painting table, a thin brush between his fingers. Strategies unfolded before him like a battle plan laid out on a board.

Tentative footsteps approach from behind, a waft of baked bread entering with them.

"Devorah," he said. "Spying is a capital crime."

"Yes, my lord. The lady will be most displeased to hear of my death. When she returns."

Clever wench.

A slow smile crept over Nebuzaradan's face, growing until it tugged at the toughened flesh of his scar. He stroked the stained handle of the paintbrush and imagined Liora's delicate fingers there, forming words of adoration for her god. "Pack up her belongings, maid. Have them sent to my tent. Take care with her paints. She'll want them," he said, "when she arrives home."

~~~

Thank you for reading!
Visit April's website and subscribe for bonus Neb content upon release: www.aprilgardner.com.
If you enjoyed the book, please let other readers know by leaving a review on your favorite online venue.
Thank you!

Book 3: *A Love Unmatched, A Novel of Jerusalem's Survivors and Babylon's Claim*

In the ashes of conquest, love becomes the boldest rebellion.

As Babylonian soldiers prod the last wave of exiles from Jerusalem, Liora is set apart, chosen for a purpose that terrifies her more than all the war machines in Babylon. With her fate tangled in politics, prophecy, and her people's distrust, every step away from Jerusalem draws her deeper into the plots of conniving men.

Liora and her God have awakened something in General Nebuzaradan he cannot silence. He is no stranger to conquest, but extricating Liora from a perilous entanglement will test not his blade, but his cunning. And this time, it's not a city he must conquer, but a love and a future he dares to claim.

He took the city. She took his heart.
Yahweh will have his soul.

Preorder on Author's Website:
www.aprilgardner.com/yokeofbabylon

Preorder on Amazon:

BONUS CONTENT

A woman stolen.
A storm unleashed.
A vow on the brink of ruin.

When Liora is taken by rebels and used as bait, General Nebuzaradan will stop at nothing to bring her back. Even if it means walking into a trap and unleashing the wrath of Babylon to do it. But as the rain falls and blades clash, he's haunted by a deeper fear—that he might have already failed her.

In this exclusive bonus scene told from Neb's point of view, witness the desperate rescue, the vow he breaks to hold her, and the prayer he breathes into the blood-soaked storm.

SUBSCRIBE FOR NEB BONUS CONTENT

AUTHOR'S NOTE

A Faith Untamed is probably my boldest work of fiction yet since I touch on the Ark of the Covenant *and* the Shekinah glory departing the temple as described in Ezekiel 10. The burden to get them right weighed on me throughout the writing process. But Scripture doesn't give us much information on either of them at this stage in Judah's history. None on the ark. And when was the last time you heard teaching on the Shekinah leaving the temple?

Confession: I hadn't given Ezekiel 10 much thought before studying for this novel. It always seemed like just one more chapter in a dense, sometimes confusing prophetic book. (I mean, chariots with wheels within wheels? *scratches head*) When it comes to major biblical events, it's probably safe to say the dramatic exodus of the Shekinah from the temple doesn't make a lot of top ten lists. Maybe because it's told only as prophecy and not included in the list of Jerusalem-destroying details recorded in 2 Kings and Jeremiah.

Still. How is it possible we rarely talk about the day the Lord's patience ran out? When He was so appalled by the sins of His people, so insulted in His holiness, that He walked away (floated? flew? rolled?) from His earthly throne? But this moment is pivotal, y'all. It's a turning point in history, the day the scale tipped from *long-suffering* to *enough.*

While studying and writing, I kept thinking of the cross when Jesus cried, "My God, my God, why have you forsaken me?" In that particular world-altering, pivotal moment, Jesus took on the sins of the world, becoming, for a time, something a holy God could not look upon. Not until our Savior Jesus Christ abolished death and brought life and immortality to light through the Gospel (1 Tim. 1:10).

Four hundred(ish) years earlier, the sins of Judah were so grievous Yahweh left the temple and acted on His promise of judgement. He first returned in the person of Jesus Christ (Luke 2), but He won't sit on His earthly throne again until "the kingdom of the world has become the kingdom of our Lord and of His Christ, and He shall reign forever and ever" (Rev. 11:15).

Oops. I seriously didn't intend for this to evolve into a Bible study. But there's no way I was going to leave Christ out of this story. Nope, nope. There is a Great Hope, sweet friend! He dwelled among us, and one day, He will return in all His Shekinah glory to fix this broken world, blessed be His holy name.

Okay, back to Liora and Neb...

Scripture isn't clear on when exactly the Shekinah left, only that it happened during Babylon's invasion. We don't even know for sure when the ark was taken, which deportation. Or if it even *was*. A wise king might have hidden the ark before the enemy arrived, but we have proof Judah's kings were not wise. Neither did they value the sacred or respect Yahweh's law or listen to His prophets or care at all for anything to do with righteousness.

The odds of the Babylonians carting off the ark? High.

A FAITH UNTAMED

It's good to ponder how it might have felt for the faithful Jews to watch Babylon defile (and possibly steal) the sacred ark, but I don't intend to give an answer to its fate. I'm no theologian or fedora-sporting archeologist. All I can say is that we see the ark one last time in Revelation 11:19: *And the temple of God was opened in heaven, and there was seen in his temple the ark of his testament: and there were lightnings, and voices, and thunderings, and an earthquake, and great hail.*

So at some point (maybe even in 586 BC), the ark was/will be transported to the temple of God in heaven. Good enough for me! The lack of answers will have to be good enough for Liora too, as you'll see in *A Love Unmatched*.

You'll see lots of other things in the next book, too, such as Liora before the king and Neb's gift of stratagem as he works to free her. We'll have to do something about that unfaithful moo-cow Aralu, and what about the most pressing question—will they *ever* kiss??

Ahem. I mean, will Neb *ever* humble himself before Yahweh? Yes, *that's* the most important question. :-D

I guess you'll just have to wait to find out...

Meanwhile, if you'd like to read what inspired Neb's axe-breaking story read here:
https://www.sefaria.org/Sanhedrin.96b?lang=bi

And if you'd like to learn what rabbis have to say about Zechariah's murder in relation to Neb, read here (be warned, it's a strange one!):

https://www.sefaria.org/Eikhah_Rabbah.4.16?lang=bi&with=all&lang2=en

And just for fun, here's an animated map of Nebuchadnezzar's campaigns: https://ibiblemaps.com/nebuchadnezzar-campaign-604-586/#open-overlay

As always, I pray this story leads you to open your Bible and dig into the events. Study to show yourself approved! (2 Tim. 2:15)

Because He lives,

April W Gardner

Acknowledgments

My perpetual thanks to God for the gift, the inspiration, and the health to write. I am so blessed.

I pray you are, too, for having read *A Faith Untamed*! Is it weird to say I felt you there beside me as I wrote? Yeah, it's weird, but then I'm an author so... That's expected, right? ;-)

Seriously though, I do think of my readers with every word that's penned, and I pray you grow closer to the Lord by exploring the Bible and its truths through story.

Others who've come alongside me and who have made this book possible:

L. Darby Gibbs, my endlessly amazing editor and friend. Jim, my endlessly patient husband. Laverne, my endlessly meticulous proofreader. Jennifer, my sweet friend, for always being ready to beta read for me. Tanya, my loyal critique partner, who sacrifices her time to make sure I'm getting it right. All my friends at my local Christian Writer's Group, for your kind support and attention to detail.

For *you*, dear reader, who took a risk on one of my stories.

Thank you!!

All my love,

April

About the Author

APRIL W GARDNER is an award-winning author of Christian fiction, an editor and book coach, and the founder of Write Start Fiction Studio. She grew up in Spain as a missionary kid and as a military spouse served the Lord in churches all over the world. She now resides in Texas with her husband. April has two grown children and two German shepherds. She dreams of learning a fourth language and visiting all the national parks.

ENJOY APRIL'S OTHER BOOKS:

Biblical Fiction/Study
A Fire and a Flame Series
Yoke of Babylon Series
Historical Romance
Beneath the Blueberry Moon Series (Native American)
Drawn by the Frost Moon Series (Native American)
Beautiful in His Sight (WW1, standalone)
Better than Fiction (WW1 era, dual-timeline)
Children's Middle Grade Historical
Lizzie and the Guernsey Gang (WW2 standalone)
Writing Craft
Body Beats to Build On
The New Author's Road to Publication

CONTACT:
Facebook: April.Gardner1
Website: AprilGardner.com
BookBub: @AprilWGardner
Email: info@aprilgardner.com

My Complete Catalogue
www.AprilGardner.com/complete-catalog

Made in United States
Orlando, FL
31 August 2025